BREATH OF MIST

LEONA WELCH

Cover art designed by: Kelly Nantes- ekilateral

Stock art by AGSTRONAUT21/shutterstock

Interior paper art: Front of book: Isa Zapata (@mysleepyblue)

Interior paper art: Bakc of book: Mori Di

Map created by: Yelena Lugin

Book Version: 3

WARNING

Breath of Mist includes elements of hand-to-hand combat, perilous situations, blood, violence, injuries, death, graphic language, and sexual activities. Readers who may be sensitive to these elements, please take note.

Author's Note

You may notice a change in spelling within this edition. The word Sidhe has been updated to Siddhe.

After publication, I became more aware of the cultural and mythological significance of the term Sidhe in Irish folklore. I adjusted the spelling for my fictional setting in order to respect the origins and folklore associated with the Sidhe.

This change does not alter the characters or story, only the spelling used within this fictional world. Thank you for reading and sharing this adventure with me.

– Leona Welch

For the dreamers, the defiant, and the daring.
This is for the ones who find freedom, even when it must be taken.

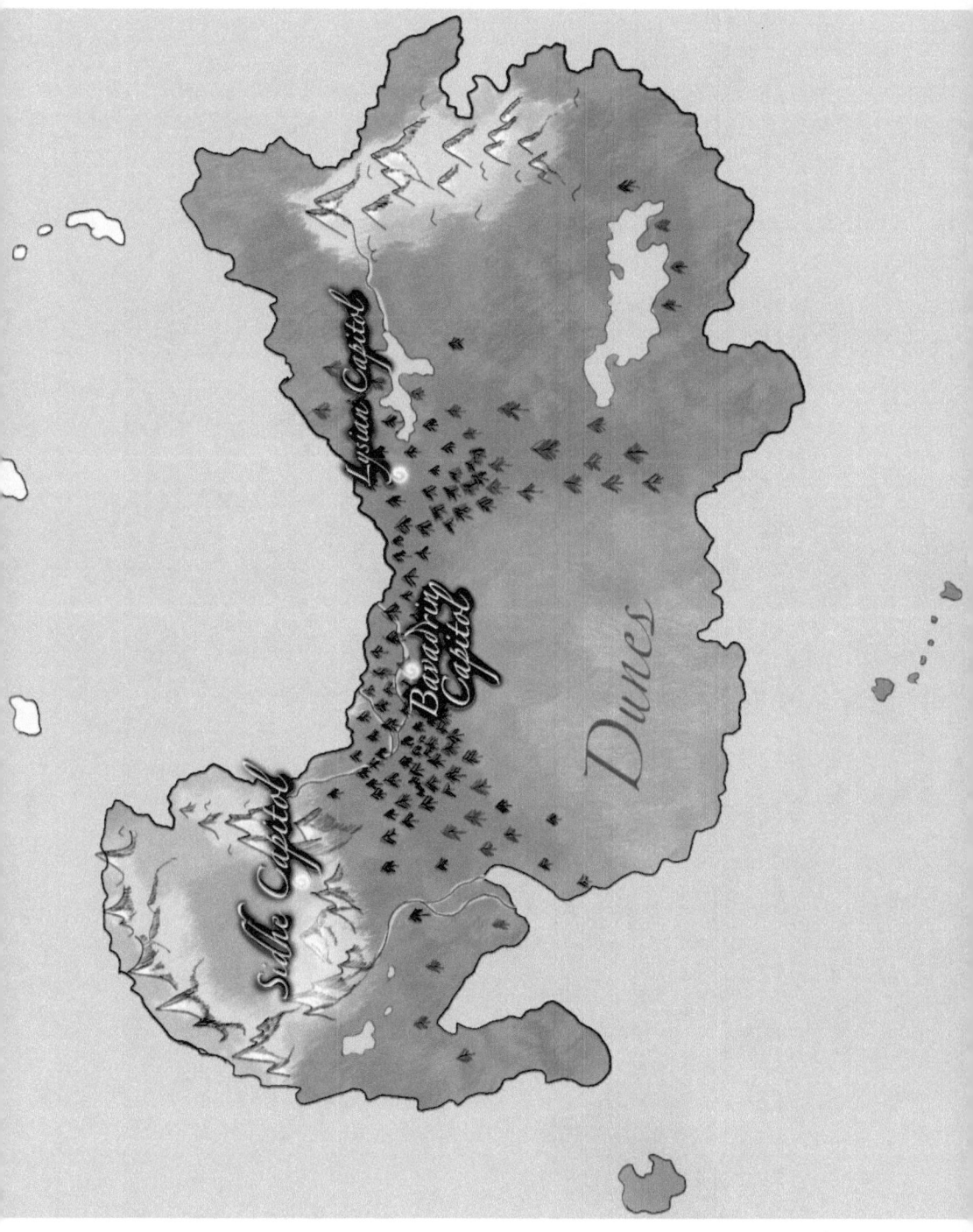

PROLOGUE

The Spirit once existed in all creatures who lived in Armenda.

It gave life to the lifeless. Gifted those who were favored with the ability to conjure. Those with the gift could open a door within themselves and connect to the Spirit realm, drawing on its mystic energy. For a time, the world of Armenda lived in harmony, conjurors using their abilities to help their neighbors. Life was peaceful.

But that time was now long forgotten.

Like a snowflake giving way to the heat of summer, the time of peace melted into the great river of history.

Too small to be remembered against the turbulent flowing water.

Some of those living in Armenda became infected with greed that spread through the lands like a contagion. Swiftly, the differences between all beings became a reason for distrust. The peace became tumultuous until, finally, a gruesome war broke out, leading to the dark years of ashes. Like an uncontrollable forest fire, the war spread corruption and hate, suffocating those who tried to ignore it and burning those who fought. No one was spared. Gray smoke clouded the once blue skies, smothering everything that the war was fought over.

Eventually, the Spirit turned away from its creations in disappointment, but not before they shed a single tear at what had become of the once beautiful Armenda. The Spirit brought the tear to the leaders of the three races and offered one last gift, a treaty. By then, the agony caused by the war was stronger than the hatred they all felt for one another, and the treaty was accepted by all three peoples.

The treaty became the covenant that separated the three beings of Armenda for centuries to pass. The great leaders signed the agreement with their blood, sealed it with the tear of the Spirit, and then burned the treaty to ash, which was carried by the wind over the land. Afterward, the Spirit was never seen again.

From then on, the Siddhe kept to the western mountains, the Lysians to the east, and the Bavadrins in between. The leaders of each race kept the sacred promises of the treaty: never to harm a fellow leader or an innocent of another race, and to remain in their own territories unless an invitation was extended, or a message sent by the leader. To break the oaths was to ensure the wrath of the Spirit.

Stories were passed down for generations, breathing fresh fear into the young, ensuring they abided by the ancient treaty, for the price otherwise was too great.

None crossed the boundaries into territories not their own, for fear of upsetting the Spirit and bringing its fury onto their lands. For centuries, each race was believed to have kept to its own lands. The treaty was believed to be maintained by all.

For generations, those in Armenda lived with a tense peace.

Until one day, a Lysian decided to break the treaty.

1

ERIK

The guard stood before me, a silent sentinel amidst the dimly lit dungeon. He might have been mistaken for a lifeless statue if not for the steady thud of his heartbeat and the faint scent of sweat clinging to him in this suffocating stone enclosure. Unlike his talkative comrades before, this particular Bavadrin did not offer a word.

His silence hinted at a mind that functioned beyond mere idle chatter. Though I suspected it to be of small intellect, it was the brain of a Bavadrin, nonetheless.

With a deliberate glare, I turned my full attention to him, a mixture of boredom and curiosity pushing me to test his reactions. My lip curled, revealing the sharp canines beneath, a wordless threat hanging in the air. Despite my attempts to unsettle him, his heartbeat remained steadfast, his demeanor unwavering. The fool believed himself safe on the other side of these bars, unaware that I *allowed* them to confine me here, *allowed* them to continue drawing breath.

With a huff, I stretched out on the hard stone bed, closing my eyes to the darkness that surrounded me. The sound of water dripping against distant stone provided a maddening backdrop to my thoughts. Drip, drip, drip, followed by a pause, then another drip. It seemed like a symphony of relentless madness, each drop echoing through the damp dungeon. Time crawled by excruciatingly slowly, dragging its feet like an old, tired beast. With every passing minute, my thoughts continued to darken.

At first, memories of my people, my family kept me satiated. But as the minutes stretched into hours, the thoughts took a sinister turn. I found myself crafting elaborate fantasies of ways to torment the guards, whose presence only added to the rank stench of the prison.

In the recesses of my mind, I could almost hear Edmond, one of my brothers, scolding me, *"Now Erik, remember why you're here."*

For my people, for my sister, I reminded myself, repeating the words like a mantra. They were a flickering light in the darkness of the cell, a reminder of the precious reason I endured this. For my family, I would endure anything.

The scowl of the guard staring at me chiseled away at what little patience I still clung to. I turned my gaze to him, and he did not look away. Either he was brave or stupid, and I was inclined to believe the latter. He leaned his broad frame against the wall, his golden eyes filled with an unmistakable hatred that seethed from his very pores. There was something unyielding about the angles of his face.

I studied him, imagining the ways I could end the guard's life if given the chance. Perhaps I would allow him to fight me, to see how many breaths it would take for him to realize his mistake. Despite his size and strength, his Bavadrin blood did little to match my stamina and agility. He was a lion in appearance, but a lamb in reality. The thought amused me, a dark smirk crossing my lips as I entertained the notion of his futile attempts to best me.

For my people, for my sister.

Closing my eyes, I took a deep breath, trying to find some

semblance of peace in the damp, heavy air. An irritated sigh passed between my lips. Time passed, marked only by the slow, methodical rhythm of my breathing and dripping water.

The voice of the previously mute guard cut through the air, though he did not speak to me directly. "You should not be here." His voice carried a stern edge of disapproval.

"It's fine, Willis," a female responded, her tone confident but betrayed by the quickening of a nervous pulse that I could almost taste in the air.

The guard offered no reply, yet his own heart quickened. While he may not have feared for himself, he seemed concerned for her.

Footsteps approached until they halted at the edge of my cage. The newcomer made no sound as she stood there, no doubt observing me. A scent of wildflowers wafted from her, a stark contrast to the dungeon's dank odor. I wondered if her nose stung from the acrid stench of this place.

Minutes passed in silence as her gaze wandered over me, a hot coal on my skin. Interest piqued, I finally opened my eyes to meet hers, sitting up to face the girl.

She appeared younger than I expected, her delicate frame and green eyes taking me in with an analytical gaze. It was likely she had never encountered my kind up close before. Her brown hair, half braided with ribbons, added a touch of strange beauty to her. The flickering candlelight cast a warm glow on her tawny golden skin as she met my gaze with unwavering curiosity.

For a long minute, we held each other's stare. If her visit had a purpose, she gave no indication, and I grew bored once more, the newness of her presence quickly growing stale.

"What is a girl like you doing in a place like this?" I finally broke the silence, my voice a low rumble.

Her eyes flicked to my mouth, noting the teeth that could easily rend flesh. Squinting, she met my stare again, questions evident in her expression. Yet, instead of voicing them, she remained silent, her thoughts a mystery.

Just as I was prepared to dismiss her as another semi-mute like the guard behind her and recline once more, she spoke.

"What's a male like you doing in a place like this?" Her question was bold, using my own words.

I couldn't help but smile at her audacity. Suddenly, everything seemed more interesting. If nothing else, this interaction promised to pass the time. Lysians, such as myself, were creatures of freedom, not meant to be caged, and her presence was as unexpected as it was intriguing.

"I believe I asked first." My lips curved upwards.

"Curiosity," she answered with a nonchalant shrug of her shoulder. "You?" Her shoulders remained squared, chin held high.

"Your people brought me here," I replied casually, making a show of looking around the sad dungeon before refocusing on her.

Her narrowed gaze revealed her dissatisfaction with my response. "What were you doing stepping over the border?"

"Curiosity," I echoed, enjoying the distraction of the girl.

Her sharp green stare continued to unflinchingly hold mine, even as she said, "You're lying." Her tone far too certain.

The girl's intelligence surprised me, and I found myself studying her more closely, wondering who this Bavadrin was who dared to venture into this dungeon.

Her clothing was not flashy, yet exceptionally well-made: trousers, which formed to her slender body, and a top that also looked as if it were made for her flesh only. Breezy, dressed for comfort, not battle or labor. From what I saw of their people on my brief trip through their little city, most wore far simpler clothing. Dressed like that, I knew she came from wealth and privilege. The fact she could come to see me in the dungeon told me she must also come from a family of power. Only one family could show up to a place like this and feel so comfortable. They had to own it.

"Careful, princess," I warned. "You don't want to call a beast a liar." My voice dropped, tone darkening. I was curious about how easy it might be to make her uncomfortable. *What does your fear smell like?*

She kept herself impressively composed, giving nothing away except for the flutter of her heart when she first entered the dungeon. The guard behind her, however, revealed his surprise at my use of the word *princess*. The Oracle had foretold that the Bavadrin leader had but one child, and here she stood before me, a fawn in a wolf's den. She had nothing protecting her except for a treaty that would soon not matter.

My heart thundered with the knowledge of my proximity to a Bavadrin with such status. She stood in the palm of my hand. I could crush her with a quick close of my fingers. Excitement spiked at the possibility, and I had to pull back. I was here for a purpose, to fulfill a duty that extended beyond my own desires. I could not be the one to break the ancient treaty first.

The girl did not give me the pleasure of a response to my comment.

"Why have you come to the border?" she pressed on, her fearlessness both admirable and foolish.

Rising from my stone bed, I approached the bars that separated us, towering over her smaller frame. She observed my movements while taking in my size. Uncertainty briefly flared in her eyes, a glimmer of vulnerability beneath her brave facade. I took in her scent, committing it to memory, the smell of a field of wildflowers. Now, when the city burned, I could find her. That was if she even survived. I hoped she would. The offspring of the Bavadrin's current leader could be a valuable asset to possess.

"Can you smell fear, or is that just a legend?" she boldly asked.

So far, she was proving herself to be far too confident for her own good. Her question too was somewhat troubling.

It disappointed me that the Bavadrins appeared to not tell the terrible tales of the Lysians. They were stories I never thought would fade, for we certainly still told stories of her kind. The Bavadrins who twisted the minds of their foes, and whose arrows bent the wind. If her ancestors had continued to speak of the legends of the Lysians, then perhaps she would have been wise enough to be uncomfortable when in proximity to me.

My lips curved at her curiosity. "It is true."

"And your hearing? How good is that?" she inquired, green eyes sharp.

Well, if her kind did little to teach her of my strengths, then I could shed some light. Hopefully, when the Bavadrin capital fell, the wisdom I provide would be enough to encourage her to give herself up without trying something stupid and getting herself killed. I wondered how bold she would be when the roles were reversed, and she was the one in a cell and I on the other side with a key. Would she then regret what her father and people had been doing all these years? Was she in on the schemes as well?

"Your guard's heartbeat has picked up since you came down here, and now even more so since I approached you." My gaze drifted to her neck, the tender flesh there, before rising to meet her eyes. It was intended as a silent threat, one she undoubtedly noted but did not respond to.

She nodded, her brows briefly drawn. I tracked her movements as she licked her lips and paused. Clearly, she wanted to say something. My head tilted in wonder at what questions burned in her now, the ones that caused her to hesitate. Would she continue our conversation, or would she be silenced now? Her inquisitiveness won over. After a brief moment, she spoke but asked no questions.

"You would have heard the guards approaching. With the

direction of the wind that day, you would have smelled them before they ever even saw you," she told me, a hint of accusation in her voice.

She was unexpectedly perceptive, quickly becoming more of a threat than I had anticipated. A simmering anger rose within me, both at her boldness and at myself for allowing her to draw me into this web of conversation. *Bavadrin indeed.*

Glancing at her delicate throat, I imagined how easily I could end her life with a single stroke. But the treaty held me back, invisible chains binding me to this cell. Soon, those chains would break.

A growl rumbled in my chest, something that she seemed unfazed by.

"What is your name?" she asked, her voice steady despite the tension between us.

Another grumble was my response, a warning.

She looked nearly disappointed that I didn't give it. "Very well. Have a good night, Lysian," she said, turning to leave as suddenly as she had arrived.

The anger slowly receded as I watched her go.

How sheltered she must have been to possess such certainty in her safety. Had she no knowledge of the dangers in the world she lived in? If she had then there would have been more caution and fear within her when I drew near. I doubted she would last in the ruins of her world. Despite her sharp mind, I was convinced that she would get herself killed. I nearly felt sorry for her.

2

ARIANA

I couldn't sleep all night.

Visions of the Lysian sitting in our dungeon floated around my mind like a dark hovering cloud, never to be blown away. No matter what I did, I could not get him out of my head. Every time my eyes would close, he came to me.

His body being behind bars was not a comfort. I was extraordinarily aware of his lethal presence during our brief encounter. The Lysian are told to be predators, and he was *content* being caged. The only inkling of discomfort that he ever showed was when I practically told him that I believed he allowed himself to be captured.

His lean muscles flexed with every precise step he made, and his keen dark eyes tracked every movement while I stood before him. His ears heard sounds I only could dream of and when he walked it was completely silent. And his teeth . . . a shiver ran through me. His dark hair was unkempt due to fingers running through it as if in frustration, but he did not appear to want to be released. He was a creature that belonged to the free night, yet he sat in a prison I was not sure could even hold him if he wanted out. The Lysian made absolutely no sense.

I scoured my mind all night for ideas of what his presence meant. If he was captured on purpose, then to what end? Did he simply have a death wish? Certainly, there were more comfortable or exciting ways to go. Death at the hands of the Bavadrin leader would not be a pleasant one.

None of it made any sense. He made no sense.

A day ago, the Lysian was found flirting with the border of our lands, a border which he overstepped. This act allowed us to do with him as we pleased. Unless he was bringing a message from his King or the Bavadrin leader invited him to cross into our territory. The Lysian had not spoken of delivering a message. He also certainly was not invited. This left him with nothing to hide behind, no protections from the ancient treaty. It was perplexing. The worst part of the situation was that our *brilliant* Bavadrin leader was going to act before even attempting to understand what exactly was going on.

The night dragged on as my mind overflowed with thoughts of the intruder. At sunrise, the perplexity bled into the day. I sat on my bed in silence, attempting to put together a puzzle with missing pieces.

Since getting up, I changed into my clothing and washed some of the sleepless night from my face. All of my actions were done so with little thought, for the questions burning within consumed me, leaving little room for anything else. I existed in a haze of uncertainty.

"Ariana." A woman's scratchy voice pulled me from my thoughts. "Your father requests your presence in the great room."

Edda stood in the doorway. Her dark eyes appraised me while she itched her elbow absentmindedly. Her extraordinarily long gray hair wrapped around her head. Wrinkles covered her face for as long as I had known her, though they never grew deeper or multiply in number. They were simply permanent fixtures of what made her who she was.

I frowned at her use of the word *father*. She knew I no longer acknowledged him as such, yet it was no use arguing with her. Edda always did as she pleased. Arguing with her never ended in my favor, anyway.

Her silver brows furrowed. She nearly looked worried.

"What's wrong?" I asked, rising and going to her.

Edda stood a full head shorter than me. Though small in size, her bite was certainly worse than her bark. For a long time, I imagined that her appearance was just an illusion so that others unwittingly underestimated her, only to be sorely mistaken.

Edda was probably one of the most powerful Bavadrins to ever have existed. Her gifts spanned beyond the mystics, for she was blessed within the soul of her being. While the rest of the world was tormented by their choices, she was not. Every decision she made was done so with absolute certainty. Edda had not hesitated in all the years I had known her. She never questioned a single decision she made. It was a skill that I could not learn, at least not fully. I still very much questioned my choices.

As a Seer, Edda could foretell things to come. However, the future was never clear-cut; it always harbored twists and turns. Following its trails could lead someone to wander dangerously close to a cliff's edge, possibly falling over, never to return. Edda's tellings needed to be taken with caution. I no longer asked her what she saw, for it was often difficult to make sense of. Instead, I waited for everything to be filtered through her, trusting her to give me what she thought necessary.

"There is a fog around everything here. The future has lost its clarity," she grumbled.

"The future has *never* been clear," I said to her, nearly rolling my eyes.

Waving my comment off with a single sway of her hand, she

nudged me into the hall. "Come, we must go to your father before his head rolls."

"If only it were that easy," I mumbled, starting down the vast stone corridor. The Bavadrin Leader Superior was neither calm nor kind. He was someone who thrived in anger.

Edda hissed, glancing over her shoulder to make sure no one was within earshot. "You must be strong." Her onyx eyes peered at me as we made our way to the great room. "Have you eaten today?"

"No," I mumbled, squaring my shoulders and straightened my spine in preparation to face whatever reason the Leader Superior decided to summon me.

"Good, nothing in your belly to lose then," she muttered.

I glanced at her, but she kept her eyes focused on the hall before her. I wondered what she meant by that but kept from asking. More often than not, when she was already being cryptic, she answered questions in a confusing fortune-telling manner. I didn't think I had the patience for such a thing, not when my attention was torn between my present situation and the mysterious Lysian sitting in the dungeon below.

The sounds of our footsteps echoed through the hall as we made our way to where Fraser waited for me. When we entered the great room, eyes turned to us, including those of the Bavadrin Superior. The room was terribly bare, made of gray stone and nothing else. It was cold and unwelcoming. There was a dais at the other end with a few seats; otherwise, there was nothing but standing room. Large windows to the west provided natural light. Despite the warmth of the sun, the windows only made the room feel colder, as if they somehow kept the sun further out of reach. A cluster of people stood in the center of the space, one of whom with skin too pale to belong to a Bavadrin.

I halted at the sight. The moment I found the Lysian's dark blue gaze, his nostrils flared in recognition. His hands were in chains and strung up on a large wooden frame that had not been there the day before. The Lysian's heels couldn't touch the ground. His shirt had been removed, placing his body on display for everyone, skin white enough to show the veins running beneath. Lean muscle covered his bones. He looked surreal, like a marble sculpture that had never been weathered by the elements. A knot twisted in my stomach at that realization.

All the stories described Lysians as scarred. They were told to be an animalistic race, wild even. The tales always highlighted their terrible strength, the acute senses, and the scarred bodies of the permanently violent beasts. The Lysian before me had no healed wounds. None. His skin was too pristine.

"Finally," the Bavadrin leader spoke, voice echoing through the room. "Ariana, come," he barked, summoning me like a master calling his dog.

I winced.

Fraser, his given name, sat in his large chair as if it were a throne and looked down over everyone in the room. His hair hung past his shoulders, gray with a few strands of black sprinkled in. One side of his head was braided with jewels and stones, marking him as the Superior. Bloodstone was always his favorite and the most prominent stone in his collection, the green of the forest splattered with blood-red patches. Brown eyes, as hard and cold as the room we were in, viewed me.

Pulling my attention from the Lysian, I did not look at Fraser's advisors nor the others present as I walked to the Superior, stopping before the seat intended for me. I couldn't keep my gaze from drifting back to the Lysian. His jaw flexed when I observed him once more.

"Sit." Fraser gave the command without even looking at me. Instead, he watched the Lysian with a dark hunger, and my stomach twisted. I once believed people were not born evil. The man who sired me proved me wrong.

Again, I looked at the stranger strung up in the center of the room. His cold eyes remained fixed on me, something almost daring stirring within them. My attention drifted over his body once more before snapping back to his stare. Despite the position he was in, power still clung to him. I felt it in the air between us.

The guard beside him stood with a whip in his hand. My stomach twisted yet again, for the guard was Willis. The Bavadrin Superior no doubt hand-picked him to act out the orders. Fraser intended to not just torment the Lysian that day.

There were many ways one could torture someone. That was Fraser's favorite lesson. It was one I learned a very long time ago—and one he'd never let me forget.

"You can't do this," I said to Fraser, turning my attention to him in time to see his sharp glare cut to me. "The Lysian has no scars on his body. He looks pristine, his muscles conditioned, his skin undamaged. I think—"

For Fraser's large size, he was quick. Abruptly, he stood, and the back of his hand slammed across my face before I could even finish. Stunned, I lost my balance, only to be caught by his hand on the front of my shirt. He pulled me threateningly close.

"You do not tell me what to do, *girl*," he said in a low voice. The smell of garlic and ale wafting off his breath burned my nose. My cheek stung, and the fresh taste of iron filled my mouth. The blow had drawn blood. It was not the first time he raised a hand against me, but it was the first time he had in such a public manner. The entire room, which was already silent, went completely void of sound, so much so that it was deafening.

My hands began shaking at my sides. Not in fear, but with the yearning to set myself free. Icy hatred burned inside me, longing to destroy the man who threatened me. Like the Lysian, my skin was not scarred, but that did not mean that *I* was not scarred. My wounds had always been within, hidden from outsiders. Still, they were deep. Scars that would be with me till my dying day.

I steadied myself from the blow. Clenching my jaw, I reined in the feeling, telling myself that I was not actually in danger, that the man holding me by my shirt was not worth placing myself at risk. To act against him, to kill the Leader Superior in front of everyone in the room, would not serve the people's best interest, nor mine. No matter how much Fraser deserved to die, it could not be by my hand. To act against the Leader Superior was to turn one's back on the sacred ways of the Bavadrins.

Often, Fraser was the one most capable of testing my patience and control. This was no different. Just another test for me to pass. He pushed me to lose control, to lash out and release myself completely, but I wouldn't.

"My Superior." Shal's voice rumbled through the room, slow and lazy. The casual tone was a thin veneer, barely masking the desperation to please Fraser or the perpetual anger that seemed to define him. He took a step towards us before letting his gaze slide down my frame.

Desire flickered in his eyes—not a yearning to love, but to possess.

"Sweet Ari spends much of her time at the children's home," he said, his words calculated, "and amongst those less fortunate. Her heart is soft, as is her mind. She simply does not grasp the magnitude of the threat before her."

It was a carefully veiled reminder to my father that I held the affection of the people while subtly belittling me before his advisors.

With a grunt of agreement, Fraser shoved me into the chair beside him before relaxing back into his. "You are correct Shal. Perhaps my daughter is in need of a firmer hand than mine. To remind her of her place."

Shal chuckled and delight sparkled in his eyes as they drifted to me once more. It wasn't hard to discern what he was thinking. He wanted to be that firmer hand.

My jaw clenched as Fraser subtly dangled my unwed status before his sycophant. The only reason I hadn't already been bound to one of his men was that he relished the power of withholding me. My availability served as a promise he could manipulate.

I bit my tongue and looked anywhere but at Shal who approached to stand at Fraser's other side. It was where the Leader Superior's second in command usually stood. Fraser had yet to name his new second since Valk's passing. The position became another promise he could manipulate, as long as the role remained vacant. No matter how much Shal frothed at the mouth for it, he was never going to be given it. At least not officially.

Bringing my shaking hands into my lap, I clenched them together, willing them to stop. Amongst those standing around the edge of the great room, I found Edda. She always offered me shelter from the storms. Because of her, I grew up feeling safe and loved despite the cruelty of the world I lived in.

Edda's gaze focused on me, an angry scowl meant for our *benevolent* Leader Superior on her face. She took a deep breath, and I mirrored her. Once, twice, a third time, until my hands stopped shaking and I regained control of myself. Edda offered a small nod of encouragement.

"Well, now is your last chance to tell me what you were doing in my lands." Fraser addressed the Lysian. There was no interest in his voice, because he did not truly care. This was mere formality, to make sure the Lysian did not carry a message from his King.

The stranger's gaze shifted to Fraser, his glare murderous. The features of his face were brutal yet not unattractive, except those teeth that appeared to consistently be threatening the world around him.

"I wish to travel northwest, for they have my kind trapped there as slaves. I want to free them. There is no other way to get to the Siddhe except through your lands," he answered simply.

I found myself leaning forward.

What he was insinuating was ridiculous. None of us crossed the borderlines, for the treaty kept it so. The Lysians, Bavadrins, and the Siddhe lived very much separately. For any of the Lysians to have been enslaved by the Siddhe meant they likely had to travel through our lands. What the Lysian proposed was simply impossible.

Off to the side, Edda's eyebrows angled in a scowl, as if she too were questioning whether to trust the Lysian or not. Edda was remarkably good at sniffing out a lie, spotting one before the words were even spoken from someone's lips. For her to appear thoughtful because of the Lysian's allegations gave me pause. Was it possible he was speaking the truth?

What's more, the Lysians were not the only ones with missing people.

"You were not invited into our lands and were not found to be carrying any messages from your King; therefore, you had no right to cross the border. You crossed the border with ill intent. For this you will receive thirty lashings to start," Fraser answered without a care for what the Lysian said.

Thirty was an incredible number of lashings. A Bavadrin was likely to pass out after ten, but the Lysians were stronger. Their bodies were more resilient to injury, or so the stories foretold. He was likely to remain conscious for the entirety of the punishment. Despite their strength and resilience, they were not immune to pain. This would not be a painless experience. It was going to be excruciating.

"Maybe we should hear him out," I offered, calmly trying to make my tone more submissive. Bavadrin's had been disappearing, enough for rumors to spread. Some said the Spirit had chosen them to ascend into a better world. The lives taken were not impactful to our leader or his rule, and thus he did not care.

Fraser's hand hit the arm of his chair with enough force that the wood splintered. Anger radiated off him in such thick waves that it was palpable.

Willis, with the whip in his hands, took a single small step in our direction before stopping himself. His golden eyes found mine, and he shook his head ever so slightly, imploring me to stand down.

Willis was already furious when I went down to the dungeon to speak with the Lysian. Yet, if it came down to it, he would stand beside me in an unprecedented act of conflict with our leader. Bavadrins were tied to their Leader Superior. No one opposed him, and definitely never threatened him. To do so was treason and went against everything we held sacred. Once the Spirit chose the Superior, he or she was to rule until their passing, and only then was another chosen to lead. The Leader Superior was born in blood and ended in death.

I felt Fraser's gaze on me, though I refused to meet it.

"Proceed," he said to Willis after a long moment passed.

Nausea rose within me as my friend moved to stand in position behind the Lysian, raising the whip. Sad and regretful golden eyes met with mine before focusing on the Lysian before him.

The first lashing sounded through the great room, and it was as if the world turned on its axis. By the fifth lashing, the Lysian began visibly shaking. His skin, which was once smooth perfection, would now never be such. For the rest of his life, he would bear the markings inflicted this day. By the tenth, the sound of each subsequent whipping changed with the wet blood dripping from the wounds being carved into his skin.

In the beginning, the Lysian remained silent, but then the pain washed over him. The grunting accompanying a lashing morphed into menacing growling. It was not a scream of agony, but one of anger. I focused on a spot on the floor and prayed to the Spirit that the torture would soon end. By the time it was over, I could no longer look at the Lysian or anyone else in the room.

After the thirtieth lash, the Lysian was dragged back to his cell. The great room quickly cleared, the first to leave being Fraser who did not say a word to me. I sat there in silence until I was the last person left. Even Edda did not approach, knowing I needed a moment. It was all I could do to keep myself together. Hardly hanging on, I focused on forcing slow deep breaths to keep from passing out.

Once alone, I could not hold the memories at bay any longer. The flashbacks flooded my mind. I heard my mother's voice, saw her blood on the floor of the very room I now sat in, saw the light slowly fade from her eyes. Heard the sound of the whips as they continued slashing at her body long after she had lost consciousness. Until she drew no more breaths.

I would have thrown up were there anything in my stomach. Edda had been correct regarding that.

3

ERIK

My back stung with every movement. It was incredible, the annoyance almost unbearable. I twitched the big toe on my left foot and my back burned from the effort. Gingerly, I lay down on my stomach, not wanting to infect the open wounds with the wet dungeon stone.

I thoroughly completed my part of the plan. The treaty offered protection to those who stepped over the border due to invitation or due to a message being sent from the leader of that race. It also offered protection to the leaders themselves and their immediate family if they were to cross a border with a message. I carried no physical letter because my voice should have been more than enough. The fools did not even ask who I was, just as I knew their kind wouldn't. Spineless leaders often could not imagine others in power having a backbone enough to risk themselves as I had.

The Bavadrins raised a hand against someone who intended no harm. A royal with a message, seeking help. The treaty protected me, and they broke it. All that was left to do was to wait. With the ancient pact violated, I had the freedom to take any Bavadrin life I pleased, without fear of the Spirit's wrath.

Destroying them from within was simple, but that was not my goal. I wanted to use them, and for that, most needed to survive. Taking control would be easier with the Lysian army at my side. A single Lysian conjuror against the Bavadrins would be formidable, but an army? That would force them to acknowledge their defeat and bend to my will much easier.

I closed my eyes, searching for relief from the pain, but the sound of footsteps kept me from drifting into sleep.

"You have got to be kidding me, Ariana," a guard growled, revealing a lack of formality that hinted at their closeness. I wondered if it was friendship or something more.

"Open it," she instructed, and I turned from the wall to see *her* standing at the door of my cell, a large bowl in her arms. The scent of herbs wafted from the bowl, reminiscent of the healing mixtures used by the Lysians. Had she come to tend to my wounds?

"*Ariana*," the guard barked, his tanned arms folded across his chest, a hard look on his face.

She turned to him. "*Landin.*"

"He's an animal," Landin said quietly, as if to warn her without my hearing. *Senseless guard.* I could hear things they could not even conceive. Lowering his voice was useless.

"Would you ever treat Willis's wolves like this?" she countered, comparing me to domesticated wolves. That was cute.

"That's not the same."

"Open the door," she demanded. "I will be fine."

I couldn't believe it when the man walked to the cell and unlocked it—a foolish move. It was even more surprising when she entered without hesitation, devoid of fear. The cell door closed gently behind her, leaving Landin standing on the other side, his heart racing.

I sat at once, my movement fluid despite the burning at my

back. The change in position caused her to pause. She froze when our eyes locked.

"Ariana," I said her name softly, finding it lovely on my tongue.

She frowned briefly before gesturing to the bowl in her hands. "If you let me, I will put this on your wounds. It will help with healing and protect the cuts from infection."

"My kind heals quicker than yours," I said to her, wondering if she would push the subject.

It did not take a Lysian to notice her discomfort when I was made an example of for a meaningless crime such as stepping across an imaginary line. She hated every moment of the punishment. By the time it was over, she had grown pale and looked as if she were going to lose consciousness. I had not expected to see her again, and I certainly had not expected her boldness to increase so much that she was willing to be in the same room as me, with nothing between us.

"Suit yourself." She moved to leave, foolishly turning her back to me. Despite the lashings I received, it did very little to slow me. It would have been nothing for me to close the distance between us and take her life in an instant.

Relief softened the worry edging the guard's eyes as he reached to open the cell and let her out.

"Wait," I said.

Ariana looked over her shoulder in my direction while the guard gritted his teeth.

"Thank you," I murmured, for once trying not to sound threatening. The words were an allowance for her to come close, to place the salve on the wounds, to touch me. My back would heal on its own, but I was not that much of a glutton for unnecessary punishment. If the girl offered comfort from the constant stinging, then I would take it.

"Sit on the edge," she instructed, and I obeyed, shifting to the corner of the stone slab that served as a bed. She stepped closer and inspected my wounds. Anger rolled off her in hot waves, sharpening her green eyes, tightening the delicate muscle in her jaw.

I almost laughed, for the princess felt something other than hatred for a Lysian, surely a rare occurrence. The Bavadrins were told to fear and hate us, but she did not seem to fit that mold. Her actions were unusual, and I found myself intrigued by her.

I wondered whether her dreadful father had hit her on the head when she was a child one too many times because she was missing necessary life-preserving senses. The comfort of being in a room with me, the false sense of security, and the misplaced protectiveness for an intruder of her lands were concerning for her sanity. A girl such as herself should have trembled at the sight of a Lysian. She should have wanted to run away, not come close enough for me to twist around and grab her by the throat.

Ariana reached into the bowl, picking up a strip of fabric that was thoroughly soaked with creamy herbs. Her fingers moved quickly, placing the strips on my back. A welcome cooling sensation accompanied each one, taking with it the stinging. It was a sweet relief.

"Why are you doing this?" I asked her when she secured the last of the strips in place. Her fingers gently pressed the fabric onto my back before she finally withdrew her hands.

I turned to find her observing me. Green eyes flitted to my teeth before meeting my gaze. She was swathed in a certain fearlessness despite likely making a mental note to keep away from my mouth. I was close enough to touch her if I wanted to. She had nothing to hide behind, yet she showed no sign of distress. None. Where a healthy sense of terror should have been instead was an almost childlike curiosity. She truly lacked fundamental survival instincts.

"You're not an animal," she simply said. "It's the least I could do."

I lowered my voice. "I'm more of an animal than you are." My response could have been perceived as a threat. Still, the princess was stoic and calm.

"I wouldn't be so sure about that," she replied smoothly.

My lips curved up in amusement. There was nothing more animal or dangerous in their Bavadrin lands than me. "You are telling me you have claws hidden in those delicate fingers of yours?"

That was impossible. Her hands were too gentle. There were certainly no claws there. However, the Bavadrin race had a different form of claws, that of a mental kind. They were known to be masters at deception and their conjuring gifts tended to be of the shadow flavor, able to alter emotions, dreams, visions. Yet she had not shown any of these traits, or she hid them well. Why was she helping a prisoner heal and feel better without asking anything in return?

Ariana raised a single brown eyebrow. "Perhaps I do." Her lip quirked at the thought. She glanced at her hands as if imagining what it may have been like. "Does having claws hurt?"

I held an open hand between us and when her attention focused on it, claws slid out, between the nails and fingertips of my hand. Her eyes widened and I pulled them back sheathing them once more underneath the nail bed.

A breath passed between her lips, and she met my stare. "Impressive." Still, not a scent of fear.

I snorted at what sounded like a complement.

The moment between us was light for only an instant before it flickered out of existence. Her gaze dropped to the stone ground in thought.

"Who are you?" she finally asked.

I peered at the guard behind her, watching like a hawk. Though his eyes were trained on us, it was unlikely that he heard a word we said with our voices so low.

"My name is Erik." I told her the truth. Everything was already set in motion. There was no way she could change the course now. "I am one of the four sons of King Sten." That was also true, though slightly misleading. I wanted to give her only enough to know of the dire situation they were now in, to know there was no going back for her and the Bavadrins.

The ancient treaty had been created by the Spirit and the leaders of the three races centuries ago. Sealed with blood, ash, and the single tear of the Spirit. The ones to break the sacred promise were to be cursed, shunned by the Spirit.

The Bavadrin Leader Superior never even asked who I was, only why I had come. My answer was the truth, and he raised a hand against me. His act broke the treaty, freeing my Lysians to attack without prejudice, for the Spirit would smile upon us and curse them.

Ariana remained quiet for a long moment. She must have realized the gravity of the situation. That which had protected her people was now shattered, and her father's actions had set events into motion that could not be undone.

"Why did you do this?" The calm she arrived with remained, though there was the slightest quiver in her voice. Good, perhaps she was understanding the dangers surrounding her.

"What I said was true. There are enslaved Lysians in the Siddhe lands," I told her.

"How is that even possible?" Anger cracked through her calm exterior. "How can you even know something like that?"

"Perhaps the Siddhe have a way to get around your lands, though the most probable theory is that they go through them," I told her, answering the first question. As for how we knew, other than their disappearance from our lands, everything was confirmed by an Oracle. But I was not going to tell her that.

Her brows drew together. Goosebumps covered her flesh.

Capturing her along with her father in the days to come was

ideal; however, it placed her life at risk to remain in the city set to burn. There was a likelihood that she would be killed, especially if she tried to fight a Lysian.

"You should run. Get away from this place before it burns," I said quietly, urging her to flee. *Before I burn it from within.* This would be the only kindness I return for hers today.

The warning served two purposes: it was true advice, and secondly, it was something that would help me if she were to stay. The burden of blame for what was to come would become partially hers. The responsibility for the destruction of her home would be shared, for she would shoulder that reality with me whether she wished to or not. And she would not see the warning as what it was: a tactic to gain her trust and share the blame. No, she would see it as a mercy, for I gave her a chance out of the goodness of my heart. It would push her a step closer to trusting me.

Ariana stood but did not leave. Instead, her mind must have been racing, for her vision clouded over with thought. Again, her senses dampened and she left herself incredibly vulnerable standing in my cell in such a manner. I did not know how the girl had survived for so long with no awareness of the danger she put herself in.

Her response was unexpected. "They are my people. I won't leave them."

"Bavadrin rulers are chosen by some form of ritual, correct?" I prodded gently, trying to give her a reason to reconsider. "If your father, the Leader Superior, dies, the responsibility of your people may not fall to you." Their rule was not passed down through bloodlines like ours.

"I already am responsible." She looked at me coolly. "If you get Fraser, what happens to the others here?"

"If they stand down, they will not be harmed," I assured her. "The Lysians seek access to your lands, but we also plan to bolster our forces with those able to fight alongside us." I would not sugarcoat the truth of her reality, for she appeared to need a good shaking to clear her head enough to lucidly see the danger surrounding her.

Ariana accepted my words, her pulse quickening with resolve. "If you succeed, I beg you not to kill those here. Spare them. It is not their fault they follow a monster. Don't condemn them for something they have no choice over."

For centuries, we had been told of the heartless and deceiving Bavadrin ways. Yet she didn't appear to fit that mold. She did not ask for her safety but that of her people. I seriously doubted that her father would ever be so noble as to make such a request as his daughter did now.

Without fully meaning to, I offered a single nod. Apparently, it was enough of an answer, for she quickly retreated after that. The sound of her steps rushed away until they disappeared altogether. Landin, the guard, closed and locked the gate to my cell immediately upon her exit before taking to staring at me with his arms folded across his chest. It appeared as though his allegiances rested more with their leader's daughter than with Fraser. Interesting. If they were a people divided, then they would be that much easier to gain control over.

As I lay back down on the stone slab, the cool sensation of the healing salve on my wounds, I couldn't help my thoughts drifting to Ariana and wondering what she would do with the information I gave her.

4

ARIANA

My soul wanted to crawl out of its skin. I was a foreigner within my body. Every ounce of my being wanted to warn our people of the threat heading for us. Sickness drifted through my stomach whenever I heard a child laugh, my mind imagining the laugh turning to horrid screams.

It had been exactly one day since my conversation with the Lysian prince named Erik, and now not a single moment went by when I was not haunted by his presence, by his words, and the looming doom which now surrounded my home and the Bavadrin race.

A storm headed for us. One that was invisible to all but me. I wanted to scream in warning, but Edda convinced me that doing so would cause more harm than good. For her, the storm threatened destruction, but with it came the possibility of giving way to something new and better. I kept replaying that conversation over and over in my head and hoping it would make me feel a fraction less guilty.

"As wrong as it may seem, sometimes the best course of action is none at all," Edda had said when I found her after my conversation with Erik.

"But they will suffer. Some will die," I countered.

Her face wrinkled with a knowing smile. "We often feel like we need to do things in turbulent times. It seems unnatural to ride the wave. However, when caught in a riptide, those who fight it grow tired and drown. It is those who allow the tide to suck them up and spit them back out who then go on to swim another day."

"We can send word to the Sparrow Archers. They would protect their home." The Bavadrin Sparrows were not in the capitol city, making it easier for the Lysians to take it. The archers would be able to see the enemy approaching, for their abilities were touched by magic. They had a way with the wind, noticing when something was amiss. The people always revered them, which our Leader Superior hated. Fraser assumed he should be the only one others looked up to. So, years ago, he sent the archers away, stating that they needed more skill and that our great city did not need their meager protection. The Sparrows now made their homes amongst the trees, about a day's journey from what was once the home they swore to always protect.

Fraser was a fool.

"No, child, this will only be the Sparrows' home once more after our current Leader Superior falls. And to bring them here will not change the outcome of what's coming; it will only add to the bloodshed."

"I could deliver my father to the Lysians. There wouldn't be a need for potential bloodshed." My mind raced with the limited choices I had.

"Then you will be seen as a threat by the Bavadrin people. They would never trust you again. Plus, how would you deliver him on your own? Your greatest power is the fact that nearly no one has any idea what you are capable of. No, you must let *them* find and take your father. And then you must let them take you."

I looked at Edda in shock. She literally wanted me to become her water analogy. To allow for me to be sucked up to hopefully be spit out.

"You have been training all these years for something. This is it. You have the patience and control to go undetected. You will learn the Lysians' weaknesses, their strengths, and then you will use that knowledge to take back control and keep it for good. It is far easier to fight an enemy you know than the one you know nothing of," Edda said with a grin.

I knew I would do as she said, for I trusted her. If needed, I could defend myself. It was not for myself that I feared for in Edda's plans. What troubled me was the risk to the Bavadrin people, something I could have prevented if only I had stood up to Fraser long ago.

"I could have protected them if only I had taken control before all of this." My voice filled with regret.

Edda released a cruel laugh. "You are incapable of bloodying your hands in such a manner. The only way to take control from your father would have been to put him down. Permanently." A glimmer of something powerful and ancient stirred in the darkness of her eyes.

"I despise him," I said sharply, angered by her response. If there was any life that I had an urge to take, it was Fraser's.

Edda's lips cut into a smile. "Indeed, you should, but that does not mean you are capable of *murdering* your father."

"So, I am to simply keep my hands in my lap, waiting for the Lysians to find Fraser and hoping that there is something left here after everything ends? And then to top it all off, I am to go with them willingly as a prisoner?" My words turned bitter. She called me incapable of murdering a monster, but what she was asking of me was to allow the death of the innocent.

"If you hope to give your people the best chance of survival, then yes."

"How can you even propose any of this?" Her suggestion was dreadful, and what was worse was that she did not seem bothered by any of it. Did she not care for the people?

"Because I see things you cannot." Edda silenced me with her words. She was a Seer, knowing and seeing things I never would.

Edda smiled pleasantly as she walked over to me, taking my hands in hers. "Your father casts a wide shadow, Ariana, and you were wise to always hide within it. Soon you will step out of that shadow, but not right now. Trust me. You will survive this, and you will have people left yet to lead."

"If anything happens to . . ." I could not finish my thoughts, for unshed tears burned in my eyes.

"The children you worry for, as well as Willis, and Landin will survive this shift we are about to experience. As will I." She spoke with enough certainty to offer the smallest fraction of comfort. Those closest to me would survive. Did that make me twisted and dark, to value the lives of some over others?

Edda then left me to my thoughts, with no further words to offer, and so I continued to sit adrift in an internal turmoil.

Later that night, while I sat on the floor before the hearth in my room, the door swung open without so much as a knock. Landin marched in, his steps heavy and void of hesitation. Dropping down on the ground before me, he folded his hands across his chest and stared at me as if waiting for a response to a question he never actually asked. His brown hair was unkempt and stuck up in nearly every direction imaginable.

"I know you're angry—" I began only to be cut off by him.

"Oh, you know that, do you?" He sounded exasperated. His gaze bore into me, and guilt coiled within. My trip to see the Lysian was not harmless; it placed Landin in danger. If anything went wrong, then Fraser would have had Landin's head for it. My actions placed his life at risk, and I did not even ask for his permission. This knowledge only added to the burden I now carried.

Landin and I had known each other since we were children, and I could count on one hand the number of times I had ever angered him. This was the second time.

"I'm sorry. I truly am," I whispered. "I just . . . I needed to talk to him."

Some of the desperation within must have bled to the surface, for the hard lines of Landin's frown softened and he unfolded his arms.

"I know that experience was probably impossibly difficult for you. Watching the Lysian's punishment. Still, you can't just walk into the dungeon and order me or Willis around. We care for you, and it puts us in a difficult situation when you ask for such things. It's reckless and not fair to us." His brown gaze eased.

"I won't ever ask you to do anything like that again and risk Fraser's wrath," I promised him.

He ran his tongue over his teeth. "Good." Landin's shoulders relaxed, and he leaned back on his hands, though his eyes remained fixed on me.

My attention drifted to the fire. The dancing flames licked the logs with long flickering red strokes. I always found comfort in watching flames as they moved across surfaces, devouring anything standing in its path. However, on that night it strangely brought me unease. As if the flames could somehow escape their confines, threatening the world around them.

"What's the matter?" Landin asked, his voice softening with concern. "It's not only what was done to the Lysian that troubles you." He knew me so well.

"Something terrible is coming." I turned to him, stopping myself before saying more.

He frowned again, shifting to lean towards me. "Something Edda has seen?"

"Yes, and no." My head was beginning to pound painfully.

"Whatever it is, I will protect you." He vowed with complete certainty.

My heart sank. "I don't want you to."

Landin looked at me, confusion surrounding him.

"Listen, if what I think may be coming truly is, then when it arrives, I need for you to stand down." I reached for his hand, taking it in both of mine. His fingers were fabulously warm against my cold ones. "Let what needs to happen, happen."

"What are you talking about?" He looked at me as if I were crazed, brows furrowed, creating a prominent wrinkle between them.

"Just do your best to stay away from it."

"Away from what?" Concern sharpened his voice. "You aren't making any sense. And if you are in danger, then I certainly will not be running away and hiding."

I lightly squeezed his hand with desperation. "Look, I can't explain this. Just know that something horrible is looming, but that I will be fine. I need for you and Willis to be fine too."

"The Leader Superior know about any of this?" he asked, pulling his hand out of mine. His brown eyes were clear and wide as they searched my face for a hint as to what I was alluding to.

"He won't listen to reason, Landin. Don't tell anyone what I shared with you, only Willis. No one else must know. Edda said that if I sounded an alarm that it would end in more death."

His frown deepened in response. He probably thought I had gone mad.

"It may be nothing. You know how finicky Edda's predictions can be," I said, offering him a sliver of comfort. I did not know if he was more worried due to what I shared with him or about my possible loss of sanity.

"Yeah, you don't seem to think this one is finicky, Ariana," he pointed out.

I drew in a deep breath. "You're right. I fear this one is true, but I hope I am wrong." A silence settled between us, only the crackling of the fire could be heard for a few minutes. "Well?"

"Well, what?" He looked from the flames in my direction.

"Do you promise?" It was as though we were children again and I was asking him to keep something silly a secret. Landin always kept my secrets—the silly ones and the big ones that could destroy everything.

"I promise not to tell, and that I will try to stay out of the unknown troubles you seem to think are heading for us. But it isn't my fault if trouble doesn't stay away from me." He shrugged a single shoulder.

I sighed while the mood instantly lightened between us. "You are truly something, my trouble-shrouded friend." I offered him a small smile.

"You know it, for you're one of the troubles drawn to me." He raised a brow.

"I wonder what it is about you that draws us troubled folk," I pondered.

"If I had a gold coin for every time I've asked that question." A heavy sigh accompanied his words, and he lay back on the ground, resting a hand beneath his head.

"You would be dirt poor," I commented, following his lead, and lying back myself.

Landin smiled at my remark.

There was a pause, and I asked, "Have you ever thought you would see a Lysian so close before?"

"I never even wanted to see one from a distance," he countered.

I turned on my side so that I could better view him.

Landin continued, "He is just so animalistic. The way his eyes observe everything. The way he moves. It's uncomfortable to watch. Fraser should have just killed him and gotten it over with."

"Did the Lysian do or say something to you?" I asked, hoping that I didn't sound too eager.

"No. And that's the thing. It was simply the look in his eyes. His teeth seem like they could rip through flesh and muscle all the way to the bone. And once they hit bone, then they may even crush their way through that too." Landin visually shivered from the thought. "Ashes, and you stood next to him in that cell. I let you go in there with him."

"Yet he didn't harm me, and he could have. After what Fraser did and being his daughter—the Lysian hardly even threatened me. He has every right to hate me, to want to lash out."

"His entire existence is a threat, Ariana. And do you mean to say you thought there was a chance he could attack you while you were in there after that lashing?" Landin scowled. He probably assumed I was certain of my safety, that perhaps even Edda confirmed it.

"There is always a chance," I stated flatly.

Landin turned onto his side and rubbed his face, needing to push the bags out of his eyes. His hair had grown longer than he typically kept it, becoming unruly. He looked rougher than usual.

"You aren't often so reckless," he commented.

Landin and I had known one another for as long as I could remember. He was one of the few who knew everything about me, keeping my secrets without fault. There are those who warn that secrets tear things apart, that they place some sort of unimaginable weight on those keeping them, a poison that's light on the lips but heavy on the soul, but that was not the case with us. Our secrets only brought us closer together. We knew what we were, and we cared for each other even more for it. We chose to lean on one other when we were hurt or weak. There was never a pressure of needing to hide anything for fear of not being accepted by each other. Our bond was pure and strong. In a strange way, I had always considered Landin my soul mate. Neither of us was perfect, but we were there for one another.

"I needed to learn what kind of Lysian we were dealing with," I told him.

His exhale was silent, but it may as well have been a sigh. "And what did you uncover?"

I pondered how to put it into words before replying. "He is dangerous; however, he doesn't seem evil."

"Well, that's comforting. The beast we have locked up is dangerous, but possibly not to an evil extent. Great." Landin rolled over, getting to his feet. "I should go. Willis will wonder where I am."

"Of course." I joined him in standing. A pang of guilt went through me, for I also owed Willis an apology for my actions lately.

Landin turned to me before reaching for the door handle. "I could stay," he offered softly, the corner of his lips curving up with the memories. When we were little, the two of us would often spend nights together, usually when one of us was upset or afraid. We would keep each other entertained, offering a laugh or a shoulder to cry on if needed. It had been a long time since we shared one of those endless nights. They seemed sleepless, yet somehow, we would always drift off together and wake to a bright new day.

"I'll be alright." I gave him a small smile.

"What you saw today had to be . . ." His hand balled into a fist and a tremble shook through him. He had held me the night my mother died as tears poured from my eyes. When I couldn't unsee the lashings inflicted upon her body.

I took his fist in my hand, unraveling his fingers. "I'm fine. That isn't on my mind."

"Yet something is bothering you." He turned fully to face me.

"Just remember what I said. You and Willis stay away from any trouble that may come our way."

With a sigh, Landin stepped close, draped one of his arms heavily around my shoulder, and pulled me into an embrace. He placed a brief kiss on my forehead. "I'll do my best, my sweet, worried Ariana. But as you know, trouble is just drawn to me."

Despite everything, a small laugh bubbled through me as I pushed him away. "Yeah, best you get home now before Willis truly gives you some trouble."

"One could only hope!" His eyes lit up with delight, and a sly smile crept across his lips.

Moments later, he was gone, and I was left alone to my thoughts once more.

Worries of the day blended into my dreams.

I woke from a nightmare, but the screams did not stop.

5

ARIANA

Distant sounds in the night caused me to stir in my sleep. A peculiar scent filled the room, burning my nostrils. The smell familiar yet odd, as if misplaced. While I sluggishly woke, my mind was slow to think. It took me far too long to place the scent. In a mental loop, I just kept wondering what it was, for it did not belong.

When the door to my room flung open, my brain finally snapped awake.

I recognized the distant sounds as screams, and the smell was that of smoke.

Edda, dressed in her silver night robe, ran to me as I jumped out of bed. Her fingers wrapped around my wrist with iron strength, and she yanked me close. Her dark eyes were wild with a mixture of both excitement and fear. An odd buzzing energy surrounded her while I felt nothing but pure terror.

"Do not use your power unless it is absolutely necessary for you to protect yourself, and not for anybody else, not even me." Her voice took a forceful tone. It was as if the chaos bred some sort of strange dark life into her. "They will likely take you with them. If they do, then they shouldn't know what you are."

It was difficult for me to hear her over the screams outside. My breath caught at the sounds. The cries continued to come, again and again, piercing my skull like needles.

I ripped my hand from Edda's grip and ran to the balcony. The doors crashed open with force.

The sight below choked the breath out of me.

Chaos had been unleashed, pure and terrifying.

Instantly, power ran through me, ready to pour out with a single command fueled by an incredible need to protect. My will melted into the gift stirring deep within. There was a pulsing in my veins, strengthening with each beat of my heart.

Edda's icy fingers wrapped around my wrist once more. She yanked me to face her.

"Do *not* release your power, child. If you hope to live to help your people, you must refrain." Her hold was painful enough to leave marks.

For days, this moment was all I could think of. And now that it had finally come, I found it difficult to concentrate on anything but the chaos. Below, Lysians and Bavadrins were running all over in an unorganized mess. Bavadrin blades basked in red blood while Lysian teeth dripped of it. The intruders did not even trigger the city's alarms. As a result, the Lysians got within the walls with terrifying ease.

I found Erik without even searching for him, for he was wholly impossible to miss. He towered above all others surrounding him. Power dripped from him as if it were too great to ever be contained. He moved with a lethal grace. Angry flames licked everything surrounding him, threatening the entire world, but not him.

I nearly threw up when I grasped what he was.

Fire danced across Erik's fingers, brilliantly red and terribly violent. He was a conjuror.

A conjuror capable of wielding fire with complete control.

My mouth went dry as a tremble moved through me.

Conjurors were not common, and I certainly *never* suspected that he was one. The thought had not crossed my mind, not even once. What a fool I was. If anyone should have considered the possibility of it, then it should have been me.

Conjuring numbers had dwindled over the years. They were disappearing. Mostly only weak ones remained, a small remnant of the powers our ancestors once had. Yet I knew strong ones could exist, and I had not once considered the Lysian to be one.

The entire time that Erik had been in prison, he had been the one in control. The lashings he received were to ensure that the battle would break out and that his people would be on the right side of things. Fraser's actions cursed our entire race.

My head spun, and my skin turned clammy.

Erik raised his hand, poised to strike and incinerate the person thrown to the ground before him. With a cold shock, I recognized the Bavadrin whose knees grew wet with blood-slicked earth, the one who raised his arm in a futile effort to protect his face from the angry flames. My heart nearly stopped in my chest. *Landin.*

Edda must have seen the same thing, for her hand tightened its hold on my wrist and her other gripped my shoulder. Bony fingers dug into my flesh and threatened to dislocate my shoulder if I made any move to use my conjuring gift. She was the only thing keeping me from diving off the balcony altogether. With Edda shackled to me, my only potential tool was my voice. So, without thinking it through or having a plan, I acted on instinct, hoping that it would be enough to spare the life in the Lysian's hands.

"Erik!" His name was a roar on my lips. Though my voice was

lost to most over the sound of the battle between us, his unnaturally keen hearing found it.

The Lysian conjuror stopped mid-assault, angling his head as
if to better focus his hearing on me. The fire still danced in his
hand.

I froze, suspended in that terrifying moment for what felt like
an eternity.

I did not yell again, for Erik likely could hear what was spoken.
They were treacherous words, but to save the lives of those I loved,
I would become whatever I needed to be. I would be a traitor to
the Bavadrin laws.

"Spare him, and I will give you Fraser." Another tremble
moved through me as I found myself completely at his mercy.
"Please. I beg you."

The fire dancing over Erik's fingers receded, and he turned his
attention to me fully then, his eyes a dark, threatening storm. An
icy touch traveled down my spine as he pinned me so completely
with a look that I found it difficult to draw in air. This was his true
predatory form. A lion dropped into a pasture of sheep. Never had
I seen the Bavadrins as sheep, but he made them seem as such. We
stood no chance, especially if Edda's warnings were true and I was
not to use my own powers or risk a much worse outcome. The
Lysians were to take control. That was inevitable, and the sooner it
was to happen, the quicker innocent lives could be spared.

On the ground, Landin followed Erik's gaze till it led to me.
Fear crossed his features, and he jumped to his feet, preparing to
protect me from the animal who now watched me. A raise of my
hand and a slight shake of my head was enough to still Landin
before he did something that would give Erik no choice but to take
his life.

Relief flooded through me when Landin did not move another
muscle towards the Lysian with the power to command fire.

I then spoke to Erik. The only other hearing my words was

Edda, who still held me in an iron grip. "Enter the building to your left through the red door. Go left, take the first right, third door on the right. Fraser will likely be there." And just like that, by our Bavadrin laws, I became a traitor to my people and the things we held sacred.

Erik gave a command to those around him and was gone in moments, leaving Landin freely staring at me. An expression of shock at being spared splayed across his handsome face. He turned, glancing at Erik, who was heading in the direction I had set him on. Landin was likely putting together what I had just done, connecting the dots. Whether he judged me or not did not matter, for he would at least live to make that decision for himself.

I fell to my knees then, struggling to breathe, my chest aching.

The Bavadrins, including myself, followed a set of rules, one of which was to never stand against our Leader Superior in a way that might bring them harm. Our words and that sacred promise were something that breathed life into the Bavadrin ways. Never did anyone act against that rule. Until now. Generations of leaders and never had they been betrayed in such a way.

Edda always said that I was the next to lead the Bavadrin people, that she saw it to be true. But how could the Spirit choose me after what I had done? I broke a promise to shield the Superior until the end. It was an unforgivable act.

"You did what you must to protect them," Edda said, and I realized I had no idea when she released her hold on me.

I nodded numbly while the sounds of screams died down. Either the battle was slowing, Bavadrins realizing their loss, or so many had been slaughtered that there were simply fewer people to cry out. Fear wrapped its talons around my neck as I tried to look back over the balcony. With great effort and dread, I forced my head to turn, to view the world below. Some were throwing down their swords, and the Lysians were shoving them against walls, but not killing them. I couldn't find Landin.

Edda left me on the balcony floor while going to retrieve something from within. When she re-emerged, she wrapped a hooded
cloak around me and handed me a burlap sack. Thin fingers
gripped my chin, forcing me to turn away from the destruction.

"You will be leaving us for some time," she said, touching the
sack. She had packed me a bag to take on my trip into a prison of
my own. Wrinkled hands took mine, and I met Edda's dark eyes. "I
am certain that you will be fine. You will soon return here. You will
free the Bavadrins of so much more than your father's horrid
rule."

When I nodded, she stood, pulling me with her and taking me
inside.

"Someone is coming for you now. It is a Lysian, but he will not
harm you." She brought an icy hand to my cheek, and I welcomed
the cooling touch. "I must go." Edda glanced over her shoulder at
the door. "Collect as much information as you can while you are
there and then return home to me. Get them to bring you back to
perform the ceremony that seals your fate as the leader of our
people. We will figure out a way to free you after you take control.
I will call upon the Sparrow Archers when the time is right. They
will return to the city and help you."

"You should take the passage," I mumbled. There was a way
through the wall of my room, which led to another empty room.
She could have gone unseen if she took it.

"No, I will be fine." Edda offered a quick hug. She released me
and turned towards the exit to my bedroom, but she never got the
chance to make her escape before the door opened.

A Lysian stood on the other side.

6

ARIANA

The Lysian looked like he was part man, part yellow bear. His shaggy blond hair was unkempt, making him appear wild. His arms and chest were enormous, in a terrifyingly brutal way. A scar carved the side of his face, spanning from eyebrow to jaw. Chilling ice-blue eyes pinned me. He looked everything that the Bavadrin stories had warned about Lysians.

As soon as the beast of a Lysian stood on the threshold, I halted in my tracks, all my focus going to him. Like a deer who had caught the sight of a hunter, I froze, waiting for him to make his move before I acted in response.

He must have seen the alarm written all over my face, for when he spoke, his voice was gentle, not harsh as I would have expected coming from someone who looked like him.

"I'm not here to harm you," he assured, sheathing his blade, and opening his hands out before him as if to show he was unarmed. "But it will be easier if you come with me willingly."

Armed or not, he was a threat. Every muscle in his gigantic body was primed to kill, and that was not even considering his teeth or claws. Someone like him needed no weapons to be deadly.

I did not move or make a sound in response.

"I have come here to escort you to the Lysian territory under orders to protect you. No harm will come to you." There was an almost effortless kindness to him whenever he spoke, which was a stark contrast to the way he looked.

When I still did not move, Edda acted. She came over and hugged me, wrapping her thin yet powerful arms around me.

"Be brave. You will return to me," she whispered before releasing me with a small push towards the massive Lysian who was surprisingly patient as he waited. I expected him to drag me away for taking too long, yet he did no such thing.

I did not reply to Edda as I took a small step towards the stranger. As I did, he moved into the hall, keeping the space between us from closing too quickly.

My ears felt as if they were filled with cotton. All sounds were muffled except for the pulsing of my heart, sending blood rushing to my head. My legs wobbled unsteadily beneath me. Tension tightened my throat.

I had no control over the events going on around me, the danger the Bavadrins had been placed in. If only I had acted sooner against Fraser or, at the very least, put up more of a challenge when he sentenced the Lysian to the lashings. Perhaps then the outcome would have been more favorable. Instead of having my world and everything I've ever known crumbling.

I tried to focus on my steps to keep upright. My head spun, feeling lightheaded.

Without saying goodbye, I left Edda in my room to follow the stranger.

The Lysian was careful not to touch me while leading me through the building. I was surprised by how he appeared to know his way around, taking care to avoid areas that were likely to be crowded or well-traveled. It was not until he led me to a side exit of the building that I finally found my voice and spoke to him.

"The people here, my people, what will happen to them?" I asked.

He paused, quickly scanning the surroundings before turning his full attention to me. "We will spare them, and if Lysians are attacked, then we were told to use nonlethal means, if possible." He turned, considering the environment. "We need to keep moving."

The Lysian told me what I wanted to hear. Was he just trying to subdue me, or was it the truth? There was no way for me to know.

He continued leading me over the terrain a short distance before we arrived at a huge dark gray horse. A long mane flowed down its side while its ears flickered towards the sound of our approach.

"From here we ride," the Lysian said, holding out his hand to help me up. A hand that could grow claws and slice through flesh with too much ease.

A glance around let me know that there was no other horse. I was left with no choice but to consent.

Accepting his hand, I allowed him to help me onto the animal before he took a seat behind me. Goosebumps covered my flesh at the proximity. Never had I been so close to a Lysian before. I could literally feel the warmth coming off his skin as his arms moved around me to grab hold of the reins. Though he touched me as little as possible, it was an impossible situation. There was no way to share a horse without contact.

The trip to their Lysian territory was nearly a day's journey. That was if one stopped for rest along the way. It quickly became apparent that Lysians did not have the same rest requirement as the Bavadrins. And their horses were insanely faster.

The sun rose and crossed the sky. We rode in silence, not stopping until we passed into their territory. I did not know how the horse didn't die of exhaustion. Even their animals were superior to our own.

The Lysian relax just a fraction behind me when we passed onto their land. Once in the thick of their forest, he finally allowed us to stop and rest just as the sun began setting.

I hadn't realized how cold it had gotten. Without the warmth of the stranger behind me, the icy air surrounded me in a chilly embrace before sinking into my bones.

My muscles groaned and shivered uselessly while the Lysian built a fire before he handed me a blanket. For his monstrous size, he continued to surprise me with his gentleness. It was not something we'd been told his kind had been known for.

Eventually, the Lysian settled down before the fire, but not before providing me with some water and bread. I shamelessly devoured every scrap of food and downed the water in record time. Wincing, I shifted into a more comfortable position. My entire body sore from riding for so long. Muscles and bones protested every movement as I settled down with the blanket wrapped snugly around me.

Several heartbeats went by while the Lysian and I simply stared at one another without saying a word. It was unnerving, having something like him silently watching me. His icy eyes felt cold even in the darkness. The way the firelight danced across the features of his face and the scar that ran from eyebrow to jaw had me tensing. Finally, when I thought he might try to attack me, he lay back and closed his eyes.

Relieved that his attention was no longer on me, I found the courage to finally speak.

"Why—why are you being kind to me?" I asked, for he was nothing like what I expected. He didn't need to feed me or give me water, didn't need to provide me with a blanket. I would have survived without those comforts, at least for a while.

His blue eyes slid open, and he angled his head my way. "Two reasons: First, my King asked it of me. Second, and most importantly, you helped my friend when he needed it. You were gentle and kind to a Lysian when you needn't be. We are returning the favor. As long as you do not give me trouble, I do not need to be anything other than that."

I shifted to better view him. "Your King was there? In the Bavadrin lands? In that battle?"

A sloppy smile softened the Lysian's features until his teeth glinted in the firelight. And suddenly, the smile looked more intimidating than comforting. "You will speak to my King soon enough." He responded to my eagerness instead of my questions.

"And Erik is your friend?"

"Indeed, he is." The Lysian closed his eyes, a smile still splayed on his face.

For some reason, I felt better knowing that he was friends with Erik. It was senseless, for Erik brought destruction to my lands. Yet, the conjuror had spared Landin's life. That act alone meant a great deal, despite what it cost me.

I glanced at the unfamiliar darkness. Never had I been in a territory not belonging to Bavadrins. Bare tree limbs reached for the sky while moonlight filtered through, creating an eerie sensation. Straining my eyes, I tried to see the forest beyond the warmth of the fire. My vision played tricks, or something was moving beyond.

Despite hardly knowing the Lysian before me, I was glad to have him near, for I could have sworn I saw the glowing eyes of beasts in the distance.

Frowning, I lay down with the blanket wrapped tightly around myself. Rest was challenging to find. Every single noise made my pulse race. As soon as it would slow enough for me to potentially drift off, there was another unfamiliar sound to set it off.

My travel companion woke before sunrise and, seeing as I was already awake after a sleepless night, we were quick to continue our journey under cover of darkness. Neither of us spoke to one another the entire time.

I would have thought that the silence between two strangers of races at war would have been uncomfortable, but it wasn't. The quiet strangely did not feel empty.

I did not know where exactly I was being taken, did not know what was to become of my people or me. Yet I felt oddly content, foolishly hoping that the worst had ended. I imagined the Bavadrin people afraid and confused but safe. Imagined myself unharmed, and someday soon returning to the Bavadrin lands. Such thoughts brought me comfort, for I believed in them as if they were fact. I had a fleeting concern that perhaps I was becoming delusional, but I shoved the notion away. If I was to survive the days to come, I needed to believe those things to be true. Edda promised that these things were clear in the future she saw.

Eventually, a city came into view. The first thing I noticed was the lack of a wall or barrier surrounding it. The second were the buildings, some of which were taller than even the trees. Nearly everything was made of stone, and most of it looked the same. I had no idea how people did not get lost navigating street after street of the similar-looking roads, buildings, doors, and windows. The only landmark was the largest structure towards the back of the city.

Lysians in the streets peered at me as we passed. I wondered what they thought of having an outsider enter their land. They probably felt as welcoming as the Bavadrins felt towards Erik.

The Lysian led me to the tall and wide structure further in the city. Was this what castles looked like? It was not flashy or architecturally appealing, just massive and stone. Once outside the thick wooden doors, we dismounted, and he led me into the building. I followed in silent awe. Yet again, hall after hall, it was all the same. The structure was a vertical and horizontal maze, one I doubted I could ever escape without a guide. It was a prison without the need for bars or a cell. What was the purpose for such a large structure?

"The first three floors are generally common rooms and spaces. Top two floors are private quarters," the Lysian informed though I was uncertain as to why he provided such information when I expected to be taken to a cell.

Eventually, he stopped leading me through the halls and opened a door to a comfortably sized sitting room. A couple of leather-covered chairs sat in the center of the space along with a small table, and a hearth. All of it was decorated in earthy tones. Within the sitting room, there were two more doors. The Lysian walked to the one on the right and opened it before stepping aside.

He angled his head. "This will be where you stay for the time being."

I hesitated in shocked surprise. The room was not a prison cell, at least not a typical one. I doubted I was free to leave or walk around. But they were going to keep me in a cageless cage? The Lysians must truly have seen me as harmless, like a puppy that was easily maneuvered, void of its strong adult teeth and muscular physique.

"You will stay here," he said when my eyes struggled absorbing it all.

It was extraordinarily luxurious. Thick fabrics hung from the windows and walls. Though the room offered more color, it was still made up of earthy lavender tones. The space was grand, nicer even than mine at home.

"Who is in the other room?" I asked, looking over at the other door in the sitting room.

"The King," he answered and laughed when my jaw dropped and eyes grew large.

Why would the King place me so close to his space? Perhaps he wanted to learn of the Bavadrin ways just as I wanted to know of the Lysians? Whatever the reason, it was clear he didn't think I was a threat. I doubted they would put the typical prisoner of war so close to their leader. The Bavadrins certainly would never place a Lysian next door to the Leader Superior.

"How long am I to stay here?" I turned to the Lysian, who posted himself outside of my door.

"As long as it is required." His response offered no timeline.

"Required for what?" I glanced at him, but he was simply staring at the far wall and paying me little attention.

"For us to save our own," he said, and in his voice, I almost thought I heard sadness.

The door to my room remained open while the Lysian remained in the small common area. I explored my new surroundings further. The furniture was made of dark and sturdy wood, the floor primarily covered by an ornate rug of creams, browns, greens, and yellows. There was a large window and two floor-to-ceiling glass doors which opened to a balcony.

My hand touched the doorknob, pushing it. I had expected it not to budge, but instead, it gave way and opened. Hesitating, I wondered if the Lysian would come running and reprimand my exploration. He didn't. Quickly, I surveyed the area, noting that I was on the fifth floor. To jump from such a height would risk injuring myself, posing far too great a risk. It would not make for a viable escape.

"If I were you, I certainly would not try jumping from this height." The guard's voice sounded from within. I spun around to find him leaning in the doorway of my new but very much temporary room. He had a casual stance, but I knew his senses were poised and alert, trained on me.

My face flushed. The Lysian knew exactly what I was doing and even thinking. Though I suppose it was easy to do given the situation. What would a prisoner do if not look for a potential escape?

How long had the Lysian been standing in the doorway, silently observing me as I familiarized myself with my prison? It troubled me, for he was so massive, yet moved soundlessly.

"Don't think I could make it?" I asked, finding no point in hiding my thoughts.

He quirked his head to the side. "Are all Bavadrins like you?" His eyes narrowed a fraction. There was an air of mistrust in the statement, in that tone.

"I'm not sure what you mean." I walked past him and into the room but kept the balcony doors open, welcoming the fresh, warm autumn air.

"I had always believed Bavadrins were cunning and untrustworthy. Yet you helped Erik, and you don't appear to lie or spin stories. Honesty seems to ruminate within you. It does not match what we know of your kind."

"Or perhaps you just haven't been around me long enough for me to spin a proper web," I countered. To pretend to be innocent and weak would not win me any favors. The Lysian guard appeared to respond to honesty, as did I. I would use that to my advantage to win his favor. He was right to be wary, but I would try to show him he could trust me, that I was not a threat to his kind.

The Lysian lifted a single golden eyebrow as he contemplated my words.

I crossed my arms over my chest as if squaring off with the beast before me. "And are all Lysians like you? Large and inquisitive?"

He smiled, canines flashing. "You should only be so lucky to have one like me tasked with keeping an eye on someone like you."

The Lysian was likely not wrong with that statement. I doubted anyone else would come off as almost welcoming to their prisoners of war. Erik certainly did not have such a hospitable experience when he was a captive. Suddenly suspicion set in, and I wondered whether the Lysian was tasked with making me feel comfortable in an attempt to find out potential secrets should I divulge them. If that were the case, then he had met his match. A Lysian like him likely believed he had nothing to fear from a Bavadrin woman, for he could easily overpower me with his size and strength. Lucky for me, I could rely on something far stronger than physical strength for protection. It was enough to help me keep my chin lifted and spine straight.

"I don't even know your name," I pointed out. We traveled together for two days and nights, if you also counted the night we left, a majority of it done so in silence. Still, it was a great deal of time to spend with someone and not know what to call them.

"Kole," he answered casually, his crystal eyes focused on me expectantly. He wanted me to introduce myself, though I was certain that he already knew my name.

"Kole, I am Ariana," I offered, and then glanced back to the open balcony door.

"You do not fear us, Ariana," he said, blue eyes not once drifting from me.

"I do not doubt that if you wished to harm me, you could easily do so." I stroked his ego with my words. "But you have yet to show that you are a threat to my life. I am cautious, but fear would not serve me well here."

"You do not fear the unknown? You are in a new world right now. You have no idea what we have planned. For all you know, you may be on the dinner menu tonight. Yet you do not fear that possibility?" He seemed genuinely curious, but his lips curved skywards. He was toying with me, trying to gain a fear response.

I wanted him to like me, not to see me as someone to entertain his boredom at my expense.

"Fear of the unknown does not serve me. I fear the things I

know, the monsters who are clear to me." I explained with a trail of breadcrumbs for him to pick up.

"What monsters?" he asked, so diligently picking up those carefully placed crumbs.

Good boy.

"You should only be so lucky never to know." My words were teasing. The suspense building, and then my stomach growled loudly.

Kole's gaze drifted to the open balcony. "Food should be brought to you any moment now," he informed me before retreating into the common room. Our conversation ended. I wondered what he made of it, disappointed that he did not ask more.

I took the time to explore the room further. The bed was extensive, with a thick wooden headboard, and a dresser with a mirror made of the same wide and sturdy wood stood alongside one wall. A leather chair was pushed against the wall in a corner of the room with a small square table next to it. I ran my hand over the table, feeling the lumber underneath my fingertips. It was smooth, with soft ripples of the wood running through it. While the dresser and bed frame were simple, the table was not. The sides and legs were carved with intricate interwoven designs, the craftsmanship unlike anything I had ever seen.

Kole had been true to his word, for food arrived shortly after he left me. A Lysian woman brought a tray and handed it to Kole, who then brought it to me. My mouth watered from the smell of pheasant and warm bread. There was also jam and sliced cucumbers. Accepting the tray, I proceeded to devour everything in record time while sitting on the edge of the bed. Kole remained in the other room, though with the door open, we had a direct view of one another.

"Are you not hungry?" I asked the Lysian when I finished my meal. He had yet to eat anything in front of me. He must have been starving. Surely his massive size required equally massive meals for upkeep.

"We do not need to eat as often as you Bavadrins," was his only response. He had withdrawn from me, no longer wishing to play with words.

The sun lowered over the horizon, darkening the sky. I retreated entirely into my temporary room and tried to calm myself enough to sleep. My thoughts were on a never-ending rotation, pushing one worry out and another took its place over and over until the entire pattern began from the beginning. My mind drifted between my people, Edda, Landin, and Willis, and what I had done by giving up our Leader Superior.

After bathing and finally washing the grime of travel from my skin, my mind must had settled enough to drift to sleep.

In the early hours of the morning, I huffed an audible breath. The soft white sheets were tangled around me, evidence of the restless night. Nightmares tainted what little sleep there was.

"You may want to get up and get dressed," a voice said from within my room, only a few feet away.

The hair on the back of my neck stood on its ends, and I sat straight up at the unknown presence, finding Kole casually standing by the balcony doors. He peered outside, consumed by whatever he saw in the distance.

"Seems that his highness is returning sooner than expected," Kole said before taking an audible breath and turning to me. "It appears as though you do fear," he commented lowly, his icy gaze pinning me before he finally walked out of the room without a sound.

My heart to thunder in my chest. I had no doubt the Lysian heard it, and I also suspected he smelled the panic that surged through me at the sudden realization that I was not alone. I sat there a few more seconds without moving a single muscle, too stunned to respond.

How long had the Lysian been standing in my room without my knowing? A shiver ran down my body. Kole could have been there all night, watching me as I slept. He was soundless.

Lysians were made of massive muscular bodies, yet they were so agile, capable of moving in complete silence. With skills like that, they could easily sneak up on an enemy and slaughter them before any form of alarm could be sounded. If things tumbled into war, the Bavadrins would need to see the Lysians coming, for we would not hear their approach.

I hoped that Edda truly found a way to send word to the Sparrow Archers to rejoin us in the city. They would likely be our best option for sensing when a threat such as a Lysian drew near. The legends always said that the forest whispered to the Sparrows. That they could see beyond their vision, around the trees, and that their arrows always found their mark.

Once my breathing returned to normal, I got out of bed and put on a top and loose pants. Luckily, I found a brush in the room and somewhat tamed the unbound hair, which was a mess from tossing and turning all night. The left side of my head was still braided with our ancestral beads and ribbons, marking me as a Bavadrin and daughter of the Leader Superior.

I approached the sitting room where Kole remained guard, wondering if he would take me somewhere to meet his King.

No sooner than I deemed myself presentable, the exterior door to the sitting room opened. Erik's eyes immediately found mine, and he momentarily paused on the threshold before entering. My focus slipped away, and I forgot what I wanted to ask Kole. My mind emptied itself and filled with the presence of the Lysian conjuror.

His gaze alone had the power to render my legs useless, for they became leaden and heavy. My breath caught in my throat. Had he always been so tall, his eyes so deep and darkly blue, like a pool of water with no bottom? Had his presence always felt like this? Authority clung to him, to every movement, every look, and I did not know how he kept so much of it hidden when imprisoned by Fraser.

Erik wore dark clothing perfectly tailored to his body. Though his shirt opened into a deep V, showing off the hard lines of his chest. His brown hair was groomed, and he appeared to have cleaned up well since his visit to the Bavadrin lands. There was no evidence of blood staining his hands, and I hoped that he indeed did not bloody them with my people.

"Your Majesty." Kole bowed deeply in greeting, but not before I glimpsed the smirk splayed on his face.

Your Majesty.

It was a title used for Kings and queens.

Spirit, help me.

Erik was not a mere prince.

He was the Lysian King.

7

ERIK

Ariana's warm golden complexion paled as she realized my identity: I was not just a son of the Lysian King, not any longer. Her eyes widened in surprise, as if finally seeing me for the first time. She stood frozen in the center of the sitting area, outside the room that was hers for the duration of her stay. It was a decent suite, but most importantly, it was adjacent to mine. Even with Kole watching over her, I felt better keeping her close. It seemed she was less likely to cause trouble that way.

Her frame was more petite than I remembered. Everything about her physical appearance was harmless. Delicate hands remained at her sides, while large green eyes viewed me with caution. Her unbound hair cascaded in waves down past her shoulders; the other half of it was still secured with ribbons and braids in intricate knots.

"I need to speak with our guest alone." I turned to Kole, who glanced at Ariana before a grin he couldn't hide spread across his face.

"Of course," he said, smiling like a fool, clearly relishing the discomfort he caused the Bavadrin. With a single wink in her direction, he left the room, leaving me alone with her.

With the door to the suite behind me, I was keenly aware that Ariana had nowhere to go. She was trapped. The thought made my heart beat a fraction faster, and it was an effort to keep my expression neutral. Ariana had always seemed confident, behaving as if she were invincible, as if I posed no threat at all.

Her understanding had expanded since then. Now, for every step I took towards her, she took steps back until she stood at the far end of her chamber. She only stopped moving when I did, pausing on the threshold of her bedroom.

"You fear me now?" I asked, noting the faint scent of it emanating from her.

The column of her throat worked, lips parting, drawing in a breath. "You're a conjuror," she stated, "and the King of the Lysians." It wasn't an answer, but both titles should have unsettled someone in her position.

"Do you not have conjurors where you come from?" I asked casually, knowing they must. Conjurors existed among all our races—Lysian, Bavadrin, and Siddhe.

She hesitated for only a moment.

"Not like you," she replied cautiously, clearly guarding her people's secrets. It mattered not, for I did not need her to offer them up. I only needed to control them. Through her, I hoped it would be easy to do just that.

The time I had to speak with her was short, and I wished there was more of it. It was rare to find someone like her, so fragile, yet so seemingly brave. Despite her hesitation and the fact that she now carefully backed away when I approached, she still held her head high, and her hands did not tremble by her sides. She displayed a certain confidence. Yet a small tendril of fear had wrapped around her.

I wondered how deeply that courageous exterior of hers

cracked by the recent turn of events in her life. Was it further crumbling while we spoke? Had she finally gathered enough sense to know the dire situations she placed herself in over the past several days?

When in battle I lifted my hand to strike the Bavadrin guard who cowered at my feet, it was partially because he opposed me, but it was also because he placed a curious thing such as Ariana into my path for me to take if I wished. She entered my cell because he opened the door for her. He was no protector, a lousy guard, and not the kind of male I needed to join my army. But then her voice called my name, rising above all sounds, and she struck a bargain. Ariana sacrificed her father for that pathetic guard who trembled at my feet. It was clear that she cared for him and so he was spared, as a favor to her. I wondered how she now felt about it all—freely offering up her own blood, to save a simple guard who harbored little concern for her safety.

To unravel Ariana's thoughts, to see her fears splayed out before me...my pulse quickened. How delicious it would have been to know those things. Her hiding behind a false shell of courage only made me more curious about what vulnerability lingered behind it. I found myself walking a fine line—wishing to show her that Lysians were not simply the monsters Bavadrins made us out to be, yet also desiring to become just that. It bothered me that she behaved as if I were harmless while in their pitiful Bavadrin dungeon.

I shoved those thoughts aside and forced myself to focus. I was the King, and as such, I needed not to play games with the Bavadrin girl who I hoped would become helpful in the days to come.

"Your people are largely safe. Some of my forces remained in your city to keep order. But your father has been brought here. He is to be executed tonight," I informed her, my tone steady though internally conflicted. "You will be present at his execution."

The Bavadrin people had their own traditions and rituals. When one leader fell, another was chosen by blood. The entire process was followed by some sort of ritual to seal the deal. I needed to know if Ariana was the one chosen to lead next. It was evident that she cared for her people, but that did not mean she would become the next ruler. Bringing her to my home was a gamble, but my gut usually proved correct.

Ariana was going to be at the execution. I needed to see for myself both her father's death and whether she was the next in line. It was simply how it needed to be, yet I couldn't help but feel a weight pressing into me for what I would force her to witness. A girl like her was unlikely to have ever seen death in such a way, a life taken by force before its time.

"I understand," was Ariana's only reply, her gaze dropping to the ground. Perhaps she regretted her decision to sacrifice the man.

"I tried to speak to your leader by the name of Fraser, but he refuses to work with me. He is leaving me no other choice," I said to her, wanting her to know that I did not seal his fate without first attempting to come to some sort of agreement. Perhaps that knowledge would help shift the weight of what was happening from her shoulders and onto his. For some reason, I wanted to bring a small amount of comfort to the Bavadrin girl. It was odd— one moment I wanted to control her fears, and the next, I wished to comfort her.

"I wouldn't have expected him to agree to anything with you." Her voice was low, eyes remaining fixed on the ground.

"And you would?" I asked, taking a small step closer as if proximity could reveal the truth.

The question caused her green stare to shift up, meeting mine. "If I say no, will you kill me too?" she boldly asked, lifting her chin. The scent of her fear had nearly vanished. She asked such a question without trepidation. Though she stepped away from me when I first approached, she now regained some of that troubling confidence.

"I would prefer not to." My words did not reassure her. Nor were they meant to as her fate remained undecided. If she impeded our purpose, then she needed to be removed. It was as simple as that. There was still the uncertainty of what to do with her if she was not chosen to be the next Bavadrin leader.

Ariana should have heeded my warning and run away from that city. Perhaps then she would not have found herself in such a position. Yet she did not listen.

"If the things you say are true—if Lysians are truly being imprisoned in the Siddhe lands—then I will help you, but not as your prisoner," she said with a calm conviction. Perhaps she had not been shaken as thoroughly as I expected. Still, she continued to carry an air of courage, even when alone in my home. A curious little thing. I would never have guessed that a Bavadrin could be so void of fear, especially one like her. The entire world seemed as though it could be a threat to her safety, yet she stood solidly before me. Any other in her place would have trembled, fallen to their knees, and begged for their life to be spared, yet she did none of those things.

"Do you know anything about Lysians being taken to the Siddhe lands?" I asked her.

"No." She held my gaze.

"But you believe me." I took another step, almost close enough to touch. "Why?"

"What makes you think I believe you?" She answered with a question of her own. It was difficult to read her intentions behind that statement.

Glancing at the window, I cursed internally. The sun was higher in the sky than expected. There was still much to be done before nightfall. I needed to meet with my brothers, a conversation that was unlikely to be pleasant.

"I have some things I need to attend to. Kole will escort you when it's time for you to join us. For today, you will remain confined to this area. Starting tomorrow, Kole can take you around the grounds if you wish to venture outside of this room," I informed her.

She only offered me a silent nod in response before I left her standing there as I exited the common room and shut the door.

Kole leaned against the wall in the hall, waiting to resume his duties as the Bavadrin girl's guard.

"It's good to see you in one piece," he grinned, his blond hair a mess atop his head. Muscular arms folded over his broad chest. Not many were larger in stature than me, Kole was.

"It certainly is good to be back home." I smiled at my friend.

His grin faltered, and he nodded towards the door I just walked from. "What are you doing with her, Erik?"

"I think she can be helpful to us. To lead her people. They will be better fighters if they feel as though they do it willingly for their leader and not because it's that or we kill them," I told him. Of course, it would only work if she was the next one to rule her people and if she agreed to help us. The plan harbored more *ifs* than I would have liked.

"She is . . . nearly likable, for a Bavadrin," Kole stated, his lip curling as if bothered by the thought.

His comment offered more relief than it should have. I wasn't the only one who felt anything other than hate for a Bavadrin, especially one whose father was their leader. The question remained whether she was truly who she seemed to be or if it was all some sort of ploy—true to their Bavadrin ways, spinning webs of deceit. My instincts always pointed towards suspicion, yet her willingness to tend to my wounds when she didn't know who I was pulled me in another direction. She certainly was an unexpected discovery.

The plan was to take the Bavadrins by force. That hadn't

changed, but perhaps we didn't need to use as brutal a force as originally planned.

"I take it she has not brought you any trouble during your time with her?" I asked.

He shook his head.

"Keep an eye on her." I was turning to leave when Kole audibly groaned.

"I am not a babysitter." Kole unfolded his hands and stepped towards me in protest.

The hair on the back of my neck stood. Irritation and heat flooded my veins. "You will do as you are told," I replied, a growl hidden beneath the words. It wasn't a request from a friend, but an order from his King.

"Apologies." Kole's gaze dropped to the ground submissively, and he gave a slight bow of his head in agreement. It had been difficult for us in these new roles. I favored Kole's friendship, but my position demanded his obedience. It was an adjustment for both of us.

Leaving Kole to his duties without another complaint, I began checking items off the mental list of things that needed to be done before nightfall. First on the list was seeing my brothers. Turning down the hall towards our family gathering room, I made my way to where they expected me.

8

ERIK

My three brothers sat in a circle, waiting. I wondered how long they had been stuck in a room together. Judging by the lack of destruction, it couldn't have been too long. Spirit knows they could only be together for a short stretch before someone pushed another with their words, and chaos quickly followed.

They lounged in three separate chairs, all facing a circular table. One chair remained open for me to take. Old family texts spanning floor to ceiling filled the far wall. Worn leather bound most of the volumes, some of which had cracked because of lack of proper handling. Years of unuse caused the leather to dry. The smell of old paper bound in leather wafted through our family meeting room. It was a scent I didn't think I could ever grow tired of.

"It is about time!" Iver growled when I walked in. He was the youngest and always the most impatient. By this point in life, he should have acquired a fraction of restraint, yet he still hadn't. He continued to run around with a rough temperament and childlike deviance. It was aggravating, more so because I longed for a time when the Lysians did not depend on me to lead. For a time when I was like Iver, free of the burden which came with a crown.

Jorn took a deep breath. "I see we were not the first of your stops since you came home." He always had a gift for scenting and tracking, even surpassing my own. Though I did not touch Ariana, in a day's time, her room took on her scent. It now lingered around me.

The other two sniffed in my direction. "Who is she, Erik? And why is she staying in your room?" Jorn asked.

"She is staying *next* to my room," I clarified.

"Why?" Iver inquired. His gray gaze settled on mine, demanding an answer.

Edmond was the only one to not first ask of the new stranger. Instead, he viewed me from head to toe. "It's good to have you back and alive," he said with a small smile.

At least one of my brothers cared for my return. Granted, it was the one who would become King if I were to ever perish. Edmond enjoyed having power, but he shied away from the burden of it, preferring to remain the brother to the King. Iver was no different, preferring the freedom to create chaos. Jorn was the one most hungry for power.

Jorn laughed. "Of course he is alive. The Bavadrins have nothing on us."

"They have the lands between us and the Siddhe." Iver rolled his eyes, pointing out the thing that they did indeed have. It was the reason for everything I did to this point.

"Not anymore," Jorn snapped at the air in irritation. The two of them often rubbed each other the wrong way.

"But you didn't leave uninjured," Edmond wished to clarify, catching the attention of the others.

The lashings on my back stopped bleeding, and no longer bothered me. I could largely forget about them until they were pointed out. Ariana was correct when she warned her father about raising a hand against me. Lysians were often scarred, for we are not a cautious group. The royals were no better, but we were superior in our skill. As leaders for our people, we were taught from childhood how to hone our senses, how to fight, and how to protect ourselves. Our lack of scars was a show of power, not a lack of danger in our lives. My brothers all remained flawlessly scarless, while I now harbored too many to even count.

"It was necessary to break the treaty," I said, hoping that we would not need to dwell on it.

"Indeed. It must have been difficult for you not to just incinerate them all." Edmond arched a golden brow.

"You have no idea," I grumbled. That was perhaps the most torturous act of all—allowing them to inflict pain when I posed them no harm, at least none that they knew of. Their actions set in motion everything that occurred after. They had no one to blame but themselves.

"Any trouble here?" I asked.

"The mountain has remained quiet," Edmond said. "You could have remained in the Bavadrin lands a bit longer."

I shook my head. "A lot of our seasoned warriors are now in the Bavadrin land's."

Iver grinned as he said, "You think we need seasoned warriors to keep the unwanted from coming down that mountain?" His smile only grew as we all ignored his comment. It was not just the exiled Lysians but a conjuror we had to deal with amongst that mountain. And even my brothers, as elite in combat training as they were, were not equipped for that. Fire had to fight fire.

"So, the treaty is broken. Why is the Bavadrin girl here?" Edmond finally joined in the questioning about the new visitor.

"She is the daughter of the current leader. I am hoping that if she takes over after him, that she can help us. If she agrees to work with us, then the Bavadrins will be that much easier to control.

They will fight harder for their leader than they would if we simply commanded them to."

"And why do you think one of her kind would ever do something like that?" Jorn asked, tilting his head in question. "They are not known for their kindness or trustworthiness." He folded his arms across his chest and leaned back in his seat.

"Because, when the Bavadrins finished whipping me, she entered my cell and cared for my wounds. She did not need to do that and asked for nothing in return before tending to my back," I said, silencing them for only a single glorious moment.

Iver whistled lowly. "So, she's lost a few marbles?" A smile splayed on his face while Edmond frowned.

"At first, yes, I thought she was stupid for her lack of fear, for coming near me. But she is not stupid, far from it. If her father listened to her, then the treaty may have never been broken. She is something else entirely. I think she can be helpful to us."

"So, this is either the Spirit bringing you two together to help us free our Lysians. Or it's her Bavadrin blood and whispers which are already casting spells on you." Jorn was clearly concerned about the latter. By the look on Edmond's face, he was inclined to agree.

"And you think killing her father in front of her will sway her to help you?" Iver asked me as if he thought I was an idiot, earning him a warning growl. He was my little brother, but he would be put in his place if needed. Never was I known for my patience, and the way I was currently wound up, there was even less room for it.

"Of course, I know it will not likely be beneficial. But I need to be there when he is put out of his miserable existence, and I need her to be there to see if there is any hint at her taking his place as the next Bavadrin leader. Also, I doubt that she harbors much love for her father. She is the reason we captured him so quickly." I no sooner finished speaking before the next question was being asked.

"She tended to your wounds. You, someone who is little more than an animal in their eyes, and you think she won't bat an eye when her own family blood is spilled?" Iver grinned at how it sounded. Either I was foolish, or she was a lunatic.

"I guess we will find out," I snapped in annoyance. How would I know how Ariana would react? All I had to go on were the brief glimpses I had of her life.

"Okay. We will find out." Edmond nodded. "We will try to show her that we are more than the terrible bedtime stories used to scare Bavadrin children. If she has a heart, as you seem to believe, then we will give her a chance to learn. But if she is not to be trusted, if she is the Bavadrin *we* were warned of, the kind who is not reliable, then I will kill her." His words were not questioning. He was telling me his position.

"Very well," I answered, knowing that he was right.

Despite Lysians having more physical strength and agility, we were not completely safe from the Bavadrins. There were reasons they continued to hold power before the forming of the treaty. They were told to have abilities capable of burrowing into one's soul and destroying it from within. They were also told to have certain fighting advantages, though I did not see anything of the sort when we attacked their capitol. Still, my brother was not wrong to worry.

I stood. "There are a few things I must tend to before the execution."

"Will you be the one doing it?" Iver asked.

"Of course not," Edmond answered, looking at Iver as if he could not believe that we were all related.

"You all are to stay away from the Bavadrin for the time being. For now, I want her interactions with Lysians to be limited," I instructed.

"Sure." Edmond and Jorn both agreed in unison.

"You are no fun," Iver whined, earning my full attention to

slice to him. He then sighed. "Fine, whatever you wish, my *King*."
He dramatically bowed his head.

"You are really asking for a spanking, Iver," Jorn warned.

"Ooh, may I choose who will give out the order?" He sat up a
little straighter in his chair, as if thoroughly interested.

My fist slammed on the table, unable to keep the frustration
from bubbling over. They all fell silent. "I am in no mood for your
childishness. You will see her at the execution. After that, you are
to stay away from her until told otherwise."

Iver folded his arms over his chest, eyes narrowing slightly.
Thankfully, he only nodded in response and kept his mouth shut.

9

ARIANA

The day dragged by slowly after Erik's brief visit, leaving me with a lot of time to myself. Thoughts swirled around my mind, jumbling together as if stuck in a vortex I had no way of controlling.

The events of the past several days were in many ways inconceivable. A Lysian King had sat in a Bavadrin prison cell. He allowed himself to be tortured, tolerating a lashing that would forever leave his body marked of that day. All of it was a sacrifice to break the ancient treaty, ensuring the wrath of the Spirit fell on the Bavadrins and luck smiled on the Lysians. The events were entirely propagated by a belief that Lysians were smuggled into the Siddhe territory through the Bavadrin lands. It was a farfetched story, yet there was a possibility that it was the truth, at least partially. The Lysians were not the only ones to have citizens disappearing.

And I was now a prisoner of the Lysians, the roles reversed.

I could have laughed at the irony.

I used to think myself powerful, though after seeing Erik, I no longer felt as confident. Were I to ever stand toe to toe with him, then I was uncertain who would emerge victorious. It took far less time to burn someone than it took to choke the breath out of them. Erik carried an ease to his conjuring which appeared completely effortless, almost second nature. He also had an entire army helping him take control of the my capital. I, on the other hand, had no army coming to my aid. All I had were Edda's fortunes.

My people's lives were at stake while I betrayed the sacred oath of protecting the Leader Superior. Technically, it was not an oath I ever made myself. It was one I was born into. Did that make my actions any more forgivable?

I was grasping at straws.

My thoughts turned back to the Lysians.

Even when held in our prison, Erik evoked dangerous confidence. Yet that now seemed like nothing compared to him in his home. Here he was comfortable enough to train his entire focus on me. The weight of that attention was extraordinary. So intense that it nearly froze me in place. The hairs on my neck stood in his presence while I forced myself to breathe steadily and keep my heart from racing in alarm. His kindness made him seem that much more lethal. As if it were a trick. Was he toying with me?

Despite being close to him when tending to his wounds, his proximity was too much when he stood on the threshold of my own prison room. The power he controlled simmering beneath his fingertips in wait forced me to stiffen, not out of fear but out of heightened senses. He was a hunter, and I was the prey. His presence pushed the surge of adrenaline through my body without him even needing to try to intimidate me. His existence alone was a threat. All of him was a threat.

That dark sapphire gaze of his was unusual, causing me to squirm when fixed on me. It was enough to steal my breath. And the way he moved, one slow step at a time, stalking me like the hunter he was. Somehow, I kept some resemblance of control when in front of him, but now just the thought of him sent my pulse climbing.

It was clear I severely underestimated his power, both physically and mystically. I still could not believe that he allowed me to enter his cell, tend his wounds, and then walk away alive. Especially when he thought I could have had something to do with the Lysians who disappeared. It was that small bit of information that comforted me, for I did not think he wanted to harm me, especially after not taking that easy chance. But how difficult would it be to push him over to the edge, for him to lose control? A part of him must hate all Bavadrins, especially when he thought we worked with the Siddhe. And the prejudicial beliefs each of our races had against one another, passed down generation after generation, instilling fear and separation between the races certainly didn't help. I doubted he trusted me, and that was something I needed to gain.

I was in way over my head and was expected to sleep in a room next to a lethal Lysian—and the King no less. The only thing separating us were walls, which he certainly could burn down in seconds if he wished to. Death by fire would not be painless.

I was working myself into a panic.

My skin burned hot, heart fluttering.

Opening the balcony door, I took a breath and focused on trying to calm my nerves. The sun had finally crawled across the sky and was setting. Turning, I expected to see Kole standing in the doorway, watching me, curious about the actions I may take with the balcony door open. But he was not there. Instead, he remained in the small common area just outside the door.

Turning towards the sun, I retreated into my mind. My eyes slid shut, and I whispered words that were meant for someone who no longer existed in our realm. Thoughts of her were often the only thing that brought me comfort when I was on the verge of unraveling. The belief that she could hear me comforted me whenever I found myself in the darkest of places.

"Mother, I am trying to be brave. Hear me, be with me, come back for me. Please, lend me your strength." As I spoke, the wind picked up, swirling around me, still warm from the fading sun. I imagined it carried my words to her, and a warmth settled in my chest at the thought. If she heard me, then she would offer me her strength.

I imagined her standing before me, brown hair gently being tugged by the wind. A kind smile on her face. Green eyes, the mirror image of mine, would stare back at me filled with love. I imagined her reaching out, stroking my cheek with a slender finger. The image in my mind was so vivid that it was almost as if I could feel her presence surrounding me.

My eyes slid open to a view of a beautiful burnt orange sky.

"You believe the great Spirit is a woman?" Kole's voice came from behind me.

I twisted to find him standing a few steps past the balcony door, closer than he usually came. There was genuine curiosity in his tone.

"No," I answered, turning back to the cloudless sunset. "We do not believe the Spirit to be male or female. The words were for my true mother."

"She's dead?" he asked after a silent moment.

"Yes. And tonight, she will have her vengeance for it." My voice grew dark as I alluded to the secret every Bavadrin knew but never mentioned out loud. Like if left unspoken, then it was never real. At first, it angered me, though with time I understood. The Bavadrins feared Fraser, but he was their leader. To act against him was traitorous, so simply keeping quiet and forgetting was a mercy. It allowed them to continue following him, believing in his leadership. I, however, never forgot. That moment when my mother was stolen from me was burned into my memory so fiercely.

"Your father . . . he?" Kole appeared at a loss for words. Surely, he must have also been relieved, for I was more likely to help the Lysians if they killed a monster and not a beloved father.

I turned to face the Lysian guard, finding that moment as good as any to give him a glimpse of the past, which shaped me into the person who stood before him. With it, I also let him know that ending Fraser would not cause me pain. It wouldn't be the reason I didn't help the Lysians if what they claimed was true. "My mother only bore him one child, a daughter, no less. He grew more and more furious with each stillborn son she had. He believed she was cursed, that she wronged the balance of things in some way. He killed her for it."

"That's terrible," Kole mumbled, looking at me as if he were uncertain about how to proceed with such information.

The worst part of the story was that my father may have been right, for she gave birth to me. I was a conjuror. And not a weak one. The balance was shifted with my birth, and she died keeping it a secret from him. Only a handful of people knew what I was capable of. There was also the grim fact of the way Fraser carried out the murder.

"It was," I said with a nod.

Gone was the warm image of my mother, replaced by the terror of her last moments with me. My chest grew tight with pain and anger. No matter how much time passed, thinking of that day evoked potent and dark emotions. The memory like a snagged thread in my mind. Always poking out of the fabric of thought and memories, never did it weave seamlessly into the story of my life. No, it always stood out.

Kole's lips parted, but he stopped himself from saying more.

Instead, his attention shifted to the setting sun behind me. "It's time for us to go." His voice carried a somber tone.

I nodded. Everything I ever knew of life was about to end. Edda was right. I hid in the shadows of my father, and it was time to step out of that obscurity. By Fraser's actions, he cast darkness over his people, and they needed the light. He no longer deserved to carry the weight of their future on his shoulders. Any Bavadrin would be a better leader than he was, even if Edda was wrong and the role did not fall to me.

Kole led me from the room and down many halls, which blurred past with our quick pace. My legs moved numbly without thought. I should have paid attention to the directions we went and where we were going. Instead, it was as if I was shrouded in a haze and my mind could focus on nothing other than that darkness. Like a frigid cape tied around my neck, pulling me back with its weight, nearly choking me. It hung around my shoulders, heavy and long enough to trip me as I continued to follow the Lysian.

Kole led me into a room and paused. There was a long table on the far wall where Erik sat with a handful of other Lysians around his age. Fraser was nowhere in sight, at least not yet. I noticed a drain in the center of the room and suddenly felt sick. How often were executions held there to warrant such a thing for easy cleanup?

I nearly jumped out of my skin when Kole gently grasped my arm. He had not touched me at all since our journey on horseback where it couldn't be helped. Suddenly the world came into crystal clear view.

"We typically use this space for customary fights. It can get bloody, but no lives are lost," Kole informed me after catching my eyes on the drain. He was trying to let me know they were not the monsters the Bavadrin stories portrayed.

I nodded, allowing him to lead me across the room.

To that point, the Lysians certainly had not proven to be monsters like the one they were about to put down.

The gaze of every Lysian in the room watched me as I crossed silently through the chamber before taking an open seat beside their King.

10

ERIK

Ariana entered the room with her head held high. Kole stayed beside her, looking particularly agitated. I wondered what the two said to one another. Her pace slowed ever so slightly, allowing Kole to walk a step ahead, bringing her closer. She followed him to the dais and silently took a seat to my right. Her green gaze drifted all over the room, taking it in, without meeting mine once.

A sliver of guilt settled within for what she was about to endure.

Iver, unfortunately, sat directly to my left. He leaned back enough so that the front two chair legs hovered above the ground as he balanced on only the back two.

"Hey, princess. This may seem a little savage, but I promise, we are gentle beasts." He flashed his teeth at her tauntingly, and I barely refrained from wiping the floor with him.

A low growl moved through me, hoping it was enough to silence him.

Ariana seemed like she was going to ignore Iver completely, but then she turned, focusing on him. "I am not a princess, *prince*."

She then held his gaze for far longer than most would have thought wise. Ariana was never told that Iver was my brother, but she guessed correctly. Of my brothers, he looked most similar to me. We both had brown hair and were on the taller side, but where my eyes were dark blue, his were a light gray. Edmond and Jorn, on the other hand, had golden hair with gray eyes, our father's eyes.

Iver laughed and allowed his chair to fall back onto all four legs with a loud slam.

To her credit, Ariana did not jump at the sound, and I realized Iver was probably trying to startle her. The scent of fear was a pungent one; at times it was nearly sweet. He wanted to smell her fear. He was playing games.

"Behave yourself," I warned my little aggravatingly uncontrollable brother.

"Oh c'mon, when did you become such a drag? You used to be more fun." Iver huffed like a child. His fingers began drumming rhythmically on the table before him as his patience began waning. Iver couldn't sit still without constant entertainment for even several heartbeats.

"I became a *drag* when I became King," I stated flatly before turning to one of my guards. "Bring in the leader of the Bavadrins."

Lysians moved at my instruction. A door opened, and Ariana's father was escorted in, his hands and feet in chains. His clothing was filthy, for he had been wearing them for days, his hair a tangled mess of black and gray. The scowl on his face was unchanged since he was taken from his home.

Ariana's heartbeat picked up its pace while she sat incredibly still next to me. Her gaze flickered to her father.

The Bavadrin Leader Superior huffed as he made his way across the room, till he was positioned before us. His lips pressed in a hard line, eyes outraged. He glanced around, noting all of us.

"We gave you a chance to work with us, but you—" I began speaking to the prisoner, stopping when he colorfully spit onto the floor.

"You are the scum of the planet." He seethed, before turning his harsh brown gaze to Ariana. "Help me," he commanded, and Ariana shifted uncomfortably beside me. What exactly did he think his daughter could have done for him? She was not in any position to help.

I visibly frowned.

The Bavadrin Superior was not willing to listen, and his position was one for life. Not that someone like him ever would give up any scrap of power. For such profound greediness, he was going to pay for his attempts at holding on to that power with his life. The only way for someone more reasonable to take command was with his death. That was the only option he left us with. I knew it. He knew it. And his daughter knew it.

"Are you in some sort of alliance with the Siddhe? Do you help them take Lysians against their will?" Edmond asked.

Fraser ignored him completely, as if he had not said a single thing. Instead, his attention remained on his daughter.

"Don't just sit there looking dumb!" he yelled angrily at Ariana. "Help me!" Again, he spoke in commands, not requests.

I didn't think that he had ever requested anything in his entire miserable life. Everything was a mandate. What he wanted, he took. Now that he found himself in such a precarious position, he didn't know how to behave otherwise. Had he expected the clouds to open and for the mystic Spirit to come and save his worthless soul? I could have laughed. The Bavadrin leader was a delusional idiot.

Next to me, Ariana closed her eyes, and she began to tremble. Her reaction only further added fuel to her father's misplaced anger.

"I should have killed you alongside your mother! You no-good wretch. You don't deserve . . ." he began, spewing such vicious words that I was stunned. My surprise quickly melted into simmering anger.

Fraser killed the mother of his offspring. What a twisted and cruel man. What's more, he desired to take the life of his one and only daughter because she did not sacrifice herself for him.

As a father, he was expected to protect his young. Discipline, sure, but the overarching theme should have been to protect and guide. The Bavadrin before me who spewed such filth at his child was none of the things a father should have been. He never protected her. I understood then that he was only ever a threat to her. Somehow, despite his irrational cruelty, Ariana managed to not follow in those same footsteps.

As soon as the shock of his behavior receded, I waved my hand in the air, signaling the execution to proceed.

Guards moved behind him, forcing him onto his knees. The Leader Superior's eyes widened, and he snarled, "Don't ju—"

A blade found the soft flesh of Fraser's neck, finally silencing his words. There was a repulsive gurgling sound when he tried to continue speaking despite the slitting of his throat. He reached for his neck, and his eyes widened further, as if he couldn't believe this outcome. Blood spilled, coating his fingers, dousing the floor, before his body finally fell into the warm red puddle.

Ariana kept her eyes pressed shut, her hands gripping the bottom of her shirt as if she were holding on to the fabric for dear life. I smelled her blood before I saw it dribbling from her eye, as if it were a tear. The Bavadrin leaders were told to always come and go with blood, and it appeared that Ariana had been chosen to lead them. I couldn't help but feel relief at that knowledge.

Pulling a napkin from my pocket, I held it out before her.

"Take it," I said when her eyes remained shut, unaware of my offer.

Her eyes snapped open, focusing on the napkin I held,

refusing to look anywhere else. After a moment, she reached out for it, bringing it to her cheek. A small gasp escaped from her when she pulled the crimson-stained napkin away. I could nearly hear the blood rushing from her head. She was going to pass out if she remained in the room.

"You may go if you wish." I offered her an exit.

She stood in an instant, Kole appearing at her side, and then they left without a word. Though they walked from the room, it was as if she ran from it.

With her gone, my shoulders relaxed. I had not realized that I was wound up so tightly.

I surveyed the body on the floor with blood pooling beneath it. Fraser looked so small. It was impressive that such an insignificant and ugly creature could have effectively ruled for such a long time. That he produced an offspring who appeared to care for others over herself while he was the complete opposite.

"Well, that was fun!" Iver balanced on the back two legs of his chair again.

"She did not seem very happy. I'm not sure she will be willing to help us," Jorn commented while staring at Fraser's lifeless body.

"She'll come around." I sounded a great deal more certain than I felt.

"And how long do you propose we wait for her to do so?" Edmond asked, eager to act. He longed for our attack on the Siddhe, to get our sister back. Edmond and I were closest in age, and he was the closest in age to our sister. Iona's vanishing was difficult for us all, but Edmond took her disappearance the hardest. And outside of our immediate family, Kole had probably suffered the most.

"Our forces will be that much stronger if Ariana stands with us as opposed to us forcing her hand." I believed she would want to help us. Even though the Bavadrins were known for their cunning ways, I did not think she was trying to be anything other than herself. Within that bravery and confidence of hers, there was a gentle kindness that I hoped was who she truly was at her core.

"I agree, but if she takes years to get to that point—"

"She won't," I cut him off. By the sound of my growing irritation, Edmond was wise to leave it at that. I did not know what would need to be done if Ariana did not come to our side quickly. The only saving grace was that our armies were largely not ready. We had been prepared to take the Bavadrins but not prepared for an all-out war against the Siddhe. And that was mostly because we were not ready to defend our home from a much closer threat.

"Clean this up," I said to no one in particular when looking at the body on the floor. Lysian guards began moving at once.

I stood. Frustration fueled every cell and if I did not find an outlet for it soon, then I might incinerate everything.

"Where are you off to now?" Jorn asked.

"Hunting," I replied before leaving my brothers.

There were still things that needed taking care of since my return; but they could wait till tomorrow. Recent events had worn down my patience, and I needed time to myself. I needed an escape.

My legs moved automatically, taking me further from the heavy weight of my responsibilities. I questioned my decision to bring the Bavadrin girl to my home. However, my suspicions were correct in assuming she may be the next chosen Leader Superior. It was good that we had her under our control. Still, a small part of me wished she had heeded my warnings and ran before we took her little capitol.

Now the blood of Ariana's father stained my hands, and I feared she might meet a similar fate. Whether she refuses to help us, and my brothers demand she pay with her life, or she agrees to stand with us, and that action thrusts in to the center of a deadly war, my mind kept arriving at the same conclusion. Despite the two paths laid out for her, she was damned. The curious woman who tended my wounds would not survive.

It should not have mattered. In the grand scheme, she was but one Bavadrin girl when many Lysian lives were on the line. Still, I could not shake the unexpected guilt. Like a sharp blade with a broken hilt, the guilt wedged itself between my ribs, and I could not pull it free.

Once outside, I began running till I hit the woods and finally felt a fraction of the freedom I once had. It was a freedom I longed for, but one I would never truly taste again. And with the actions of that night, Ariana too would never taste such freedom, for the lives of her people would forever rest on her shoulders. Though I doubted that she experienced many liberties with a father like hers. Perhaps that was for the best. She was less likely to miss a freedom she never had to begin with.

11

ARIANA

Kole and I stood at an open window in the hall just outside the room where Fraser's body lay as it grew cold on the floor, on full display before the Lysians.

Was that the destiny of my family's bloodline? To die bloody and by execution? Both of my parents had perished in such gruesome ways. It seemed only right that I would eventually meet the same fate.

The thought only made me feel numb.

I threw up out the window, thankful that no one stood directly beneath it. There was no way a Lysian's keen nose would miss the pungent smell of vomit. But I did not care for anyone else's discomfort. Not when I felt so horribly empty.

"You going to be okay?" my personal prison guard asked while standing next to me. Concern flashed across his face.

"Fine," I grumbled, righting myself. I didn't want the pity of a Lysian or anyone.

Kole frowned, as if not believing me.

Slowly, we walked down the halls. My legs were unsteady beneath me, as if on the verge of buckling. When we arrived, Kole remained in the small sitting room while I went to my fancy prison cell. As soon as I entered, an awfully claustrophobic sensation pressed up against me, despite the generous size of the room. Feeling trapped, both physically and mentally, my breathing turned quick and shallow. Again, I went to the balcony door and opened it. A breeze instantly surrounded me, cooling my clammy skin. I drew in a deep breath, my panic slowed, and muscles loosened. Gradually, I lowered myself, taking a seat on the floor outside. The stone was cool and soothing against my skin.

An odd numbness enveloped me. The feeling was so pungent that it pushed out everything else, leaving a deep emptiness. In that moment, if the entire world ceased to exist, I don't think I would have cared. My core hollowed out and left a shell of the person I was.

My mother's murderer had been slain. It was a moment I dreamt of nearly my entire life. Typically, they were my favorite dreams, and acknowledging that made me feel as though I truly was my father's daughter. What kind of twisted soul replayed someone's imagined last breaths over and over, as if it were their favorite lullaby?

I tried not to. I tried to think of other things. Yet time and time again I soundly fell asleep to the imagined end of Fraser's life.

Was I a monster for my lack of guilt?

I heard others say that revenge was destructive. Was that because it destroyed the person seeking it more so than the one paying the price of their sins? I gave Fraser to the Lysians, and I did not lift a finger to help him. Instead, I wished for his ending to come true more than anything else in the world. I think I even wished for it more than for my own freedom.

Tears streaked down my face, and I hadn't the slightest clue as to why they were even there. Was I crying for the man whom I led to his death? Were they for my mother? Or was I crying because I felt sorry for myself and the position I found myself in? Perhaps they were a joyful release for obtaining something I had long desired. The worst and most troubling was that I did not know. Tears fell from my eyes, and I did not understand the reasoning for their presence.

It disturbed me.

I always knew myself, known who I was. Yet, in that dark moment, I did not.

Somehow, I lost myself without even realizing it. I couldn't even pinpoint when it happened.

Movement caught my attention, and I was fairly certain that I saw Erik run into the woods in a blur. After that, there was very little going on outside my balcony besides the occasional bird flying by.

Time appeared to drag by while energy leached from me as if trying to fill a boundless pit that endlessly demanded more. I was drained, unable to move from where I sat. My legs grew numb and still, and I couldn't put in the effort to get up. I didn't want to even bother with trying.

Nausea remained, threatening to worsen if I left the freedom of the night in favor of the room with a comfortable bed. Eventually, I lay back on the stone ground of the balcony and stared at the stars above.

It was not a simple thing to focus on my breathing and the night sky when all I wanted to do was think of my mother, the Bavadrin people, and Fraser. My muscles tensed and then relaxed, moving from toe to head. I focused on that sensation, what I physically felt. Eventually my body calmed, the nausea nearly vanishing. Still, I doubted I could get any rest.

A door in the distance gently opened and shut.

"How is she?" Erik asked in the other room, his voice low.

"Her heart no longer sounds like a vibrating drum, and she hasn't thrown up in a while," Kole informed his King.

Erik released a sigh. He entered my room and slowly made his way to the balcony. The only reason I even heard him was because he wanted me to know he approached and probably didn't want to startle me. I wondered how much effort it required for him to actually make sound when he moved.

My gaze shifted from the dark sky to Erik's face as it came into view.

"How are you?" he asked, his tone gentle.

"I'll be fine," I replied, turning my attention to the stars once more.

A moment passed when neither of us moved or spoke. I thought he might have left, but instead, he lowered himself to the ground beside me and gazed into the darkness above. He stared at the stars for a while before turning to me.

"If there was a way for me to spare you from what happened, I would have." His voice was barely above a whisper. There was a warmth there, a departure from the usual threat that emanated from him.

Remarkably, Erik dialed down that predatory intimidation of his. Or perhaps I simply didn't care enough to feel its effects.

Had he been feeling guilt over Fraser's death? If so, then it was needless. The only one who should have been guilty was me. I brought my Leader Superior to the slaughter. If Erik had given me a choice, to attend the execution or spare myself of it, then I would have chosen to go. I was unable to refuse the darkness within myself an opportunity to be in the presence of Fraser when he finally drew his final breath.

"I don't blame you for any of it," I said without looking at him. "I was not the bystander in Fraser's death. You all were."

I wondered what he made of my comment.

Several minutes passed before Erik spoke again.

"Your father killed your mother," he said. The words were not phrased as a question but a statement, allowing me to either expand upon it or simply leave it. I had no intention of elaborating, but as he waited, the silence pulled the words from me. I couldn't help but fill the void with the story, one that most Bavadrins desperately tried to forget.

"I watched her die," I admitted softly, feeling Erik's gaze shift towards me. "The great Bavadrin Leader Superior forced me to watch as he had my mother whipped to death before my eyes. That was the day he stopped being a father to me. Children often see their parents as these great beings, constantly seeking their approval, no matter how destructive or wrong they may be. But after that, I saw him crystal clear for the monster he was. One deserving of far worse than what he received this night." Erik watched me without a response. "I often wonder if I will have the same fate as my mother," I whispered, the words meant more so for myself than anyone else.

I sensed his entire body tense before he said, "I won't let you be tortured in such a manner." Erik did not promise me life, but a death void of suffering. It told me everything I needed to know. My kindness towards him saved me from a painful execution, though the threat of it would continue to loom. He could not offer me safety. Living amongst the Lysians was not an endless sentencing. Eventually, the decisions made moving forward would outline my fate.

"Then, in what manner do you propose to take my life?" I asked, meeting his gaze.

Dark eyes focused on me and under the night sky, they looked as if they were endless pools of shadows. In them, I found an odd mixture of both danger and security. Having his attention fixated on me caused my pulse to quicken.

I was a lost bug caught in a web, and the way he looked at me made me want to squirm and risk getting even more stuck. Still, in those terrifying eyes, I saw fairness too. Erik was not a heartless Lysian, but someone who cared for his own. I remembered his warning when he was in the Bavadrin prison cell, when he told me to run. He showed me kindness then, and again when fire danced in his hands, and he spared Landin's life.

I looked away first, searching for solace in the darkness above.

"I don't propose such a thing," he finally answered, his voice gentle once more.

"Yet if I do not do as instructed, then you will, won't you?" I challenged. My life was a bargaining chip. Do as I am told and then I may live long enough to return to my lands.

He shut his eyes, bringing a hand to the bridge of his nose. He would harm me if he needed to protect his own. Erik's largest problem was that I did not behave as a threat, giving them no real reason to hurt me. Therefore, my life was threatened simply for not doing as I was told. It was a far less noble reason to take a life.

Erik appeared oddly unsettled by the conversation about my potential death.

"Why are you trying to be kind?" I asked. It was clear he attempted to bring me comfort in some strange way.

He chortled cruelly. "I forced you to watch your father's life be taken, and you think I am trying to be kind?" There was a bitterness to his words.

"One act does not exclude others," I commented. My attention snagged on his ear, and the single black stone that hugged his left earlobe. From what I could see of his brothers earlier, they all had one as well.

"Does it not?" His focus shifted to the star speckled sky above us.

Pushing myself off the ground, I sat, turning to him. "The situation we find ourselves in is not a comfortable one. I have found myself in many difficult positions and doing so I can tell when someone is trying to be kind, even in acts of cruelty." Now it was he who remained silent. "Who are you looking for in the Siddhe lands? Who do you think the Siddhe took?" I asked him, shifting the conversation. Someone important must have been the catalyst for all that had come.

"My sister." His voice sounded distant, as if his mind drifted off to another place.

Sister?

"How long has your sister been missing?" Could it have been possible that the Bavadrins too were taken by the Siddhe? We also had disappearances over the years and always believed it to have been something to do with the Spirit, as if the Spirit wished it. We believed that those missing were chosen for something grander than the life they had. Never did we question it, for even Edda supported that theory. But what if we were wrong? What if Bavadrins were taken by the Siddhe the way Erik thought Lysians were?

"Three years," he answered.

Years? "Why act now?"

"My father ruled until a few months ago."

When he didn't elaborate, I asked, "And he didn't want to find his daughter?"

A muscle twitched in Erik's jaw. "The answer is complicated."

I had run into some sort of wall, though I had no idea how the question could have been threatening or what he could have possibly been hiding by not answering it.

"And you think she is alive and in the Siddhe lands?" After three years, he and his brothers still held hope that she lived.

"Yes." Erik shifted to better see me.

"How do you know any of this?"

He watched me while seeming to consider his response. "My father saw an Oracle after she went missing. It is confirmed that the Siddhe have her."

My eyes widened. An Oracle was told to be able to sense all of time, able to sift through it for answers, moving forward or back. Unlike a Seer, who was shown only glimpses of a possible future.

An Oracle could sift through it all, searching for specific answers. "Where is this Oracle?" My heart threw itself against my ribs at the threat of such a being under the Lysian's control.

Erik's head moved slowly from side to side. "Not information you are privy to."

I swallowed, willing my pulse to slow. Maybe the Oracle was not in their capitol, if they were then surly Erik would have sought out answers already regarding me or the Bavadrins. They would have told him we were not involved in his siter's disappearance. Erik said his father saw the Oracle regarding his sister. So, Erik had not been there? Was the Oracle somehow out of reach? That would have been a Spirit's blessing.

"Are you willing to help us?" Midnight-blue eyes viewed me intently, waiting for a response.

"I already told you that *if* what you say is true, then I will, but not as a prisoner." I needed it to hit home with him as much as possible that I was not a threat. That I would be of use, even when I returned home. Edda was correct. It was time for me to forge my way, and I needed to be free to do so.

"If I release you, then you may go to the Siddhe and side with them against us." Erik shared his dilemma out loud. And if I knew anything about Siddhe, perhaps I would have sought their help with ridding my lands of the Lysian control.

I did not respond, as several things became clear. Erik wished to not need to hold me against my will, but he seemed powerless to do otherwise, for he feared the risk to his people. A risk he would never take, and thus I would never be released. Freedom was not something that was going to be offered. I needed to take it.

My path was laid out before me. If the Lysians wished to use me, then the ceremony for me to claim the power as the Bavadrin Leader Superior needed to happen soon. And after it did, then I would use my people to help break free of the Lysians.

Though Erik gave me a room with a bed and a window, it was

still a prison. I was not freed from the confines of my father's shadow to stand in someone else's. My decisions were going to be my own.

I would break free of my temporary shackles. No one other than a Bavadrin born would lead my people. Ruling under the thumb of another race was simply unacceptable. Surely, even Erik understood that.

Silence spread between us for some time before the Lysian King turned to me. "May I ask you something?"

I glanced at him. His features were sharply striking in the moonlight. "Sure."

For the time being, I was stuck in his world. I may as well welcome his questions and allow him to get to know me so he could learn to see Bavadrins as more than the evil people the Lysians believed us to be.

"Where does your bravery come from?" He paused before elaborating. "From the little I understand of your life, it seems you have experienced things that could break a person, send them running for shelter. But you do not hide behind anything or anyone. You do not close your eyes to the horror of the world. Instead, you step forward and approach the dangers with very little hesitation."

In a way, he was correct. With time, I learned to face demons, for the other option was to let them completely have their way. Had that made me brave or simply a survivor? The picture of who I was would never be complete without exposing my biggest secret.

I could not simply answer such a question.

So instead, I said, "Is it not more dangerous to run from a wolf than to face it eye to eye?"

His lip twitched. "Am I the wolf in this scenario?" Did he enjoy being seen as a predator? Yes, clearly.

I thought it over for a moment. "No, you are more of a bush between me and the wolf. An obstacle."

Amusement touched his dark eyes. "A bush?"

"Don't worry, you have thorns," I answered, realizing that perhaps I should not have called the Lysian King a plant. Thankfully, he found it more humorous than insulting, for the corner of his mouth turned up.

"Then who would the wolf be?" he asked, not taking his eyes off me.

"Destiny," I stated.

A low laugh rumbled through him, the sound surprisingly warm. "You believe that all that is happening to you is your destiny? That I am but an obstacle in your path towards your destiny? Which is what exactly?"

"When I was young, a Seer told me I would live a long and tumultuous life. That I would know much happiness and much sorrow. I was to meet many strangers on my path, some friends, and some foe." I hoped Erik would not be the latter, for I did not want him as a foe. Even in trying to be cautious, I said too much. Though I left out the fact that the Seer was someone close to me and very much still a part of my life.

"So, you are brave because you assume the Seer is correct and that your life will be long, meaning that it isn't actually in danger right now?" He held my stare, and the power behind those eyes was breathtaking.

"I am not brave. I simply do not wish to die, nor do I wish it for my people."

"You entered my cell when I was in your prison," Erik pointed out. "That action was the opposite of wanting to live."

I swallowed. His gaze tracked the movement, falling to my throat, lingering there before lifting to my eyes once more. I clenched my hands into fists to keep from touching my neck, refusing to let him see my discomfort and the threat that even his gaze possessed.

My actions were foolish that day I entered his cell. Still, I did not like what he was insinuating. "You were an unknown danger. I will say it again. Is it not more dangerous to turn and run from a wolf than to face it?"

"It sounds like I am the wolf in that scenario," he said with a smirk that seemed to evaporate the threat I felt just moments ago.

I might have found a nerve. The stories of the Lysians' admiration of physical strength rang true, for the King preferred to be seen as a predator and not a simple plant. "In that scenario, perhaps you were."

We both turned to view the stars once more.

Erik stayed with me on the balcony, even as the moon began crossing the sky.

We did not speak again but simply existed beside one another. Being around him when his focus was on the stars was easier. In the moments when his gaze drifted back to me, it became difficult to think clearly. My focus gravitated to him as if monitoring for signs of aggression from a wild animal I found myself in close contact with. Yet when his attention shifted to something else, his presence was almost comforting in those moments.

I shouldn't have wanted the company of the Lysian who took me as a prisoner and had my father killed before me, yet I found an odd security in him. Everything Erik did was for his sister, to protect his family and the Lysians. Even in his confrontations, he was compassionate. He spared my people from unnecessary bloodshed when his Lysians attacked. He spared Landin.

I just didn't know if his behavior was true to who he was or if it was a tool to win my easy compliance with his endeavors. I wanted to believe that he was good. But there was a thread of suspicion that I couldn't shake. He was a Lysian King after all, and I had always been told that Lysians were aggressive and unpredictable.

12

ARIANA

The last thing I remembered was looking up at the stars. It was as if the night sky covered me in a blanket of twinkling darkness that felt strangely safe. I eventually fell asleep only to wake in my bed still dressed in the clothing worn yesterday. Erik or Kole must have moved me from the balcony.

I frowned, for they touched me without my knowing.

Light seeped in through the window. Golden strands filtered through in bright rays, landing on the wooden floor, warming wherever it touched. Nothing in the room appeared out of place, even the bag I brought from home still lay in a chair, appearing untouched.

The door was shut, and I wondered whether I was locked in.

Rising out of bed, I crossed the room. My hand hesitated over the knob for a heartbeat before trying it. The heavy wood creaked open, and I nearly sighed in relief.

Kole sat in a chair, staring in my direction. The sight of him gave me a start, and I jumped. I would have fallen backwards had my hand not still been on the door handle for support. It was creepy. Who stared like that?

"Do you ever sleep?" I squeaked the question, my heart somer-saulting with surprise.

His lips twitched, undoubtedly hearing the galloping in my chest. "Hardly. And I'm terribly bored. Care to go for a walk?" he asked, and I could have leaped for joy at the invitation. Was I ever ready to get out of that lovely prison of a room? Yes, I certainly was.

"Just let me get changed." I closed the door, splashed water on my face, and put on some clean clothing, the last of what I brought from home.

The time for collecting intelligence was finally upon me, and I was about to have a tour guide. Everything was perfect. A smile found its way to my lips.

The empty feeling from last night still lingered in the dark corners of my mind. However, it was largely pushed to the side, no longer holding me in its grip. I focused on the task at hand: to gather information. The rest did not matter and so I held those thoughts in the shadows, keeping them from stepping into the light and being fully observed.

When I emerged from the room once more, Kole rose to his feet with ease. He shifted as if stretching stiff muscles before leading me through the halls. Once outside, he took me through the streets, which earned me curious and at times ugly looks from the Lysians. Knowing the stories we told of the Lysians, I could only imagine what they must have told themselves of us.

Kole picked up his pace to a brisk walk, placing me on the verge of a jog. I hoped to get a better sense of the immediate surroundings, but he guided me through and away from the densely populated areas until we were at the edge of the woods.

I bit back a frown. The woods were not likely to offer much information. Glancing back at the town, I tried to think of a way to get us to explore that area. What was their capitol like, or other

Lysians for that matter? Where were their closest cities? It seemed like there weren't any between my capitol and theirs.

When I turned back, I found Kole's crystal eyes watching me.

He did not trust me. Until I earned some of that trust, he likely planned on keeping me as far away from the others as possible. The area permitted for me to explore was unlikely to change anytime soon. I glanced at the forest, trying to keep the disappointment from my face. Either way, I gained access to more than a single room. It was progress.

Though my home was also woodland in nature, it was vastly different. The trees that surrounded my home were impossibly tall, at least three times the size of the trees in their forest. It also smelled different. Both carried the scent of green earth but there were subtle undertones that were unfamiliar. Despite the differences, being in nature brought me comfort, at least while in the sunlight.

Kole shifted from leading to following, allowing me to explore. As we moved deeper in, I relaxed at the peace there. Nature often had that effect, as if it welcomed me. I found myself wanting to move faster and faster, to feel the freedom of it.

"Is it okay if I run for a little?" I asked Kole after walking a while.

"You like to run?" A confident smile graced his brutal face.

Not exactly. But I had become accustomed to training physically and mentally. Since my mother's passing, Edda developed a regimen for me to follow, and I always had until the past several days.

"Sometimes," I answered. "My muscles are sore from sitting all day. I'd rather them be tired from exertion."

"Sounds like fun." He grinned, and I realized I wasn't the only one who was burning for a physical release.

I bit my lip with apprehension. "You won't attack me? Instincts kicking in or anything like that?"

When dealing with wild animals, the trick was to always frighten them away. Fearful running risked the opposite. It provoked a predator, leading to a chase.

Kole snorted. "I'm not *hunting* you, Ariana. You will be fine." He shook his blond mane of a head.

"I'll try not to lose you," I commented casually, knowing fair well that I likely stood no chance. My words were just light banter in attempts to soften the walls Kole erected when it came to interacting with me. Though he did not trust and was cautious, he also did not openly hate, and that was something I could work with.

He opened his mouth to respond but never got the chance, for I took off into the woods in an all-out sprint. I was ahead of him for only a few seconds before he caught up and kept pace with me.

Kole grinned. "Try not to hurt yourself. You won't outrun me."

I pushed myself harder.

Kole remained beside me the entire time with complete ease while I struggled to keep the pace I originally set. Eventually, I slowed and settled for a jog. It was evident that I truly could never hope to outrun one of them.

The Lysians' list of advantages continued to grow. They were faster, incredibly silent, and had heightened senses. With dread, I wondered if the Bavadrins could ever hope to truly stand against them. The now broken treaty between our lands might have been the only thing keeping Bavadrins safe for all these years.

Blood surged through my body with every powerful beat of my heart, sweat coated my skin, and my breath became ragged. It was glorious, the physical freedom of running. Yet no matter how hard I pushed myself, unease still clung to me like an impossibly permanent stain. The forest surrounding me was not my forest, the land not my home. I was not free, and neither were my people.

I considered slowing when Kole broke our silent run with a sharp, "Wait!"

His sudden alarm startled me as he grabbed the back of my

shirt, keeping me from falling over as I abruptly halted. He pulled back, maneuvering me so that I stood a step behind him.

"What are you doing?" I complained, shaking free of his hold while he scanned the surrounding area. His complete attention focused on the woods. Something unsettled him. The hair on my neck stood. It troubled me to see the Lysian alarmed, even if he was my prison guard.

Kole then sighed with what sounded like relief. "You shouldn't sneak up on me, Iver!" he called out into the forest.

Nearby, someone laughed and came out from behind the brush. I recognized him immediately. The one who had been sitting on the other side of Erik when Fraser's life was taken, the one who called me *princess*. One of Erik's brothers.

"It's getting easier and easier to do just that." He grinned.

Lysian senses were excellent, but this was impressive. Hardly anything could be heard over the sounds of my own footsteps and the pounding in my ears. There was no way I would ever have been able to find someone silently hiding in the woods the way Kole had.

The prince turned to me. "My name is Iver. It is a pleasure to finally have the opportunity to properly meet you." He held out his hand.

I eyed it coolly, leaving it suspended in the air. After making no move to touch him, his hand dropped to his side and the smile on his face widened, exposing even more of his teeth.

His unruffled gaze turned to Kole. "And what would my brother say if he knew you were out here running about in the woods with our *guest*?"

"I wouldn't be here if he did not approve." Kole sounded bored. His body went from poised for an attack to that of complete comfort. I wondered if he was actually comfortable or just trying to pretend to be.

Iver's head tilted, his eyes darkening. "Is it difficult for you to need his approval for anything you do when you used to be pretty much equals?" His smile turned cruel. "Constantly bowing to Erik. Subservient."

Kole and I were not friends. I was a captive and Kole's responsibility. He intended to keep me both safe and imprisoned. There was no reason that someone being rude to him should have bothered me. I just hated when some found the need to be rude and hurtful for no other reason than to bring themselves a sick pleasure.

"I'd say that it's probably no more difficult than it is for you," I said, unable to hold my tongue. Both of the Lysians turned their attention to me.

Iver became the brother of the King. He no longer had free rein to behave however he would like toward Erik. I'd bet that for someone like Iver, that would be quite the adjustment. He only pointed something out that bothered him himself.

"My, my, the little Bavadrin girl speaks." The prince took a step towards me. "And even has a bite, despite her lack of teeth." He flashed his canines to make a point.

When I did not back down or hide, Iver tilted his head like a curious mongrel observing something which it did not understand.

"Don't you have more important things to do, Iver?" Kole said casually, though his muscles stiffened ever since Iver's attention turned to me.

"Of course I do," he replied dismissively before turning to me. "Till we meet again, *princess*." A devious smile flashed my way before he casually strolled away, disappearing into the forest as suddenly as he appeared. Though he was no longer in my line of sight, it was as if his presence still lingered. Unease coated me in restlessness, and the falling of a single leaf could have startled me.

Kole and I remained in that area until we were certain he had truly left us.

"He's terrible," I mumbled to Kole, whose brows were drawn in thought.

"Indeed. Let's go. This has been enough adventure for now." We made our way through the woods at a brisk pace led by Kole. He remained quiet, neither of us speaking the entire time.

Upon entering my prison room, it surprised me to find new clothing folded tidily, along with three books stacked neatly on the bed with a note.

May these take you on brilliant journeys. -Erik

I frowned. Never being much of a reader to begin with, I doubted the books would bring me any form of enjoyment. Nor did I see a reason for them, not when I had plans of learning all that I could about the Lysians.

Unfortunately, progress in information gathering proved harder to come by than initially thought. Kole made sure I always avoided areas that may be of importance. My limited freedom confined me to places where there was no knowledge to gain, and my conversations with him also proved fruitless. No matter how I tried to approach him whenever I sensed the smallest of cracks in his mental defenses, he would retreat as if noticing that he had come dangerously close to sharing something I could find a use for.

It took me two more days before I grew restless enough to open one of the books Erik left. It took me two more days to finish the first book. I assumed I was reading at a pretty pathetic pace, as I was an extraordinarily slow reader. But given that I had no place better to be, the story offered a much-needed escape. When I wasn't conducting limited and often unrewarding information gathering, I was yanked into a different world by the words on a page. It was extraordinary. It felt as though I partially wasted my youth by not allowing myself to go on more of these magical adventures. Journeys that were at my fingertips the entire time; all I needed to do was turn the page.

The next several days were uneventful, and all began roughly the same way. I was getting used to Kole's presence, and I think he was getting used to mine. We fell into a rhythm. In the mornings we went for a jog. Slowly he began letting me spend more time in the town and wandering around certain parts of the building. Though Kole continued keeping me from wandering off into spaces that he deemed too risky for my eyes or presence. I still caught the lining of mistrust when he watched me, but it also became easier for me to pull a smile from him, one that was not at my expense. Typically, we rarely spoke of things that truly mattered. It was the way Kole preferred it.

I did not know where Erik vanished. I hadn't seen him since that day I fell asleep on the balcony under the stars with him lying on the ground beside me. Besides my brief encounter with Iver, it appeared no one wished to interact with me, except for Kole whose job it was to monitor me. I asked him once how long they intended to keep me, Kole only said I would know when my time was running out.

In my free time, which there was a lot of, I read.

I had been devouring the second book when the story hit a lull and my stomach began growling. Putting the book down I padded over to the door to my room and cracked it open to find Kole lounging in a chair, a book of his own in hand. Blue eyes snapped to mine.

"Is there anywhere a girl can get a snack around here?" I asked with a small smile.

"At this hour?" he grumbled, looking me over before giving in. With a sigh, he shut his book and stood. "Fine, let's go see what we can find for you."

I followed him through the dark hallways to a unique part of the building, one which I had not been to before. He led me to a kitchen-like area and began rummaging around, collecting various things onto a plate. It was a decent-sized room filled with pots and pans, capable of making enough food to feed a small army. Kole began humming a strange tune to himself as he focused on gathering my snack. He was distracted.

The door to the room was left wide-open when we entered. Beyond it was an area I had yet to investigate. While Kole busied himself, I very slowly backed into the hall.

It was considerable, lined with large windows spaced uniformly down its length, dark blue drapes framed the glass. Moonlight streamed in through the windows. My skin prickled at the thought of wandering around without the Lysian shadowing my every movement.

I thought back to the first book I read about a band of thieves. One of the characters was incredibly nimble and silent, a collector of secrets. I tried to embody that character as I slowly moved further into and down the hall. *I am as silent as a shadow.*

"Look what we have here," a voice murmured, followed by a chuckle.

My heart stammered, and the blood in my veins turned to ice. Spinning around, I found myself face-to-face with *two* Lysian males.

"What a sweet little rabbit," the other said, raising his hand as if to stroke my cheek. We were way too close to one another. I stepped out of his reach and they both laughed lowly. "Run, little rabbit," he said as they both stepped towards me.

They were faster and stronger than I was. Running was futile. I knew it. They knew it. Yet at the moment, I tried to do just that. There was no thought behind it, just a terrible instinct.

I made it only a few steps before foreign hands circled my waist, pulling me towards a muscular body. Immediately, I bent forward, throwing my weight to the ground. The motion forced the Lysian forward. His hold on me did not break, but it loosened enough to provide room for me to turn and send an elbow to his face. I felt the crunch of his nose.

He cursed, abruptly releasing me.

I barely stumbled away before the other Lysian shoved me.

Like a rag doll, I flew into the edges of one of the windows with my shoulder before tumbling to the ground. The blow forced the breath from my lungs.

Adrenaline rushed in rivers through my veins. Power within came alive at the threat and the stinging at my shoulder. I cursed, for I could not hope to fight two Lysians, not without the use of conjuring. But doing so would reveal me. If the Lysians knew what I was capable of, then I would not be free to leave a cell. They would see me as a dangerous threat, and my future escape would be nearly impossible. I needed them to see me as a Bavadrin girl and a potential Leader Superior to her people, nothing more.

My only other option was to scream. Kole would hear and come. I opened my mouth, but sound did not come. The way I hit the wall squeezed all the air from my lungs.

Placing a hand underneath my ribs, I moved on the ground to turn and face my attackers. I needed to figure a way out of the situation without completely compromising myself.

"I will break off the next part of you that touches her." Kole's voice was low and bitterly cold.

Thank the Spirit, I thought while rolling to my side and backing away, putting more space between myself and the two Lysians.

Both of them retreated from me at once, their focus on my Lysian guard. They did not speak to him, did not offer an excuse for their behavior, nor did they offer an apology. Without a single word, they ran, leaving me alone with Kole and the platter of food in his hands. He did not take his eyes off them until they disappeared completely.

Kole grumbled with thick displeasure, "I told you not to leave my side." His icy eyes narrowed on me, drifting briefly over my body and then back to my face.

"You did not say such a thing," I countered, wincing as I moved. It was true, he hadn't, though I knew it was very much implied.

He growled, not liking my response. His crystal-blue eyes fixated on me with a lethal focus.

I knew not to push him any further and so I remained silent on the ground.

With a frown chiseled into his face to the point I did not know if he would ever smile again, Kole practically stomped towards me. When he finally closed the distance between us, I fought the urge to shimmy away from him.

He held out his hand.

I nearly flinched before realizing that he was only offering to help me up and not to strike me. Taking his hand, he pulled me up with ease, cursing when he saw my shoulder. I followed his gaze, finding a nasty cut with blood dripping down my arm.

"Let's go," he said bitterly, turning away as he led me back to my room.

13

ERIK

Footsteps from the hall entered my living quarters. By the darkness outside, it was deep into the night. There shouldn't have been anyone entering or leaving this area at such a time. Something was wrong.

I was instantly out of bed and at the door. As soon as it opened, Ariana and Kole froze in their tracks, the way rodents often did when trying to sneak by, believing that they might have gone unnoticed if they just remained still enough when in the presence of danger.

Taking a sharp inhale, I smelled blood. *Her* blood.

A slender red stream dripped down Ariana's arm stemming from her shoulder. Instantly, a wave of heat surged through me.

I turned to Kole. "Why is she bleeding?" The anger in my voice was sharp.

His gaze dropped to the ground, knowing there was going to be no patience on this matter. Ariana was to be protected. That was his duty, and he failed miserably. What excuse could there possibly have been for whatever events led to this?

"She ran into a couple males in the hall," Kole answered, while shifting on his feet, unmistakably nervous.

"And where were you?" My voice dropped an octave with simmering fury. Not only had Kole done a poor job of watching her, but other Lysians were involved. They *harmed* her. The girl who was too brave for her own good.

"She was hungry." Kole offered a pitiful excuse.

My claws slipped to the surface of my fingers, barely kept sheathed. A growl ripped through me, and I refrained from taking a single step towards my friend, for I could have shredded him. My hands balled into fists to keep them at my sides.

Ariana appeared to have re-discovered a sliver of her briefly shaken bravery as she stepped forward. "It was my fault. I was reading the books you left and was trying to be like one of the characters. You all are so silent with your movements, and so I just . . . I didn't know anyone would be roaming the halls." Her voice wavered ever so slightly, her pulse racing while her eyes focused on the threat before her, me.

My attention snapped towards her. Kole nearly winced, allowing his attention to flicker from the floor to me.

Ariana was trying to make light of the situation, and I was not in the mood. Despite being a prisoner of war, she was to be treated as a guest. For her to side with us, she was not to be injured. Kole's job was to ensure that.

Her being harmed without my desiring it was unacceptable.

Anger consumed me, quick and efficient, burning hotter and hotter. I felt nearly unhinged, capable of tearing apart anything that got in my way, even if it was her. The lives of Lysians—including my sister's—depended on what happened in the next several weeks. Nothing could jeopardize that.

In an instant, I stood before Ariana and she recoiled at my sudden movement, bumping against the wall at her back. Good. We were not simple people; we were Lysians. She needed to understand that, to have a healthy caution towards us so that this would not happen again.

Her body reacted to mine, to the space that disappeared between us. A single tremble moved through her when I leaned toward her, baring my teeth. "I want no one touching you."

Her body stiffened.

Taking in a deep breath, I caught the scent of the Lysians mixed with hers. Though I did not lay a finger on her, she responded to every single movement I made. Pulse climbing, breath shaky. When I stepped away, Ariana's shoulders relaxed. Yet her green eyes stared at me as if she were afraid to look away.

I glanced at Kole and his gaze dropped to the ground once more. His behavior was submissive, and it only further angered me. I didn't need his submission. I needed him to do his damn job.

Neither of them spoke as I exited the room.

I left without saying another word. Instead, I focused on those who dared to touch her.

I pushed the thought of Ariana and Kole from my mind in favor of finding another two, the Lysians who laid their hands on the Bavadrin.

I hunted them.

They were still wandering some of the castle halls. I pursued them until they had no outlet left. The fools cornered themselves in an empty room. When I approached, words came from them, but I did not care to hear any of it. It was just noise.

"You will both regret so much as glancing the Bavadrins' way," I snarled. "Let alone laying a hand on her."

My fists connected with their faces as soon as they were trapped with no exit besides the one at my back. My vision blurred till all that could be seen was red. If they begged for forgiveness, I could not hear it over the sound of the blood rushing in my ears and the rage in my head.

They put everything in danger. My sister's life and the lives of countless other Lysians hung on the hopes that we could get to the Siddhe lands, which would be easier if the Bavadrins fell in step with us. The Bavadrins were far more likely to cause less trouble if Ariana took control and did as we instructed her to. I was still trying to figure out what exactly to do with her, and how best to broach the subject. She needn't fear for her life while under my protection.

Ariana stated she would not stand with us as a prisoner, but there was no other way. Bavadrins were told to be cunning. It may have been easy to take control of their lands now, but there was a reason they withstood the great wars before. They had gifts unlike ours. Gifts that could compete. If given a chance to regroup and prepare, then they may become a formidable force to deal with.

As much as I wished her promise to be true, I did not trust it. If the Bavadrins were working with the Siddhe, then as soon as she was freed nothing was stopping her from running and requesting aid. My soldiers were powerful, but I didn't want to risk losing unnecessary lives by fighting both Bavadrins and the Siddhe. The entire situation left me infuriated and desperate for an outlet to release that frustration.

Kole and Ariana did not know, but this was exactly what I needed. Something to clear the rage and frustration from my body.

There was a welcomed sting every time my fist connected with one of the Lysians who harmed the Bavadrin. Blood seeped through broken skin, mine mixing with that of those I struck. I did not mind it; in fact, I welcomed the feel of the warm, thick liquid covering my hands.

Time did not exist. It was as if I were trapped in some sort of cyclone with the sole desire of inflicting pain. Even though there were two of them, they stood no chance against me. The constant roaring in my head slowed. The assault continued until I grew tired of it.

When finished, I left them both whimpering on the floor. At least they were alive. Hopefully, now they knew better than to venture too close to their King's belongings. Not that I owned Ariana, but she was in my home and my responsibility.

Stopping by the kitchen, I washed my hands of the blood. With my mind the clearest it's been over the past few days, I began putting together a few herbs and creams into a small bowl, crushing the mixture together before returning to my living quarters. Ariana gave me something similar when I was wounded while a prisoner. It seemed appropriate to return the favor.

Kole rose from his seat as soon as I entered and dropped to one knee, head bowed.

"I'm sorry," he said.

"Get up," I replied, and he hesitantly did as instructed.

"Those two Lysians, are they in training?" I asked Kole once he stood upright. They were too young to have been anything more than trainees.

"Yes." His lips set into a thin line.

"Not anymore." There was no need for Lysians of that character to be a part of the royal guard. "They are never to step foot in here again. And be sure to remind whoever oversees them that recruits are not permitted onto these grounds after hours."

"It will be done." His chin briefly dipped.

I nodded, taking a step towards Ariana's closed door. "You know, she tried to protect you and take the blame," I pointed out.

"She doesn't know when to back down," Kole mumbled. "Sure, she started out trying to take the blame, but then once you left, she wanted to sit out here with me. When I told her to go to her room, her eyes turned cold and she was all 'call it what you may, a beautiful cell is still a cell' and then slammed the door. That Bavadrin female has some bolts loose. Are you sure you know what you are doing with her?"

"She wanted to stay out here to protect you," I pointed out, unable to keep the amused smile from my lips. Despite being Bavadrin, Ariana continued to wish to protect Lysians. She was sweetly misguided, trying to protect those whom she needed protection from.

"From what?" Kole looked confused, as if unable to comprehend what a Bavadrin could hope to protect him from?

"From me."

Kole glanced at her closed door and back to me, scratching his head as if the thought made his brain itch. He then shook his head. "She really doesn't comprehend who you are."

I chuckled, for she truly did not seem to.

Despite my temper, I was capable of self-control, most of the time. I'd never truly hurt Kole. Though if there ever was a dark day when I wished to take someone's life, Ariana could never hope to stop me from it. For her sake, she shouldn't ever try.

I knocked on Ariana's door. The soft sound of bare feet on the floor pattered closer, then a pause before the door opened. Wide green eyes met mine, and I couldn't help but notice the way her nostrils flared, taking in the scent of the healing herbs in the bowl I held. Without a word, she shifted aside, letting me pass into her room.

Silently, she moved through the space before taking a seat on the edge of the bed. With a careful hand, she removed the rag covering her shoulder, revealing a red, angry cut that left jagged marks over her skin. The sight of it fueled my anger anew.

Taking a seat beside her, I gently smeared the healing mixture over the injury. She hissed at the stinging, her hand briefly grabbing my arm before releasing it as if my touch burned her. Her hands clenched into fists in her lap, her pulse quickening beneath my touch.

"What did you do to them?" Ariana asked, her voice barely above a whisper.

I glanced at her face briefly before returning my focus to her arm. "They were put in their place, but they will live."

She nodded, biting her lip. "Can Kole train me to fight?"

My hands paused at her request, my gaze pinning her as I considered her words. "He has agreed to that?" I asked, a hint of surprise in my voice. If Kole agreed, then I would need to have more than a few words with him about his recent behavior.

"No, I don't even know if he would want to. . . It was just a thought." She nearly held her breath at the request.

"Kole will protect you. What happened tonight will not happen again. Plus, you broke one of their noses. It doesn't seem like you are without defense." It was impressive for her to break a bone of theirs, no matter how minor of one.

"A lucky elbow to the nose is not defense," she said with a displeased grumble, then her eyes boldly narrowed on me in a challenge. "What, are you afraid I would learn enough to take your entire kingdom down? Breaking one nose at a time?"

I smiled at that.

Her sarcasm faded, replaced by a genuine plea. "As silly as it may sound, it will help me feel less defenseless. Please."

I watched her, considering the request. She would still be vulnerable, even with training. A slender Bavadrin woman stood no chance against a Lysian warrior. But there was something about the fire in her eyes, the determination in her voice, that made me want to grant her request.

"Fine," I relented. "I will allow it. But Kole will not go easy on you. I doubt it will be a pleasant experience for you."

Her eyes briefly widened as if she had not expected my response. "Thank you," she murmured.

I focused back on her shoulder and felt her stare tracing the lines of my face.

"What's with the earring?" She asked after a moment.

"Don't like it?" I glanced at her.

Green eyes narrowed in open appraisal as she tilted her head. "It... strangely suits you." Her voice was smoothed even though her cheeks flushed. "You and your brothers all seem to have one."

"It's my mother's doing. Believed the Onyx would give us strength and protection. She had several stones all cleansed and blessed by some strange conjuror before she ever even had children." I didn't know why I was sharing any of this with her.

"What happened to her?" Ariana's voice softened with caution.

"Died in childbirth."

She did not apologize for the loss as so many might. Nor did she shy away from the topic. Instead, she simply said, "It's difficult not having the guidance of a mother." Ariana looked at my ear, and the stone there. "I suppose she still offers guidance and protection, in a way." Her green eyes met mine again, uncertain only a heartbeat before asking, "Iver?"

I nodded, finished with talking on the matter. She seemed to acknowledge this and lapsed into silence as I worked on her shoulder.

When we were little, Jorn and Iver often got into fights. During a particularly nasty one, Jorn blamed Iver for our mother's death. Not that he believed it to have been our little brother's fault, but it was a way to injure with words. I then injured Jorn in return with my fists. No one threw the blame at Iver again, except for himself.

Withdrawing my hands from Ariana's arm, I wiped them on a rag and set the bowl down. Hesitation kept me from rising, wanting to stay in her presence a while longer. It had been several days since I found myself in the same room as her. Truthfully, I was avoiding her while considering how best to approach her with the tasks required.

"Where have you been?" she asked before I got up to leave. It appeared I wasn't the only one thinking of how long those few days of absence were.

"There were things I needed to take care of," I replied vaguely. She did not need to know how I oversaw the training of my warriors, the plans of how I intended to fatten my forces with her people. Nor did she need to know about the male I sent to seek out the Oracle, only to have his severed head left for us to find on the edge of that mountain which acted as a border between what's mine and what's my cousins. The disease my father had allowed to fester and take root on that damned mountain.

It was obvious that Ariana did not like my response by the way her brows shifted down and together, her jaw clenched.

"I too have things I need to take care of," she stated. When I did not respond she continued, "I would like to see my people."

"That isn't a good idea." The words slipped out before I could stop them. In reality, I knew she needed to be reunited with them, otherwise how else would they know she was their new Leader Superior?

"Let me guess," she said, her tone slightly mocking. "You've enclosed them in the main city with no way out or in? The problem is that the city is not prepared for something like that. I expect they will be running out of food soon."

Of course, I already knew this. The Lysians left behind remained in contact with me and they did a thorough evaluation of her so-called capitol, which was more like a town.

"Why would you share such information?" There was a flash of distrust pulsing within me. She was openly voicing a valuable weakness of her home. For the Bavadrin stronghold to have been so easy to destroy was remarkable. They had planned nothing out in the event of an attack. Though they likely saw no necessity to prepare for one because of the protection the treaty offered. Still, even as a precaution, they should have been more equipped. Instead, they looked to have gotten lazy and careless.

"Because if you don't know, then they will all die," she replied evenly, her gaze unwavering. "You will have no additional army to help your cause, and I will have no home. Both of us lose if that were to happen."

I contemplated her words, knowing that bringing her to her people was necessary.

"There is a ceremony that must take place for you to claim control of the Bavadrins, correct?" I asked to confirm what I already knew.

"Yes." Her voice softened. "It is one they would need time to organize for."

"We need at least five days to prepare, but I will take you there," I said, deciding.

"You?" She looked surprised, and a hint of confusion crossed her features. "But you are the King to your people. Certainly, they would want you to be safe and not at risk?"

My teeth flashed at such a cowardice insinuation. "Lysians do not hide behind their own. The King leads and sets an example for his people. I cannot expect them to risk their lives if I cower behind them."

She seemed taken aback by my words, but there was a flicker of something that nearly looked like respect in her eyes. "The Bavadrins typically protect their leader." Her voice then dropped to a whisper. "Except I didn't." Goosebumps spread over her flesh. It was clear she harbored some discomfort with her actions against her father and what that meant for her.

"You protected your people and for that, you will be a better leader for them," I said with certainty. Ariana showed me a few sides to her, and each portrayed the potential of a far better ruler than the Bavadrin before. If she was the one in charge when I came to destroy the treaty, then I may have failed to do so. She could have ruined everything. Or perhaps the treaty would never needed to be broken in the first place. Maybe she would have listened to me and agreed to help despite my being a Lysian. I both wished that to be true and false. If it were true, then I was right to feel kindness towards her, but if it were false, then there was no reason to feel guilty for what I was now doing.

"That is, only if they accept me as their leader." She frowned in thought.

"You bled when Fraser died, is that not a sign to your kind that you were chosen?"

"How would you even know that?" She stared at me. "The Oracle?" She asked when I did not reply.

"No." We had journals from before the treaty was enacted. Old documents on the verge of turning to dust, but they had slivers of information regarding our enemies.

She nodded, accepting my refusal to give her more information. "The choosing can still be opposed until the Ascension is finalized. My people need to accept me."

"They will." For her sake, they'd better. I had an idea what my brothers would want to do with her if she ended up not being the Leader Superior. They certainly wouldn't wish to return her to her people. Fearing the possibility that she learned some secrets while living here and then using that knowledge against us.

"And if they do, what sort of leader would I be under the thumb of another?" Ariana challenged, and the conversation turned sour.

"This is the position we find ourselves in."

"You have the power to change it."

I stood, collecting the bowl. "I will not change a thing." The words came out harshly.

Power, for all its allure, is but a mirage—a fleeting illusion that conceals the burden it carries.

I was a King, bound by the chains of my people. Their lives intertwined with mine, each decision weighed against their survival. My refusal to unnecessarily endanger those lives narrowed my choices, leaving little room for personal desires. Even if I wished to release Ariana, I could not gamble my people's safety on the fragile hope that she might prove an ally. No ruler who truly cared for their people was ever free.

I left Ariana without another word.

14

ARIANA

My lungs nearly collapsed from the force of being thrown to the ground. It took several seconds to get my breath back or move. With a groan, I slumped to my side before finding the strength to stand.

"You need to not focus so hard on one thing," Kole commented while watching me struggle to get onto my feet.

"Make up your mind, Lysian." I snapped, sounding embarrassingly winded. "One day you're telling me to focus more, and the next, that I am focusing too much."

"That's because before you were like a little butterfly, just wandering about, dazed. And now you are so hyper-focused on one thing that you miss the complete picture," he countered.

"If I were a butterfly, then I would have been crushed by now," I grumbled with frustration. Things did not always come easily to me, but they rarely stagnated for so long. I was no better now than when I first began training with Kole a few days ago. Granted, a few days was not much time, but I feared I had gotten worse.

"If I used my full force, then you very much would have been a crushed butterfly," Kole stated, folding his arms across his chest.

"You were so focused on my teeth and hands that you missed the rest of my body, leaving you open."

"Show me an attack to try on you," I demanded, growing tired of chronically being on the defensive.

"You need to learn basic defense first," he answered with a frown.

I learned basic defense when I was a child. I was decent at it when sparring with Bavadrins. Lysians were impossible, their moves and skills incomparable. On behalf of my entire race, I felt a bit defeated.

Despite everything, I tried to charge him.

He moved with ease, even *sighing*, leaving a leg in front of me while shoving me with one of his arms. I went flying to the ground, eating dirt.

"Ashes and bones," Kole muttered for the first time, sounding a trace concerned for throwing me to the ground, but his gaze drew to the side. His words were meant for someone else.

I followed his line of sight to Erik. He was standing with a Lysian female, the two of them watching me. I flushed with embarrassment at what they just witnessed. Erik appeared to nod in agreement to something the female said, dark blue eyes appraising me once more before he turned and left. The female then sauntered down the small hill, heading straight for us.

"Get up," Kole mumbled under his breath before plastering an incredibly fake smile on his face and turning towards the female approaching. Never had I seen him try to be anything but himself until that moment. Emotions other than happiness tainted his smile.

"Eislyn, it's good to see you." He greeted her as I got to my feet. Did he think anyone believed those words with the smile that looked more like a scowl on his face?

The female looked me over with brilliant green eyes. She was fair, like all the Lysians. Of the skin showing, it was pristine with nary a scar, indicating her skill. Her clothing was dark brown and loose-fitting. Her blond hair was unbound, cascading over her shoulders and down her back like golden rivers. She looked beautiful until her smile exposed those sharp canines.

"Tell me, Kole, how is someone so talented as you are in hand-to-hand combat so awfully terrible at teaching?" Her voice was lyrical and sweet-sounding even as the words jabbed at him.

Kole rolled his eyes, folding his hands over his chest. "What do you want, Eislyn?" The smile completely evaporated. He quickly gave up his pleasant façade.

"I would like to teach the girl if she is willing," she stated, before turning to me. "My name is Eislyn, and I am certain that you would get a better experience if I were to help here..."

"Yeah, she would get an experience alright," Kole bit out.

Eislyn's green gaze cut to him. "Better than any you could offer." Icy tension spread through the air.

Kole did not respond, though his face flushed.

She turned her sights back on me. "Would you like for me to teach you? I promise you won't spend as much time on the ground unless you want to."

"Absolutely not," Kole answered, irritation lacing his voice. Whoever this female was, she was incredible at igniting his anger with minimal effort. I had seen him annoyed and bored, but he was never quick to anger until that moment.

"It's not up to you. Erik already agreed." She glanced at Kole. "If the Bavadrin wishes it then it is a done deal." Green eyes narrowed triumphantly as her lips curved into a smirk.

Both of the Lysians then turned to me, waiting for a response.

"I—I'd like that," I said. It was a chance to get to know another Lysian and learn more about their weaknesses if they had any. Unfortunately, Kole was difficult to pull information from; his mind was like a fortress. So perhaps I'd have better luck with someone else.

"Have it your way." His entire stance was rigid.

"I'll return her to her room at sunset. You're dismissed." Eislyn waved a hand in the air, shooing him away flippantly.

"If anything happens to her . . ." he warned, and by the intensity, I imagined that his hackles would have been raised if he were a wolf.

"Don't worry. I don't break things. That's your realm." She spoke with a calm that only fueled Kole's temper.

He stepped towards her. Eislyn held her ground, not giving him an inch. Though claws slid out from her fingertips in a silent threat to not come any closer. Kole noted them and stilled.

I cautiously moved away, having no idea how far this might escalate. What would I do if they actually physically attacked one another?

"At least I'm trustworthy," he muttered while turning to leave.

"I'm pretty sure Erik trusted you to protect her when she got herself in trouble with a couple of Lysians." Her voice dropped. There was anger simmering within her, mirroring his.

Kole paused, and I thought he would turn on her, but he didn't. A moment passed and then he continued walking away from us. Though he did not acknowledge her response, it was clear by the way he moved it bothered him, his body tight and direct as he left.

"What should I call you? Is Ariana fine?" Eislyn asked, seeming to forget her entire encounter with Kole. Her displeasure evaporated into a smile. The claws retracted.

"Yes, Ariana," I answered her.

She looked me over with sharp observant eyes. "Well, Ariana. You look like you can use a break. Are you hungry?"

"Am I ever!" My stomach nearly growled in agreement as I smiled. I wanted the Lysian to like me, to see me as nonthreatening. The warmer she felt towards me the easier I hoped it would be to learn something of use.

"Alright. We will go grab a bite and then get back into training." She looked over her shoulder as if in thought. "Have you been to the west wing dining hall?"

"I—I haven't really been anywhere, at least not where there are gatherings of Lysians. Normally, I just eat in my room." I stammered over my words, surprised by her question.

A slow smile spread across her face. "Don't tell me that you have primarily been around Kole your entire stay?"

I nodded.

Next thing I knew, Eislyn placed an arm around my shoulders and began moving me towards one of the buildings. My new companion didn't have the same boundaries that Kole had. She clearly was comfortable with little personal space. I, on the other hand, wished to peel her arm from me.

"You poor thing. To think Erik wants you to feel comfortable and safe, yet he placed that large dumb ox as your only source of Lysian interaction." She shook her head as if she couldn't believe it.

"He isn't too bad," I offered, feeling off-kilter about the sudden change of events. With my time in the Lysian lands, I learned the things Kole responded favorably to, and those he didn't. His familiarity had become a comfort, and without either him or Erik with me, I felt more out of place than usual. I tried to focus on the opportunity before me. This new change presented me a chance to learn more and hopefully aid in my eventual escape.

"That's because you do not know how much better it can be," she stated flatly, apparently not caring for my favor towards Kole.

As we entered the building, her arm finally fell from my shoulder, and I was happy for the freedom of it. Lysians were lethal, and I didn't particularly enjoy having one of them casually draped over me. A few feet of separation offered no great protection, but it gave me a morsel of peace.

Eislyn led me down an inner hall and then into a dining

room. The hum of conversations and forks scraping plates greeted us as we rounded the corner and entered the room. There were a dozen dark wooden tables throughout the space with four to six seats per table. When we entered, half the Lysians present took obvious note of me. The other half appeared to ignore me entirely, though I was sure they monitored my movements from where they sat.

It was as though I was thrust into a den of serpents, each of them capable of striking me dead. They slithered in place, poised to attack while I followed Eislyn deeper into their stronghold. Even if I used my conjuring, there were too many of them in such proximity. I wouldn't stand a chance. My heart raced despite my attempt at keeping myself calm.

Eislyn peered at me from the side, though she said nothing. Instead, she turned her attention to an older Lysian female who guarded the kitchen behind her. I followed Eislyn until we stood before the kitchen guard. She had withered skin, her hands covered in scars that came from a lifetime ago. A tie pulled long dark hair with streaks of gray back into a low bun. Her face was set with an unreadable stone expression.

"Good afternoon, Brie. We want three plates of potatoes, turkey leg, and pickled cabbage." Eislyn smiled at the Lysian.

Brie grunted with the same stone expression, her hazel gaze turning and boring into me before she finally disappeared into the kitchen.

"We can sit over there." Eislyn nodded to an open table by the wall. She took a seat, gesturing for me to take the one before her.

"Is someone joining us?" I asked, cautiously sliding the chair out before sitting. The last thing I wanted was for it to loudly scrape across the floor and draw even more attention.

"Nope, one plate for you and two for me." Eislyn grinned and then rolled her eyes. "*Ashes*, you have only been around Kole and so probably have no idea how the rest of us live. That lunatic eats his body weight in food maybe twice a week. Others, such as I, typically eat one large meal a day."

I nodded in response, unable to keep my focus on her. Instead, my attention darted around the room, noting every Lysian. There were too many threats to keep count. A warmth spread across my chest, and my heartbeat slowed a fraction as the power within me stirred. Like a lazy cat waking from a long nap, I felt it stretch, sending warmth through my limbs. A humming sensation came to my fingertips, and I kept it from going further. The Lysians, though terrifying, were not acting violently against me.

My life is not in imminent danger, I told myself, taking a deep breath. There was no need to conjure. My power finally settled, licking its paws in anticipation of the time when I would finally set it free.

Eislyn watched me, her green eyes unreadable.

I squirmed under her gaze.

"You're uncomfortable around us," she observed out loud.

My mouth went dry, and I desperately hoped that the food would arrive with some water. "You are all predatory compared to me, and I haven't been around so many Lysians in one room before."

"If we are so predatory to you, then why did you help Erik when he was your prisoner?" she asked, her head tilting inquiringly, eyes narrowing ever so slightly. Nearly all the Lysians in the room froze mid-chew, as if waiting for my response.

"Erik was never *my* prisoner," I clarified, "and he was mistreated. But, up to that point, he had caused no harm to the Bavadrins. It was the right thing to do."

"You don't view him as dangerous?" A secretive smile spread across her face, making her appear even more intimidating.

"I guess I felt as though he may not harm me if I was trying to help him." I shrugged, unable to keep my gaze from darting around the room once more. Unquestionably, most of them were listening to the conversation while pretending not to.

"You often gamble with your life in such a way?" Eislyn leaned back in her seat, raising a single eyebrow. An air of cautious mistrust settled between us. Though she appeared warm to that point, it was clear that I should not mistake her friendliness for trust.

"No." I did not add more than that simple answer. What more could I say? I couldn't tell her I was a conjuror and felt safer than I probably had a right to when entering Erik's cell. But, of course, reflecting on my actions now caused my stomach to turn. That he could have been a conjuror too never crossed my mind. Even if he wasn't, I let him come too close to me; I knew that now. He probably could have had me subdued without even using his power, and before I even had a chance to use mine.

Thankfully our food arrived, and Eislyn asked no more questions. I could eat only half of my plate while Eislyn devoured the entire two others. A Lysian also brought out water and I greedily gulped it up. All of it was a welcome distraction. Though Eislyn ate nearly four times the amount I did, we somehow finished at the same time.

She leaned back in her chair, patting absentmindedly at her stomach. "That was just what I needed." Finally, she rose to her feet with ease, and I followed suit. She nodded to the older female Lysian. "Thanks, Brie, that was delicious as always."

Brie again turned her gaze to me. "And you, what do you make of it?" she asked me.

"I . . . it was delicious. Thank you." I stumbled over how to answer, not wanting to upset the Lysian with the cold expressionless demeanor.

Eislyn chuckled softly. "Bavadrins don't eat as much as we do in one sitting."

Brie looked back at our table, at my plate which was still half full, and her lips may have curved down into a frown ever so slightly, though I couldn't tell.

"Let's go." Eislyn bumped her shoulder against mine and I smiled awkwardly at Brie before following Eislyn out of the dining room.

We left the dining hall, taking a roundabout way back to the area where I had been training with Kole earlier. The walk allowed for some of the food to make its way through my stomach, so I no longer felt too full.

When we arrived, Eislyn began stretching her arm behind her head. "So, let's start with the obvious. You are a female and a Bavadrin, which means you have a lot of disadvantages, especially when fighting against a Lysian."

"I have noticed," I mumbled.

She smirked. "But sometimes the disadvantages can be a strength. When Kole attacked you, you tried to fight it. But sometimes, it's best to go with the hit, to let yourself fall. Instead of falling flat on your back and having the wind knocked out of you, be prepared. Go down in a way that doesn't render you useless for any amount of time. Often, women end up on the ground when they're assaulted. The good news is that most males are not skilled ground fighters."

"Somehow I doubt Lysians are poor ground fighters."

"Some are better than others." She shrugged a shoulder. "But they certainly would not expect you to be any good at all, and that gives you an advantage."

Eislyn took me through several maneuvers. She went slowly, explaining what the point of each movement was. We then practiced, also with slow steps so that I could get comfortable with the motions. Eventually, she was content enough with our exercise to allow for a brief water break, and we were back at it again.

For the first time, I felt that I might have been learning something. Eislyn was true to her word and better at training than Kole, though I would never admit that to him.

15

ERIK

The sword glinted as it scraped against the whetstone, the edge perfecting with every pass. There was something therapeutic about the sharpening of a blade, the rhythmic movements of the act. The repetition brought forth comfort. It relaxed me, as if the sharper the edge, the smoother it cut through the grime of life, leaving behind a peaceful purity.

Fire from the hearth provided both light and warmth for the small room while I worked on the blade. I always sharpened my own swords ever since my father taught me how. As a King, the responsibility of keeping my weapons pristine didn't need to fall to me. Though I never asked anyone else to do the work. Not that I did not trust others to do the task—I trusted them to do their best—but I just knew I could do better myself. So, I always did.

"You actually ever use any of your blades?" Iver asked from the open door while he leaned against the frame. Edmond peered into the room from beside him.

"I admit it is not terribly often that I resort to using them. But better to have them ready in case the need ever arises," I answered without breaking stride.

Edmond turned to Iver as if waiting for his next words. That act alone gave away that my brothers conspired to come to me. Meaning that they were also not going to be easy to get rid of.

"You are teaching your Bavadrin to fight?" Iver's gray eyes narrowed, rimmed with curiosity. And there it was, the true reason they found me.

"She is not *my* Bavadrin," I grumbled.

"Of course she is. You control who interacts with her and keep us at bay." He smirked.

Edmond ran a hand through his golden hair. "You know, Erik, he has a point."

"I always have a point, brother," Iver stated casually.

Jorn grunted in disagreement from somewhere in the hall, earning a searing glance from Iver. The three of them funneled into the room without invitation. Iver took a position in front of the hearth, casting a long shadow, making it nearly impossible to continue my work effectively.

"You mind? I am in the middle of something here." I turned to view all three of them.

"Please, continue. It won't bother us." Iver remained standing in front of the fire, placing his hands in his pockets.

With a slow exhale, I laid the blade down on the table before me. All hope of continuing vanished, along with my peaceful serenity. "What is it you three want?"

"I want to better know our guest." Iver spoke first.

"No."

"We want to know what you are doing with the girl. Why is she learning to fight?" Edmond asked as if concerned.

"She asked to," I answered with a sigh. A Bavadrin woman could not hope to physically take us. His worry wasted energy and time.

"And you allowed for it?" Jorn placed his hands on his hips.

"Clearly."

"Why?" Jorn and Edmond asked nearly in unison.

"A few reasons. One, she asked, and I saw it as a way to please her by easily giving her something she wished for. Second, for her to feel like we may have something to offer her people if we worked together. We have strength. Third, to solidify her understanding that she nor any Bavadrin can ever stand against us. Never will she or they physically beat us."

"What if she learns something that can be used against us?" Jorn frowned.

"C'mon." Iver laughed sharply. "You are afraid of that little girl?"

"She is a Bavadrin—who knows the depths of her scheming ways," Jorn snapped.

Edmond continued our brother's line of thought. "There is a reason the great war lasted so long between us all. We currently have control because Bavadrins had no clue we were coming and so we took them by surprise. Now we have their chosen leader, which helps maintain control. But what if she learns something she shouldn't? What if she brings that information back and the tides turn? Bavadrins were told of having gifts that differ from ours. That they can burrow into minds, though the truth of those tales is uncertain. We need to use them as warm bodies to fight against the Siddhe, but we also need to not allow them to regroup and stand against us."

Jorn nodded fervently. "They ultimately should not be trusted. Deceit is in their blood. They—"

"And hotheaded anger and destruction is in ours," I interrupted. "The stories we tell of the Bavadrins and the ones they tell of us have slivers of truth, but they are vastly oversimplified. She is not wicked, and neither are we."

"What if she is a conjuror?" Edmond asks.

"She has shown no sign of gifts."

Edmond shook his head. "Would you even know what to look

for? It is written that Bavadrin gifts do not always fall into the realm of elemental control like ours. If only you had let the two-" He silenced himself when my eyes widened with sudden realization.

"Tell me that you did not send those two youths to lay their hands on her the other night." I barely managed to keep my tone neutral.

Iver's head swiveled to Edmond. "How devious."

Edmond paid Iver no mind, instead keeping his eyes locked on mine. "Fear and threat of death is often useful in flushing out such things. And it would have never even come from you. She wouldn't have been the wiser for it."

My jaw clenched. "I said to stay away."

Edmond did not back down. "And I have. We all have. But she is a potential threat. If she is more than just a Bavadrin woman then we need to contain her and not allow her free reign."

"I will not tell you again," I said slowly. "Keep away from her." My claws lengthened on their own accord.

Edmond's gaze dropped to my hands before he dipped his head. "I apologize for overstepping."

Iver chuckled under breath.

There was a knock at the door, and Kole stuck his head in. "Your Highness, may I have a word when you have a moment?"

Iver smirked, enjoying Kole addressing me so formally and unbothered by the tension trapped within the room. "And where is your delicious little friend?"

Kole ignored him. "When you have a moment," he said to me once more and began backing out of the room.

"Kole, now is as good a time as any." I was fairly certain that I knew what he wished to discuss. It seemed everyone wanted to debate our guest's activities. My claws retracted.

Kole glanced at my brothers before entering.

"Well." I moved my hand through the air invitingly. My

peaceful evening had come to an abrupt end and there was no point in dragging out the torment. Kole and my brothers wished to discuss Ariana and so we would. Of course, there was a chance that Kole wanted to speak of something else, but I would bet otherwise.

"You are letting Eislyn teach Ariana to fight," he stated, thinking carefully about his next words.

"Your issue is Eislyn. However, she is a splendid teacher and a skilled fighter." Iver spoke before Kole completed his thought. "From what I recall, she could have you lying on your back with hardly any effort."

Kole clenched his hand into a fist, though he did not rise to Iver's comment.

"Eislyn is . . . untamed." Kole's eyes were icy cold as they focused only on me. The strain of not responding to Iver's methodical jabs was clear in the thinning of his lips.

"Just because you could not control her does not mean she is untamed." Iver's tone remained casual as he continued to prod with his words.

Kole gritted his teeth. "Do not push me, Iver."

"Why? You going to push me back?"

"Ariana will be fine spending time with Eislyn," I said before they could escalate things any further.

Iver made his remarks partially because he was a fool who enjoyed playing with fire, using his words as sparks to set the world ablaze, only to then run away and watch the destruction he created from a safe distance. He also pressed Kole on this particular matter as a misguided attempt at helping him. Iver saw the history between Kole and Eislyn as something that Kole needed to get over. So Iver pushed him, crawling under his skin and driving him mad in an effort to numb him to the pain.

"She took her to a dining hall." Kole informed me of something I already knew.

"I told Eislyn she could take Ariana wherever she believed was safe to do so."

Edmond frowned. "You are letting others get to know the Bavadrin yet keep her away from us. Why?"

I shot him a glare. "We want her to see us as friends. That is more likely to happen if she spent time with those who did not look forward to killing her."

"I do not look forward to such a thing." Edmond's eyes grew larger as if he took offense. As if he had not set forth a plan to have her attacked in the middle of the night. He had no qualms about taking a Bavadrin life.

"You have a reason to want her dead if she does not comply. And though you are typically the most patient of all of us, you are not on this matter. You simply lack the tolerance to pretend otherwise," I pointed out. "I hope that you all will have your chance to better know her in the future. However, at present she needs to be protected and shown that we are not vicious. She needs to *want* to help us. That is the only way this is going to work."

"What if we promise to be on our best behavior for just a short time? Dinner perhaps?" Jorn suggested. "We are curious. It is not every day we have a Bavadrin living amongst us."

"It is unreasonable to have us as confidants and advisers to you when we are some of the least informed Lysians here when it comes to our *guest*," Edmond added. They were going to continue to press on this matter, and my brother's point held validity.

I learned long ago that when it came to my brothers, especially when they teamed up against me like this, it was best to wisely choose my battles. If they indeed behaved themselves, then one dinner was unlikely to drastically change anything.

"Fine. Once we return from our trip to the Bavadrin city, we will all have dinner together." My attention drifted to Kole. "I know it's difficult for you to have to interact with Eislyn and for that, I am sorry. But I believe she will do well with Ariana."

"As you wish," Kole replied, void of any emotion. His response came automatically, a subordinate following his King's commands. With a brief bow of his head, Kole turned and walked from the room.

My brothers also scattered, pleased to have gotten the outcome they wished for.

Finally, I was left to myself once more, yet I could not bring myself to pick up the blade again. So instead, I leaned back, staring at the hearth and the flames.

16

ARIANA

The horse stables were immaculate. Each pen clean, with fresh straw covering the floor. Stalls lined the stable, surrounding an open area in the center where several horses stood. Lysians moved around the magnificent animals, saddling them and securing packs of supplies.

We were always told that all animals fled from Lysians. Birds flew away, horses turned unruly and bolted, for fear was uncontrollable when in the presence of one of them. Even wolves avoided them. Yet there were many horses in the stable and many Lysians, and they appeared as comfortable as our own were around us.

The Lysian horses made ours look like simple ponies. I could not help but feel the sharp edge of disappointment, for not only did Lysians have physical advantages but even their animals were superior.

For all the stories our children were told of the horrors of the Lysians in order to scare them away from the border of our lands, I wondered why stories of their weaknesses were never also passed down. Surely there were some flaws, for otherwise how did the

Bavadrins stand their ground during the great war and not completely crumble out of existence?

We had one potential advantage: the Sparrows. They could attack the Lysians before they ever even got close. That was the only way I could see us standing against them. We needed to fight from afar, not in close quarters. No wonder our archers were so revered and loved in the past. They were our greatest defense until Fraser sent them from our city. What a fool.

"I know you have seen a horse before," Kole mumbled, gently pushing me forward.

I had not realized I stopped moving.

"You ride with me," Erik informed me when we approached the group. With us there were five other Lysians whom I had never met nor seen before. Half of them watched me while the others finished tying supplies to their mounts.

Erik looked at me expectantly, and I frowned. I glanced around the stable, and it was clear there were many horses left to choose from. It was not a matter of short supply.

"What if I promise to not run off?" I turned to the King.

"You're riding with one of us," he stated flatly.

Apparently, I was not to be trusted with my own mount, even when surrounded by Lysians. I wondered if the animals were faster than the Lysians. If they were, then for how long? Undoubtedly, some were faster than others. They could give me the slowest one.

Erik's stony expression told me that pushing the matter would be fruitless. He wasn't going to budge, not even an inch. And with the promise of finally going home, I found myself desperate and agreeable.

"If I have no choice," I grumbled under my breath, resigning myself to the situation.

A couple of Lysians finished getting two horses equipped with small carriages filled with supplies of food for my people. The animals only pulled the carts of food; no Lysians rode them. I hoped that perhaps once they emptied the carts, I could use one of them on our return to the Lysian lands.

Soon enough, we were all mounted and ready to depart with the Lysian King sitting behind me. His arms reached around to hold the reins, his presence so close that his breath ghosted the nape of my neck. It sent an involuntary shiver down my spine, and I instinctively wrapped my cloak tighter around myself. I was surrounded by him, in the grips of a Lysian, without him actually holding me. His warmth at my back was both comforting and unsettling.

My heart raced in my chest, the rhythm matching the hoof-beats of the horses.

"I promise not to bite." Erik's voice was a soft murmur, his lips nearly brushing against my ear. His words were teasing, a hint of amusement in his tone, and it only served to make me more flustered.

The intimate proximity was unnerving. I struggled to keep from squirming.

Erik chuckled softly, the sound sending another wave of heat through me. It was as if the air between us had thickened. I gritted my teeth, wishing I could turn the tables and make him feel as vulnerable as he was making me.

"Why do you seem to relish making me uncomfortable?" My face warmed with the admission.

He shifted his hold on the reins, his arm brushing against mine. It was the lightest and most fleeting of touches, yet my skin heated at the contact.

"Your feathers are surprisingly difficult to ruffle. It's endearing when they finally are," he answered in a low voice, though I could hear the smile in the tone of it.

I did not think he had ever seen me with my feathers unruffled. Irritation surged through me, though it also mingled with a strange thrill at his words. My life had been tumultuous since he entered it, turning everything I knew on its head. In some ways, he had shackled me, yet in others, he had freed me. Freed the Bavadrins from a tyrant leader and freed me from the shadow of my past.

"I'd imagine that you would be smart enough to not cause unnecessary discomfort when you are *desperate* for my help," I commented, forcing myself to sit a little straighter. If he wanted to play, then let's play.

"I'd imagine that you are quite comfortable at the moment," he purred in response.

A wry smile tugged at my lips. "Oh yes, abducted by a Lysian King, on horseback with his arms around me. Truly, a fairy tale come to life." My voice came out steady, even as my cheeks heated.

He released a small laugh that skimmed over my skin. "Sounds like a fairy tale, no?"

"Sounds like a nightmare, no?" I shot back.

A chuckle was his only response.

We rode out of their city and through the Lysian woods in relative silence. I could not hear a thing over the horses' hooves as they met with the hard ground beneath. Hours passed, and the sun began setting, yet a proper break never came, only one stop to relieve ourselves. My body ached with every step the horse took, as if I were the one carrying it and not the other way around. My eyelids grew heavy, and it became an incredible effort to keep myself up so that I did not lean back into the Lysian King behind me. It was not until we reached the grasslands that we finally took a break.

Kole grabbed my arm as soon as I stumbled after dismounting, leading me a few feet away before pointing to the ground. "Rest here," he instructed.

I sat at once on the ground without a second thought. Kole

handed me a napkin wrapped around bread and an apple. I devoured it while numbly watching the Lysians set up camp.

Their tents were massive, and I wondered why they needed such big ones. It was really quite extravagant and not anything like what I would have expected Lysians to use. I only witnessed them pull one of them together before exhaustion stole my attention away. As soon as my belly was good and full, I lay back in the grass. With the distant sun filtering through enough to just barely warm my face, I drifted off.

There were no dreams. Everything was just black. That was the way I preferred it. Without dreams or nightmares, I woke with a clear head. No questioning of what the dream potentially meant —if it was a sign of something to come or a warning of some sort. A dreamless night meant a fresh start to the day. A clean slate.

I woke from a dreamless night. The sun's rays heated my arm. My lids parted, and I blinked the blur away. Realizing that the warmth I felt was not from the sun, my eyes snapped open in surprise. Only dull darkness surrounded me. The heat near me came from a large body resting next to me. If we were a hair closer, then we would have been touching.

Startled, I looked up and saw Erik, his eyes closed, face strangely serene yet still terrifying, for I knew the power simmering within him.

In the darkness, I could make out that I was in a tent, a very large one. With dread, I came to realize that Erik was not the only Lysian within it. Dark living mounds, half under blankets, surrounded me. There were at least five.

My heart jumped into my throat.

I made absolutely no sound, yet somehow, I woke every single one of them. Large bodies moved, rolling over, blankets falling off. Their eyes all appeared to open at once, turning to me. It was a horrifying nightmare.

A squeak slipped past my lips. They surrounded me. There

was no escape. Lysians were in front of me, behind me, at my sides. I was in the center. My ears were ringing from the pressure building in my head.

The Lysians were alert, all their deadly senses directed towards me. Dangerous eyes pinned me, and I froze, unable to move a muscle.

"You're okay." Erik's voice came from behind me.

I spun around on my heels to face him. The last thing I remembered was sitting up. I hadn't even noticed myself moving into a crouch.

Erik's hands were out in front of him, palms open towards me. "You're safe," he said calmly.

There was a cough to the side, breaking a sliver of the tension building in the tent. "Seeing as everyone is up now, let's get out and start preparing to leave." Kole's familiar voice addressed the Lysians surrounding me.

Erik nodded in agreement and in moments the tent was alive with movement until it was just the two of us left.

A shiver racked my body, and I sat back, taking a large breath. My hands flattened on the ground before me to keep from shaking.

"I'm sorry," Erik said, shifting to take a cautious seat in front of me. "You had fallen asleep, and I didn't want to disturb your rest, so we moved you to the tent once it was ready. It didn't cross my mind that it may be frightening to wake in here surrounded by us." He seemed truly regretful, which was peculiar since he also appeared to at times enjoy my torment.

Control. That was what he enjoyed. Having the control of my torment.

"Why do you all sleep in a tent together?" I asked, still shocked to have had been in a den of them. Inches away from me while I slept, and I had absolutely no idea.

"Why not?" He appeared genuinely confused.

"I don't know, privacy?"

Erik's lips tugged up at the side as if I said something funny and he was trying not to laugh. "It's safer when we are all together. Plus, the thin fabric of the tents doesn't do much to hinder what we hear or smell. It's practically useless for privacy. The only thing the tent is good for is shelter from the elements."

Sleeping all together like a pack of wild animals.

"Why did they all wake at the same time and stare at me as if I was their dinner?"

"Your heart rate spiked. Adrenaline and fear moved through you. Your alarm at the situation was like an alarm to us. They looked at you because you were the thing to wake them, and they were searching for any sign of threat." He laughed. "They certainly were not looking at you as if you were their dinner."

I swallowed the unease and wondered what the difference would have been when they looked upon their dinner.

Erik rose to his feet, offering his hand. "C'mon, let's head out so they can dismantle the tent."

His palm was warm as my fingers brushed against it before he closed his hand around mine. Erik pulled me up with ease and led me outside. The other Lysians were busy readying the horses while I made myself useful by folding some blankets.

"Here." Kole held out a cup as I finished folding the last blanket. "I'll take that." He held out his other hand for the quilt. We exchanged a cup for a blanket. A soothing warmth seeped into my fingers. The aroma of lemon and ginger drifted from the liquid.

"You made me tea?" I asked, unable to hide my surprise.

"To settle your nerves," Kole answered, turning to continue packing up. I couldn't help but smile, for he took the time to make it for me. I attempted to get Kole to drink tea with me at times. He always refused. I even once made a brew very similar to the one I now held. I relished drinking it while he frowned, making a comment of how it tasted like dirty water, and he had no idea how I could stomach it.

This act, him making me a cup, I could not help but wonder if I was finally bridging the distance between us. Was he finally taking a small liking to me?

I downed the tea and welcomed its warmth. Sadly, the moment ended too soon and again, we were on the move.

My body ached when we mounted the horses. The single night's rest was far from enough. Tight muscles groaned as we began the journey. A sharp discomfort eventually subsided into a dull nagging that remained no matter how I shifted my weight or changed my posture.

The day dragged on as we set a good pace across the lands, making camp one more night before our scheduled arrival in my home city. The Lysians traveled remarkably quick, making the journey at least half a day quicker than Bavadrins would have.

With a frown, I understood how lazy we had become. After the Sparrow Archers were removed from the city, the Dunes Clan to the south then vanished along with their conjuring gifts. Our military was in poor form compared to the Lysians who seemed put together as if they were training for war this entire time.

Eventually, familiar grasslands surrounded us. We approached my home painfully slow. Were I riding on my own then I would have sent the horse sprinting, but they did not give me that opportunity. Erik kept the pace unfalteringly steady.

It was a challenge to keep from moving in anticipation. A mixture of excitement and uncertainty pulled at me. The feelings mixed with the discomfort of the unknown. What would greet us on the other side of the city's gate? All I had to go by were the promises Erik made.

Erik halted the horse, the other Lysians following his lead without question. I glanced over my shoulder at him to find his gaze focused on something in the distance. Turning, I followed his line of sight till I saw the thing holding his attention.

A wolf crouched in the grass, its ears and eyes directed towards us. Though I knew it to be gray, it somehow blended into the dry grass surrounding it.

"Shay." Her name was a whisper on my lips, yet she recognized it. The wolf rose from her crouch, standing straight, amber eyes not straying from mine. She was one of Willis's, and now that she knew I was coming home, so did he.

I turned to Erik, who watched the wolf, brows drawn.

"She is one of ours," I said to him. "She will not harm us or get in our way. Please, leave her be."

"One of yours?"

"Yes. We have a few domesticated wolves, primarily used for hunting."

"Fine, as long as she does not come any closer," Erik said, finally moving his horse forward. As we continued, his gaze periodically fell to the side, looking at the wolf running parallel to us. Not once did she get closer while accompanying us all the way to the gates.

The city looked whole from the outside. The protective wall still stood. A dark cloud of smoke did not hover over it. Yet a strange, ominous feeling surrounded it. As if the city held its breath, afraid to exhale in case it all came tumbling down. It felt oddly still with a stale air encompassing it.

We paused outside of the entrance, waiting to be let in. The wooden gate opened, now controlled by Lysians, and we entered what used to be the stronghold of the Bavadrins.

Normally upon arriving, one caught the sounds of life: children playing, friends laughing, and elders lecturing. None of those things were present. It was eerily quiet.

"Would you like to go on foot from here?" Erik asked gently.

"Please," I answered, eager to be free to move around.

A moment later, we were strolling down the path that cut down the heart of the capitol. Whispers rumbled from the edge of the street, but above that, the strange silence persisted. It broke my heart. How frightened everyone must have been when the city was overtaken by the Lysians and their Leader Superior ripped away from them. Even if Fraser was a terrible leader, he was someone they would have turned to at a time of need and they no longer could.

"Can you hear what they are saying?" I looked at Erik. Surely his Lysian ears could make out some of the distant whispers.

"They are confused and scared. They don't know why you are with us. Some thought you died in the battle," he answered with a slight frown, as if he may have heard more, but did not wish to share it.

"Where are the Bavadrin warriors kept?" I asked, not seeing any of them when normally there were many stationed around the walls of the city.

"They could stay in their homes as long as they didn't cause trouble," he answered while monitoring the surroundings. Even though the Lysians now controlled the city, he remained very much alert, watching for potential threats.

"And if they caused trouble?"

"Then they were gathered and put into cells."

Cells? For how long and how many had that happened to?

"Ariana!" a familiar voice yelled out, drawing the attention of our entire Lysian party.

Breath left me in a whoosh of relief. I had not realized how frightened I had been for the safety of those I cared most for. It was as if I locked away those emotions while I was gone, only for them to be released now. Though I thought of them, I realized those worries were only a shallow scratch of the full force stirring deep within.

It was Edda. She was okay.

That realization nearly crippled me. I could have fallen to the ground and wept, but I didn't. To fall apart and show such blatant weakness would not serve me well. The need to remain strong for my people and the Lysians who imprisoned my city kept me upright.

Edda stepped out into the open, heading straight for us. Lysians reacted in unison, shifting into a protective stance. They prepared to keep her at a distance, primed to use force if necessary.

"No, please let her pass." I turned to Erik, who searched my face for something before finally nodding. Instantly, the Lysians around us relaxed, stepping away to allow for a path for Edda while keeping a wary eye on her. Old age and small stature did not mean she was harmless, and they knew that.

Edda and I moved towards each other, and I couldn't help but throw my arms around her. She held me in an iron grip, and it felt as though the two of us exhaled in relief together. Tears lined my eyes as I released her.

"I am so glad you're okay," I said to her.

Edda huffed, waving a hand in the air as if trying to wave off my needless words. "I told you I would be fine, and that you would return."

By the Spirit, why did she speak like that out loud in such a company? Did she want the Lysians to know she was a Seer? It was not a secret I wished for them to know, for I did not know what they would do with her then.

"You look well, considering," she stated while fearlessly making a pointed glance at those surrounding us. "Have you returned for good?"

"Just visiting. We brought food." I answered. Looping an arm through hers, I led her past the Lysians to Erik.

"Edda, this is Erik, King of the Lysians." I then turned to him. "This is Edda. She often gave insight and advice to the Leader

Superior." I would try to play her off as simply an old, wise, and witty woman.

"Not that he ever listened," she muttered to herself before smiling at Erik. "Well, you are handsome for your breed. You always had quite the powerful physique but now seeing you up close there is clearly more there." She alluded to the last time he was in the city when Fraser had him strung up and whipped. My fingers gripped her arm, burrowing into her flesh as a plea to stop speaking. If she felt an ounce of discomfort, then she showed none of it.

A tight smile found its way to Erik's lips.

"Egh, that is, unless you expose those barbaric teeth of yours," Edda stated without care of potential reprimand.

Kole coughed to either suppress a laugh or pure shock at how someone was speaking to his King. Erik's smile evaporated into a thin line. Edda was testing his patience, and we hadn't even made it halfway into the city yet.

"Edda!" I looked at her in surprise.

She carried on as if nothing happened. Reaching into her pocket, she retrieved a small burlap bag, beads clinging against one another as she held it out to me. "I have collected these stones over the years for you. It brings me great joy to finally gift them to you."

My eyes would have bulged, but by the grace of the Spirit, I mastered myself. What did she think she was doing? It did not appear she was trying to hide what she was at all.

"What are they for?" Erik asked before I could even respond.

Edda's dark gaze turned to the King, void of apprehension. "They are for her to wear in her hair when the ritual will be performed, marking her as our Leader Superior."

Blood instantly drained from my face. She was basically announcing that she was a Seer.

"How did you know she would be chosen next to lead the Bavadrins?" he asked.

"How did you know?" she asked him in return without missing a beat.

"I didn't." His stare bore into her, and she met it full force.

"Yet in your short few interactions with her, you knew enough to consider the possibility, so much so that you took her when your army attacked." Edda then smiled. "I have known Ariana since she was but a child. You don't have to be a Seer to know she should be the next to lead." I nearly choked on air and Edda turned to me. "Or am I wrong? Were you marked by blood when your father was killed?"

Erik's sapphire gaze narrowed, though he waited for me to answer the question.

"I was," I confirmed.

Edda smiled. "Well." She held out the satchel with stones once more. "Then these are for you."

I took them, not knowing how to remedy her lack of caution regarding hiding what she was. "Thank you." The words were a mumble.

Edda turned to Erik once more. "I would like to go with Ariana when she leaves with you to head back to your lands. She will need help to prepare for the ceremony to ascend, and I am now the closest thing to family she has left. It would be wise to allow her to have my guidance as she takes on this new role."

Erik's sapphire eyes narrowed even further. He looked at Edda from head to toe.

"That will be fine," he finally said in agreement.

I nearly sighed in relief.

17

ERIK

Ariana walked nervously between me and her elderly friend, Edda. The old-timer was peculiar. A boldness encased her in an impenetrable shield. It was clear that she had a hand in raising Ariana, for the girl harbored a similar stubborn confidence. However, Ariana's held cracks; her shell could weaken when applying the correct type of pressure. I could push her out of her comfort, forcing her heart to pick up its pace as it now did.

Edda's attention swung to me. "Tell me, Lysian, when do you intend to bring Ariana back for the ceremony?" There was something I appreciated about her forward questions.

Frustration radiated from Ariana and had to suppress a smile at her discomfort. She clearly hated that Edda continued to address me.

"When would it be best for the Bavadrins?" I asked.

"The sooner the better. We would only need a few days to prepare." A darkness flickered in her eyes, almost as if a dare of some kind. I did not yet know what to make of it.

"We could return twelve days from now," I said, needing time to oversee a few things before coming back.

"Good, and then afterward, do you intend to leave her here or take her back with you?" she probed.

"That's none of your concern." Kole stepped up beside me, answering Edda with a stern voice, which she appeared unfazed by.

Edda's tone dropped so that no one around except for us could hear her. "If you wish for her to be your puppet while keeping her under your watchful eye, then you will need to bring her here at normal intervals." Ariana grabbed Edda's hand, trying to hush her, but the old bag continued to speak. "She has no bond to the Bavadrins as their Leader Superior. Ariana will need to build those. Otherwise, there will be unrest amongst the people. They won't want to follow a figurehead they do not know."

"Given your customs, once she is Leader Superior, what choice will your people have but to follow her?" I asked.

Edda snorted a low laugh. "Was Fraser not handed to you, despite our customs?"

Ariana tensed, her steps turning ridged. "Edda," she warned, glancing around as if to make sure no one else could have heard.

"If she returns every twelve days, for the time being, staying for a couple of days at a time after we complete her Ascension, will that suffice your people?" I asked the old-timer.

Edda's gaze, filled with unreachable shadows, looked me over. It was void of any warmth. The daring edge of the darkness that seemed to surround her reminded me of the warnings about the Bavadrin race. She nodded in agreement before finally turning her attention back to Ariana, who scolded her for her behavior.

They had a strange relationship.

"That's going to be a lot of traveling," Kole said under his breath.

I nodded absentmindedly. "If that is what's needed to gain easy control of the Bavadrin forces, then that is what we will do."

"Your brothers won't like this," he mumbled before turning his attention towards two quickly approaching Bavadrin guards. Kole advanced, placing himself between us and the strangers, baring his teeth in warning.

"Wait." Ariana reached for Kole's arm. She was lucky he didn't react aggressively to her touch. Typically, when Lysians were on edge and alert to potential threats, they functioned on instinct. Harmless distractions could easily lead to amplified hostile responses.

Kole only looked at her hand before meeting her eyes.

"Please, they are my friends." Her green gaze then turned to me. "I would like to greet them."

I only had to nod once, and she was running towards them, throwing her arms around their necks. It was not the first time I had seen either of them. Each of the men at some point worked as guards in the dungeons, both allowing Ariana to have access to me. One of them, Landin, would have been burned out of existence were it not for Ariana giving up her father to save him. And the other left me with scars on my back.

As Landin wrapped his arms around her, his hate-filled stare found me in the background.

"Thank the Spirit you are unharmed," the guard murmured before releasing her.

Ariana caught him eyeing me. "Don't look at them, look at me." She grabbed his chin, turning it to better view a healing scar near his jaw. "I'm glad that you both are alright. I was so scared. If something had happened to either of you . . ." Her head shook as if she couldn't handle even the thought.

The guard with the hateful gaze pulled her in for another embrace. "Don't, we are fine. Because of you, we survived."

Though his voice had dropped incredibly low, my hearing easily caught the words, along with Ariana's small sob.

Edda stood beside me, watching the encounter from the distance.

"Are they lovers?" I asked, earning a quiet glance from Kole.

It would have been valuable to know such a thing. Despite the days Ariana had spent on our lands, under the same roof, much remained a mystery. Whatever of her past and present, I wished to know it.

Edda released an irritating laugh as if she were not laughing at the question but at my asking of it. "When Ariana and Landin were little, there was talk of possibly arranging a marriage between the two. They were best friends, both attractive, and he came from a prominent family."

"Such a prominent upbringing didn't spare him from being my prison guard in a dungy, dark, smelly prison?" I asked. I had imagined he came from a less fortunate upbringing.

"Fate was not the most kind to him. Ariana has protected him. She is the reason he and Willis had the positions they did. Now, with her ascending to become the Leader Superior, they will rise with her." The old bat didn't exactly answer my question.

"What did she protect them from?"

"It is the reason she and Landin could never be more than what they are. Ariana and Landin love one another. That is true. But they do not love each other in that way." Edda turned, viewing me with a thoughtful expression.

"I'm afraid I don't understand."

"It is not my place to say more." She smirked.

"Does she wish to be with him?"

Edda laughed again. "Landin and Willis are both like brothers to her. There is absolutely nothing romantic between them."

My attention turned back to Ariana and the two men.

"I saw Shay when we approached the city," Ariana said to the large Bavadrin with dark amber skin.

His golden eyes met with mine before turning back to Ariana. "How did she seem?"

"Fine, healthy."

"Good." He smiled tightly. "Did the Spirit choose you?"

"What do you think?" Landin cut in with a heartfelt smile.

Ariana nodded in answer.

"Then perhaps there is hope yet for us," Willis said. His attention briefly drifted to where I stood with Kole and Edda. The scars on my back no longer bothered me but, in that moment, they itched. "How long are you staying?"

"I think it's just the day."

Willis frowned. "Better keep moving then. I know the old advisers will wish to speak with you."

The smile slipped from Ariana's lips. "I will need to get some new ones," she grumbled under her breath.

I watched from a close distance as Ariana made her way through their small town with the two Bavadrin males. She stopped by what seemed to be a home of children. Kids greeted her with squeals, cries, and hugs. Ariana made a point of speaking to each child, leaving the keeper of the home with a large supply of food. It was clear that the little ones loved her, and suddenly I felt a sliver of guilt.

From what I knew of Ariana, she had a difficult go at life. Her father killed her mother, and I recently took her father's life. Though raised in a harsh environment, she did not allow it to harden her against the world. Instead, she gave the world life. She tended to the unwanted children of her village. She even tended to my wounds, and I was the Lysian who threatened her entire world. I would have destroyed countless amounts of her people to get to her father without an ounce of remorse, all because I thought I knew the truth.

There was a saying that nothing was more dangerous than someone certain they knew the truth when they were wrong. I was sure the Bavadrins were not blameless for taking my sister even when I had no proof. And now, I still had no evidence. Instead, I was getting to know one of them and learning that possibly they were not as evil as I had always assumed.

One child pointed a dirty finger at us, fear in his big brown eyes.

Ariana kneeled and grabbed his hand, taking it in hers.

"You needn't be afraid. They will not harm you," she said to the boy in a gentle voice.

"But they attacked our village," the boy whispered in rebuttal.

"They did that because they were afraid . . ." Ariana said. Kole scoffed beside me, not liking that she called us fearful. "Someone very important to them has gone missing, and they thought we had something to do with it. They were afraid, and so they attacked, but that is all over now. No one will harm you. I swear it."

The boy's brown eyes glanced at me, looking as if he were on the verge of tears before turning back to Ariana. "But you are very important, and now they have taken you from us."

Kole released a low whistle to replace the curse he would have said otherwise. Just like that, I became like those who had taken my sister. I stole someone precious from them.

I believed the Bavadrins were not to be trusted. Evil. All of them. They worked with the Siddhe and kidnapped my sister. But perhaps I was wrong for thinking that. Perhaps in Ariana's life story, I was the villain who destroyed their home. I was the monster.

Ariana pulled the boy close, embracing him. "Sweet child. I'm here with you now, and soon I will be back for good."

"Promise?" He sobbed against her.

"I do," she vowed, while gently stroking his hair.

"She's always been good with the little ones," Edda stated,

turning towards Kole and me. "She is a blessing. You may have ensured that the treaty broke so that the curse fell upon the Bavadrins, and it may have benefited you up till this point. But the great Spirit favors Ariana and if you ever try to bring her any harm, it will be your greatest regret in life." Her tone turned icy.

Kole's eyes grew large in pure surprise. "Have you lost all the marbles in your head? That is not how you speak to the Lysian King, not when he can destroy you without lifting a single finger."

Edda smiled. "Far scarier creatures than a couple of Lysians have threatened me in my very, very, long life. Yet here I still stand." Her bold fearlessness coupled with her blatant careless comment, which bordered on a threat, infuriated Kole.

"What scarier creatures?" I asked before Kole could reply.

"What's going on?" Ariana joined us, her eyes darting between myself, Edda, and Kole's red face. She then turned to Kole and me. "Whatever Edda foolishly said, I apologize. Unfortunately, she has a habit of speaking without fully appreciating how her words affect those around her."

"These two big grown Lysians can't handle a few words of wisdom?" Edda commented, and Kole immediately growled under his breath.

Ariana spun around, grabbing the old woman's shoulder. "Stop it. If you want them to let you come with us when we leave, then you need to quit burrowing under their skin."

Edda's dark eyes twinkled as she glanced at Kole and then feigned a brief confusion with a shrug of her shoulder. "Whatever you say. I didn't mean to upset anyone."

None of us believed a word of it.

Ariana sighed and twisted towards Kole. "Please don't kill her." Her words were spoken lightly as if it were a joke, one that she used to gauge just how much damage her elderly friend had done.

"Put a muzzle on her and maybe I won't," Kole gritted out through his teeth.

Ariana winced, grabbing Edda's arm and pulling her away from us. For the rest of our short walk to the main compound, Ariana did not permit Edda to be left alone and certainly not to wander back towards us.

I glanced at Kole, who still fumed, and couldn't keep my laugh silent. "Why did you let her get to you so much?"

"She is senile," he commented, only further fueling my intrigue.

"That isn't an answer. But, seriously, look at her. How many more sunsets will she get to see before the sun sets on her life entirely?"

"If she were a Lysian, then she would pay for the way she spoke to you." He growled lowly.

"But she isn't. She is elderly, a Bavadrin. We need not make it even harder for Ariana to bend her people to our will."

Kole's gaze narrowed. "Since when do you let things like this roll off your shoulders? Perhaps when you were a prince, you would. But your patience had worn thin with the crown. And now you allow for this disrespect?"

"So, you are angry that I am not as furious as you think I should be?" Had he forgotten that I allowed them to put me in prison? That I had permanent scars across my back from this place? An old woman's words mattered little compared to the *disrespect* I endured previously.

Kole glared in my direction before looking back towards Ariana, who walked several paces ahead of us. "Just forget it," he muttered under his breath.

"Seriously, what has gotten under your skin? Usually, only Iver or Eislyn get you this wound up."

"The wrinkled onion is a threat." Kole folded his arms across his chest, trying to keep his anger from turning towards me at my humor at the situation. "When she speaks this way to our faces, can you imagine the things she will say to Ariana in private? Do you not think she may come between the progress we are trying to make here?"

"*The wrinkled onion* practically raised Ariana. I don't think Edda will have any more sway than she already had over Ariana's entire life." Though I spoke with certainty, Kole's concerns were not unreasonable. Invisible shadows encased the elderly Bavadrin, and it inclined me not to trust her. However, that was my inclination towards every Bavadrin. I had not been around enough of them to tell how different that mistrust was with Edda compared to the others.

After the brief journey through the small city, if it could even have been called a city, we entered the main building. It was one of the few structures made of stone, as everything else was primarily made of wood and highly flammable.

Kole and I remained standing together, watching as a few others gathered in the very room where their previous leader had me whipped. It seemed like a lifetime ago.

Ariana stole a flickering glance in my direction, her green eyes regretful. It lasted only a fleeting moment. The emotion in her gaze froze me in place before she averted her eyes.

My guards silently stood behind us. Ariana took a place between her two warrior friends and Edda between them and me. The few others joining completed the makeshift circle so that we all were facing one another in the cold room. It was a peculiar gathering, void of tables, chairs, or any form of comfort. Standing in such a manner should discourage any distraction from the conversation at hand. To discuss unnecessary things would prolong the need to remain in the dreadful frigid room. Which was strange, for it was not physically cold, yet it felt uncomfortably icy in the stone structure.

Edda audibly inhaled, quick and deep, instantly pulling the attention of all in the circle. "For those of you who haven't yet guessed, our great Leader Superior no longer draws breath.

What's more, the Spirit has chosen Ariana to take his seat. She will return in twelve days for the Ascension ritual," she informed everyone, pausing just a moment to allow for a response.

"Why have you come?" One of the Bavadrins turned to me. "You forced the breaking of the treaty, destroyed our home, and now you keep your mutts here to guard us, turning our home into a prison."

"If you think I have destroyed your home, then you are sorely mistaken. If I wished destruction, then this place would be nothing but ash," I replied, glancing at Ariana in time to see her frown, though I did not know if it was for the person asking the questions or my response.

"The Lysians want our help. Some of their kind have gone missing and they believe they have been taken to the Siddhe," Ariana was quick to add, slightly shifting the conversation from the *terrible* Lysians to those who require help.

"So, this is how they ask for help? Bringing terror to our children?" Another one of the Bavadrins spoke, voice rimmed with disgust.

Kole stepped forward. "We tried to reach out to your Leader Superior, but he was not interested in anything we had to say. However, for the Siddhe to take ours, they would likely have to travel through your lands. We assumed that you all were helping them."

"What if he speaks the truth?" Ariana shifted on her feet, forcing a deep breath. "What if that is where our missing have gone to as well?" Her eyes did not meet mine while I stared at her in surprise. Never had she mentioned Bavadrins disappearing.

"The Spirit has taken them, for they are blessed." Edda offered an excuse, her large dark eyes staring intently at Ariana.

"But how can we be sure of that? Maybe that's just something some have come up with to appease the people. What if it's a lie?"

she challenged, and the unfamiliar Bavadrins looked at one another wearily. The scent of unease increased amongst them.

"Ariana, what you are saying?" Edda began, voice rimmed with a warning.

"It's possible, is it not? Edda, tell me you know for a fact something different. Swear it upon the Spirit, but if you cannot, then you must know that this is a possibility. The Dunes Clan vanished without a trace—an entire group of people. Over the years, others with conjuring abilities have disappeared, too. We thought it was the Spirit's will, but what if we were wrong? What if the Siddhe took them?"

Edda shook her head with the barest of movements, and it felt as if the room turned even colder.

The first unfamiliar Bavadrin to have spoken did so again. He addressed me as before, with palpable distaste. "So now that you know we had no hand in any of that nonsense, why not leave us in peace?"

"I do not know that for certain." It was the truth. There was nothing that proved the Bavadrins' innocence. Without that proof, I would not risk Lysian lives.

"And you plan on using Ariana to do your bidding?" He scoffed.

"I plan on keeping her close until I know I can trust you all," I clarified.

The man twisted towards Ariana and Edda. "Shal should be here for this meeting. Fraser would have chosen him as his second in command."

Ariana's green eyes sliced into him. "After Fraser's second died, he never officially chose a replacement. Shal has no place here."

"Fraser made a mistake taking so long to hand you over to Shal. You should know your place is on your back instead of assuming you could stand and lead," he sneered.

I was struck by his words. Foolishly not expecting any opposition to Ariana's claim. But no one witnessed her being chosen, only outsiders and her. This was an oversight on my part.

Energy shifted around Edda, darkening in a way that pointed towards her being something more than she appeared. "I suggest you be careful with how you speak to your future leader," she warned.

"What if she never ascends?" There was a threat in the comment. His chin jutted forward as he looked down his nose.

Edda stepped towards him. "The Spirit has chosen Ariana. She will ascend." Though she answered calmly, her black eyes whispered with dark fury. She would protect Ariana to no end, which I felt was the most genuine thing about the old Bavadrin woman.

"So that we can all be puppets for the Lysian who destroyed our peaceful lives?"

I chortled, earning glares from nearly all but Ariana. "Your previous Leader Superior should hold as much blame as I, if not more. He trapped a Lysian who wished him no harm and tortured him without the decency of hearing him out. He did not even ask whether I was of royal blood." I reminded them of the actions which placed the Bavadrins in the situation they were now in.

"This is ridiculous. You and your puppet will not lead me." His gaze cut to Ariana pointedly.

"You have no choice," Ariana said, void of emotion. "Someone will ascend, and you will follow that person. If not, then you are no longer a Bavadrin. If at the Ascension you wish to challenge my claim, then you or anyone else is free to do so."

No one spoke for a few heartbeats.

"What about food?" It was the meek Bavadrin woman's first time speaking. Up till then, she had not made a sound. Her eyes darted from me to Ariana. She was looking to her for advice, already seeing her as a leader. Finally, at least one of them seemed willing to accept her. "We are running out and quickly. The Lysians have allowed none of us outside of the walls."

"Have they harmed any of you?" Ariana asked.

The Bavadrin glanced fleetingly in our direction before focusing again on Ariana. "If we do what we are told, then no," she cautiously answered.

"Considering the circumstances, have they harmed anyone unjustly, in your opinion?" Ariana pushed.

"Not that I am aware of," the woman replied, her voice calm.

Ariana nodded, turning her attention to me. "I understand your hesitance to trust us, especially considering what you have to lose. But in your actions, my people are suffering. If any of them are unjustly harmed, then I will not help you in your search. I wish for this to be clear."

"I don't think you have a choice here," Kole answered.

Some questioned Ariana's intentions and abilities to lead. She had to show them she was on their side, a Bavadrin. I did not fault her for needing to take some power into her hands, though she really did not have many options except to do as we told her.

"I give you my word that they will harm no one unless they are a threat," I agreed.

"What good is a Lysian's promise? They are beasts. Do they even know the meaning of a promise?" the Bavadrin male snapped.

A growl vibrated through my throat.

Ariana's voice silenced it. "Enough. You have made your feelings clear, but you do not know Lysians. All that you know are the stories passed down by elders to frighten children."

"And you know them?" His eyebrows reached for the ceiling.

"I know more than I used to. Lysians feel like we do, bleed like we do, and die as we do. Trust is not linked to any bloodlines. It is linked to the soul within the being. The Spirit created us all, and therefore all creatures have the capacity for good and evil. Or do you believe the great Spirit made a mistake in creating the races?"

"Interesting choice of words. All have the capacity for good and evil. Even a Bavadrin could be evil," he said in mocking thoughtfulness.

"Yes, a Bavadrin could," she replied coldly. When he did not reply, Ariana turned to me once more. "We brought rations with us, but they will not last long. Can Bavadrins leave the city to gather food and bring it back?"

"I could allow two groups at a time. There are four extra Lysians who accompanied us today. Two can leave with each group," I offered.

She frowned. "Our farms are small, usually family owned. It would be better if it were small groups and many of them. Two large ones would not suffice and would be a poor use of resources. It would not be enough," she countered, and I cursed myself for not discussing this more with her before our coming here.

"What if each family were to leave a loved one here while they went out to ensure they returned within the allotted time?" Edda offered. Ariana's eyes grew large, as if she couldn't believe what the elderly Bavadrin had suggested.

"You propose we leave our own as prisoners?" Ariana's voice turned rigid.

"They are already prisoners. They would just now have a sliver of a risk of death if their loved ones do not return in a reasonable time. The farming families are close. This shouldn't be a problem. They will all return."

Ariana's heart galloped.

"We could just throw them in the dungeon if their families were not to return," the meek Bavadrin woman offered. "That way, they wouldn't need to die for something they have no control over."

"But then, what would be the point of returning at all?" Kole countered. He was right. Edda's option was the only one if they wished to send out many parties at once. The consequences needed to be dire enough to avoid trouble.

"He is correct. The punishment needs to be severe for this to be effective." Edda agreed with Kole, then turned to Ariana, whose lips pressed into a thin line. "I know you will not like this. But our people will not let their loved ones be killed. This will work. The city will have food, and all will be well." Ariana shook her head without a response, and Edda placed a hand on her shoulder. "To this day, I have not steered you wrong. Do not lose your trust in me now. This plan will be good for not only you but all Bavadrins."

"If anyone dies because of this . . ." Ariana's voice grew low.

"You are not Leader Superior yet. It is not on you," Edda responded, her tongue sharp yet offering an oasis.

I took the opportunity to remove the weight of the decision from Ariana's shoulder. It was not her decision to bear. I could spare her. "It is not on you at all," I cut in, and all eyes fell on me. "This city is under my control. And I accept these terms."

The Bavadrin male smiled darkly to himself. "Yes, we all have the capacity for good or evil," he commented before turning and leaving the room with another one following in tow.

The other Bavadrin female looked at Ariana. "I look forward to your return and your Ascension."

"Thank you." She gave a nod of her head and a forced but polite smile.

Once it was only Ariana, Edda, and my Lysians left, she spun around to face me. I thought she was going to say something, but she held back while fury burned in her green eyes. "I'm done here. When do we head back?"

"We can leave now if you are ready."

"You aren't staying the night?" Edda asked in surprise.

"We will stay the next time we come for the Ascension ceremony. But we are leaving today," I answered.

"Very well." Edda turned to me. "We have some who live outside the city. If the food-gathering parties run across others, would it be alright if they brought them back to the city to witness the Ascension?" When I hesitated, she added, "The more who are here for it, the easier it will be for Ariana to have full control of all Bavadrins."

"I see no problem in more Bavadrins joining, but they better come planning to stay a while."

"That likely won't be an issue." Edda agreed. "I will go gather my things and then meet you at the gate if that is alright with you." I nodded, and she vanished at once.

Landin and Willis took turns hugging Ariana goodbye.

"It was so good seeing you both," Ariana said to them.

"I won't let them hurt anyone," Landin whispered to her.

"Don't be stupid. I need you alive," she replied lowly.

"But..."

"No." Ariana took Landin's hands in hers, silencing him. "I need you both at my side when I ascend and moving forward. You are not to get yourselves killed. Understood?"

"Understood," they replied in unison.

She then turned to Willis. "Make sure he stays out of trouble."

"You know how trouble feels about me," Landin said before Willis had a chance.

A slow smile found its way to Ariana's lips, as if he had made a joke. "If you don't behave in my absence, I will give you trouble when I return."

Willis sighed. "I will do my best to keep him contained."

"Thank you." Ariana hugged them both once more.

We made our way back through the city. Ariana worked hard at avoiding the rest of us. Once her elderly Bavadrin friend joined, it appeared as though she, too, was not spared from the cold shoulder the future Leader Superior was giving.

18

ARIANA

I was still seething, days later, as we made way through the Lysian lands. Fury held me in its clawed grip, a relentless force fueled by the knowledge that I left my people vulnerable to death with every farming party that dared to venture out of the city walls.

Edda wisely gave me space, though she found entertainment during her time riding with Kole. It surprised me he had managed not to rip her head from her shoulders with how effective she was at making his blood boil.

Erik kept his words to a minimum for days until we approached his city. His horse further slowed its pace.

"I'm sorry that your trip home has left you in a dark mood," he said finally, his voice low and gentle. It was the first genuine attempt at conversation since we began our journey back. I glanced briefly at Edda and Kole, who were pretending not to hear, though their bickering had abruptly ceased, a telltale sign that they were listening.

I considered not responding, but the words spilled out anyway. "It wasn't the trip itself. It was the increased risk my people are now facing because of Edda's *wise* idea and your agreement with it. That's what soured my mood."

He exhaled heavily, his breath brushing against my cheek. "If there was a better way, then I would have taken it."

There was a better way. His response only grated on my nerves. I clenched my jaw, gritting my teeth to avoid speaking without considering my words carefully.

"Do you think I'm working with the Siddhe?" I asked, my tone sharp.

Erik paused before saying, "I do not know."

I stared at the horse's ears in front of me, refusing to turn and look at Erik. "That is not what I asked. You very well may never truly know the answer, given your inclination to mistrust. I did not ask what you could prove, but what do you *think*? What way do you lean?"

"No, I don't think you are," he admitted, the surprise evident in his tone.

"Then you have a better way," I said bitterly.

"Ariana, I—"

"I understand that I'm your prisoner here, with zero power," I interrupted, frustration bubbling within me. "But if you have any shred of kindness in your heart, could you please just leave me alone? Before I lose what sliver of sanity I still cling to?"

Erik's hands tightened around the reins, and the horse picked up the pace. He did not say another thing as we approached the stables.

Once we got there, Erik immediately dismounted and left without a word to any of us.

"Help me down," Edda commanded, and Kole cringed, though he held out his hand to her. He unfastened his fingers from hers as soon as her feet touched the earth. It was as if he could hardly bear to touch her.

"You will stay in a room on the same hall as Ariana's," Kole informed her as he began guiding us to our rooms while others took our horses.

"And where do you stay, Lysian?" Edda asked with an arched silver brow.

"Wherever I am needed," he grumbled in response.

"Which is?" she probed.

I sighed, feeling a headache coming on. "He practically lives where I do. Probably sleeps in a chair outside my room," I answered, feeling a surge of irritation toward Edda's persistent pestering. "Now, leave him alone. I'm sure he's tired of your incessant questions."

Edda bristled but did not reply.

Kole mouthed, *Thank you,* to me.

We dropped off Edda at the door to her new living quarters, leaving her to explore and make herself at home. A Lysian was stationed in the hall, ensuring she would not go anywhere that was not permitted. When we got back to the rooms, I hesitated on the threshold.

"Are you alright?" Kole asked, sounding concerned.

"No, I'm afraid I'm not," I replied without moving another inch. It felt as though every muscle in my body was tight and not just from the travel on horseback.

Kole approached till he stood next to me. "You are doing the best you can for your people. They will be fine." He softened his tone with me surprisingly quickly. When we were in the Bavadrin lands he was stern, on edge, and easily angered by anyone standing up to Erik or the Lysians in general. After leaving, he regained some of his kindness.

"Am I? Is not having a choice in things supposed to make me feel better?" He did not respond, and I turned to face him. "I cannot just sit here. I need to move."

"We can go for a run?" Kole offered.

"Do you think Eislyn is free to spar?" I asked instead.

For the first time, Kole didn't cringe at the mention of her name. Instead, there was genuine concern in his icy gaze as he considered my request.

"If she isn't available, then I can step in, if you'll have me. But it could only be for a few hours for you have dinner plans tonight with Erik and his brothers."

Of course, I had forgotten about that dinner. A night with the Lysian royals while I was in a dark mood. What could go wrong? At least they did not wish to kill me ... yet. Maybe.

"Fine," I agreed, resigning myself to the evening ahead.

By the time we got outside, I told Kole to forget about looking for Eislyn. I did not want to waste the time. My muscles burned for a release. Even my power began searing through my veins. I wished to conjure, but that was impossible without risking being found out, so I needed to thoroughly exhaust myself in other ways.

Kole was perfect for the task. He was relentless, offering a consistent challenge and never going easy. Unlike the first time he ever tried to train me, I could actually land a few blows on him. They weren't harmful, but they pleased me, nonetheless. I was improving. Still, I doubted I could ever physically hold my own against him. Hopefully, I would never need to.

My muscles ached from exertion, sweat coating my skin. My heart raced from effort and my breath left me in heavy gulps. It was a wonderful release.

We moved around our makeshift grassy arena for a few hours before he glanced to the sun and straightened. "We need to head back. You have dinner to attend."

"Thanks for this ... I needed it," I said as we began making our way back.

"You aren't the only one," he commented, his icy eyes glancing at me sidelong. "You okay?"

I frowned. Why did he keep asking that? Nothing changed

from when we started sparring till when we ended. The issues at large remained. But I answered, "Yeah. You?"

"I'm fine." He said it as if he did not know why I even asked.

"You were on edge before," I pointed out.

"I was out of my element."

"You were more on edge than the day you took me from my home." I couldn't help but stare at him while we walked, as if I could uncover his secrets if only I looked hard enough.

"Yeah," he answered. It sounded like him admitting to something other than my question.

"Why?" I asked.

"Perhaps someday I will share it with you."

"But not today?"

"No, not today." He grinned playfully while stretching his enormous arms overhead.

I sighed.

We were nearly back to my room when I asked, "Any advice for tonight?" Up to that point, my interaction with the Lysian royals was largely limited to Erik. I knew little about his brothers and even less about what they thought of me.

"Erik will make sure they are all behaving," Kole replied.

"I don't need his protection," I said. Irritation coated my words.

Kole's lips curved at the side. "You do not know them. You may appreciate the protection yet."

"And here I thought you knew me better than that," I answered, and he smiled fully.

"Well, I look forward to hearing what you make of them," he said with a grin.

When we got back, I quickly showered and prepared for a dinner that I did not want to attend. I did not know what Erik's brothers thought of me, but I was fairly certain they neither liked nor trusted me, though I did not blame them for that. Unfortunately, I was not in the mood to try to sway them otherwise.

19

ERIK

Tension flooded the room. It simmered in the space between us, making its presence known yet withdrawing enough that it was difficult to pin down where it stemmed from. Ariana had entered silently with Kole by her side. She did not appear happy, but she at least seemed more at ease.

I went around the table, introducing everyone by name to her. She smiled tightly and gave brief nods by way of greeting. The dinner began awkwardly, my brothers stealing glances at the Bavadrin while she did her best not to acknowledge any of it.

"So, how did the trip go?" Edmond asked casually, after taking a bite of meat.

"Fine," Ariana answered shortly.

Iver released a low laugh. "What went wrong?" His gaze drifted from Ariana to me, eyes rimmed with an edge of playful intrigue. He was completely undisciplined. "Well?" he probed when neither Ariana nor I leaped to answer.

"Ariana wanted farmers to leave their city to gather food. But the way their farming is set up, many groups would need to go, and we did not have enough Lysians to accompany them all. So, Edda offered for each family to leave a loved one behind who is to be executed if any of them do not return within the allotted time," I explained to my brothers, hoping that shining a light on the dark cloud that enveloped the room would cause it to evaporate.

"Ashes, that's one brutal old bird," Edmond commented. Not that he cared, but it was unusual for someone to willingly put their own in danger so easily. Iver's mouth hung open. Thankfully, it was not filled with food.

"I think I'd like to meet this old bird," Iver said once he stopped gaping.

I couldn't help but sigh. "I agreed to it."

"It seems reasonable enough," Jorn stated in support with a nod.

"I'm sure our *guest* thinks otherwise," Iver pointed out, his gaze lingering on Ariana. Her jaw clenched, and she stopped eating. She stared so intensely at the table in front of her that it would have caught flame if she had my conjuring abilities.

"She does," I replied, earning Ariana's gaze to cut to me.

"*She* isn't really your *guest* though," Ariana said, truly speaking for the first time since dinner began. "*She* is a pawn. *She* is a Bavadrin, not a Lysian. *She* should not be trusted." Her eyes carved into me as she spoke. "*She* is nothing more than a means to an end."

Silence spread through the room like an angry river drowning us in its stream. Even Iver made no sound. Gone was any flicker of delight he had previously shown.

"You are more than that," I answered.

Ariana laid her fork down gently. I had not even realized she had been holding it. "Please, tell me what I am, Erik."

"You haven't exactly spent much time with her," Iver chimed in, seeming to go to Ariana's defense. Gone was any ounce of hesitation he had just shown. Back was the air of amusement.

I gritted my teeth in an attempt not to snap his neck.

Turning, I looked at Ariana. "You are someone who has been put in an impossible situation. You have endured much pain in your life, enough to ruin someone's outlook on it entirely. Yet, you still harbor kindness. I regret the pain I have been responsible for inflicting on you, but this is something I need to see to the end. That does not mean that any of this will be your end. Ariana, I do not wish you harm."

She released a huff of breath as if none of what I said surprised her, nor was it enough for her.

"We only wish to get our sister back," Edmond stated. It was also the first time he appeared warmer towards her. Since Ariana's arrival, he began planning her death in the event that she did not side with us when everything was done and over.

Her gaze turned to him, holding it. "So, you took me from my home, just as the Siddhe took your sister from hers. We both are held against our will, those who care for us worrying for our safety, wondering if we will survive the situations we find ourselves in. You should be ashamed for following in the footsteps of those who took your sister, for it is not noble of you. I have no idea what kind of Lysian your sister was, but I will assume she was decent for all of you to care so much about her. I wonder what she would think if she knew what you were now doing in her name."

Her words were like an ice storm, dropping the temperature of the room. Thankfully, she left my brothers too stunned to react, for I had no idea whether what was said would leave them thoughtful or angered. One thing was clear: the short dinner had already gone on for far too long and Ariana was hating every moment, as was I. There was no need to prolong it.

"If you wish, you need not stay for the rest of the meal." I offered her an escape, and she took it with greed.

"I wish I could say this was a pleasure, but I am not a liar." Ariana stood; her gaze boldly met with each of us before she finally left with Kole. She did not show a speck of fear despite being surrounded by Lysian royals. Ariana's head remained held high as she walked away, her shoulders back. There was not an ounce of regret for the words she spoke. Had a Lysian spoke the way she did, they would have been trembling and begging forgiveness for the rude slip of their tongue.

Iver laughed when she finally exited the room. "Brother, you have royally messed everything up with that girl."

"Do you ever shut that gaping hole you call a mouth, Iver?" My voice lowered in warning. "Your need for drama and amusement is insatiable."

Iver shrugged a shoulder and reached for the glass in front of him. He must have noticed my thinning patience, for his only response was the small smirk on his irritating face.

"You need to fix this, Erik." Edmond leaned back in his seat. In his hand, he held a glass of water, moving it just enough that the water kissed the edge of the glass without spilling over. Then, with a frown, he set the glass down and looked up. "Her words have validity, but so do our concerns. Unfortunately, we find ourselves at this crossroads. This is the situation we are in. You need to bridge our differences into one single goal that we may unify behind, the Lysians and Bavadrins."

"She wants to be freed," I stated. There was an easy way to unify when she desired to be let go and trusted not to betray the Lysians. But, unfortunately, it was a risk that I would not take.

"Of course she does. Does that matter to you?" Jorn leaned forward in his seat to better view me as if he were uncertain of my answer. He asked one question, but truly intended for another.

"Clearly." Iver answered with a small chuckle. "Our King sent one of ours to seek out the Oracle for answers regarding the girl." His gray eyes danced around the table before settling on me. "Unfortunately, the poor thing got himself killed and no answers."

I bared my teeth at Iver before turning to Jorn. "I do not like that she continues to suffer due to my decisions, but I will not release her because of that," I answered, and Jorn leaned back, pleased to know that I would not free her just because I felt sorry for her.

"She will not back down," Iver stated. "There is a viciousness to her, beneath her docile exterior. In her heart, I believe she is a beautiful savage."

Edmond rolled his eyes.

"You're saying she is not to be trusted and to be put down?" Jorn raised a brow in question at Iver.

I did not like the insinuation.

"Not at all." Iver turned to Jorn. "I only mean to say she is not a simple Bavadrin. She will not be easily controlled, but I do not necessarily see that as a fault, for if it's difficult for *us* to control her, then it would be the same for the Siddhe. I do not think she works with them."

"You would bet Iona's life on that?" Edmond's words held a dangerous edge. Both he and Jorn shared the common thread of mistrust of the Bavadrins, something that all Lysians were born with. However, my thread appeared to be frayed, losing bits of that warning strand. To my surprise, it seemed Iver stood closer to me than our other two brothers on that. Rarely did Iver and I ever agree on anything anymore.

"Of course not." Iver lazily turned his head to face my brother. "I choose our kind over any other." Though he said the correct thing, and I believed him to be a proper Lysian in the sense of not being capable of betraying our kind in favor of another, he harbored a softness towards our Bavadrin guest. He hardly knew her yet was already giving her the benefit of the doubt.

"What makes you so qualified to entertain such opinions of Ariana?" I asked.

Iver shrugged, jutting out his lip. "Nothing at all. I only know what I think. And I think you know her enough to agree with my assessment." His gaze narrowed, challenging.

"Well," Edmond's voice broke the stare between Iver and me. "The fact is, she is stuck here, and you, as King, need to soften her a bit more towards our cause. Our army is nearly ready. We need to figure out how we wish to spread the Bavadrins amongst our forces before we make a move on the Siddhe."

My brother was not telling me anything I did not already know. Despite hardly eating a thing, I found myself feeling nauseatingly full.

"Consider it done." I stood from my seat, tired of both the conversation and the company. Though I was not confident that the company I was trading theirs for would be any more welcoming. Ariana's anger likely remained, yet there were things we needed to discuss. Time was not something either of us had to waste.

"Good luck. I expect you will need it." Iver smiled mischievously, and it took a great deal of self-control to turn and walk away instead of landing my fist in his smug face.

Edmond leaned over towards our youngest brother. "Careful, Iver. You keep pushing him, and our King may snap your neck," he warned.

I could hear Iver's smile in his voice. "He would have to catch me first."

It irritated me that he was right.

Iver had always been incredibly fast. No one was ever capable of catching him if he did not wish it, not even our father, and he was the most powerful Lysian I had ever known. What Iver could do, it went beyond physical capabilities. It bled into the realm of conjuring. My gut was certain of that, even though Iver never admitted to such things.

My little brother had secrets, and I allowed them—for now.

20

ARIANA

Knuckles rapped against the wooden door to my room, the sound echoing in the quiet space.

Turning from the darkness beyond the open balcony, I faced the entrance. "Come in," I said, my voice steady.

A chilled breeze drifted from the balcony into the room, riding on the draft created when the door opened. Goose bumps spread over my arms as I faced the Lysian King.

Erik strode into the suite, shutting the door behind him, locking us in. His broad frame shifted with each confident step until he stood in the center while I remained on the edge of the open balcony. Dark blue eyes absorbed the room, likely looking for signs of threat before finally landing fully on me.

The sheer power in his presence, in his gaze, caused my heart to miss a beat. I forced a deep breath, willing my body not to tremble.

As we stood there in silence, my pulse climbed with each passing second. Erik had yet to say a word, and I could only guess at his state of mind. All I had were the facts: I was his prisoner, and I was now cornered by a lethal male.

"Do I frighten you?" He finally broke the silence, his voice low and smooth, yet holding an underlying warning that sent a chill skittering down my spine.

"Do you wish to frighten me?" I asked, somehow managing to keep the tremble from my voice.

His eyes darkened before they flickered briefly to my throat. A silent threat.

My hand moved to my neck as a reflex, the vulnerability of the gesture not lost on either of us.

"I did not mean . . ." Erik seemed momentarily thrown off, his tenor softening. "No, I do not wish to frighten you."

"Right," I said, my tone laced with skepticism. "You enter the room, cornering me without an escape, ask me if I am afraid, and then look at my throat. *Threateningly*. How should that be perceived differently?" My hand fell to my side as I squared my shoulders, refusing to cower.

"That's not what I was doing, not what I meant to do," he replied, his voice a mixture of frustration and apology as he glanced around the room before gesturing to a leather chair in the corner. "Mind if I sit?"

"It's your castle," I replied indifferently, though indifference was the farthest from the truth.

In reality, I felt torn. A part of me resented Erik, fearing the destruction he was capable of. Yet another part was drawn to him, wanting to understand better. I desired to help him find his sister; I did not have any siblings of my own but could imagine the pain he felt. If someone ever took Landin or Willis, then I would not stop till I freed them.

Erik lowered himself into the chair, his gaze never leaving mine. "I looked at your throat because it is a weak point," he stated.

"It's what you would target if you wished to kill me," I clarified, finding no comfort in his response.

"No. It's what someone else may target if they wished you harm. I do not want to hurt you, Ariana." He seemed exasperated. "I want us to be friends."

Someone needed to teach him what it meant to be a friend and the best ways to make them.

"Friends typically choose the relationship; they are not forced into it." If no one else would educate him, then I could at least offer that advice.

He tapped his thumb against the wooden armrest of the chair for three quick beats. "Why do you have to be so difficult?" he muttered, more to himself than to me.

I stiffened. "You prefer it otherwise? For me to pretend to be whatever you wish?" Just because I did not bow to him the way his Lysians did, he saw me as challenging. I think it bothered him that I refused to fold in his presence. He had no idea how *difficult* I could be. He was lucky I was trying to gain their trust. Lucky that I wanted to be an ally and help.

"I suppose not." Erik was quiet for a moment, as if in thought. "Are you agreeable to having a meal with me every other day? It will give us a chance to understand one another better."

I hesitated, unsure whether it was a question, or a demand dressed up as one. Accepting allowed me to learn more, to possibly find his weaknesses if he had any.

"As long as I am not to become the meal," I replied, earning a small, genuine smile from him.

"I swear to the Spirit you will not." Amusement glinted in his eyes before retreating, replaced with muted concern. A rift formed in our already tumultuous relationship, and he likely wanted to mend it but didn't seem sure of how. It was the first time I had ever sensed actual discomfort in him. Erik had been furious before, after the whipping he had received under Fraser's orders, but even then, he had a certain confident calm to him. This was different.

"The Spirit will hold you to it." I moved deeper into the room, taking a seat on the edge of the bed, facing him.

"I hope so." He leaned forward, propping his elbows on his knees. His gaze drifted to the ground in thought and when his eyes met mine once more, gone was any spark of humor. "Ariana, I hope you know how truly sorry I am for the pain I have caused you and for that which I will continue to cause."

I wished to hate him for everything. For tormenting the Bavadrins, for tearing apart our lives, and now threatening lives with Edda's ridiculous plan. I wanted to feel nothing but disdain towards him, but at that moment, I did not. On the contrary, I found myself feeling in some ways sorry for him.

"I believe that you wish for peace between us and that you do not desire to harm my people or me. But that does not change the position we find ourselves in. You hold the power to alter the road my life takes yet refuse to take that chance. I hope that someday you recognize that I do not wish to be your enemy, just as I think you do not wish to be mine."

Erik's head moved ever so slightly, as if nodding without fully committing to it. "How is Edda settling in?" he asked, leaning back in the chair and changing the subject to something lighter.

My gaze drifted over the masculine features of his face. The bridge of his nose was straight, lending a regal quality. His lips held an edge of firmness that suggested he was not easily swayed, and behind them were teeth that could slice through flesh with ease. Though somehow his eyes were more terrifying than his mouth. It always took more effort than expected to meet his stare. To hold it.

"She will be fine in any situation. I worry more for Kole's sanity," I said.

A smile spread across Erik's lips, softening his features, and I couldn't help but meet him with one of my own.

"Kole certainly will have his hands full between the two of you. I have never seen someone so quickly get under his skin."

I nodded. "Edda has a talent in that way."

"You two are very close," he observed.

"She is one of the closest things I have to family. I would not be the person I am today were it not for her years of guidance." It was the truth. In a life where I nearly lost my way every day, Edda was the compass that kept me centered and able to continue on my path. She had been my protector and shield, and she had been the one to push me to grow and become someone worthy of guiding our people.

"Then I am glad she is here with you, even if Kole must suffer for it." A handsome crooked smile pulled at his lips.

"Careful, you may hurt his feelings by talking like that," I teased.

Erik's smile widened, and for a moment, it felt like we were just two people having a conversation, the weight of our circumstances nearly forgotten. "He has survived worse."

I lifted a brow at that statement. "Neither of you have survived Edda yet," I pointed out.

Erik grunted out a laugh, rising to his feet.

I too stood as he moved closer. He stilled, just barely out of reach.

"Do you think me evil?" he asked, and I found myself stunned by the question. His eyes stayed on mine for several moments before he finally turned to leave without hearing an answer. The question tugged at something from within, and again I felt sadness for the Lysian King. He was being pulled in various directions, including one to set me free.

He was lost.

"I've known evil," I finally said, finding my voice when his back was to me. He angled his body so that I could just see the side of his face. "I have stared evil in the eye, felt its cold talons as they ripped apart everything good. I disagree with your actions, for I believe them to be misguided, but no. I do not think you are evil, Erik."

Though the words spoken were true, shadows still danced in his eyes.

"Goodnight, Ariana," he said, turning his back to me once more as he opened the door to leave.

"Goodnight, Erik," I replied softly.

The room felt emptier without him, the lingering warmth of his presence fading as I was left alone with my thoughts.

21

ERIK

Ariana already sat at the table when I entered the reading nook of a room where we would share a meal. It was a small space where I often read. That seemed like a lifetime ago. Still, it remained one of my favorite places. Cozy and warm, the room had one wall made entirely of windows, keeping the space from feeling claustrophobic. Each of the walls bordering the windows was crammed floor to ceiling with books. All filled with fantastical stories of adventure.

In the center stood a single rectangular table, large enough for four, and it was already fully set. A delicious aroma wafted through the air, causing my mouth to water.

Ariana smiled politely when my gaze met hers.

I nearly returned the smile before noticing that there were only two plates set out.

I turned to Kole. "I told you that you could join us."

"I'm not hungry." He shrugged.

"He has already had his one meal for the month," Ariana commented, earning a cool glance from Kole. To which her lips tipped up.

"I eat more often than that," he snapped, though it was more friendly than angry.

"Whatever you say. Though, you may be more pleasant to be around if you stop going hungry for so long." Ariana's eyes sparkled as she teased him.

"You have been spending too much time with some who are clearly a bad influence on you," he replied before turning to me. "If it's alright, I have a couple of things I would like to take care of."

"It's fine. I'll bring Ariana back to her room when we are finished eating."

Kole dipped his head before excusing himself.

"This smells divine." Ariana inhaled deeply as I took a seat across from her. Her unbound hair flowed in soft waves over her shoulders. She ran her fingers absentmindedly through the bottom section of her hair while her eyes scanned the table before her. Was she nervous? I worked at keeping my smile hidden at the realization.

Ariana was a peculiar creature. Brave when she had no reason to be. In many ways, she seemed fearless. Yet this, sitting in a room with me when I promised her that no harm would come to her, made her fidget.

"Help yourself." No sooner had I said the words than she began loading her plate with various meats and vegetables. She seemed relieved to have something to occupy herself with.

Ariana hesitated with a spoonful of cooked mushrooms hovering above her plate. Her eyes were enormous when they met mine, as if just then noticing I had not moved. "Don't tell me I'm the only one who is going to be eating here."

I smiled, finding her surprise and concern for eating alone curious. "I will join you. You seem ravenous, so I wanted to grant you free rein at the table."

Ariana finished placing the serving of mushrooms on her plate and sat. The barest hint of a flush painted her cheeks. Had I embarrassed her? That would have meant that she cared how I viewed her, which was vastly different than when we first met. Her actions always were her own. She never seemed influenced in the slightest by my opinion of her.

"I didn't mean to embarrass you," I commented, wondering if my pointing it out would cause her further to squirm. It was perhaps cruel of me to do it, though I couldn't help myself.

"You didn't." She reached for her water, taking a few large gulps. Did she use the cold fluid to cool her body from within in hopes that the flush would not spread? Smart girl.

"The flush to your cheeks says otherwise." I shrugged and stood to load my plate with food while Ariana eyed me.

The blush began spreading to her neck though her voice did not waver as she said, "You always so observant?" It was not a denial. She did not shy away from my gaze when it drifted to her before retaking my seat. Typically, when others stared in my direction, their gut reaction was to look away when I turned to them, but not hers. Instead, she held my gaze, breaking contact only after making the point that she refused to be rattled by my company. A part of me desperately wanted to rattle her.

It was as if we were playing some sort of implied game with unspoken rules.

"When something catches my interest," I answered honestly.

Tension filled the small room, causing her to shift in her seat. "And how quickly is that interest typically lost?"

I leaned back in my chair, openly observing her, neither of us touching the plates of food before us. "You're going to hurt my feelings, making it sound like you don't like my attention."

Her lips lifted ever so slightly. "*You're* making it sound like I caught more than just your interest if it's that easy for me to hurt your feelings."

I let out an amused breath. This woman was lethal, and this game, or whatever this was, was dangerous. Despite my best efforts at not continuing, I found myself saying, "And what is it you think I have caught?"

"You tell me." Her mouth twisted into a smirk, eyes glittering. "Unless your ego cannot handle the embarrassment of announcing how you are desperate for my favor." Any hesitation I may have seen within her when we first sat had evaporated.

Her words cause me to genuinely laugh. "My ego is not so easily bruised." She arched a slender brow in disbelief before I added, "And maybe I am desperate for your favor."

Her head tilted, brown silky locks spilling over her shoulder. "I must confess, I am surprised you admit it." A tendril of hair curled against her throat.

"How does one go about winning that favor?" I reached for the glass of water before me, needing a distraction to keep my thoughts from wandering to a dangerous edge.

"Get on your knees and grovel," she answered with a completely straight face, though she could not hide the shine in her eyes. But something shifted, and the light dimmed from her face as she said, "And free me."

All brightness vanished from our conversation. The pleasant tension altered into an uncomfortable one.

My gaze dropped to her plate, untouched. "Food is getting cold."

Both of us took a few bites, neither making a sound other than the forks scraping.

"So," Ariana broke the silence while pushing some food around her dish. "This time is intended for what? For us to learn more about one another?"

"Ideally," I replied, leaning back, making myself more comfortable while looking at her.

The chair Ariana sat in rose well above her head and shoulders, making her look so small and delicate. Though I was well aware that things were not always what they appeared.

"Who asks the first question?" She tilted her head, waiting for a response. An air of curiosity surrounded her.

"You can go ahead."

"What do you fear the most?"

"There is nothing," I answered nearly immediately with a smirk. I indeed harbored fears, but they would not be shared with anyone, certainly not a Bavadrin woman. The question was ridiculous, and she could not have expected any other answer.

Her eyes narrowed. "That is a lie, but fine. I will ask something that does not make you feel less masculine if you tell the truth." She tapped a finger against the glass in her hand. "Tell me about the white night."

That sparked my interest. The white night was tied deeply within my culture. I was not aware that the Bavadrin stories held that information.

"Anything in particular you wish to know?" I asked, surprised that she even knew of it.

Ariana studied me as she considered her words. "I know that we are told to stay inside and far from the Lysian border on that night. Our stories paint the Lysians as going mad by the light of the moon, tearing everything apart. That you become more unhinged than usual."

A smirk pulled at my lips at that, *more unhinged than usual*. "And is that what you believe to be true?"

"I think there is some truth to it. There is a reason for the warnings." She looked at me expectantly, waiting for me to fill in some of the holes to complete or confirm what she already believed she knew.

"On that night, the moon is the closest to us out of the entire year and full enough to cast a white light that is so bright it chases most of the night away. Lysians are linked deeply to the planet and its phases. We do not go mad, but we tend to act more on our instincts. Most of the Lysians who have scars on their bodies got them on the white night. Lysians become more territorial, which certainly could bleed into viciousness and a need to prove superiority through physical means." I smiled and added, "But it can also be a night of far more pleasure. Whatever one is in the mood for."

"What do you typically do on the white night?" she asked, her green gaze unwavering, unfazed by what I said.

"I used to have fun." I shrugged a single shoulder. It was once one of my favorite nights of the year when I could run wild with Kole, Eislyn, my sister, and my brothers. However, that life felt foreign now.

"Used to?" Her brows drew together in question.

"The past few years, I joined my father, who patrolled the border between our lands. I will now continue that tradition on my own."

"You patrol the border?" she asked, surprise clear in her tone.

"Yes. We wanted to make sure some Lysian drunk off the freedom given by the white night did not feel free to risk the consequences of creating trouble in your lands. And that is still something I feel is true for today."

She nodded, glancing at the windows and outside in thought. "My people, and the Lysians watching them. Will they be safe?" The white night was nearly two months away, it would be upon us in no time.

"Yes. The guards there are good. They will not create trouble and will do what they are told. Your people will be safe, and you, too, will be safe. The guards will probably be more tense that day but will not unjustly cause harm."

Ariana reached for her glass again and finished off what water was left.

I felt as though we needed a change of topic. The goal of this time spent together was not to further upset her. Instead, it was partially to attempt to build a bridge between us so that she would be more willing to follow my lead.

"What do you think of our food?" I asked, realizing that I had no idea whether the things we ate differed from what she was accustomed to.

A subtle smile found its way to her lips. "It's fine. You eat basically the same things we do. It's just very separated."

"Separated?"

"Yes. For instance, you have a plate of meat, one of mushrooms, bell peppers, pickled tomatoes . . ." She moved her hand out over the table, gesturing to each she mentioned. "It's all served individually here, while we typically combine a few of these to make a dish."

"Give me an example of something you may like," I said, my interest piqued.

"Well, one of my most favorite dishes contains finely chopped eggs, meat, potatoes, pickled cucumbers, peas, and onion, and it's all combined with an egg and oil–based cream."

I couldn't keep from making a face of disgust. "That sounds horrendous."

The sound of Ariana's laughter filled the room. It was probably the first time I ever saw her appear so comfortable. It was undoubtedly the first time I ever heard her freely laugh. The sound brought a smile to my lips. I liked hearing it.

"It is absolutely delicious. You do not know what you are missing."

"It seems lazy. To simply combine everything into a bowl," I commented with a look of disgust while shock caused her mouth to drop open.

"Lazy!" she exclaimed, her eyes wide in surprise. "You clearly have never cooked anything in your life. Do you have any idea the time or patience it takes to finely chop and cook all those things?"

I laughed at the conversation. "I suppose I don't."

"I thought Lysians fended for themselves. Yet here you are, a simple spoiled highborn." Her words were teasing.

"I simply took on training other than culinary," I answered. Though I never was a fan of being teased, there was something different about it when she did it. I was not angered. Nor did I feel disrespected. Instead, in some odd way, it left me feeling lighter.

"Like fighting?" Ariana mentioned one of the things she assumed I trained in other than cooking.

"Amongst other things," I affirmed her suspicion.

"Care to show me some moves someday?" Her eyes narrowed slightly.

Did she hope to find a weakness in practicing with me? I chuckled, amused. "You've already surpassed Eislyn's training?"

"No, but I find it best to learn from multiple sources." Her lips curved.

"It can be a nuisance having too many voices in your ear," I answered, as though I was not entirely on board with her suggestion, and I wasn't. Yet, some part of me was fascinated by the possibility of actually feeling what she was made of. I got glimpses of her work with Kole and Eislyn. Ariana still had a very long way to go. Though some of the advantages we have, she could never hope to compete against as a Bavadrin. Yet I was still interested to see how she might hold her own against me.

"I don't easily get confused," she countered.

"No, I don't imagine that you do." I couldn't help but feel that there was more to her. It was tucked away, kept hidden, but I sensed it. I wanted to know what it was, what the secrets she kept close to her heart were. There was something unattainable about her, and I desired to obtain it. Mysteries surrounded her. She remained layered in them. Yet I did not see her as a liar. Strange.

Far too often were secrets and lies used synonymously, yet they are not the same. To lie is to deceive or to portray something other than the truth, while secrets are simply undiscovered truths. I typically harbored no fondness for either.

I wanted to peel back every layer of hers and examine what

was underneath. I wanted her stripped of it all so that when she stood before me, I could see her in her entirety. My pulse climbed at the thought.

I forced myself to refocus. To stay in the present and not run away with my thoughts.

We continued our meals, eating until we were both good and full before finally making our way back.

"If I made you my favorite dish, would you try it?" Ariana asked when we turned onto the hall which our rooms were off.

"That ridiculous concoction?" I asked, and she nodded eagerly. "You wish to make it for me?"

"You hate it and haven't even tried it. Yes, I want to make it for you and for myself. I just need the ingredients and a space where I can work it without angering any of the cooks you have around here."

"The cooks aren't as angry as they look."

"Speak for yourself. You're their King. Of course, they are soft towards you."

"Don't ever let them hear you call them *soft*. But sure. I will make it happen for you. Though I can only promise one bite. Our senses are superior to the Bavadrins'. I will not torture myself by promising to force down an entire bowl of that stuff."

"Oh, Erik." Ariana sighed. "You will be *begging* me for seconds. You truly have no idea."

We shared a brief laugh. One that was cut short after opening the door to the small joint sitting space connecting our rooms.

Kole looked up at us, his blond hair a mess on his head as if he just lived through a battle. The only thing lacking was blood, which would have stained his hands and sword.

"Ashes, I never thought you would return," he growled at Ariana.

Before I could ask what was going on, Edda marched out of Ariana's room.

"It's about time!" She placed her hands on her hips. The balcony was open in Ariana's room, and a fall scent mixed with fresh green grass wafted through the space.

"Seriously," Kole mumbled under his breath.

Edda ignored him. "We have so much to discuss. Your Ascension is coming up!"

"I told you I was going to eat with Erik, that I would get you once I returned." Ariana made her way across the small space towards her bizarre friend.

"There's no time to waste, child." Edda stepped aside, waving her into the room. Ariana glanced back apologetically to Kole and me before disappearing into her chamber. Edda closed the door without ever acknowledging my presence.

"She is a viper," Kole mumbled.

"She is an old woman," I commented.

He just shook his head, looking as if he were in an exhausted daze.

I did not intend to stay.

But Ariana's balcony door stood open, and my hearing was quite good.

I entered my quarters and made my way to my balcony, cracking the door.

22

ARIANA

As soon as Edda followed me into my room, she began asking a series of questions.

"What were the two of you laughing about when you walked in?" Her eyes narrowed as if accusing me of something. Coldness emitted from her, which had never been present before, at least never directed at me.

"I was trying to convince Erik to try my favorite dish," I informed her, confused as to why she carried such negative air around her.

"Try it? You mean you plan on cooking for him, like a *servant*?" Her words nipped at me.

I straightened, startled by her demeanor. "No. It is more a show of friendship."

"You think that Lysian King is your friend?" she asked smugly, folding her hands over her chest.

I expected Bavadrins to be wary of Lysians, especially after what happened in our city and to Fraser. I knew it would be a challenge to move past everything. But Edda was partially the reason I now found myself in this position. Though she wanted me to play nice with the Lysians, Edda was bound to question them and their intentions. However, I never expected to feel as though she questioned *me*.

The room we stood in was charged with an air of anger and distaste, all of it stemming from Edda. None of it made much sense.

I looked at the open balcony door, thankful for the warm breeze wafting in. However, it did little to warm Edda's icy demeanor.

"I think he would prefer us to be friends rather than enemies. I don't think they wish me or our people harm," I said. Erik was many things. Sometimes he clearly tried to make me uncomfortable, which was infuriating, but there was also a kindness to him. Were the circumstances different, I believed that we could have been friends. The more time I spent with him, the more I found the raw power oozing from him less threatening.

"Don't be stupid," Edda spat angrily. "They are using you. Any ounce of friendship you see in them is a false picture they paint to control you better so that they get what they want in the end. They care *nothing* for you."

The way she spoke, her eyes rimmed with judgment, wounded me.

Why? Why are you saying this?

I was not someone easily hurt by words. My upbringing made certain of that. But Edda was my weakness. She was never anything other than a pillar of strength for me to draw upon, until that moment. The pillar cracked, crumbling, and the weight that I was left supporting was crushing. Suddenly, the ground beneath my feet trembled, and my knees threatened to buckle.

"I do not need you lecturing me on any of this." My voice grew callous. "*You* were the one who told me to come here, to not fight, promising that the Lysians would not harm me nor those I care for. And now you dare to speak as though you judge me. After all that I have been through."

Edda scoffed, a cruel smile finding its way to her lips. "You are still no more than a child. Tell me, do you fancy this Lysian King? Giggling like a little girl instead of behaving like the Leader Superior of the Bavadrins. Think he will protect you from the evils of the world? Because I can tell you he cannot do that for you. No one can truly protect you, not anymore, not with what is coming. You need to pull that head of yours from the clouds and start using it."

Her words opened a wound within me. It took a long time for me to stop doubting myself. Ever since my mother's death, I began questioning myself and my existence. Edda was the one who helped me the most, supporting and helping me grow from within. She always had her odd ways, but she was also always nurturing. Yet now, she's trying to tear me to pieces? For what reason?

There had to be a reason.

I hid the pain within myself, locking it in some deep, dark corner of my mind, and surrounded it with fury.

"I do not need anyone's protection, including yours," I replied, sounding oddly calm though my heart cracked.

"Really?" It wasn't just a question—it was a gauntlet thrown, a flicker of defiance that shimmered like the edge of a blade. Her gaze locked on mine, unyielding, as if daring me to falter under the weight of it.

"I have no idea what is going on with you today, Edda. But I will not be made to be some foolish girl by you. The fact that I do not absolutely hate the Lysians is not a weakness. I do not let prejudices cloud my judgment, and you should know that better than anyone, for you used to share that view with me."

I paused, shaking my head gently in disbelief. "I feel as though I have always been a decent judge of character, and I believe that there is an opportunity that we could work with the Lysians." I took a step back from her, feeling as though I did not know the person before me. "The way you have been behaving—so willingly offering Bavadrin lives as a sacrifice for farming parties, and this, now, today—never in my life have you spoken to me in such a way. I do not even recognize who you are. You are not the woman I grew up loving. Why are you doing this?"

A look of hurt briefly passed over Edda's features before disappearing altogether. "This is who I have always been, child. I am doing what I always have: helping to direct you to do what is best for you."

Though a sliver of something other than bitter peeked through her words, it did nothing to help the pain in my chest.

"You no longer have that authority. If I am chosen to ascend, then you will be an adviser, but you do not direct me anywhere. I will choose whether to heed your advice, and that privilege will only be if I don't lose all recognition of who you are. Frankly, Edda, you are scaring me. Never have you been so unnecessarily cruel."

Her black eyes were shadowed. She offered no explanation. No apology.

My voice lost some of its edge. "It's clear that you are trying to hurt me, and I have no idea why. But I think it's time for you to go now."

Edda approached me without an ounce of emotion. I half expected her to say some sort of snarky remark. Instead, she raised her hand, placing a featherlight touch on my cheek. Tears swirled in her dark gaze, though she did not shed a single one.

She stunned me, for never in my life had I seen her with tear-glazed eyes.

"I am proud of you, Ariana," she said before dropping her hand back to her side. "But you are right. I am only an adviser to you, nothing more." A sad sort of smile softened her features and then she simply left, leaving me alone in my room, completely dumbfounded.

I am only an adviser to you, nothing more. Those words swirled in my mind, and they cut me deeper than anything else said.

Edda always had been so much more. She was a shelter from the storm, something warm within the cold. She was the family I chose. And with her words, she stole all of that, as though it were nothing. As though she was not the reason I survived all those years under Fraser's rule.

Everything shifted.

I stood in the room motionless until I heard the door leading into the hall close and I knew Edda truly left. I remained there a few more heartbeats before finally finding the strength to move. Walking out to the balcony, I greedily took a deep breath of fresh air.

I was completely fine until I wasn't. Tears filled my eyes till there was no more room and they spilled over. Edda never attacked me before. And though in life I experienced so much worse, her words were strangely more painful than most of the darkness I lived through.

She was my shield until that moment. At that instant, she became a blade that was shoved into my heart.

The door to Erik's balcony opened with a soft creak.

"How much did you hear?" I pointlessly asked while continuing to look over at the distant forest, knowing with my balcony open and his keen ears that he heard everything.

Erik was not quick to answer. "Lysians were raised to hate and distrust the Bavadrins, just like the Bavadrins were taught the same of the Lysians," he replied, trying to offer Edda some form of defense. He believed that she acted so aggressively because I did not outright despise Lysians, but that was not the case.

"No." I turned to find him standing in the center of his balcony. A short iron wall separated us. "You were just a convenient cover.

She used it as a reason to attack me with her words. Edda's mind is not clouded with prejudicial hate. Her point was to wound me. That was her goal."

And she so easily succeeded.

"Why would she do that?" He moved silently until he stood next to me. The slightest hint of concern swirled in his deep blue eyes.

"Why would she try to sever the single tie I have to something familiar, something that has always felt safe, and to do it while I am trapped in a foreign and unknown land? I have no idea."

He did not respond, and I filled the silent void myself. "She is either pushing me away or she is testing me in some way." The worst part was how incredibly alone I felt at that moment. I was brought back to when I was a child who just lost her mother, learning how unsafe the cruel world could be. The loneliness reclaimed its place within me. My knuckles began turning white as I held on to the iron bar before me, squeezing it with everything I had in an attempt to crowd out those horrid feelings.

"Would you like to go for a walk?" Erik offered, his voice gentle.

"No, I wish to be alone right now," I lied. That was so incredibly far from what I wanted, but he was a Lysian, and I was his prisoner. No matter how much kindness he tried to show, it would not make up for the fact that I was not free.

I refused to seek comfort from my imprisoner, no matter how tempting.

"Alright," he finally answered and though his steps were silent, I felt it when he moved away from me. Did he have any idea how potent his presence was?

"Thank you for dinner. It was nice," I said while looking out over the forest before me.

"I'm sorry, Ariana." His voice was low but very much heard. I wondered what exactly he was sorry for.

With the soft click of his balcony door closing, my eyes filled with tears anew. I stood there as they rolled down my cheeks, falling to the floor. I was feeling sorry for myself and that only made things worse. How pathetic I had become. *Poor little Ariana. Mother killed for her existence. Father an abusive and sick individual. The person closest to family turned their back on her. Her friends and her people living under the threat of the Lysians, and little Ariana stolen away from all of them.*

Anger rose within me at how whiny my thoughts became. I grabbed on to that rage like a lifeline and the fire of it grew until it evaporated my tears.

No, I am not some sad, helpless girl. I said to myself.

I am a conjuror. I have strength.

I will return to my people and free myself of the invisible shackles placed on me. I will lead the Bavadrins to a life void of the fear and oppression they had long endured. Even if I lost Edda, I was not alone. The Spirit chose me as the next one to lead, and I would not fail. My mother's death would not be in vain.

One way or another, I would change the path of the Bavadrins.

One way or another, I would change everything.

23

ARIANA

Clumsily, I made my way down the hall, carrying the large bowl filled with my favorite dish. Perhaps I overdid it a little and should have cooked a smaller amount in case the Lysians hated it. However, my certainty that they would like it won out, and I made a ridiculously sizable amount. My arms trembled from the weight of the bowl as I stopped before the door, waiting for Kole to open it.

Kole raised a single golden eyebrow.

"Open it, please." The words huffed out of me in spurts of breath.

Instead, he folded his hands across his chest. "You know, this is an excellent exercise for you."

"I am about to drop it, and if I do, you will be licking it off the floor," I replied through clenched teeth.

His crystal eyes grew more prominent. "Ooh, I do not think you have the authority to make such demands, tiny Ariana."

"Your King is expecting this," I countered.

"Well, in that case . . ." He then *leaned* against the wall, making a point that Erik may in fact appreciate my dropping it.

"If you do not open this door, I will ensure that Edda spends all her time with us from now on," I threatened. Edda and I had not spoken since that day when she lashed out at me. I certainly was not planning to end the silence over a ruined dish, but Kole did not know that.

He winced at the threat, having developed a healthy dislike for Edda. Without another word, he reached over and opened the door.

"Thanks." I shoved my way past him.

We were in the same room where I shared a meal with Erik a couple of days ago. However, this time there were three plates set out.

"Take a seat," I instructed while placing the bowl on the table and shaking out my wobbly arms.

Kole frowned and remained standing. Looking as if even sitting next to the bowl was possibly going to make him ill.

"You promised me you would join us and try this," I pointed out.

"I have no idea why I agreed to this," he mumbled and reluctantly made his way to one of the seats, dropping into it.

I placed a large scoop on each of the three plates and was heading towards my seat when Erik entered.

His dark sapphire eyes pinned me, and I froze. He glanced down at his plate before turning his attention back towards me. "I only promised one bite."

"I couldn't find a smaller serving spoon." I shrugged a shoulder and watched as a smile slowly spread across his lips, softening his features.

He made his way through the room with a silent grace while I settled into my seat.

"Nice of you to join us this time, Kole." Erik regarded his friend, who was wearing a scowl.

"Wouldn't miss this," Kole replied, looking down at his plate as if he couldn't make out what was on it.

Erik chortled, turning to me as he lowered himself into his chair. "How did you get him here?"

"He lost a bet," I quickly answered while probably grinning like a fool. Winning that bet was the biggest feat for me. It was rare that I landed a hit on a Lysian.

Erik's eyes widened. "You don't say." Kole somehow managed to moan without actually making a sound while Erik leaned forward, fully invested. "What was the bet?"

Kole's jaw flexed, though he did not respond.

"I slapped him." I glanced at Kole. "He didn't think I could."

Erik's eyes instantly filled with boyish excitement. Suddenly, he did not seem like someone who would harm a soul. His world did not rest on his shoulders, and he was no more than a normal person. At least it was easier to think that when excitement poured out of him, and his focus was on someone other than myself. Not having to feel the weight of those dark eyes made everything easier.

"Oh, c'mon, wipe that ridiculous grin off your face," Kole barked at his King. "She cheated." He held out a thick finger, pointing directly at me.

"You underestimated me." I rolled my eyes.

Of course, he would say that the only way for me to win would have been to cheat. But, that was not the case. I won fair and square. You cannot cheat if there are no actual rules.

"I thought you were hurt! Do you have any idea what would become of me if I harmed you?" Kole made a pointed glance at his King, who watched us with a smirk.

"Give me a break. You threw me around outside like a rag doll when I first began training. I am sure Erik would not love the idea of my being injured, but he won't kill you if it were an accident."

"I'd rather not bet my life on your assumptions," Kole

muttered. He was staring at his plate again. Looking as if what was on it offended him nearly as much as my landing a hit on him.

"So, you tricked him?" Erik quirked an eyebrow.

"I fell. Kole walked over, bent down to help me, and the rest is history." I could not hide the devilish grin itching to surface.

"Who hits someone who is trying to help them?" Kole sounded exasperated.

"You should have never let your guard down," I pointed out, telling him the same words he had told me many times.

"You were raised without manners," he snarled in response.

My jaw nearly dropped. "Manners? You wish to speak to *me* about *manners?* You held out your hand in training only to shove me back down to the ground, telling me to not let my guard down."

Kole growled.

"You are such a sore loser," I said under my breath, knowing they would all still hear it clear as a beautiful, bright day.

"I am not a loser." Kole's voice dropped, edged with what sounded like anger. It would have been worrisome if he was not technically supposed to protect me from harm. I may be held in the Lysian lands against my will, but I was not to be hurt, at least not yet. The thought of that instantly dampened my mood, and I shoved it to the back of my mind. The time I spent with Erik was not going to be soured, not when I needed him to set me free. Or at the very least, not when I wanted him to refrain from killing me when I finally freed myself.

"In this instance, you are," I shot back.

Kole snarled.

"Oh, c'mon. You win some, you lose some. A big bear of a Lysian like you should be able to let small things like this roll off your back. Spirit knows your back is large enough to roll a boulder off it," I said, complimenting his size. Sometimes that was all Kole needed to feel better, for someone to stroke his ego just a little.

He was silent for a beat, then finally relinquished some of that grudge. "Fine," he mumbled.

"I'm sorry, I couldn't quite catch that with my lowly Bavadrin hearing." I brought my hand to my ear and cupped it as if to better hear him by.

"FINE!" he roared.

Erik chuckled. "Kole here has hardly ever been less than a winner. It's one of the reasons he will never spar against me. He does not want to lose. But, as you have now learned, a loss severely damages his mood."

"What is this? Pile turds on Kole day? Was I invited to a meal just to entertain you both by having someone to poke at the entire time? And for your information, *Erik*, I choose not to fight you because it would be an embarrassment for a King to lose against one of his subjects." Though he sounded big and mighty, we all knew that was not true. Erik could take him, and it was not even because he was a conjuror. In a match between the two of them, conjuring aside, Erik would win. There was little to go by for this judgment. I never saw the two of them physically compete in any way, but it was a strong feeling. For Kole's size, there were likely very few who could truly best him. I believed Erik could.

"Oh, really." Erik's eyebrows shot up.

Kole's face was reddening.

"So . . ." I pointedly glanced at the dish in front of Erik with food already spooned onto it, figuring it was time to give Kole a break from being the center of our attention. "You have yet to try the deliciousness before you."

Deep blue eyes flashed in my direction. "It's not like it's going to get cold," Erik answered with a crooked smile. The dish was served cold.

"No, but I am starving." I grinned.

"We're not stopping you from enjoying your meal." He held my gaze and a glint of something dangerous moved in his.

I was the first to look away.

"Fine." I reached for my fork. "I will begin only to prove to you both that this is edible."

"You eating something does not prove it's edible." Kole frowned, looking at his plate. "Maybe we should wait till tomorrow to try this, just to make sure you aren't poisoned and die in your bed."

"For someone so strong you have an awfully weak stomach," I commented.

"It is not weak."

"Oh, pardon me. I forgot that we weren't allowed to call any part of you weak or risk damaging your fragile ego."

Kole grabbed a spoon nearest to him, shoveled some of the salad on his plate onto it, and shoved it into his mouth. He chewed with zero expression before swallowing and then shoveling another spoonful into his mouth.

Erik and I briefly glanced at one another before turning back to Kole.

"Well?" I asked.

"It's not as terrible as I expected," he commented before taking another bite.

My eyes narrowed. "It's not terrible at all. Look at you. You're basically inhaling it." I nodded towards Erik. "It's your turn."

His attention settled on me once more. "You first."

Obliging him, I took a bite, savoring every moment. "Mmmm, so good."

Erik looked down at his fork, suspended just above his plate, ready to be eaten. His expression was unreadable. Finally, he brought it to his mouth, and I could hardly contain my eagerness. He chewed painfully slowly before finally swallowing.

"Well?"

Erik reached for his glass of water, taking a leisurely sip without paying me any attention. When his eyes finally locked with mine, he worked at suppressing a laugh, knowing that the wait was torturing me.

"It isn't bad," he answered and took another bite, smiling while he chewed.

"Why can neither of you just say that it is good, and you enjoy it!"

"You want us to lie to you?" Kole asked, with the plate in front of him completely cleaned.

"You devoured it!" I pointed to his plate, and then to him. "And now you are getting seconds!"

"I don't want to be rude," he commented, spooning a rather large serving of seconds for himself.

"You have zero qualms with being rude," I informed.

"I take offense to such accusations," he replied with a full mouth. "I am a gentle Lysian."

Taking a deep breath, I sighed and took another bite of what was on my plate. The taste reminded me of home. So many feelings were linked with the flavor, most of them of joyous occasions from a time where I remembered very little for my mother had taught me to make this. I found myself savoring it.

"Honestly, I did not expect to like this at all." Erik's voice pulled me from the thoughts I was slowly burrowing myself into. "But I am finding it enjoyable."

I couldn't help but smile. "I'm glad."

"Me too," he replied, and his smile faltered. "There is something I need to ask of you." The way he said it made it sound like I had no true choice in the matter.

"Ask or demand?"

Erik ignored my question as he continued, "My brothers . . . they would like it if one of them came along for your Ascension ceremony."

"Why?"

He licked his lips. "You and your kind are still largely unknown to us, and your customs—"

"Are private." I couldn't help but interrupt. "What happens when a new Leader Superior ascends is sacred. Never have outsiders been present. It's not some special event for your brothers to enjoy."

Erik remained silent a moment, though by the look in his eyes, it was clear he was contemplating his next words. "I am going to be honest with you."

Kole looked to Erik with a completely unreadable expression on his face. They both were so good at becoming impossible to read with a snap of a finger.

"Please do," I said, putting my fork down, and giving the Lysian King my full attention.

"I need them to see you in your world, to understand you better."

What did it matter whether they understood me better? "You think this would help them agree to let me go?"

"No."

"Then why?"

"It may help buy you more time," he stated matter-of-factly.

More time. More time for my life to hang in the balance. He wanted me to change my mind, to decide to simply do what I was told while under the thumb of the Lysians. If I took too long to fall in line, then Erik would likely feel pressure to do something about it. If I became an unruly obstacle, then his brothers would probably call for my *removal*. Erik likely thought more time would cause me to switch my view on things, but he was wrong.

"I do not need more time," I replied, and Kole turned to me with hope in his icy blue gaze.

"You will help us?" Kole asked while Erik's lips pressed in a thin line, for the King knew my answer.

"Not until I am free to go home and the Lysians leave my city."

"As long as that remains your answer, then you need more time," Erik pressed.

He was wrong. I refused to be controlled in this way, not anymore. I was determined to get myself out of this situation. But that was not known to him, and I needed to keep it that way. If I was to pretend that I had no hope of freedom, then I needed to grasp at every extra second I got to keep breathing.

"Why do you think allowing this would help me?" I asked, genuinely curious about his thoughts behind this request.

"When I saw you in your lands, the way you interacted with your people and even us, the Lysians—it will help them see you as more than just a Bavadrin in the way of their goals. They would be forced to see you for what you are: as someone deserving of life."

Was that what changed? Erik was never unkind, but he was certainly making more effort to get to know me, his prisoner. Was it because he no longer viewed me as the lying monster they assumed Bavadrins to be?

"Fine. Which of your brothers is coming?"

"You may choose."

"All of them wish to go?"

"It does not matter what they wish," Erik answered flatly. Clearly, some preferred to stay.

I thought back to his brothers. My interactions with them had been relatively brief. The eldest had eyes filled with cold hate whenever he looked at me. Without saying it out loud, he obviously saw me as an obstacle between him and his sister and wanted me removed. The other brother Jorn also seemed shrouded in a cape of suspicion. Iver, on the other hand, looked at me with curiosity, and when he spoke it was direct. If he plays games, then it is clear he is doing so.

I wanted none of Erik's brothers in my city, but if one of them had to join, then it was better if it was the one who desired my death the least.

"If it is my choice, then I suppose I choose Iver," I answered.

Kole sighed but did not speak a word after catching a glimpse of Erik's dark gaze settled on him.

"That is a fine choice," Erik replied in agreement while Kole shook his head to himself as if he could not believe what was being agreed upon.

The rest of dinner flew by, just as the days did. Between my training with Eislyn and the dinners with Erik, I found myself too busy to worry about Edda. From the very sparce information I could gather through snippets of conversations I was able to over-hear, there was some sort of issue regarding the safety of the Lysian lands. Their forces were planning on being split. Some will stay behind, protecting the capitol, while the rest would attack the Siddhe. Did they expect the Siddhe to somehow retaliate and threaten their capitol? But the Bavadrin lands were in between the two. I did not understand the concern or the tactics. And it wasn't like I could ask Eislyn or Kole about it.

It was not until the day before we left for our trip back to the Bavadrin land that I finally saw Edda. At this point I didn't even know why she bothered to come with me to the Lysian lands only to alienate herself from me.

Edda helped fix the sacred stones to my hair, twisting strands in various ways and braiding others till one side of my head was intricately decorated as one expected of a Leader Superior. We hardly spoke to one another during that entire time except for her directing me to turn a certain way or hold a strand of hair for her.

Edda did not apologize, and I did not ask her to, nor did I ask her what her reasoning was to hurt me. Whatever it was, she would have told me if she wished for me to know.

The pain of it all was a weight that sat deep within my chest. For someone whom I trusted so explicitly to go out of their way to force distance between us left me confused and wounded. Edda never acted rashly or without reason. She didn't hate that my feelings towards the Lysians softened. What she wanted was to place a wedge between us. To pull our bond and relationship through thick mud which now clung to me, weighing my limbs down, and making it difficult to move on.

As soon as she finished my hair, she left without a word, leaving me incredibly confused, angry, and hurt. I didn't see her again until we went to the stables to leave.

I was given my own horse. A large gray beast with a dark luxurious main was to be my riding companion. Kole let me know that her name was Rain, for she had dark splotches of gray marking on her hide, as if wet by rain.

I greeted the enormous animal with caution.

"Hello, Rain." I spoke calmly, lifting my hand to her. The horse moved its nose into my hand, and I ran my fingers over her. Slowly, I moved around her, running my hand down her muscular body. She shook her head but did not bolt or revolt against my touch.

"She likes you." Erik approached us holding an apple, which he handed to Rain. "I was going to have you bribe her, but it seems that is not necessary."

"She is beautiful," I commented, stepping back to get a better look at her.

"While you are here with us, she will be yours to use whenever you like."

"Am I able to ride her even when we are not traveling?" I asked, turning to view the King, who was patting the horse's side.

"As long as Kole accompanies you," he answered with a smile.

Kole approached with his mount. "Mine is the strongest and fastest," he stated, and the message was received.

"Here, let me help you up." Erik came around the horse as I readied myself.

"It's alright, I can . . ." I began refusing only to feel his hand under my leg, pushing me up higher until I could throw over my other leg.

"You're welcome." He smirked, then left to get his stallion.

While I was allowed a horse, Edda still seemed not to be trusted. She was forced to ride with a Lysian, and Kole, again, was the unlucky one stuck with her. I couldn't help but feel sorry for him.

24

ARIANA

T hree days later I stood lost amongst the mass of my people, with a few Lysians lingering around me. It was the day either I or someone else became the new Leader Superior.

I felt foolish for believing that I could lead my people toward a brighter future. As I stood amongst them, doubt doused me in anxiety. What made me special enough to lead? Conjuring abilities did not make a good leader. Had the Spirit meant to choose me? It was as though I was an imposter.

I had been bathed and dressed up appropriately for the part. Edda made sure of that. I was swathed in a cream dress with whimsical patterns threaded throughout. The fabric hugged my body until it reached my hips, where it then flowed down the length of my legs. Several slits cut into the skirt of the gown, allowing for effortless movement. I was packaged as if I already was the Leader Superior, but I was not—at least not yet.

I stood before my people with Lysians at my back. In a way, I had welcomed their control. By giving them Fraser, I ensured my people had no choice but to bend to the Lysians. I betrayed the

Bavadrin oath and gave our leader to an enemy who invaded our homes, spreading fear and doubt. Before ever becoming a leader, my choices brought so much unease and turmoil to my city.

But what choice did I have? Fraser was the one who truly brought the destruction to our home. The decisions I made after were to keep things from completely falling apart, and to spare as many lives as I could.

And now, as I stood before my people, it was their choice whether to accept me. No matter what they decided, I would continue to fight for them. That realization brought me a sense of peace.

Familiar golden eyes found me from across the room while we waited for things to begin. Willis. We nodded to one another in recognition. I wanted to run to him, but the weight of what was about to happen kept my feet cemented to the ground. A hand-some smile found its way to his lips, and he winked. People moved between us, and he disappeared into the crowd. I lost track of him just as quickly as I found him.

Edda clicked her tongue, and the room went silent. "I have news to share. The Spirit has chosen our very own Ariana to ascend to become the Leader Superior of our people." Her voice floated through the space as if carried by the wind though there was absolutely no breeze.

"Why does everyone listen to her?" Erik bent down and whispered the question in my ear. His proximity warmed my skin.

"She was an adviser to the past Superior. And she is ancient, which equates to wisdom for some. So, the people listen," I replied, trying to focus on anything but the feel of the Lysian King standing so close to me.

Edda's black gaze snapped to me as if she heard my remark before she turned and addressed the room once more. "Is there anyone who opposes Ariana's claim as the chosen Superior?"

"I do." A male's voice cut through the space. I immediately recognized it and cringed. *Shal.*

Of course, he was going to be the one to think he should rule. There was no way *he* could take our people anywhere good.

Erik and the entire Lysian party turned to look at the man who voiced his challenge. They looked out of pure curiosity, for there was no need to size him up. Any Lysian could crush him with little effort. No matter who became the next Leader Superior, the Lysians would remain in control. They had the power, the fire conjuring King.

The Lysians had no skin in what was about to happen. They would simply take whoever was chosen to lead next.

I thought back to what I knew of ascending and what happened when someone opposed a claim.

The Leader Superior is chosen by the blood of the Spirit's choosing, and the opposed will fall by blood drawn. I needed something to draw blood.

Cursing under my breath, I turned to the Lysians near me.

"I need a dagger," I whispered to Erik and Kole, my voice low. Bavadrins already did not like Lysian presence, let alone the fact that they were hovering around me. I did not need them seeing Lysians helping me too.

The two turned to me in unison.

"Why?" Erik asked, brows drawn. His jaw set tight, lips pressed into a displeased line.

"I don't have time to explain." I glanced to Edda, who was making her way toward Shal. "I swear I will not use it against any of you." My attention shifted towards Erik's narrowed gaze. Were they nervous I would somehow turn a dagger on them and be victorious with nothing more than a single blade? More likely, they were afraid of losing their prized Bavadrin, though it should not have mattered. No matter who won, the Lysians would keep their control, at least for the time being. "Please."

Iver placed a hand on his brother's shoulder. "Awh, come on Erik, just let her have one. She clearly can never hope to defeat a Lysian with no more than a little dagger."

Evidently, he and I agreed, though I was unsure if I liked that.

Across the room, Edda stepped in front of Shal, viewing him coldly. "Very well." She turned. "Any others?"

The moment of silence fell thickly. The pressure of it weighed heavy on my chest.

"In that case, I ask that everyone clear the center of the room, and the two laying claim to please move into the opening. Shal and Ariana."

Time was up.

"Fine," I murmured in irritation. It was up to the Spirit to help if I was deemed worthy enough.

Erik moved before I took a step toward the center. His hand took hold of mine and I felt something cool slide into my palm. His fingers let go of my wrist, freeing me. I took the blade and shoved it into the dagger pocket of my dress.

"Be careful," he warned, his voice low. Dark blue eyes pinned me before I peeled my attention from him.

"Thank you." I was already moving towards Edda and my opponent in the opening created as people parted, leaving the center of the room empty as they pressed closer to the walls.

Shal stood in full view, a scowl splayed on his face. He was taller than I yet seemed somehow shorter than I remembered. His brown hair was bound by a single thick braid running down his back. He threw his shoulders back and his chest forward as if to make himself appear even larger. Perhaps it would have caused me to hesitate at one point in time, but I now lived with Lysians. Shal could try to make himself seem as big and robust as he desired, none of it would ever compare to the strength and skill of those I just stood amongst.

"The two of you will remain in this circle until either one of you recedes your claim or blood is spilled. The one who bleeds will be marked as not worthy to lead." Edda's voice echoed throughout the room.

Glancing around, I found myself surrounded by my people. There was a potent strength in their presence. My entire life, I feared being noticed in such a manner, always surviving in part by hiding—but not anymore.

I would help pull my people from the shadows Fraser thrust upon them, for I was not the only one tormented by him. No longer would they need to live in fear. No longer would the women be used as a currency amongst those deemed the select. No longer would our own be driven out of the capitol. I would take back the Bavadrin people from the Lysians, and I would protect them till my dying breath.

When I looked at those surrounding me, fear shone in their eyes, in some I saw hate, but overwhelmingly, there was hope. Despite the blood running through my veins, they believed in me. They did not fear me. I was not simply my father's daughter.

Edda cut across the room and rushed to the Lysians. She firmly placed her hand on Erik's chest. Was he afraid of harm falling to his prized prisoner? I wondered what Edda said to keep him in his place.

"I wish I could say it's good to see you, Ariana, but you reek of them." Shal's voice was cold, bringing my attention to him once more. Tanned skin stretched over a solid muscular body. However, most of it was for show. Muscles did not make someone strong, especially with a mind as weak as his. It was easy to turn cruel when life was hard. Shal used the pain of others as steppingstones for his success, climbing till he reached the highest tier possible. Unfortunately for him, he reached his top and was about to tumble back down to the bottom. He was so starved for Fraser's love that he blinded himself to the fact that most did not harbor the same affections for Fraser, and for his little follower.

"Not pleased to see an old friend?" I asked. We were friends, once. That seemed like a different life.

It was before he decided to crawl up Fraser's butt and make a home there. And began wishing to put a collar around my neck. Ever since I turned of age, he watched me with a darkness in his eyes.

I wondered how different Shal may have ended up without Fraser tainting his soul. I never knew why as a boy he turned to such a bitter man, seeking affection from the one who was incapable of it.

"I would have preferred to see Fraser instead," Shal replied with a cruel smile.

Anger blossomed inside my chest. After everything Shal witnessed, he wished for Fraser's continued rule. Shal was there when that monster butchered my mother. He stood by my side when my world turned upside down. And now he craved for that monster's rebirth.

The man before me could not be allowed to take control. He was no leader. He was only a follower of a madman.

I always did my best not to hate people. To try and understand that most hurt others because they themselves were in pain. Yet, I couldn't help but feel bitter hatred as a pit in my stomach at that moment. With every breath, that loathing grew fiery roots and spouted. It moved through my limbs, intertwining itself with the anger growing within me. It was as though the flame within was consuming me, leaving behind a cold stone void of any feeling at all. With that hate, I found myself enveloped in a strange calm.

"That can be arranged," I answered lowly.

The threat didn't go unnoticed.

If he wished to be with Fraser so severely, I wouldn't stand in the way of such desire.

His smile widened in response. "Tell me, were you the cause of his death?"

It felt as though ice slid down my spine. Had he assumed I had a part in it, or did someone tell him something?

I did not reply. To say no would have been a lie, and I was not going to enter the seat of the Superior on a blatant lie. I wanted to look at those around us to see whether his insinuations gave them pause, but if I did so, I risked showing an unease with the question. If I had nothing to hide, then I would not need to confirm their belief in me. So instead, I kept my eyes trained only on Shal.

Instead, I said, "Fraser's actions led to his ending." That was undoubtedly true.

"And now *you* hope to lead *my* people?" Shal's gaze narrowed. Confidence rolled off him. It was impressive. He never possessed a spark of such potent confidence before. He worked at the will and pleasure of Fraser. Our late Leader Superior had been Shal's entire world.

"I plan on leading *our* people," I clarified.

He opened his mouth to reply, but I cut him off. "You and I have hardly spoken a word to one another over these past several years, so why all of a sudden are you so talkative?"

"Fine." He pulled a sword free. "I fight for the great Fraser and the Bavadrin people!" His lips curved at the side into an arrogant smile, as if he had already won before ever beginning.

Shal was not the brightest.

He was so blinded by admiration that he did not realize just how much favor Fraser had lost with his people. They followed him because of his title, not because they genuinely wanted to, and certainly not because they harbored love for him.

Briefly, my eyes slid shut.

Spirit, help me. Guide me.

Something otherworldly flowed into me, bringing with it an odd sense of peace.

With a deep breath, my eyes fluttered open.

Mother, give me your strength.

Standing in the ring, I didn't fear the outcome of that day. Instead, I pitied the soul that dared to oppose me.

I stepped forward, accepting Shal's challenge.

Both of our lives were about to be forever changed.

25

ERIK

T he little old Bavadrin's hand pressed to my chest, keeping me back. She was impressively strong for both her small size and age.

"Don't you dare interfere with this." Edda sounded vicious.

I was not sure who she thought she was. Did she desire to be reduced to ash?

Iver stood beside me. His gaze fell upon Edda, her hand pressed into my chest, and then back to the makeshift arena. For the first time in his life, he appeared serious and focused on what was occurring around him.

Ariana stood in the open circle, while her opponent, who was both larger than her and more muscular, pulled out a sword.

The hand fell from my chest, but the hag stood there looking up at me. "That girl is the only thing in this entire world that I love," she said with such viciousness that I believed her. "If you think I would allow her to place herself in harm's way with no hope of a victory, then you are sorely mistaken."

An intense desire to toss the nuisance of a woman out a window came over me.

"How is she supposed to stand against someone with a sword when all that she has is a dagger?" Kole asked Edda, whose black eyes lit up at the question, and she released a small laugh.

"That idiotic boy is trying to fight with force because that is all he has ever known. Ariana needs the dagger only to draw his blood, not to win." She smiled devilishly.

"I don't understand." Kole looked at Edda as if she had just lost her last marble, though I was reasonably sure she lost it long ago.

Edda laughed. The sound was unbelievably irritating. "The girl fights with something much more powerful than a simple sword. She has the hearts of her people. That is why she is the one to become Leader Superior."

Edda turned to me. "You have seen the way the people respond to her when she walks through the city. They are drawn to her, and they are drawn to her now." The little terror of a woman then turned to watch, her back to me. "Prepare yourselves. You are about to witness a rebirth. The Spirit will guide her today." She sounded giddy, and I was pretty sure that she must have been far too old for that mind of hers to function correctly.

Ariana and her opponent walked the perimeter of the circle they were in and then stopped. He flexed his muscles with each step as if to show his strength. In contrast, Ariana moved with a sense of calm surrounding her. She squared her shoulders, keeping her chin held high. Not a shred of fear or uncertainty lingered in her eyes. I found myself pulled in by her, intrigued that despite all that had happened to her that she was able to find herself on steady ground. Able to face opposition without a shred of doubt.

He looked down his nose at her, raising his blade. "Last chance —give up."

Ariana merely stood there, hands at her sides.

"No." She did not yell, but every soul in the room very much heard her words.

The simple word sent her opponent flying across the circle, blade poised to strike. If not opposed, then he would have done more than bring her to her knees. He would have killed her. The hair on my neck stood. My palms instantly heated as I tapped into the power which always hummed through me.

Before I even took a single step, Edda moved.

"Don't you dare interfere!" she hissed. "This is not something Lysians have any right to involve themselves with." Her arm splayed out before me as if it was strong enough to stop me.

I would have shoved her out of the way had others in the room not started shifting, pulling my attention again towards Ariana.

While Shal ran to close the distance between himself and Ariana, others stepped into the circle. Two Bavadrin men drew blades, flanking Ariana protectively. Shal came to an abrupt stop, a look of surprise gracing his face. Then, two others stepped out, flanking him with blades drawn as if to assist the scumbag. His ridiculous smirk did not get the chance to fully form before four others emerged, blocking Shal's men. The entire thing was like something done by design. To call it random acts seemed unlikely.

Landin, the Bavadrin whom Ariana saved by giving up her father, positioned himself behind Shal, kicking the back of his knees. Shal dropped to the ground, his sword slipping. Landin brought a thin blade to his neck when he looked up. The room stilled completely.

The warmth in my hands receded. My attention trained on *her*, drawn to the woman who controlled the entire area without even moving a muscle. Fear did not touch her steady green gaze as she observed the man on his knees before her.

Ariana remained where she stood when Shal had first been poised to attack. Those loyal to her protected her, fighting for her to ascend. She did not give a single order. No command was spoken, yet the Bavadrins acted so fluidly.

Ariana tilted her head, eyes narrowing. "Do you give up your claim to Superior?" Her voice moved through the chamber as though it were alive. Like a cat, her words slinked around every soul before setting its sights on the man on his knees before her.

The room held its breath, waiting for the response.

Shal looked at her with such hate-filled eyes. "You don't deserve to be the Superior."

"Very well." She pulled my blade from her pocket and looked at it.

At first glance, it appeared simple and silver, but if given the time to be observed, its intricate carvings on the handle and the blade could be seen. She turned the dagger in her hand, taking the time to view it while running a thumb down the handle. Then she shifted her attention to Shal, walking over till she stood before him.

"Final chance," she said, giving him yet another opportunity to give up.

"Your father should have taken care of your mother before you were ever even born!" Shal seethed, and the room soundlessly gasped, lips parted, jaws dropped.

From where I stood, I could hear Ariana's breath leave her. Her eyes momentarily slid shut, and she inhaled slowly and deeply. A slight tremble moved through her, likely unnoticed by all others.

The nerve of that maggot to use such emotional words in his pathetic attempt to derail her. He was honorless. If he were to take over as the Leader Superior to the Bavadrins, then I would have seen to it that he would have met the same fate as the previous one. My hands itched to feel the warmth of his blood on my knuckles.

The old bat standing before me balled her hands into fists at her side, her heart rate raising ever so slightly. Edda's entire stance turned rigid. The male's words triggered something in her as well.

Ariana stood motionless before Shal, her gaze turning uneven and difficult to read. If the man's comment hurt her, she did not show it on her face.

Something changed as if the air vibrated with a power stemming from Ariana, and I couldn't look away from her. Smoothly, she kneeled down, balancing on her toes before him, my blade in her hand. There was something otherworldly about her at that moment. As if she were not the same woman I came to know over the past several weeks. As if she possessed the power to shift the entire world.

Her head tilted, features softening ever so slightly. She was completely captivating. Ariana brought the blade to Shal's cheek and placed a roughly two-inch cut beneath his eye, deep enough for a decent stream of blood to coat the dagger's edge. Shal flinched, but Landin kept a firm hold on him, keeping him from struggling.

My heart punched me in the ribs.

Ariana casually observed the blade, the blood on it. Her gaze then locked on Shal, and she brought the weapon's edge to her lips.

This was unlike anything I had ever experienced. My chest tightened till I could not draw a full breath.

Her full lips parted, and she ran her tongue along the side of the blade. A sigh passed between those lips, sounding as if she just tasted the sweetest thing in the entire world.

My mouth watered.

Spirit, help me. What is this woman doing?

Her eyes remained locked on Shal as though there was no audience. She was a vortex I could not escape.

My lips parted, drawing in a shaky breath.

"Well, looks like she is even more savage than I thought," Iver commented lowly, his eyes wide with a spark of excitement as he observed the scene unfolding before us.

I didn't seem able to form a coherent response.

"Mmmm, delicious fear," she said, naming the taste of his blood. "I wonder if this is how your blood would have tasted that night Fraser butchered my mother. The night you stood beside me, squeezing your eyes shut and pissing yourself."

"Shut up!" He jerked forward with rage. The men behind him kept him from lunging at her.

Ariana smiled, though it did not touch her eyes, before rising to her feet. She wiped the remaining blood from the blade on Shal's other cheek. "What's the matter, Shal? Do you not like remembering where you came from?"

"You traitor! You killed our true Leader Superior!" he growled, looking more and more like a desperate animal.

"Your accusations bear no merit. The Spirit has chosen," she replied coolly.

"I will kill you for killing him!"

She ignored his threat as if it were never even spoken. "There is something I have long yearned to know, Shal. Why do you love him so? You and I were friends once. Then that night, when my world came tumbling down around me, you went to his side, acting like the son he never had. Why?"

"You should have had the same fate as your mother. For if I ever get my hands on you, that will seem like a mercy."

Edda visibly shook as anger dug its claws into her.

Ariana slowly turned her head side to side, a sad look in her eyes. "I feel sorry for you. You sought the affection of someone incapable of it, and that has left you a shell of the person you could have been."

Shal opened his mouth to respond. He never got the chance. Willis's fist connected with Shal's jaw, drawing a fresh stream of blood. Ariana's friend had also grown tired of subjugating everyone to the filth coming from Shal's mouth.

"You are finished talking," Willis informed the Bavadrin on his knees. Landin, who stood behind Shal, nodded in agreement.

"I banish you, Shal," Ariana said to him. "When our city's gates are under our control again, you will be exiled. You will live out your days as a Bavadrin, but I will never welcome you into my capital again."

I wished to allow the exile to be executed immediately to get him as far away from Ariana as possible. But that was not wise. Given the circumstances, we could not trust a man like him not to run to the Siddhe. It would have been best if his sentence was simply to no longer have the privilege of drawing breath. That, I would have gladly allowed for.

"She should just have him killed," Iver said under breath.

Edda glanced at my brother. "She is not yet ready to bloody her hands that way."

"Not yet?" I asked. Was she insinuating as if some day Ariana would be ready for something like that.

Edda gave me a cold smile before turning away from me.

Shal spat a bloody glob on the floor, similar to Fraser's actions before he was executed.

Landin and Willis pulled Shal up, dragging him from the room.

"The Spirit has chosen!" Edda yelled, drawing the attention of the room. "Ariana is our new Leader Superior!" The room erupted in cheers.

"That's it? It is all over?" Kole asked no one in particular.

Edda turned, answering him anyway. "Not yet. Tonight, she will spend the night in the Spirit realm. And then she will truly be the Bavadrin Leader Superior."

"Spirit realm?" I tore my eyes from Ariana as the crowd surrounded her.

"Yes. There is a herbal potion that thins the separation between us and the Spirit's realm. There, the Superior meets with the Spirit and ascends to their position."

"Sounds intoxicating," Iver stated with a smile, throwing an arm over Kole's shoulder only for him to shake him off. "What is in this potion?"

"That is a Bavadrin secret." Edda flashed a smile. "But the only one who ever sees the Spirit is the new Superior at the time of Ascension. Otherwise, it just makes you feel more vulnerable to the beauty of the world around you."

"It is mind-altering?" I was hesitant about Ariana taking something like that.

"Are you not listening, brother? It's magical juice," Iver stated, clearly intrigued. He turned back to Edda. "Mind if I try some?"

"Will she be guarded?" I asked over my brother's ridiculous questions.

Edda laughed. "We will lock her in the temple. She will be fine. And if you want her to lead the Bavadrins, then this is something she must do. Now, I need make sure the next steps of the ceremony are prepared." She vanished into the crowd of cheering and celebrating Bavadrins.

"That was . . ." Kole began without being able to find the words.

"Invigorating." Iver finished the sentence. "Perhaps our little Bavadrin is more Lysian than we ever knew." He grinned, nudging me with an elbow.

"That was not Lysian," I replied while scanning the crowd, catching sight of Ariana being whisked away by Edda.

It was something else entirely.

She was something else.

26

ARIANA

After extinguishing Shal's claim to the Ascension, Edda had me taken away and prepared for the ceremonial party. I was swathed in a beautiful deep green dress with embroidered flowers and vines running the length of the skirt, along the edge of the bodice and down the sleeves. There was something whimsical about it. Even more of the stones Edda gave me were braided into one side of my head, creating various knots before flowing into the rest of my hair. The other side was left with soft waves that fell past my shoulders.

For a moment I was allowed to look at my reflection before being taken away for the celebration. In the mirror, I saw a woman, mature, brave, and fierce. My eyes were a reflection of my mother's. I couldn't help but reach out, touching the glass.

"I will never forget all that you sacrificed. I take these steps today for you," I said to her.

A gentle knock on the door let me know it was time.

No one announced my presence when I entered the large room, but that did not stop them from noticing. A hush spread through the space and those closest to me all turned, viewing me.

As I moved through the room, they parted to make way. With their eyes on me, I felt the weight of responsibility for each of them. They were mine to protect and lead.

Looking over the crowd as I passed, it was easy to spot the Lysians. Edda stood with them, likely keeping them contained. Erik watched me. His gaze unreadable. Iver stood beside him, his teeth flashing with a bright smile when my eyes connected with his. He nodded as a way of greeting across the sea of people between us. Kole stood scowling at Edda.

I focused my attention forward, making my way towards the dais as those who had helped me get ready instructed me to do.

I stepped up to the platform, where Edda greeted me. She managed to move incredibly fast from the Lysians' sides to mine.

"Kneel," she commanded, the word rolling over the crowd even though she did not raise her voice.

Without hesitation, I dropped to my knees on a small rectangular pillow.

A boy moved onto the dais, holding a bowl. His large brown eyes focused on what he held, careful not to drop the thing he carried. Once he stood beside us, he held out the bowl to Edda.

She glanced at it, giving the boy a nod of a job well done, and turned to continue addressing the room. "On this night, a new Leader Superior Ascends." The entire room was hanging on every word. Like a crevice had opened up on the stage, and everyone was being pulled into it.

Edda stuck her thumbs into the bowl, coating them in white paint. Her dark eyes settled on me and softened just a touch. There was kindness in them, though I now hesitated to trust in it. "Tonight, you will reunite with the Spirit." Taking my face in her hands, she pressed her thumbs under my eyes. Moving down, she painted lines underneath and over my cheeks. "May you see clearly in your journey."

The boy provided a cloth which Edda took, wiping her hands.

He then disappeared with the bowl of paint, and a girl stepped forward, taking his place, holding a golden goblet.

Accepting the goblet, Edda addressed the crowd. "May this flow through your veins, taking you from our world to the Spirit's." She then turned to me, holding it out.

The goblet was nearly overflowing. My stomach clenched at the sight.

"Drink the entire thing," she instructed.

Without a second thought, I poured the concoction into my mouth. The consistency was nauseatingly thick, tasting of dirt, grass, and twigs. Despite its repulsiveness, I got it down in a few disgusting seconds.

"Good." She took the goblet back before passing it along to the girl who then disappeared.

"In three hours, you will be taken to the temple where you will spend the night," Edda informed me. "Until then, this ceremony is for you." Though she only spoke to me, the entire room erupted in applause and cheers. "You may rise." She smiled softly.

As soon as I got to my feet, silence spread once more. Hundreds of eyes viewed me, waiting to be addressed.

"On this day, I swear to you I will do everything in my power to protect you. Till my last breath, I will defend you. I will fight for you, and if need be, then I will die for you." Murmurs went through the room. "You all have always been a shield for your Leader Superior, but I will not hide behind it. For I, too, am a shield. I am your shield, and I will stand side by side with you as we move forward into a new day." The room erupted into cheers once more. It hummed with excitement. The energy was unlike anything I had felt before. A mixture of joy and hope lifted everyone, and for at least a night, worries appeared to melt away.

Once everyone settled once more, Edda stepped forward. "For the Ascension, Ariana will need someone to stand guard while she is indisposed in the temple. This person will become her second-in-command."

I couldn't help but smile, for I knew who that person would be.

"I call Willis forward," I said, and after a second, he was moving towards the front. Golden eyes found mine and softened just a touch. Once he stood before the dais, I focused on only him. "Willis, would you do me the honor of being my second?"

"The honor is all mine." He slapped a fist across his chest, over his heart, and bowed his head. When he looked back up there was no hiding his wide smile, nor mine. We grinned at each other like children who had no worries in the world. I even thought I heard the howling of wolves in the distance. Had he shared the news with them? Were they also rejoicing?

"Well, now that that's settled, let's celebrate!" Edda yelled out, and the entire room erupted in cheers once again. Festive music played from one end of the room. Those closest to it could not help but dance. The sheer excitement in the air was remarkable and, in a way, sad. Desperation tainted the happiness as if finally, they had been freed from dark oppression. But, they were still not truly free.

I made another vow, silent to all but very much real. Today the Bavadrins were liberated from the shackles of my father, a new Leader Superior born, and the next time I returned home, they would also be released from the Lysians' command.

I stepped off the dais no sooner than someone shouted my name.

"Ariana!" a woman called out. "My, you are certainly taller than you were before."

I spun around and met face-to-face with a ghost from my past.

Kiora. I had not seen her in many painful years.

There are some in the world whose destinies were meant to be commingled. Those friendships forged of the most powerful substance, completely unshatterable. The souls recognize one another, finding a forever home in each other's presence. A bond so powerful that it withstands the test of time.

Kiora and I had now spent more time apart than we ever had together, yet it did not matter. She was the same as she had been. Her eyes were bright and hazel. Her skin kissed by the sun, and her hair bleached by the same sun from brown to a dirty blond color. She greeted me with a warm and welcoming smile.

Tears lined my eyes.

"Kiora," I whispered her name and instantly threw my arms around her. She hugged me back, and the two of us laughed like we were giddy children.

"*I'm* tall?" I exclaimed as we released one another. "Have you looked in a mirror?"

Her own eyes were lined with unshed tears. She laughed, hugging me once more, as if unable to believe that we were here sharing the moment together. That we were finally physically in the same room again. "It has been ages. Yet it feels like I have known you this entire time. That nearly no time has gone by."

"I cannot agree more." I beamed. "How is this possible?"

"Well," she casually glanced around the room, "some of the farmers came by and let us know you were Ascending, and that is definitely something I would not miss." She grinned. "I would have loved to join you when that scoundrel challenged you, but figured my presence may have been more distracting than helpful. Besides, Willis and Landin had everything under control."

I smiled, probably wide enough to look like a lunatic. "I can't believe this is real life."

"You? I return to you becoming the new Leader Superior! You were just a kid when I last saw you." Her smile was contagious. She was so full of energy that it spilled over.

I laughed. "You know what I mean. You are here, finally."

"I am," she said with certainty and hugged me once again.

"Your *guests* are coming to greet us," she whispered before releasing me.

I turned to find Erik, Kole, and Iver closing in.

My eyes locked with Erik's sapphire ones, and my face warmed before I tore my attention away from him.

"Kiora, let me introduce you. This is Kole." I contemplated calling him my friend, but that seemed forced, and *my guard* did not sound any better, so I settled for just a name. "and Iver, brother to the King. And this is Erik, King of the Lysians."

"King?" Kiora exclaimed. "Ariana, you never told me that you ran with such an impressive crowd." Though she smiled at them, her hazel eyes gained an edge.

I mumbled out a laugh, hoping she would be able to contain her distaste for them. When we were young, Kiora was always honest, to the point of wearing her emotions on her sleeve. Not that she was overly emotional, but if she did not like someone, she had no qualms about letting them know. And if she was ever angry, Spirit help whoever that was, for the stubborn girl could hold a grudge like no other.

"Everyone," I addressed the Lysians. "This is Kiora. She is one of my oldest friends."

Kiora made eye contact with Erik and dipped her head ever so slightly to show respect in the greeting.

"If you both know one another so well, why are you two so weepy?" Iver asked.

Kiora assessed him, running her gaze down the length of him before snapping back to his face. "We are not weepy. But we have not seen each other in a very long time. My family moved out of the city when I was young, and I have not returned until now." She left out the part where her family was forced out of the city, for my father believed that the Sparrow Archers were no longer necessary. The truth was, he was jealous. They had always been in a way worshiped, and that was the real reason he sent them away, because he couldn't bear the Bavadrin people worshiping anyone except him.

Kiora reached out, taking my hands in hers. "We have all returned here for you. I have returned for you. And my tailoring is better than ever. I can send a needle soaring, never a stitch out of place." There was a wicked gleam in her eyes.

Never had Kiora picked up a needle in her life, but she had picked up a bow and arrow. She was telling me she had joined the ranks of the Sparrows, that her skill was as impeccable as those who had come before her.

"There was never any doubt in my mind that you could achieve greatness at whatever you set yourself to." I smiled.

"I won't keep you from your celebration any longer." Kiora's lips gained a fierce curve, matching the unwavering certainty in her eyes. She hugged me once more.

"We will catch up soon," I replied, not wanting to let her go.

"Definitely," she agreed, her attention moving briefly to the Lysians. "Enjoy the party."

Kiora disappeared into the sea of bodies moving throughout the room.

"Why did she not return here for such a long time?" Kole asked after she was no longer visible, and I nearly thought I had perhaps imagined her into existence.

"Her family moved away," I replied.

"Yeah, but they are here now. Surely, she could have come to visit, or you visit her."

I was not sure whether he was suspicious or simply could not comprehend. "Fraser would not allow for me to make that trip. As for her family . . . you have to understand we were forced to follow our previous Superior. That did not mean that they wanted to. Sometimes leaving was a way to keep the peace."

"It was that bad that your citizens avoided the capitol?" Kole's crystal eyes watched me as I considered how much I wished to share.

"Taxation has gotten steep, and for no reason other than Fraser wished to widen the gap between himself and those he viewed as beneath him. We have also had a population decline. Fraser began encouraging reproduction efforts. As a result, some began viewing women as currency. Those living outside the capitol found ways to avoid some of these changes. The closer to Fraser, the more likely to be required to aid in his efforts."

"Do you have children?" Iver asked curiously.

A bitter smile curved at my lips. "I was spared because the price of my womb was a bargaining chip Fraser enjoyed wielding."

Kole and Iver appeared disgusted, and I couldn't bring myself to look at Erik to see what he thought.

Kole decided to change the subject saying, "By the way, you were remarkable today."

"Yes, very savage but lovely," Iver voiced before draping his arm across Erik's shoulders, and pulling him in. "I think this one nearly fainted."

My cheeks flushed, embarrassed that they witnessed me like that. I don't know what got into me when facing Shal. Never had I behaved in such a manner before. It was suddenly difficult to meet the Lysian King's eye.

"That reminds me." I dug into my pocket, desperate for something else to focus on. Pulling free the blade, I held it out for Erik. "Thank you for this."

Dark sapphire eyes observed the beautiful silver dagger in my hands before rising to view me. Reaching out, his hand pushed my fingers, curling them over the hilt. "It is yours to keep."

I couldn't keep the surprise from my face. I wasn't certain what was most shocking: that he was gifting me something of his, or that he thought me so nonthreatening that he allowed me to keep a weapon.

"You're sure?" Never had I seen a blade like it. Intricate carvings etched the silver with a detail that would have taken someone a great deal of effort to make. The weight of it felt good in my hand, perfect even.

Erik nodded. "After tonight, that blade is more yours than it ever was mine." His lip quirked up at the edge.

My cheeks flushed. "Where did you get it?"

"It belonged to my father." He smiled.

"Erik, I can't have this." I held it out to him once more.

"You already do. Besides, it's not like my father did not have an entire room of weapons." He nodded towards the dagger. "But you should probably pocket it for now. You wouldn't want someone running up to hug you and ending up with a blade in their gut."

"Ariana is not that careless," Willis said from beside us, surprising me with his presence.

"Willis!" I exclaimed.

"Superior." He dipped his head. A single dimple pressed into his cheek with his smile.

"You don't have to do that," I said, finally pocketing the blade.

"Of course he does," Landin spoke as he, too, joined our growing group that was now half Lysian and half Bavadrin. Though he smiled at me, it turned into a scowl when he turned to the Lysians. "You lot planning on letting her enjoy the night or are you going to remain hovering around her and scaring off those who wish to pay her their respects?" His tone was cold and dismissive.

No. Do not do this. Not tonight.

"Landin," Willis said in warning, beating me to it.

Erik tilted his head, his attention fully on Landin as he took one small step toward him. Willis stiffened but otherwise did not move.

"You can pretend to be big and strong, but I know how you tremble with fear. How you *reek* of it," Erik said, his voice deathly calm. His jaw clenched in a way that made it seem like he was going to say more but stopped himself.

"Does it look like I am trembling in fear, Lysian dog?" Landin sneered.

The blood drained from my face as the surrounding air turned uncomfortably thick.

Kole grunted, hand casually moving to the hilt of his sword.

Erik's face became completely unreadable.

Instantly I moved, stepping in front of Landin. "I want you silent," I hissed between clenched teeth.

I then turned to Erik and his terrifyingly indecipherable expression. "He is just worried about me. He did not mean it," I said as if it were an excuse.

Landin *scoffed* behind me.

If he survived this, I was liable to peel his skin from his body myself at this rate. And yet, I said, "Please, Erik."

Erik looked past me, kept his focus trained entirely on Landin. The Lysian King took yet another step towards us, nearly trapping me between the two of them.

Surprisingly, no one around the room noticed, or they were pretending not to.

"Erik." Though I said his name, he did not respond to it.

The Lysian King invaded my space as he leaned towards Landin. "The only reason you draw breath is because Ariana saved your miserable life. The way I see it, the only reason you are a sliver more than worthless is because *she* deems it so. I would prefer to erase you from this world, and if you continue to push me, then despite her love for you, I am afraid I won't be able to hold back. After all, I am no more than a Lysian dog." Erik looked down, meeting my gaze and holding it. The power running through him felt electric, buzzing, poised to strike. Without saying a word to me, he turned and stalked away, Kole stiffly following suit.

I pivoted. "What in Spirit's name is the matter with you! He is the Lysian King!"

"I don't care the least bit what he is." Landin folded his hands over his chest in defiance. His jaw set with a stubbornly rigid demeanor.

"Do you wish to die? Is that what you want?" I could have wrung his neck.

"I want you released," he stated flatly.

Willis, who still stood beside him, looked around the room as if to make sure we were not drawing unnecessary attention.

"And you think angering the Lysian King is a way to get that outcome?" I pressed.

"He holds you hostage. Who knows what is being done to you while you are under his control." His gaze narrowed on me. Was he angry with me?

"What exactly do you think is being done to her?" Iver asked, drawing all our attention. Why had he not followed Erik as Kole had?

"You tell me, *Lysian*," Landin replied with growing anger.

"You should take a walk," Willis said, grabbing Landin by his arm, but he twisted out of the hold.

"How can you be okay with this?" Landin asked Willis.

I reached for Landin's shoulder. "That Lysian King spared your life when he thought that we may have had something to do with the disappearance of—"

Landin cut me off. "Don't be stupid. Do you think he did that for you? For me? He did that so it would be easier to control you. So that you would feel as though you owed him something." Though he was likely not wrong, the fact was that Landin's life had been spared. We still were living under Lysian authority and because of that, he needed to regain control of himself.

"That's enough," Willis warned Landin.

I focused on Landin. "You didn't actually think I did not know that. The sacrifice I made for . . ." I stopped myself from saying more or implicating myself in Fraser's death. "It is only because I deeply know you that I will excuse your behavior this time. Though I thought you had grown out of these outbursts. I am not a little girl. Not someone you need to protect from every danger in the world. I will not be gone from this city forever. It and the people within our lands are now mine to lead as I see fit. If you think me dumb or unworthy, then you should have challenged me for the position, but you did not."

Surprise touched Landin's features, stealing away some of the anger that had encased him. It was as if he realized the poor choice in his words and actions for the first time. "You're right. I'm sorry," he whispered, gaze dropping to the ground, as if he could not bring himself to meet my eye once more.

"You are not to speak to the Lysians like this again."

"I won't," he submitted, tempering his anger.

I nearly sighed in relief. Though when my shoulders relaxed, a wave of dizziness hit me.

"We'll go get some fresh air," Willis stated.

"See that he makes it home alright and then return at once," I instructed him.

Willis's golden eyes drifted over my face, concern coloring them. "You alright?"

"Fine. I'm beginning to feel dizzy, that's all." I offered him a small smile and a shoulder shrug as if it were no big deal.

"I shouldn't leave you." Willis scanned the room, likely looking for someone else to help make sure Landin went home.

"I don't mind keeping an eye on her until you return," Iver offered.

Willis frowned and turned to me.

"It's fine. I will be fine. Just go and hurry back." I nodded.

With his lips pressed into a thin line, Willis turned from us. He disappeared into the crowd, leading Landin from the room.

"Can I get you something? Water perhaps?" Iver offered, looking me over.

I shook my head. "I just need to have a seat."

He nodded, taking my arm and guiding me to a chair near a small table on the outskirts of the room. Then, like a gentleman, he moved the seat out for me, surprising me with the gesture.

"Thank you," I said, taking the seat.

"It's the least I could do for such entertainment." He grinned, leaning against the wall. His gaze moved over the crowd, observing the Bavadrins who were celebrating.

"You can go. No need to stay with me." I gave him an escape.

"Please. If anything happens to you, either your Bavadrins or my brother will have my head," he stated casually. His hands were in his pockets, and his shoulders relaxed. Fine clothing covered his body. He appeared as though he didn't have a care in the world. Someone who was truly free of burden.

"I doubt you fear any of them," I observed. Iver always seemed to be the one to stir up trouble with others. He never behaved as if he were afraid of reprimand.

"Everyone fears Erik," he commented, turning his attention to me.

"Even you?"

"Would that surprise you?"

"The way you behave towards him, yes, it would."

Iver smiled. "Your friend would be wise to have a bit more fear."

I shook my head in disagreement. "Unfortunately, that would only serve to make him worse. Not better." Landin was a complicated person. He did not lash out because he lacked fear; it was the opposite. He likely was terrified for my safety and that of his people. That was the reason why he behaved in such a manner. In his way, he was trying to protect me.

Iver tilted his head in thought while holding my gaze. It felt as though he was looking right through me. "What did he do to deserve your love?"

"You aren't actually interested to know such a thing," I stated. He was a Lysian royal, and one of the least tamed of them. Someone like him did not care to know those types of stories.

"Why not?" He frowned. "We are keeping you in an effort to have you help our cause. Seems it would be important to know the things you care for and why in order for us to better be able to make use of you."

Though his words should have angered me, they did not. Instead, his blunt honesty was why I wished for him to be the one of Erik's brothers to join us.

"What makes you so forward?" I asked.

"No point in wasting time pretending things are not what they are. It is no secret that we are keeping hold of you for a reason," he answered.

Oddly, I found his candor welcoming.

"Well? If you have nothing better to do than sit here and entertain a Lysian prince, then I would like to hear the story of you and that very angry Bavadrin guard."

I told him that story. How Landin and I both had things in our pasts that we trusted each other with, though without divulging what those things were. How we were there for one another since childhood. How he was the brother I never had. I shared everything with Iver except for the biggest secret of all, for I could not have them know what I was, at least not yet.

They were all going to find out soon enough anyway.

27

ERIK

The breeze felt wonderful against my skin. Crisp night air settled over the land with a chilled edge. It aroused the senses without causing discomfort; it was revitalizing. I craved the open night sky, seeking it out to get away from the Bavadrin mass inside. Not that I cared what they thought of me, but being the object of silent attention was draining. They stole glances, eyes filled with a mixture of fear and hate. Their whispers were no better. My senses were buzzing with the desire to permanently shut them all up, and so I left, allowing myself a few seconds of peace and quiet before returning.

"Alright, there is a step here. Be careful." Iver's voice snagged my attention to where he exited the building out of a side door.

"I know there is a step, *little* Lysian," Ariana replied warmly, leaning on my brother for support.

"What's going on?" I approached them in a few quick strides. Ariana swayed at the sight of me, surprise widening her eyes as if my presence was completely unexpected.

Iver turned towards me, a mischievous glint in his eyes. "This little princess has officially been hit by the magic juice. We were just getting some fresh air."

Green eyes slid to him. "This *little* Lysian has officially been appointed as my guard."

He chuckled. "Calling me little does not make you taller."

"I could say the same for you . . . *little Lysian*." She smirked to herself as if proud of her reply. For someone who usually maintained a high level of control over her responses, this was... amusing. The easy smile on her lips, the warmth in her gaze. She felt reachable. Less hidden.

"I have a feeling it is close to time for you to go to your temple." Iver tapped her on the nose with a finger. She snapped at it with her teeth, too slow to actually catch him. He smiled and turned to me. "I can go get Edda, if you want to keep her from faceplanting."

Ariana gasped. "I would not fall on my face."

"I'll stay with her." I stepped up to them, my hand sliding around Ariana's waist before she leaned her weight onto me, even as she said, "Not mean Edda."

"You know, Kole calls her a wrinkled onion," Iver said once he released her.

Ariana's eyes grew large before she tipped her head back and laughed. It surged up like a pure and clear spring, captivating and heartfelt. A melody of pure joy wrapped around her. I couldn't help but smile.

Iver laughed lowly, looking at her before turning to me. "I think I like her like this."

The giggling stopped. Ariana narrowed her gaze in feigned irritation. "Hey. I am *always* likable." She flicked her hand out before her, waving him off. "Better go and . . ." her lips curved skyward, "get that wrinkled onion." Another giggle burst out of her. "Oh Spirit, Edda is going to love this one."

"I'll return with the old one," Iver said with a grin before disappearing back into the building.

"How are you feeling?" I asked Ariana once we were alone, my arm still around her waist, liking the warmth of her against me.

"I'm fine," she replied softly, her voice slightly breathless. Her eyes darted between mine then dipped to where her shoulder leaned into my chest. She released me as if she just realized we were touching, and my hold loosened enough for her to sway before I pulled her back. Her hand gripped my arm for support. "I am just dizzy."

"I won't let you fall."

Green eyes found mine. Her head tilted as if in wonder. There was not an ounce of hesitation in her gaze as it drifted between my eyes, over my face.

"What are you thinking?" I asked.

"You're handsome," she replied with zero regret, her gaze lingering on my features. "It is a shame you are so stubborn."

"Stubborn?" My lips inched up at the unfiltered comments I was receiving.

"I won't stop fighting until I am free," she announced, brows furrowing in determination. Her thoughts had already moved on.

"You can fight me all you want. You won't win." Some part of me felt a thrill at the notion. Of the roles we currently held—I the predator and she the prey. My fingers tightened at her waist and she leaned into me even more, her body flush with mine.

To my surprise, her lips curled as if she also enjoyed this. "With a belief like that, it will be all the sweeter when I do." Her gaze dipped to my lips before lifting once more. "I wonder. What will you think once we are on equal ground? When you finally truly see me for all that I am."

Ashes. My pulse spiked at the thought. It was part of what drew me to her. The fact that she did not cower before me. I enjoyed her defiance. Perhaps I even craved it.

She tensed, gaze dropping to my chest, lashes fluttering briefly. The drumming of her heart shifted its beat, becoming erratic.

"Are you alright?"

She sagged as strength slipped from her. "I—I don't feel so well all of a sudden," she murmured. Any trace of humor vanished.

"Is this normal?" Being under the influence of what she drank was one thing. This was something else. With every irregular beat of her heart, she got worse.

"I don't know." She squeezed her eyes shut.

"Edda will be here soon." I hoped the words brought her some sliver of comfort. *Ashes, Iver, what was taking so long?* My thoughts appeared to bring the old hag to us.

"Hurry up," Edda hissed as she exited the building out of a side door.

"I am," a deep voice replied, Willis on her heel.

Edda observed Ariana, whose eyes remained shut, as I held her upright. "It seems the potion took effect a little quicker than expected. We are taking her to the temple now."

"Give her to me." Willis held out his arms.

I hesitated, not wanting to release her when she was in such a state. As if I could somehow help her.

"Mhhh, Willis," Ariana murmured, turning towards him. She reached for the Bavadrin guard, and I forced myself to let her go.

Ariana looked even worse than just a moment ago. A sheen of sweat coated her forehead, skin pale. I reached out to touch her brow, but my hand only landed on air as Willis stepped out of my reach.

"Keep your hands off of her," Willis instructed flatly. He managed to keep the hate from his tone, but his golden eyes spoke volumes.

"It's fine," Ariana said softly. Her eyes opened, but she seemed to have trouble finding me. "I'll be okay, Erik." Her gaze went in and out of focus before her eyes slid shut, and her head rolled to rest on Willis's shoulder.

"I don't like this," I stated, a sense of unease settling over me.

"You think *we* would harm her?" Ariana's now second-in-command asked.

"I didn't mean . . ." I began, my own frustration gnawing at me.

"Save it for later, Lysian," Edda cut in sharply. "Right now, we need to get her to the temple." She looked to Willis and nodded towards the street, as if telling him to get moving. He carried Ariana away, her limp form in his arms. I trailed a step behind them.

Once we reached a small round wooden building near the center of their town, Edda turned to me once more. "You are not permitted to enter. You may stay out here if you would like while we set her up inside, but you remain out here."

I nodded, accepting that this was a part of their ritual and rule. I would not disrespect their belief, especially when I could monitor Ariana's heart rate and breathing from outside. If anything went wrong, then I would know.

Edda and Willis entered with Ariana and emerged without her a few minutes later.

"She is to remain in there until she walks out herself," Edda informed me. "Willis will stay here with her. You may go."

"I am staying here," I told her. There was no way I would leave Ariana while she was drugged. She was in no condition to create trouble. However, her Bavadrins were another story.

"Suit yourself." Edda waved a hand in the air as if it did not make a difference to her and turned to leave.

"You hurt her," I found myself saying to the old bat, bringing up the time she attacked Ariana with her words. "When you spoke to her that way. Why did you do it? Was it just for me to hear her defend the Lysians?"

Edda turned. A look of surprise passed over her features. "Well, aren't you a clever beast? But you would do well not to try to understand the reasons for my actions. However, I will offer you this. No, it was not just for you to hear her defend you, though I realized that may be a benefit, and for that reason, I left the balcony door open. The only thing you need to know is that everything I do is for that girl. My actions served to help Ariana. There is a darkness that looms, and the thread that tethers me to her is unraveling. I am afraid that it may break, and before that is to happen, I must help her see that she no longer has a genuine need for me. She is more than capable of standing on her own."

"You are a Seer," I stated what I long suspected. If she was truly a Seer, it was no use for me, for I could never hope to trust her or the things she says.

The Bavadrin smiled darkly. "As if you had not already assumed this about me." She then turned to the night sky before looking back at me. "I hope you have a lovely night, Lysian." She then left.

Willis took a seat on a step outside the entrance to the small temple, and after a minute, I followed suit. A breeze ran a lap around us before disappearing, leaving nothing but still-chilled air. Soft noises began to come from within the temple. Ariana mumbled something incoherent in between the sounds of her teeth chattering. Her pulse picked up. I wondered what the discomfort she felt was like.

"What are you listening to?" Willis pulled my attention from the temple.

"What makes you think I am listening to something?" I turned to find him staring at me. The scars on my back suddenly itched, as if knowing I sat with the man who had put them there.

"I have been around enough animals in my life to know the gentle shift of their heads when searching for sound," he replied. "Is it Ariana?"

Animals. I nodded. "I can hear her shivering and mumbling incoherently."

Willis turned, looking out at nothing in particular. "She will be fine," he said with certainty.

In the new silence, I couldn't help but continue to monitor what was going on within the temple. None of it brought me any peace. Ariana was going through something uncomfortable, and in turn, it made me uncomfortable. I needed to focus on something else. Anything else. For this was perhaps even more tortuous than when I sat waiting in one of their prison cells.

"What do you make of the Lysians and me?" I asked Willis with genuine curiosity. His eyes were cold when they looked upon us, however he did not lash out like Landin, nor did he smell of fear.

Willis chortled. "It does not matter what I think."

"Still. I would like to know." I shrugged.

He sighed, turning his golden gaze towards me. "You and your kind are very lost and confused. You assume you have power, and in some sense, you do, but you have less than you think." Again, certainty was very much present in his words. He truly believed what he said.

"And what power do you think you have that I do not?"

"We have Ariana. You may have her physically for the time being, but you do not have her, not really, and you never will," he answered, turning from me and looking into the darkness before him. There was a stoic silence around him.

"You wish to kill me?" I asked simply. Whatever his answer, it would not upset me, for I could understand why he would want my death.

"No." He kept his focus on the darkness before him.

"No?" I asked in surprise. I would have bet otherwise. Despite his calm and lack of outward hostility, it was obvious he did not have any favor towards us.

"You spared Landin's life, and you have not brought harm to Ariana. If I was to kill you, then who would take your place?

Would they be worse? That is not a decision I am equipped to make, nor do I have the power to make it." He alluded that Ariana would be the one to make such a decision. What would she choose if she were given the option?

"Landin is a curious one," I stated.

Willis ran his tongue over his teeth and nodded in the darkness. I nearly thought my attempt at continuing a conversation with him over, but then he spoke. "Landin is afraid. When fear takes hold of him, he loses all sense of empathy. He lashes out and tries to force things to go his way. But, of course, it never works out that way for him, yet he is stuck following that same pattern."

"He should have been afraid when he allowed Ariana into my prison cell." I pointed out the first mistake he ever made in my presence.

Willis viewed me. "We underestimated you and your kind. That will not happen again."

"You were always silent, never tried to talk to me while I was down there," I pointed out.

"I had nothing to say to you," he answered with a shrug.

"And now?"

"Now, Ariana has decided to see good in you and your kind, and so I will try to understand her decision."

I nodded, and again we fell silent. The darkness around us grew still, allowing for my mind to wander under the backdrop of Ariana's distant murmurs.

Remaining outside that temple was for no one other than myself. If Bavadrins tried to revolt, then we would easily regain control. If anyone harmed Ariana, then we would just take whoever was chosen as the next Leader Superior. It was not for my Lysians that I sat on the steps of the entrance to a Bavadrin temple. It was for her. I was protecting her, only to be tortured by the discomfort she felt while under the spell of that poison she drank.

Why did I find myself wishing to protect her? Was it because in her own way, she tried to protect me when I was a prisoner? Was it because I believed her to be a compassionate Bavadrin and not the witch I first thought she may be? Did the reason matter? Eventually, my brothers would lose their patience and demand either her compliance or her life. My stomach clenched at the thought.

Since I've known her, Ariana always held her head high. She never hid or ran from the horrors biting at her heels. Every obstacle she faced head-on, and with a grace I never could have imagined a Bavadrin to have. I was fairly certain she would not agree to stand with us while under Lysian control, which left her ultimately forfeiting her life. Would she also face her death with her head held high, or would she finally break and beg for mercy? Could I order her death? Could I do it with my own hands?

I refused to force Lysians to do something I could not do myself.

"I want you to know that I do not intend for any harm to come to her," I found myself saying to Willis.

He nodded without looking at me. "We shall see how good your word is."

28

ARIANA

I was freezing, yet strangely numb. It was as if death bound
me in his icy embrace. Like iron bars wrapped me so tightly
that I did not know where my skin ended and the cold
began. My body vibrated as it uselessly tried to warm itself.

Everything was made worse by the endless spinning. I could
not decipher whether it was I or the room that spun. Nausea beck-
oned, threatening whatever remained in my stomach to come up. I
forced it down, squeezing my eyes shut, but that only made things
worse. When my eyes snapped open, things got worse yet again.
There was no escape.

Then abruptly, the obscure spinning room stilled. Darkness
turned gray, before lightening further. My body stopped shaking,
and I no longer felt cold or alone. I sat on the stone where I had
been placed in the temple, though I was no longer in that same
room; I was in a white realm of nothingness. In the distance, a
figure approached, coming into view. Its skin was as white as the
place I sat in, evident by the visible long thin fingers peaking past
dark sleeves. Its face and features were unknown, hidden by a

dark hood. Without asking who they were, I understood. Their heavy presence seeped into my bones. It was the Spirit.

I felt almost nothing at that moment. Fear vanished, along with caution and joy. A strangely simple peace surrounded me. I existed in that place to speak to the Spirit. There was no need for anything else. Yet, I was still myself. My emotions were known and present, though it was as if they were behind a curtain, hidden away so that my mind was uninhibited by them.

The Spirit stood several feet from me, motionless. No sound came from it. A moment passed, and I broke the silence with the question I burned to know the answer to.

"Are the Bavadrins cursed?" I asked, knowing that the Spirit could answer such things. That was the entire reason for the Ascension ceremony. The Spirit chose the Leader Superior who thus met the Spirit to be enlightened, to better be equipped to lead their people.

The Spirit appeared to shift without moving, its face remaining hidden. "No. Far from it," it answered in a voice neither masculine nor feminine.

"How so?" I asked, my tone mirroring its calm demeanor. Though I could not make out the features of the Spirit, I knew it was peaceful. I also knew myself to be safe.

"Look in the mirror when you ponder that question," it replied, and I frowned. It seemed that the Spirit answered questions in riddles similar to Edda's style whenever she answered about her visions.

"Are the Lysians to be trusted?" I asked instead.

"Do you trust the Lysians?" it asked in turn.

"I want to," I admitted.

"That was not the question."

"Then yes, I suppose I do. Is that foolish of me?"

"Not at all."

"Why me? Why was I chosen for this position? And why was someone as horrid as Fraser ever even chosen?"

The Spirit tilted its head unnaturally. "Fraser served his purpose. As for you, would you have preferred that the boy who challenged you be the victor? The one with the sweet-tasting blood of fear?"

"That was you. Who made me behave so . . . wild?" While standing before Shal, I felt as if I were on a boat and someone else began steering it. I was not in control, stuck on that bit of wood in the middle of an ocean while someone else manned the helm.

The Spirit's shoulders shifted as though it laughed, yet no sound came from it. "Today, the veil between us is the thinnest as you Ascend. Yes, I was present within you when that child challenged you. Did you not enjoy the taste of your enemy's blood?"

I gritted my teeth to keep from making a face of disgust. No, I didn't particularly enjoy that part.

I shifted the conversation. "Tell me what I need to do."

"Ariana." The Spirit said my name without my giving it. "You are on a path that is very much your own now. It will bring you great pain, but it may also bring you and those you care for peace. Some have been placed in your path to help you on this journey. You must never lose the trust you have in yourself. Trust in your choices, and the path you are set on may be less painful."

"Path I have been set on? You make it seem like I have no choices, at least not really."

"*Some* choices are now out of your hands."

"Are they in yours?" I asked, wondering if the Spirit had set me on the path.

"No, they no longer are."

"But they used to be?" It made no sense. The Spirit was a god. How could anything be outside of its control?

"Many things are at work here. Your ties to the Spirit realm are strong; do not fear using those ties. Pull on the power, draw it into you. But know, the power will not be able to protect you from everything." The Spirit was alluding to my conjuring, for that was what tied me to its realm.

"What is it I need protection from?" I asked. Did the Spirit not just imply that the Lysians could be trusted?

"You will soon know the answer to that."

"You do not wish to give the answer yourself?"

The Spirit seemed to smile, though I still could not make out its features. "You remind me much of your mother."

My breath caught. "You knew her?" My mother never ascended to Leader Superior. She could not have even been in a realm such as the one I was now in. Of course, the Spirit oversaw everything and thus knew her in some way.

"I must go. Time has gotten away from us," the Spirit suddenly announced, and I felt my chance at obtaining any answers slip through my fingers.

"Wait. There is still so much I don't understand. Can I truly trust the Lysians? Are the Siddhe behind the disappearance of conjurors from our lands? Will Bavadrins be injured if I free myself? What about the broken treaty and the curse?" I found myself rattling off several questions to which I desperately wanted answers.

"I will answer one question. Ask wisely, for some of which you asked may offer information that is of no true use to you."

"The treaty. Did the curse die with Fraser's death, or is there something else I could do to free the Bavadrins?"

"No, the curse did not die with your father's death, and there is nothing you can do, for it was your birth that was the curse," it answered plainly, and my heart nearly stopped in my chest.

"What—what do you mean?"

"I will leave you with one more bit of knowledge. There is one other on a path that will cross with yours several times. It is a conjuror of illumination. You will need their help. The two of you

are drawn towards one another, for your futures are intertwined."
The Spirit then moved till it stood directly before me. I looked up
at it and still could not make out a face or features. It was as if
darkness clung to the shadows created by its hood, hiding the face
behind it. "Those you have met in your brief life are lucky to have
you in theirs."

Conjuror of illumination? Did the Spirit mean fire? Was it
speaking of Erik? I should have questioned it, but instead, I found
myself asking, "How are they lucky if I am cursed?"

"I never said you were cursed. We have waited a long time for
you." The Spirit tilted its head as if looking down at something.
"Your left hand, don't drop it."

Those were the last words said before it vanished altogether.

I woke up in the temple.

Gone was the mystical entity and the otherworldly feeling of
its presence. Thankfully, so were the nausea and the cold in my
bones. Though I was far from back to my usual self.

We have waited a long time for you. Who was this *we*? The Spirit
and others have been waiting for me? I did not understand.

Rising to my feet too quickly caused the world to spin, and I
sat back down as my body slowly adjusted to the change in position. After a moment, I tried again. My head protested. The floor
was unsteady underneath my feet, but I managed one small step
after another.

Your left hand. I looked at my hand to find nothing out of the
ordinary. *Don't drop it.* I then looked at the ground, seeing nothing.
Slowly I shuffled my feet, moving around the stone altar to the
other side. There was a rolled-up piece of paper on the ground.

I lowered myself to the floor, not trusting myself to bend over
to pick it up without falling. It was small and rolled tightly with a
single piece of red yarn holding it together. The string slipped off
easily, and I unraveled the paper to find words written by Willis's
hand.

. . .

We are prepared to take the city back. A few days before your next return, we can take control from the Lysians here. None of them appear to have conjuring abilities, and with the return of the Sparrow Archers, they will be easy enough to handle. When you come home, the archers will line the walls as they had years ago. They will protect you, should you need it. I need to know that you will be prepared for this. I also need to know what you wish to be done with the Lysians here.

I took a deep breath. Somehow, the Spirit knew the note was in my hand. Without the warning, I would have left the temple without seeing it. And now I needed to destroy the evidence.

The hearth in the temple was nearly dead. Fire no longer burned, but the coals still had a dull glow, barely producing any significant heat. I made my way to that hearth and shoved the rolled-up piece of paper in. The coals were hot enough for the paper to catch fire. It was a flash, a sudden spark that turned the note to ash in moments, leaving behind no trace of the plan.

After the embers returned to their dull glow, I pushed myself up and made my way through the room.

The door to the temple creaked open with the thrust of my hand. Fresh air and light rushed in, and I suddenly found myself again disoriented. I took a step, but the ground was not where it was expected. Stumbling forward, I fell.

Willis moved, grabbing hold of me before I hit the ground.

"I got you," he said, pulling me against him.

After a moment, I felt my feet beneath me and regained my bearings once more.

"I am prepared for this new beginning, Willis," I said to him, and by the look in his eyes, I knew he received the message that I would be ready for the power to be returned to the Bavadrins. "I will rule, unlike my predecessor. No harm will come to Bavadrins or any others if it can be helped," I said, answering the other question of what to do with the Lysians once we took back control. They were not to be harmed.

"It is my honor to serve you," he replied, his lip curling up ever so slightly with an otherwise hidden excitement.

"I'm okay," I said, gently pushing away from him.

Willis hesitated but reluctantly released me.

After taking two steps on my own, I found myself again uncoordinated. This time it was Erik who stopped my fall. Without a word, he scooped me up into his arms.

"How are you feeling?" Erik asked while Willis ground his teeth, hating that a Lysian was holding me.

"Better than I seem," I answered, offering him a weak smile.

"You are a terrible liar," he said without a shred of anger. Instead, in his sapphire eyes, I found a tinge of concern.

I smiled, turning to Willis. "Where is Edda?"

"She went to gather the people so that you could address them as soon as you woke."

"Now?" Erik seemed surprised.

"Yes. Ariana is now the Leader Superior. It is customary to address the people after the ceremony and share parts of what the Spirit said." Willis stepped forward, holding his arms out. "I will take her."

Erik stepped back. "I don't think she is in a condition to be giving a speech."

"It is tradition," I said, silencing the needless dispute, and turned to Willis. "It's fine. Show Erik the way."

As we began moving, I found my eyelids closing for brief moments, which stretched for a longer and longer time. My head leaned against the Lysian King's shoulder, and he briefly tensed in response to the movement.

"Did you actually see the Spirit?" Erik asked in a hushed tone.

"Yes," I mumbled, and he did not ask anymore.

My eyes slid open once more when we stopped moving. Willis was silently watching us.

"This is far enough. I must walk now. Please put me down," I said to Erik.

Erik did what was asked without complaint. Once I felt the ground beneath my feet, I looped my arm through his and felt him stiffen to offer me better support.

"Walk out with me?" I asked.

"I don't know if that's a good idea," Willis spoke before Erik had a chance to answer.

Erik's gaze moved past me to Willis before returning to me. "Are you sure you don't want a Bavadrin to help you?" They both feared the implication of how it would be taken by the Bavadrin people to see their new Leader Superior being helped by a Lysian. Perhaps I would have worried about the same; however, the Spirit essentially told me to trust my choices and to follow my gut without fear. And my heart was telling me that the Lysians were not evil, that in the end, we would stand on the same side.

"Yes, I'm sure," I answered them both.

Erik smiled softly and nodded.

He walked with me a couple of steps before turning the corner to the courtyard area where a large gathering of Bavadrins stood; we appeared on the steps above them.

Murmurs moved through the crowd when they caught sight of me.

"My people," I began addressing them, my voice loud as it carried across the space between us. The particular spot where Erik and I stood thankfully had good acoustics so that all could hear me without my needing to yell. "I stand before you, exhausted from my journey last night and excited to share that I spoke with the Spirit."

Again, murmurs moved through the crowd.

"I asked questions, but the Spirit only offered a glimpse of answers for a few. During that time, the Spirit answered one key question." I paused, and the purest form of silence settled between all around. "We, the Bavadrins, are not cursed due to the breaking of the treaty."

There were some audible sighs of relief.

"But then, what of the Lysians?" a voice rose above all the whispers.

Erik tensed beside me.

"I asked the Spirit of the Lysians." The Spirit did not tell me anything about them other than for me to follow my gut. "They are not our enemy," I announced. Erik's gaze turned, boring into me while I remained focused on the Bavadrins before me. "I do not yet understand the path we have been set on, but the Spirit confirmed that there is a good reason the Lysians are in our lives, and we are in theirs."

"Will you stay in the city?" another voice asked, and I felt myself weakening.

"No. I am leaving now, but I will return in twelve days, and when I do, I hope that more of your questions can be answered. I wish to leave with a vow that I will bring us back to the lives we were always meant to live. For far too long, we have been burned by the world, by those who wished to harm us, and even by those who had promised to protect us." I alluded to Fraser without saying his name.

My gaze found Landin in the crowd. "Some of us had to hide parts of ourselves to survive. I will not support the notion of causing my people more pain and difficulty when life is hard enough. Love does not have bounds, and we will no longer try to bind it." Landin's eyes glazed over.

My attention shifted, moving over the crowd of people. "It is time for us to rise from the ash. We will take our lives back, and the land will recognize the Bavadrins as people of character, strength, and compassion. I must leave today, but I promise that I am coming for you all."

Cheers erupted through the crowd.

"Let's go," I whispered to Erik, who reacted at once, taking me away from the mass, and sheltering me from the excitement, which only further drained my energy.

29

ERIK

It pleased Kole to learn that he did not need to ride back to the Lysian lands with Edda. Given the state Ariana was in, I insisted she ride with one of us. She was in no condition to keep herself upright on a horse. Thankfully, she must have come to the same conclusion, for she did not fight me on it.

Ariana agreed to ride with me while Edda happily took Rain.

Despite the occasional jostle of the horse, Ariana quickly fell asleep when we began our trip back home. Her body leaned into mine. Now and then, her head would roll to the side across my chest. Every breeze blew the scent of wildflowers from her hair and skin around me, encasing me in her. I kept my arms firmly positioned around her to keep her from sliding off the horse.

Even unconscious, she was distracting, taking up room in my mind and drawing my attention. Wind blew an unbound piece of her hair wildly around her neck, pulling my eye to her throat. Strange how most went about life with their necks exposed and it did nothing to me, yet in that moment it felt somehow intimate. The way my gaze drifted over her skin, across her jaw, the corner of her lips.

I forced my eyes up, refocusing on the land surrounding us.

Despite my gaze being on everything but her, my mind could not escape the strange pull she had on my thoughts.

Thankfully, even sleeping, Ariana appeared better than before. Her body no longer shivered; her eyes focused whenever they were open. Despite these improvements, she remained frail, unable to effectively walk on her own. Whatever that concoction was that supposedly brought her to the Spirit left her vulnerable.

Ariana seemed so small for someone who now carried so much weight on her shoulders. The responsibility of her people fell to her just as the responsibility of the Lysians fell to me. We shared that now. I had been bred for it, trained throughout my entire life to take my father's place, for I was his first-born child. Ariana did not know whether the Bavadrin crown would fall to her after her father's death. She did not have time to prepare as I had.

It was unfortunate for her to have such a burden placed on her in the middle of something like this. Siding with us would be the easiest choice for a smooth progression in the days ahead.

Yet, what if she did not need stability, as I assumed? Ever since I met her, she had the strange ability to stand on her own in a way she never should have had the power to. Every step of the way, no matter how much I challenged her, she did not bow. Yet she remained flexible enough to keep the pressure from snapping her. She moved with the change while somehow keeping her head above the water and facing the uncertainty with calm clarity.

Perhaps this new role would not make it easier to sway her to our cause, and if that were the case, what then? During the long night I spent outside the Bavadrin temple, I had plenty of time to consider the options. However, every thought led me to the same realization that I could not bring myself to take her life.

I looked at her face as she leaned against me. The slight wrinkle in her brow, the way her lips lightly parted, all of her was captivating. She seemed so vulnerable, and I longed to shelter her. *Ashes. What is this woman doing to me?*

Ariana dozed off again, but this time dreams accompanied her sleep. She mumbled something incoherent, even for my keen hearing. The sound of her heartbeat climbed. A moment later, she flinched, and then a small whimper escaped from her. And though she did not appear to be in any blatant distress, I couldn't help but feel as though the dream was unpleasant.

I moved my hand to her thigh, jostling her gently in an attempt to wake her before the dream had a chance to turn into an all-out nightmare.

"Ariana," I said her name.

She woke, though it was not gentle. Her heart rate spiked, and she leaned over, nearly plummeting from the horse. Caught off guard myself, I almost missed grabbing her. She was practically falling before my hand captured her waist and yanked her back. Her hands flung to my arm, holding it as if startled by my presence.

Quick breaths rattled from her. "Sorry, I'm fine," she said, and the pressure of her shoulders lightened as she tried to lean forward, but my arm prevented her from it. "I just need a second. Will you release me?" she asked, her voice unsteady.

I slowly let her go, afraid that she may lose her stability and fall. Instead, Ariana leaned forward while keeping her balance, and I realized she was trying to touch me as little as possible.

My stomach sank at the thought that she was having a nightmare that had anything to do with me, but with the way her heart raced and her leaning away from my touch, that was the only thing it could have been.

I asked her what I already knew. "What was your nightmare of?"

Me. It was of me.

30

ARIANA

The dream began with me wearing the dress I wore when I ascended. All around me, the room was shimmering, casting various light patterns in my peripherals. I stood in the center of a chamber filled with Bavadrins and Lysians. They were celebrating together as friends. The scene brought me so much joy that I needed to find Erik to show him we could be more than enemies, to show him that my kind and his could share in the joy.

Scanning the crowds, I could not find him, so I moved, searching for him. I ran past the faces that surrounded me, but I was lost. No matter where I went, I was not getting anywhere. It was as if I were trapped in that room. So, I ran harder, my legs moving faster till the faces all blurred together. It felt as though an eternity passed.

Finally, familiar deep blue eyes caught my attention, and I halted before them. My hair flung around me in a wild mess from the sudden change in motion.

"Where are you running off to?" Erik asked, his voice deadly soft.

"I was looking for you."

His eyes studied me as if they were burrowing into my soul, rendering me speechless. Before me stood a King, dangerously powerful and focused so entirely on me it was difficult to even draw breath.

A small smile graced his full lips, and he brought his hand up to my neck, moving my wild hair back over my shoulder. When finished, he did not withdraw his hand. Instead, he grazed my jaw, his fingers brushing past my neck so that his fingertips caressed the base of my skull. My skin burned wherever he touched, sending my pulse climbing. His grip tightened, forced my head up so that I could not look away from him.

"Erik, what are you doing?" I asked, finding myself breathless.

The people in the room began shimmering out of existence until it was just the two of us.

With a ghost of a smirk on his lips, he stepped closer. Nearly all the space between us was stolen in one move.

"Erik," I warned, though I was not sure what I was trying to warn against. Would I use my conjuring to bring him to his knees? No, I didn't want to do that.

I found myself both frightened and intrigued by the situation. The feelings competed for control. To run or to stay?

He leaned in, the space between us dwindling. "Tell me to release you, and I will." The words were a whisper. He surrounded me, holding me captive, and I couldn't formulate a response.

His hungry gaze dipped to my lips.

My mouth went completely dry, and it felt as though my heart catapulted into my throat. Then, when I didn't move, didn't make a sound, he leaned even closer.

His hand gripped my thigh, his voice calling my name. Yet it couldn't have been him.

My eyes opened even though I thought they were already open.

The floor disappeared beneath me, replaced by a quickly moving ground that I wasn't even standing on. Startled, I shifted to the side and found myself completely thrown off-balance. Before I knew it, I was falling face-first toward the ground at an incredible speed.

An arm gripped my hip and yanked me back, throwing me solidly into someone behind me so that my breath left me in a whoosh.

Suddenly, everything came together.

I was on a horse with Erik, and I had just woken from a very troubling dream. I couldn't catch my breath, while behind me, I could feel the steady rise and fall of Erik's chest. My face burned hot. I tried to lean forward, but his arm remained wrapped around me with a firm grip.

"Sorry, I'm fine." My voice quivered. "I just need a second. Will you release me?"

Without a word, Erik removed his arm, freeing me to lean forward, putting some space between us. The adrenaline from nearly flying off the horse began to subside, leaving me with a shocking embarrassment for the dream I just had.

"What was your nightmare of?" he asked.

"Nightmare?" I parroted his words, unable to wrap my mind around why he thought it was a nightmare while being relieved that he believed it to have been that. Thankfully, Erik could not see my face and how incredibly red it must have been.

"Yes," Erik replied, waiting for my elaboration.

I wished that we were not on horseback and that I could put some space between us. "What makes you think I had a nightmare?" I faced forward, unable to bring myself to turn and look at him.

"You stirred in your sleep uncomfortably, mumbled something incoherent, flinched, and then your heart rate spiked, and you tried to take a nosedive from the horse to get away, and now you seem to be unable to bear touching me in any way." He laid out all the things he picked up on as proof that my dream was a nightmare and apparently may have had something to do with him. Still, I had no intention of explaining my dream and why it was not exactly the nightmare he expected.

"It's fine, Erik. It was just a dream. I only need to collect my wits. Let it go." I tried to sound calm, hoping there was no desperation in my voice. The last thing I needed was for him to feel like he caught the trail of something that he was determined to follow it to its end.

Though I did not see him, I very much felt his eyes on me.

Gripping the mane of the stallion, I gritted my teeth.

"Kole!" Erik called out.

Kole was on horseback beside us in an instant. His clear blue gaze fell on my face, and I did not know what he saw, but he looked at me confused.

"Take the others onward a few hundred yards and begin making camp. We will catch up soon," Erik instructed before bringing his horse to a complete stop.

"Sure thing," Kole replied, and just like that, the small Lysian party and Edda, who raised a single eyebrow as she passed Erik's very stationary horse, went to make camp.

Spirit, help me. He will not let this go. I cursed myself for ever falling asleep in the first place. Wasn't anything private? Wasn't I allowed to have my own personal thoughts, hopes, and dreams? Sure, I was under their rule for now, but they wanted to work with the Bavadrins, and to do so, they needed to allow for some respectful privacy.

Once everyone left us, Erik dismounted, and I followed suit, having no idea if I should have remained on horseback or not.

Once we both stood with our feet solidly on the ground, his sapphire eyes observed me, probably taking in the embarrassing blush on my face. The weight of his gaze was substantial, and I feared he would somehow uncover my bizarre dream before I even made sense of it myself.

Erik took a single step towards me, and I mirrored his movement, taking a single step away. It felt as though if he got closer, he would better be able to see my thoughts, and so automatically, my body reacted, trying to keep the tiny bit of space between us from closing further.

"Do you fear me?" he asked, and the question instantly angered me.

What precisely was the correct answer in this case? Because to me, it felt as though the correct answer changed depending on the circumstance. Erik oscillated between wanting me to tremble in his presence and wanting me to trust him. But I was not some toy for him to play with for entertainment, just as my people were not simply tools for the Lysians to make use of however they saw fit.

"What exactly would the correct answer be?" I asked, eyes narrowing.

"The truth."

I snorted. "You don't want the truth. You only wish for the answer you want to hear."

"That isn't true." His brows drew together as if he couldn't comprehend my accusation.

"Isn't it? Wouldn't you have loved for the Bavadrins to have been working with the Siddhe so that you could have a simple path before you? But the truth is that we never have done anything like that. Half the time, you want me to be comfortable around you, and the other half, you want to have me fear you. So what mood are you in today? I am at your service and will respond however it may please you." I was irritable, part of which could have been because of my growing hunger. I was never happy when hungry.

But, it wasn't just that. I was furious at *him*. It was as if the dream were not simply a dream but something that truly happened, and now, I stood before him thinking, *How dare you do something like that? I will not be some pawn for you to use and play with as you see fit.* My anger continued to grow. I was not just some lovely Bavadrin doll they could poke at and use. I was the Leader Superior. I was a conjuror, and I was a person with worth.

Erik's gaze dropped to the ground, and I tensed, preparing myself for his rage, but it did not come. Instead, he lowered himself into a squat, propping his elbows on his knees, and looked up at me. He was trying to appear smaller and less intimidating. Though it did nothing to lessen the threat of his presence.

It was possibly the most foolish thing I had ever seen him do.

There was no way getting close to the ground could ever shift the vortex of the power dynamic we were in. In an instant, he could have my throat in his hands before I could even blink. Despite my conjuring abilities, I doubted I would win against Erik if we had to fight at that very moment with so little distance between one another. If he truly wanted me dead, then he was probably one of the few people I had ever met who was capable of so easily making that desire a reality.

"I deserve your anger, and I will take it." He finally spoke, looking up at me. "But I ask you to please tell me the truth."

He remained incredibly still except for the gentle rise and fall of his chest. His response was calm and controlled. Some of my anger wavered, but it was far from extinguished.

"Fine, you want the truth, then I will give it," I began, hesitating for a moment. My instinct was always to not show fear, to show no sign of weakness. Yet Erik asked for raw truths, and so that was what I would provide.

I licked my dry lips and continued, "I have feared you since the very moment I first laid my eyes on you in our dungeon." Erik's jaw clenched, but he did not say a word. "It was not just that you were a Lysian, something I had never seen before, but there was something powerful surrounding you. I didn't understand it then,

didn't understand your position or abilities, but I felt it crackle in
the surrounding air. Right away, I sensed the danger when near
you. It felt as though we were all sheep who had brought a wolf
into our home without even realizing it, and though you were
caged, it may as well have been made of straw. And then I learned
you were a conjuror and capable of destroying everything I ever
cared for."

His gaze physically froze me, and we stared at one another
with my truths laid out for him to see. He always assumed I had
no fear. It was clear by the way he tried to constantly bring it out of
me. He *wanted* me to fear him. I wonder if it upset him that I
wouldn't outright tremble in his presence. He had mistaken my
calm and courage for fearlessness, yet that was far from the truth,
and now he knew it.

"And now?" Erik asked, his voice low.

"And now?" I shrugged. What did he want? "I suppose the fear
is still there in ways. It's different, though. You can still destroy
everything of mine, but I don't think that it's something you would
do unprovoked. I guess my biggest concern is not knowing what
you are thinking or what you are going to do."

"You always seemed so fearless." He looked at the ground,
speaking as if it were a thought passing through his mind that he
hadn't intended to make heard.

I knew it. He assumed I had zero regard for the danger I had
been in. He probably thought I was half nuts for not fearing
him.

"To be completely fearless is to be reckless," I answered.

He nodded and rose.

His eyes lifted slowly to meet mine, and his head followed
until he stood fully upright. "I want to make you a promise,
Ariana. I will not harm you, and I will not allow for harm to
unjustly come to your people."

My heart skipped a beat. I hadn't expected him to say anything like that. Were his words the truth? It was possible that he could have been lying, but I found myself believing him.

"Why now?" I asked.

"Honestly?" His lip curved up at the side, though it did not touch his eyes. It looked more cruel than happy.

I nodded, *yes.*

"I usually get a thrill from others' fear of me. Some part of me craves it. Yet, I find myself not wanting that from you. At least not anymore." He looked down towards where the others likely had camp fully set up by now. "You probably think I'm twisted in some way."

I took a single step towards him and froze when he turned back to face me. "To desire power is not abnormal, especially in your Lysian culture and with your position. I have told you before that I have seen monsters up close, and that is not what I have seen of you, nor your kind."

"Was I in the dream you just had?" He pressed the question he wanted to know this entire time.

My cursed heart beat faster from embarrassment, which he would likely confuse with distress. "Yes."

It was as if a band had been wrapped around us, invisibly pulling us towards each other, and it just snapped. Erik twirled away from me, grabbed the horse, and shoved the reins in my direction. "Take the horse and join the others. I'll go on foot from here."

"That's unnecessary," I said, surprised at the abrupt change.

"Please, just do as I asked." His voice turned reserved and cold. He withdrew from me.

Something about him seemed defeated. It was strange to witness him in such a manner. Not knowing the best way to handle him when he was in that uncommon state, I settled for simply doing what he asked.

When I took the reins, Erik began walking in the opposite

direction of the camp. He moved with a silent and powerful grace until he disappeared into the wild.

It didn't take long for me to find my way to the camp the Lysians had set up.

Kole walked over, taking Erik's horse from me. He looked me over as if to make sure I was alright though he did not say a single word. Instead, he gazed over my shoulder, back towards where I parted ways with Erik.

"He said he wanted to go on foot." I let Kole know.

He nodded over towards a small fire. "Go warm up. I'll bring you some food."

Again, I simply did as I was told.

31

ARIANA

All the Lysians were busy being productive except for one lounging by the fire, accompanied by Edda. Iver's and Edda's laughter greeted me as I approached them. They were giggling to themselves, probably at the expense of someone else.

"Ah! Princess!" Iver welcomed me, patting the ground beside him. "Come, join us."

Edda snorted. "She is no princess. She is the Leader Superior now, you clever little Lysian."

"Little!" he exclaimed. "Have you by chance seen your own size? The two Bavadrin women, going around calling *me* little."

"Physical size has nothing to do with it," I commented.

"Indeed, you are correct." Iver grinned, turning to observe Edda. "There is certainly something darkly dangerous about you." He playfully wiggled a finger at her. Though the way he said it made it sound more like a warning than a joke.

Edda laughed lightly. "Of course there is." She yawned, bringing a hand to her mouth. "I'm exhausted. Most of us did not have the Lysian King acting as their personal armchair to sleep against during this leg of the trip." She arched an eyebrow, and I felt my cheeks warm. When I did not rise to her bait, she got to her feet. "Goodnight," she said with a small smile.

I didn't respond, still harboring anger and hurt from the time she ripped into me about my relationship with the Lysians. She never tried to apologize or talk about it. The wound was left open.

"Sweetest dreams to you, old-timer," Iver commented and turned his attention to me. "My brother run away from you?"

"He didn't run away," I stated flatly.

He laughed, though his eyes trailed Edda. "Sure, whatever you say."

"What did you mean about Edda?" I asked, watching her as she walked towards the single massive tent, disappearing into its shelter.

Iver leaned back onto the grass, placing his hands behind his head, observing the night sky. "I'd like to think I am a pretty spot-on judge of character. Give me a few seconds looking someone over, and I could tell you just how annoying or dumb they may be with remarkable accuracy."

I rolled my eyes. "You cannot possibly know all that just by a quick glance at someone."

"That's where you are wrong, my tiny princess. I can." The confidence coming from him was substantial.

"Fine, say I agree with your ridiculous skill of being able to judge one's entire being with no knowledge of their experiences, thoughts, or feelings. What do you make of Edda?" I asked, playing along as if agreeing with his ridiculous skill.

"She gets by having everyone around her think she is some sort of loony old woman, but she is much more devious than that. Apart from myself, I think she may be one of the smartest people in this camp, which makes her dangerous."

It was difficult to keep my jaw from dropping with a remark like that. "Do you ever tire of thinking so highly of yourself?"

"Never, only 'cause it's true." He grinned, flashing his teeth.

I sighed and lay back on the grass. "Well, then, wise Lysian, what do you make of me?"

His eyes narrowed. "I rarely share my thoughts with the subject itself."

"That is such a lie."

His chest rumbled with a small laugh. "Yeah, you're right. So, you wish to know my thoughts about you, eh? How brutal do you want this to be?"

"As brutal as it requires." I smiled, welcoming the evaluation.

"You're not too bad," he finally said without adding more.

"What? That's it?" I rolled over onto my stomach, propping myself up on my elbows. "C'mon, I'm stronger than I look. I can take it."

Iver shrugged. "I could say that it is obvious you care for others. You are kind. I think you downplay your strengths. You certainly have not shared your secrets, and I am intrigued by that. But honestly, when it comes to who is more of a threat to my family, Edda has you beat there. Despite the secrets you continue to try to keep, you are no threat to us."

"You think me weak," I commented.

"Not the least." His gray eyes turned to me. "You just do not possess the personality of someone who would concern me. However, that does not mean I view you as weak. I believe having you as an ally would be quite useful for us. So, Ariana, do you intend to go to war against the dark and evil mysterious forces of the Siddhe alongside us?"

"Do not badger her with such questions." Kole approached, holding a bowl of potatoes and sausage. "It is not your place to ask her such things."

I rolled over and sat straight up.

"Oh c'mon, we were just having a casual conversation." Iver's grin sharpened.

"If Erik heard you asking such things . . ." Kole growled.

Iver sat up, shrugging. "He would what? Where is the great King anyway?" He made a show of looking around.

"He hasn't returned yet," Kole informed us, holding the bowl out for me to take. It warmed my icy fingers, steam rising from the soup.

"Do you think he is alright?" I asked Kole, but Iver answered first.

"Of course he is. A single unpleasant conversation will not harm our great King."

I turned to him. "What makes you say we had an unpleasant conversation?"

"He's run off to clear his mind, hasn't he?"

"Mind your mouth," Kole growled.

Iver rolled his eyes. "You used to be so much more fun before . . ." His words trailed off, though there was a dangerous glint in his gaze.

"Before what?" I asked, turning to Kole, who was now deathly still. Rage simmered beneath that stillness. Clearly, this was not a conversation he was planning on having.

Kole took a single step towards Iver, and the intent of it was deadly. I was not the only one who picked up on the shift.

"Why don't you scamper off before your actions result in something regretful?" Iver commented, his voice low. Though he remained sitting on the ground, his demeanor changed, his focus concentrated on Kole, poised to act if needed. Unease settled over me at the thought of this possibly escalating.

Kole's entire body tightened as his muscles stiffened. He then angrily pivoted and stormed off without another word. Iver relaxed back onto the ground.

"Why do you do that?" I asked.

"Do what?" he asked, looking innocently at me as if unaware of his actions.

"Push everyone with your words to no end."

"Do I push you?"

"You try by calling me *princess*," I pointed out.

He chortled. "Sweet princess, that is me simply joking around with you." Then, smirking, he turned his attention to me. "Would you like for me to push you further?"

"Not really." I focused on the bowl of soup in my hands, beginning to greedily eat.

"Well, then consider yourself lucky."

"But why do you do it?"

He shrugged. "Why not? It keeps life a bit more interesting and fun to oppose the firm beliefs others have about the world and themselves."

"I don't imagine it wins you very many friends."

He viewed me. "Those who stick around are the only friends I need. If they don't like it, then they can get lost."

We fell into silence as I ate my meal. Once good and full, I lay back on the ground, staring at the cloudless dark sky.

I'm not sure how long we lay in silence before Iver asked, "So, you never answered the question. Do you intend to stand beside us against the Siddhe?"

"I don't know that they had anything to do with the disappearance of your sister," I stated. Erik mentioned an Oracle had informed them of this information, but I had no way to confirm.

"I have an inkling that you agree that there is something wrong over there. It's like something tainted the land in darkness in that direction."

I did not respond, for he was right.

"So?" Iver pressed.

"My answer remains the same. I will help you, but not as someone forced to because I am your prisoner."

"So, a trade for your freedom?" He turned, looking at me.

"I wouldn't call it a trade."

"We both get things we want. Sounds like a trade."

"If the Siddhe are truly responsible for the disappearance of conjurors in both of our lands, then I *want* to stand with you against them. I am not trading anything for it."

"But you would withhold help if we do not give you your freedom," he said as if again to clarify.

"I will not subject my people to fighting for something they have no faith in. How could I ask them to risk everything when they believe I am doing it only to save my own life because I am a prisoner? I vowed to be better than the last Superior."

He turned his attention back to the stars above.

Silence fell over us once more.

Eventually, a breeze rushed around us, and I peered at the fire, which had turned to embers. How long had we been lying outside? No Lysians except for Iver were around. Were they all sleeping?

"When do you think Erik will return?" I asked with a whisper, not wanting to disturb the peace that surrounded the camp.

"He has been back for a while now," Iver replied, tilting his head to look at me. "You want to lie down?" He nodded towards the tent.

Go in there? With all the Lysians already inside? Usually, I was the first one in and the last one out. I liked it that way. Going into the tent now felt like entering a den of lions.

Iver appeared to read my emotions and laughed lowly. "Would you like a blanket and pillow? We can just stay out here."

"Oh no, I don't want to trouble you."

"It is absolutely no trouble at all," he said with a smirk, then louder added, "Kole will bring them out to you."

"It's really okay," I said, but Kole was already emerging from the tent, carrying blankets and a pillow. He made his way towards us with a scowl directed at Iver.

"Thank you," I murmured, taking the bedding from him.

"If you need any help, just scream," he said to me as if he were wishing good night with those words.

"Help with what? I can protect a single Bavadrin from the scary woodland creatures without a problem," Iver commented, and Kole ignored him as he turned and walked back to the tent.

Silently, I shook my head while wrapping the blanket around me.

"What?" Iver asked in mock surprise.

"Both you and Edda burrow under his skin to no end. You are both lucky to still have your heads attached to your necks."

Iver's teeth flashed with a smile. "He could never hope to separate my head from the rest of my beautiful body."

I smashed my hand on my forehead, knowing Kole likely heard everything and was fuming even more. Iver chuckled. The sound grew quieter until all we heard were the distant crickets and the periodic breeze sweeping through blades of grass and rustling the leaves still attached to the trees. Slowly, I drifted off to sleep. Thankfully, it was void of dreams.

The gentle and distant sound of bickering eased me out of sleep. Edda and Kole were back at it, with Edda driving the oversized Lysian mad without care. Was it time to get up already?

"Ariana," Erik's voice from nearby forced my heavy eyelids to finally open.

He was crouched down in the grass beside me.

"Oh." I sat straight up, which was challenging with how the blanket wrapped thoroughly around me. "Hi." I couldn't think of anything else to say.

He smiled. "It's time to go."

"Okay."

"If you're feeling well, then you may ride on your own. Kole will be fine riding with Edda."

I glanced behind Erik to Kole. His shoulders tensed. Even from that distance, it was clear. Though he did not look at us, I knew he likely was listening.

"No, it's fine. I'd like to finish this trip with you if that's alright," I said to Erik, but caught the easing of Kole's shoulders in the background. He was *definitely* listening.

I also needed them to find comfort in Edda riding on her own. So this was good exposure for her.

"Very well." His lips inched up at the corners. Erik rose to his full height and walked over to his brother, who was fast asleep a few feet from me. He nudged Iver's side with his foot once. When Iver did not stir awake, Erik nudged him again, harder that time.

Iver growled. "Bloody ashes. What is the matter with you?"

"It's time to go," Erik stated, voice void of warmth.

Iver groaned, sounding like he was speaking without opening his mouth. It was unintelligible.

Erik sighed, head tilted to the sky, eyes closing as if saying a prayer to the Spirit. The way the sun glistened against his dark hair, it was as if the edges had an ethereal golden glow. "If you're not up and saddled by the time everyone else is ready, then we will leave you here," he warned as he stalked away to join the other Lysians.

I quickly rose, smoothed out my clothing, folded the blanket, gathered the pillow, and was ready to go while Iver still lay motionless on the ground. The other Lysians were nearly finished deconstructing and putting away the tent. Half the horses were already saddled and ready to go.

"Hey, Iver. We need to go," I urged, but he did not move. Had he fallen back asleep? "Iver!" I contemplated physically waking him but did not want to startle a Lysian with predator instincts, so I kept a safe distance and chucked my pillow at his face. When he did not move, I turned towards the others.

Two steps later, I was shoved forward by something soft,

thrown with force. At my feet was a pillow. I twisted around, yet Iver still lay on the ground as if he had not moved a single muscle.

Picking up the pillow, I chucked it at him once more.

He did not react.

I took a cautious step backward. Nothing. Four more steps and still nothing. He remained still as the dead. Turning, I made it a couple of feet before the wind was nearly knocked out of me, and I dropped the blanket I was holding. Never had I thought a pillow could have such strength, though never had I seen it thrown by a Lysian before.

I spun around, but he was gone.

"It isn't nice to attack someone while they sleep." Iver's voice came from behind me.

With a sharp but silent inhale, I spun again, meeting his gray eyes with my own. He stood right behind me and holding the blanket I dropped. It was alarming how silently he moved and at such speed. It almost seemed like magic. Was it a conjuring ability of some sort? The thought made my throat tighten.

"I was just making sure you didn't get left behind." I stepped around him, shaking off my surprise and leaving him holding the blanket. Iver trailed me with a smile as we joined the others.

32

ARIANA

The lake was stunning. Glistening water reflected the sun's rays, stretching out nearly as far as I could see. The surrounding forest was bright and warm despite the autumn air. I could not believe that Kole had not brought me sooner. I nearly felt giddy, capable of jumping for joy at the beauty of it all.

Kole cursed softly. "We should go."

"What?" I looked at him in shock. "We just got here!" And the walk was *long*. No way were we turning back already.

"Yes, but I didn't know that Erik would—" His words cut off, and he looked out over the water at something. "You're certain?" he asked someone I could not see.

Squinting, I searched for whatever it was he saw, but there was nothing. Just the sparkling lake and surrounding distant forest.

"Erik is fine with you remaining here." He turned to me.

"Erik? He's out there somewhere?" I looked even harder over the water, but nothing.

Kole nodded. "He likes to come here and swim sometimes."

"At this time of the year?" Sure, it was warm in the sun, but the water was undoubtedly frigid. Kneeling, I touched it with my fingertips to confirm.

Kole chuckled softly. "You already forget about his conjuring?"

That was something I could never forget. Being a conjuror of fire apparently also meant he never got cold.

I took a seat on a sizable flat stone that overlooked the lake. Kole joined me after a moment. It was tranquil. I could have stayed in that spot for eternity and never gotten bored.

Something glided through the water, and it took me a moment to realize that it was Erik. Powerful arms and legs propelled him across the lake at an unnatural speed. I thought fighting a Lysian on solid ground was challenging, but in water, it was possibly even more terrifying when they could move like that. A shiver ran down my spine.

"I'm sorry. I didn't know you were here," Kole stated once Erik came within several yards of us.

"It's fine." He didn't sound the least bit out of breath, despite the distance he just covered. "You may go, if you wish. I'll bring Ariana back after a while."

"Well, if you're certain," Kole said, rising to his feet. His attention moved over the lake before landing on me. "See you later." He nodded in farewell.

Erik swam closer till he was at the stone I sat on and turned, looking out over the view with me. "It's beautiful here, isn't it?"

"I have seen nothing like it," I murmured in agreement.

Sapphire eyes glanced at me, a slight smile playing on his lips. "You do not have lakes in your land?" Water dripped from his hair onto his face, a few droplets clinging to his jaw before falling. There was a brutal beauty to him.

I shook my head. "We have one, but it's only used for sending off our dead. The water mostly flows through our land in rivers. We have nothing quite like this."

Erik turned to me fully. "If I swim another lap, will you still be here when I return?" There was a sliver of a challenge there in his tone.

My mouth dried. *Would I be left alone?*

I nodded in agreement, afraid that he would see the uncertainty as it spread through me if I spoke.

Erik smiled, his gaze holding mine for a moment. Without another word, he dove back into the water, each powerful stroke carrying him further away. As he distanced himself, my heart raced with a mix of excitement and apprehension.

I could run. The thought entered my mind. Even if Erik took chase, I could conjure and drop him. But that was only if I heard or saw him approach. Something told me that even racing to catch me, he would be soundless. And once he got to me, what then?

No, I couldn't run, at least not yet. I would keep my plans to leave once we were at the Bavadrin gates on our next trip home. There was less room for error that way.

Did Erik leave me as a sort of test to see what I would do? Curious to see if I would try to escape. If that were the case, then he believed that I would not be able to make it very far.

Picking up a nearby pebble, I tossed it into the water, watching it bounce before sinking. I imagined that my thoughts of Erik, running away, and all concerns were tied to that pebble, sinking with it.

It was a while before the Lysian King returned, his powerful strokes bringing him back to the shore where I sat waiting. He emerged from the water, droplets glistening on his skin.

My face warmed at the sudden realization that I did not know what he wore as he swam, if anything.

Without hesitation, he rose out of the water. The liquid ran down his neck. His shoulders. Chest. Stomach. Waist. I looked away. Heat rushed my face.

Erik chuckled softly, though he said nothing as clothing rustled off to the side. A moment later, he appeared beside me, the bottom half thankfully covered while his chest and back were left exposed. Droplets of water fell from his hair, gliding over the smooth skin of his neck. His dark gaze found mine, and it nearly stole my breath. He was striking. There was no other word to describe him. Again, my face flushed, and I turned, looking out over the water while he took a seat beside me.

"This is my favorite place," he said after a while.

"It is beautiful and incredibly peaceful," I commented.

"When I need to get away and clear my head, I often find myself coming here," he murmured, shifting his weight and leaning forward. The movement gave me a full view of his back. My heart sank at the sight.

Angry scars, which were now smooth, covered his otherwise flawless skin. They were everywhere, from shoulders to lower back. What pain it must have been to endure such a thing, even for a Lysian. I couldn't look away from them. Pain and anger settled in a pit in my stomach.

I reached for the scars as if compelled, hypnotized by the markings.

Erik's head turned ever so slightly, and I knew he tracked my movement. When my hand hovered over his back and he did not stop me, I touched one of the countless markings. He flinched when my finger tips brushed against his skin, and a pang of sadness stirred within me. Everything could have been prevented if only I had been stronger. If only I had taken control from Fraser long ago.

I traced a scar, following its marking across and down his back. His muscles tensed beneath my touch.

"Ariana." My name was a breath on his tongue.

My fingertips moved along his skin, feeling the smooth, angry markings he would carry for the rest of his life. A tremble moved through him.

Suddenly, Erik turned at the waist, his hand grabbing my wrist out of the air.

"I'm sorry . . ." I whispered, my voice barely audible, my heart aching with the pain he must have endured. *For what was done to you.* "I'm sorry for not stopping this from happening."

Erik's grip on my wrist tightened for a moment before easing. A wrinkle formed between his brows as he viewed me. "You could not have stopped it," he said, but he was wrong. I could have if only I was not afraid to stand up to Fraser.

He then clarified, "*I* did not want you to stop it." His thumb moved against my wrist, stroking the skin there twice before finally releasing me.

"Why?" My eyes met with his. "If you believed that we worked with the Siddhe and if they have taken Lysians against their will, then that would have been a break of the treaty. You didn't need to put yourself through that."

A cunning smile caused his features to darken. "The treaty was burned long ago, its ashes scattered over the land, so we cannot confirm the exact wording of that ancient promise. Does it take one break for the entire thing to crumble? Or was every race locked into an individual promise to the others? I needed to be certain that no matter what, the wrath of the Spirit would not come down on what's mine."

"You think this is what the Spirit wished for when the treaty was made? For us to try and cruelly trick one another into the breaking of it?"

"Someone unworthy of such an outcome would never have been able to be tricked so easily." His lip turned up with a sad smile. "*You* would not have been tricked into breaking the treaty." Sapphire eyes held my gaze as his words settled over me.

Goosebumps ran across my skin, and I was not sure how to respond.

"We better head back," he said finally, the conversation seemingly over as he stood up from the stone.

The trip to the lake had been roughly a two-hour walk with Kole. Erik and I were about one hour in on our way back when without warning, he grabbed me under the arm, stopping me cold. Erik's hold was nearly painful. For the first time, it appeared his attention was everywhere but me.

Always I felt the overwhelming pressure of his notice. It was enough to steal the breath from my lungs. There were days I desperately wished for his gaze to not land on me. Yet now, at that moment, with his concentration honed on everything around us, my pulse spiked. Something startled Erik, and in turn, I felt a terrible dread wash over me.

Nothing ever had alarmed him before. *Nothing.*

His gaze darted around as he scanned the surrounding area. He searched for something. His jaw clenched when his eyes finally settled in a particular direction of the forest.

Erik grabbed me roughly, moving me till I stood with a tree solidly behind me. Finding myself too dumbfounded to say a thing, I remained silent. Erik then stepped in front of me, baring his teeth.

"Do not speak and do not move." His words were a command directed at me.

I would have bristled if fear had not wormed its way into my stomach. Whatever placed the Lysian King on edge could not have been good.

A silence so deep settled over the forest that the loudest noise was the sound of my breathing. It felt as though we were suspended in that impossible moment for a long time, frozen except for my heart, which drummed against my ribs.

A dark chuckle came from somewhere in the forest. The sound danced along my bones. The hairs on my neck stood. My conjuring hummed to life, awoken by my fear.

33

ERIK

The scent of fear filled the air surrounding Ariana even though she did not yet see what I knew headed straight for us. Silently, she remained behind me while I faced where they approached, cursing myself for not bringing my sword. I had not expected Ariana or anyone to be with me, so I left everything at home. The sword I carried was not to protect myself, but those with me. Sometimes fighting with fire was riskier than using a blade.

A chuckle sounded before me, followed by Hedrek stepping out from behind a tree. His blond hair was loose and flowing down to his middle back. His cold gaze settled on me. A scar I had given him a few years ago pulled at the side of his lower lip, slashing over his chin and down his neck. Five other Lysians also came into view. If I was on my own, it would have been no trouble handling them all. But having Ariana with me changed everything.

"Who do we have here?" Hedrek tilted his head as if to better see the Bavadrin standing behind me.

I shifted, blocking her from his view.

Damn it. In the single move, it was clear I wanted her unharmed. Hedrek would use that.

He tsked softly. "What are you doing with that little thing, Erik? A girl like that could easily be turned to ash." Holding out his hand, fire flared over his fingertips.

Ariana's breath hitched behind me.

"Go back to the hole you crawled out of, and I will let you live to see another day," I stated flatly.

Hedrek had been born outside of the main Lysian group. His great-grandfather and a few others left long ago, exiled to live on the edge of our lands where the mountains met the ocean. I frequently monitored their movements in the past, and if any of them dared to come down from the hills, I killed them. My skills sharpened on the bones and blood of his followers. The exiled Lysians had turned me into a proper killer.

However, since my father's death, my focus was redirected to retrieving my sister and our stolen conjurors. My attention shifted, and that opened a window for the exiled pack. I never expected them to so quickly become so bold as to wander this close to the main city. I had been reckless. After this day, my errors would be amended. They would think long and hard before stepping foot off their mountain again.

Hedrek smirked. "Where is the fun in that?" He took a couple of steps to the side to gain a better view of Ariana. "It has been a while since you have come to massacre our family, Erik. I was beginning to wonder if something had happened to you. But I now see that a young Bavadrin seems to have drawn your attention elsewhere." His gaze moved to her. "I suppose I owe you thanks, girl."

A growl rumbled in my throat, bringing his attention back to me.

He smiled, the movement shifting the scar running through his lip. "I'll tell you what, seeing as the two of us can burn everyone else here to a crisp, I'll make you a promise: I won't use my conjuring if you agree not to as well. Swear it on our families."

It was his lucky day and his best opportunity at standing any chance against me, no matter how tiny that chance was.

By the looks of his men, they were trained fighters. Each bore swords and weapons on their hips, while I had none. Conjuring would have been the easiest way to end them, but that exposed and risked Ariana to my cousin's flames. Hedrek used that to his advantage. Fire could only be controlled so much, and I was uncertain whether I could protect her from his flames. Though I had no doubts regarding my strength or skill, the five with Hedrek only had me to concern themselves with. Taking them all down myself was going to be a challenge.

Behind me, Ariana's heart thundered in her chest, yet she remained unmoving except for those wide green eyes that stared at the danger before us.

"Fine," I agreed.

Hedrek's smile widened. "Marvelous." He then addressed his men, "Do try and keep the King alive. I'd like for him to witness the fall of his family's rule."

What he didn't say was that I was also *his* family.

Hedrek came from *my* family line, one that broke off because my great-grandmother ruled the Lysians, and her greedy little brother thought it should fall to him and not a female. He rejected her claim. Instead of killing him, my great-grandmother took pity on him, allowing him to flee. He and a handful of others who shared his beliefs fled to the distant mountains at the ocean's edge, making a home there.

I bared my teeth, claws lengthening, before Hedrek's men attacked. They lunged at once, swords drawn. Staying close to Ariana was a greater risk than protection, for a blade aimed at me could quickly strike her if I dodged an attack.

A flash of steel thrust towards me. I sidestepped, avoiding it.

The Lysian snarled just as another came from my side. Again, I managed to evade the blade, though he didn't evade me. My claws sliced through his side, deep enough to scrape against his ribs. He stumbled forward before turning on me once more.

Adrenaline pumped into the chambers of my heart, shooting through my veins, sharpening my senses. My eyesight enhanced and muscles tightened. Fire burned underneath my skin as I kept the power leashed. I was going to kill them all.

Four of them surrounded me, taking their turns attacking. Meanwhile Hedrek stood at a safe distance. He had always been afraid to truly dirty his hands for as long as I had known him. Instead, he watched. The fifth Lysian was standing before Ariana.

"It isn't fair if you come at me with a blade when all I have is my hands to defend myself with." Ariana's voice was surprisingly steady when she spoke to him. "Unless you are afraid of a Bavadrin girl, in which case, please keep the weapon."

The male grunted, tossing the sword to the side.

Smart girl. She got rid of her opponent's blade with only her words.

Two of the Lysians attacked me at the same time from opposite sides. That was a mistake.

I moved, grabbing hold of the faster one. Using the momentum, I swung and shoved his body so that the blade of the other cut into his chest. Blood soiled my clothing. The impaled Lysian's hand loosened on his weapon, and I took it in time to stop the blade of another's from slicing my neck. That was aggravatingly close. With a grunt, I shoved him back.

My attention swung to the Bavadrin.

Ariana moved cautiously around the male who targeted her, trying to catch her. She avoided him three times before he finally grabbed her arm. He yanked her forward with ease, for she did not resist. As she fell into him, her arm pulled back before flying forward, and she landed a hit to his throat. The male coughed, suddenly gasping for air. However she had managed such a hit, it was unlikely to happen again. I moved, taking three long strides before shoving a blade through the Lysian's back. Ariana gasped as red droplets rained over her. The Lysian fell before her feet as I turned back to the three who had been busy with me.

Another lunged. I blocked, but there was a flash at my side. I dodged too slowly. His blade kissed my thigh before biting deeper into the flesh there. It burned. The edge of his sword came away painted with my blood.

Damn it.

I didn't have to look to know the wound was extensive. Warmth coated my leg. A red river flowed from the cut. I was losing blood quickly. Rage fueled me as I whirled on them. This needed to end. No longer waiting for their moves, I attacked first. The Lysian swung, and I ducked. He lost balance when his blade missed my flesh and slashed air. I used that moment to shove the sword in my hand through his throat. He dropped to the ground before he ever even knew he was dead.

It took five more seconds for me to drop the other two.

Hedrek and I were the only Lysians left.

My gaze pinned him as he picked up the blades closest to him. Not to fight with but to simply not waste resources. He was likely going to hand them off to others who were bred for this sole purpose: to fight me and mine.

Hedrek's icy gaze cut to Ariana before returning to me. "A promise is a promise. Till we meet again, cousin." He backed into the forest, and once more trees separated us, he finally turned and took off.

I remained still until I no longer heard his steps as he disappeared. Even as the edges of my vision began to blur. It took everything in me to remain upright. As soon as Hedrek was gone, I lost my balance, falling to my knees. There was so much blood covering me that the fool had not noticed the deep gash in my leg, utterly unaware that I was bluffing, for there was no way I could have effectively fought him hand-to-hand.

Suddenly Ariana was there, studying me, pausing at my thigh.

"You are losing too much blood," she stated and went to stand. Grabbing her hand, I stopped her.

"Run," I said to her. "Hedrek may return. You need to leave." She stood no chance against them. None. She needed to get as far away as she could and as quickly as possible.

Her gaze hardened, looking as though I had insulted her. "You will die if I leave," she bit out, pulling her hand from mine.

I fell back, suddenly finding my head too heavy to hold up.

Ariana disappeared only to return with a sword in her hand. She used the blade to cut a strip from her tunic. I felt her hands on my thigh as she wrapped the fabric above the wound. Taking a smooth stick, she used it to tighten the fabric around my leg.

Unable to help it, I winced. My vision was darkening.

I should never have left home without my sword.

A hand firmly grabbed my jaw, forcing me to look upon her. "Whatever strength you have, I need you to use it. We need to get you closer to your city. I can help you, but I cannot carry you by myself. Can you do this?" Fear touched her features, though her voice came out confident and strong.

"Yes." It sounded like a hiss from my lips.

With a frown, Ariana stood, awkwardly helping me to my feet. She found a sturdy branch for me to use as a walking stick. Grabbing a sword in one hand, she slipped her other around me, positioning herself under my arm. I tried to keep my weight off her, but it was useless. She nearly stumbled at first, her hold tightening on me as she regained her footing. Finally, we began making our way back, one painful step after another.

It felt like we had been walking forever, though I was certain that if I looked back, I could likely still see the place we had started from. We were not moving fast. Each step zapped more energy. More and more of my weight shifted onto Ariana. She began shaking in effort, though no complaint came from her.

My mind was slowing, a haze settling over it. I glanced at the Bavadrin who struggled to keep me upright, who took one small step at a time with me. I was entirely at her mercy. I would have laughed if I had the strength, for this was certainly something to behold. A young Bavadrin woman trying to save a Lysian King, one responsible for keeping her against her will. She indeed was something unexpected, entering my life without an ounce of hesitation. Even after everything, she now stood beside me, trembling as she struggled to hold my weight.

Ariana whistled, a long and steady sound.

I cast her a sidelong glance.

"Lysian ears may pick up the sound." She forced the words out between her clenched teeth, answering my question though I never asked.

Again, she whistled, low and steady.

We made it four more steps before I lost my balance, and we fell into a tree. Ariana used her body to pin me and somehow kept me from falling entirely to the ground. She stilled while leaning into me, trying to regain her strength.

Footsteps and a familiar scent drew my blurred gaze up past her.

"Iver." His name was a rasp in my throat.

Startled, Ariana turned, finding my brother. A sliver of tension left her at the sight of him. Iver's gray eyes were wide as he looked over us.

"Lysians attacked," Ariana said. "He has lost a lot of blood."

"Don't move," Iver stated. "I will be back in just a minute." He took off into the woods, leaving Ariana too stunned to even respond. His steps moved further and further away before disappearing altogether. My head became heavier, and I was uncertain how much longer I could remain conscious.

When Iver reappeared, he helped Ariana as he took the brunt of my weight from one side.

We began at a quicker pace, moving in silence.

My eyes slid shut, and though I tried to open them again, they wouldn't.

34

ARIANA

E rik lost consciousness, and I nearly fell with his weight, crushing me beneath him.

"Sorry." I braced myself against the weight of the Lysian King.

Iver grunted in effort. "It's fine. We can lower him to the ground. Kole is nearly here." He must have heard and smelled Kole somewhere in the distance, heading our way. Slowly, we lowered Erik to the ground. His only acknowledgment of the change was a low moan.

Kole emerged full sprint, heading towards us. To his back was strapped something made of wood in a rectangular shape, with a tight fabric stretched over it. Kole took the device, lowering it to the ground beside Erik. Iver helped settle Erik onto it, the two of them then lifting him into the air with ease. Erik's head, back, and hips were supported while his legs bent at the knees hanging.

The two Lysians moved wordlessly into position around the device that would help carry their King.

Iver and Kole began a quick pace towards the city. I nearly had to jog to keep up. Several minutes later, we entered the castle where Erik lived, but we moved to an area I had never been to before. Down the hall, there was a female Lysian at the far end standing by an open door.

Iver and Kole entered with me on their heels. They lowered Erik onto a slated wooden table bed, one allowing for various adjustments.

Kole cursed. "What happened?" It was the first time he had spoken since joining us.

I answered with a shaky breath. "Lysians attacked. One of them called Erik his cousin. There were six of them. Erik killed five. The sixth ran off."

The female Lysian moved, a frown etched into her otherwise smooth face. Her hands flew over Erik's leg, and she gritted her teeth. "There's no time. He will lose his leg if I don't start right now." She looked up at Iver, silently asking for permission. Iver gave it with a nod, and her focus shifted to the horrendous wound before her. The sight of it was enough to turn my stomach. Her hands barely grazed Erik's skin, and he jerked violently.

"Hold him down," she hissed.

Kole and Iver went to Erik, grabbing his shoulders and legs.

The female began again.

There were no herbs, no tools in her hands. She merely touched him with her fingertips. *Conjuror.* She was healing with her touch.

I glanced around the room. Jars of familiar herbs and some I had never seen before littered the shelves. She was a healer. I took a quick inventory of what she had, noting the herbs and roots I recognized. They had pretty much everything needed to . . .

"He is burning up," Kole said through clenched teeth, drawing my attention back to Erik. His entire body was trembling. Had fever already taken hold?

I reached out, fingertips barely grazing his forearm. He was not just warm from fever. He was literally burning. No average person could survive such temperatures.

"Stop." I spun towards the female whose sharp eyes flicked to me.

"You may wish for his death. I do not," she stated, sounding surprisingly calm.

"You can't save him if we all die," I snapped and turned to Iver. "I can make a tea that will help to numb some of the pain, and it will also serve to numb some of his conjuring abilities, just for a short time. If you do not do this and continue, then he very well may set the entire room ablaze."

"We have things for pain, but they take half an hour to work, and we do not have such time," the healer cut in.

"This will begin working almost instantly and will help temper his conjuring so that you can heal without fear of injury." I turned to Iver again, for it was clearly going to be his decision. "All the supplies I need are already here. It will take me less than a minute. Please, let me help."

Gray eyes looked down at his brother. "One minute," he stated.

The healer removed her hands from Erik, and he stilled.

Instantly I moved, pulling herbs from the shelves, while the female watched me in surprise. Most healers I knew were very particular and guarded regarding their herbs, yet she did not seem uncomfortable with my prying and using her supply. Or she was good at biting her tongue.

"Is there any hot water?" I asked, grinding herbs and roots in a cup, just enough to release the oils from the leaves.

"Silver pitcher. It was freshly boiled just before you got here," she answered.

"If possible, sit him up so that he doesn't choke," I said to no one in particular.

The healer moved. With Kole's help, they adjusted the wooden table, raising Erik's upper body to a gentle angle. Kole stepped aside, giving me access to him.

I brought my hand to his burning hot cheek.

"Erik," I said his name, my voice calm but firm. "You need to drink this." I poured a little into his mouth, and he coughed it up, spewing it all over himself.

I gripped his jaw. "Erik. We are trying to help you, but you need to drink this. If you do not, then you may kill us all. Do you hear me? Please. Trust me and drink this." It seemed like his eyes may have opened briefly into thin slits before closing once more.

Again, I tried to pour the tea into his mouth.

He swallowed.

The relief I felt was extraordinary.

I poured more of it until it was all gone.

He drank the entire thing.

Thank the Spirit.

Moving out of the way, Kole helped to lower Erik back down, flat on his back. The healer's hands found their way to the wound at Erik's leg.

"Cut the bandage," she ordered, and Kole moved, snipping the fabric. I hesitated, fearing the sight of blood gushing through the wound, but it never came. Had she already done enough to stop the bleeding? *Amazing.*

"Amazing," the healer murmured, looking from Erik's face to mine before returning to the gash. Her hands remained on him the entire time, and slowly I could see the wound heal, the sides gradually coming closer together, the skin stitching together.

I jumped as the door into the small room swung open with force. Edmond entered, his gaze traveling over Erik's body, before looking at each of us.

His attention ended on Kole. "Get her out of here." His voice was frigid as he gestured to me.

"But I—" My words were cut off when Kole grabbed me under

my arm, guiding me through the room and out the door. He did not release me when we exited the chamber, practically dragging me down the hall.

"Let go." I bit the words out, trying to wedge my arm out of his hold. He only released me once we got to a narrow staircase. His enormous body stood squarely between me and the floor we had left Erik on.

"Go." His voice was firm.

I took a step towards him, entering his space. Anger flooded through me. How could they treat me like this? I was the one who cut off the blood to Erik's wound and who half dragged him back to this wretched place, and they treated me as though I was not even worthy of being in the same room as him. Within that anger was a sliver of hurt, which only further fueled the rage. Kole knew me, yet he stood between his King and me as if he needed to shield Erik from me. As if *I* were the dangerous one.

There was no way of getting around Kole, and so I reined in my emotions the best I could and pivoted, taking the stairs to the fifth floor. He trailed silently behind me till we finally made it to the small sitting room leading to my individual room.

Only when the door closed behind us did Kole finally speak. "Thank you. For everything you did today." His tone was gentle.

I whirled around. "You have some way of showing it. Treating me like . . ." I stopped myself, for I was a prisoner. That's all I was to any of them. I had no rights, nothing except for what they allowed me to have.

"Edmond is overprotective and wary. He does not know you as well as we do. I am bound to follow his orders within reason until Erik is back on his feet. Though Edmond may not yet fully appreciate what you did today, I do." The sympathy in his voice was disarming.

Some of the anger left me, though most of it remained. A tornado of fire burned inside my body, searching for an escape.

With a sigh, I took a seat in one of the chairs. Bringing my hands to my temples, I made several circular motions before dropping them in my lap.

"Do you mind telling me a little more about what happened?" Kole asked.

"It all happened so quickly. The other fire conjuror and his pack of Lysians appeared. They attacked. Erik took care of them, but clearly, he was wounded. Thankfully, he could keep it together until the other fire conjuror vanished." A shiver ran through me at the thought of what might have happened if that other Lysian had noticed the severity of Erik's injuries. If he had not used that opportunity to burn me where I stood, I would have stolen the air from his lungs, but after that, I would have had no choice but to run, for they would know what I was. Would I have left if it meant Erik's death? An uncomfortable feeling skittered down my spine.

"They just left you alone?" Kole took a seat in the other open chair.

"No. One tried to attack me. I managed to get him to not use his sword. Somehow, I dodged a few of his attacks, and when he finally grabbed me, I hit him in the throat. He choked, and a moment later, Erik was there, killing him."

"You were brave," he stated.

"I had no choice."

As if I summoned her with my thoughts, Edda knocked on the door and without waiting for a response, she entered. Onyx eyes pinned me before sweeping over my body, taking in the dirt and blood covering me.

"By the Spirit," she whispered, moving through the room till she stood directly in front of me.

"There was a Lysian attack. I'm fine," I said to her, voice clipped.

"Lysian?" She turned to Kole with a storm brewing behind her stare.

"Not our Lysians," he clarified.

"Who?" Her eyes darkened.

"I am afraid I cannot answer that," he stated flatly.

Another knock at the door drew my attention, and I jumped out of my chair, foolishly hoping it was Erik, though he never would have knocked to enter his own living quarters.

Iver and the healer entered, and suddenly the comfortably sized but cozy sitting room felt incredibly cramped. I fell back into my seat, energy leaving me.

"Well, this is a snug gathering," Iver commented.

"How is he?" I asked.

The healer answered, "The King will be fine. We are keeping him in the healer's quarters for the night but come tomorrow afternoon, he will likely be up and going about his business once more."

"Thank you," I said to her and truly meant it. Of course, she was bound by duty to do all she could for her King. Yet relief washed over me all the same with hearing that they were able to help him, that he would be fine.

With dread, I also realized that I would never have left him, even if my conjuring was discovered. I would not have let him die. The revelation only upset me further. Was Edda right? Was I nothing more than a stupid girl, caring more about a Lysian's life above her own? Meanwhile, they still wouldn't even let me remain with Erik when he was wounded. As if seeing him in that manner somehow weakened his position. Ignoring the fact that I had done everything in my power outside of using conjuring to help him.

Iver spoke, "I am afraid in the chaos I never properly introduced you two. This is Roan, one of our very talented healers." Then, he turned to me, "And this is Ariana, Leader Superior of the Bavadrins."

Roan smiled politely, taking a small step towards me. "How did you know how to make that tea?"

That was a ridiculous question, or perhaps I was in a ridiculous mood.

"How does anyone know anything? Someone taught it to me," I answered flatly. My attitude rapidly managed to turn incredibly foul. All energy was zapped from me and an unspoken grudge tainted what little of it was left. I was angry at Edda for how she had been behaving towards me, mad at the Lysians for keeping me against my will and then treating me as little more than an irritating gnat. I was also angry at the Spirit for not telling me more when I ascended. I was angry at the entire world.

Edda's head snapped to me. "What tea?"

"It worked nearly instantly, lessening pain and dampening conjuring abilities," the healer stated with awe, clearly not offended by my lack of pleasantries.

Edda did not say a thing, though her eyes threw daggers my way.

I ignored her.

"Listen, Ariana." The healer took another small step towards me. "Would you be willing to show me how to make what you did tonight? If you would share what you know, then it could help a lot of the innocent moving forward."

"Is there such a thing? Innocent Lysians." Edda commented with a fury of her own. She was likely upset that my life had been in danger and that I then shared something so dangerous with the Lysians.

"Is there such a thing as an innocent Bavadrin?" I snapped, silencing her. Forcing a deep breath, I turned to the healer. "The answer is yes, just as there are innocents amongst the Lysians and likely the Siddhes as well. We would all be wise to remember this. And to answer your question, yes, I will teach you."

She smiled, dipping her head in gratitude. And could there possibly have been a tinge of respect as well? Seemed as though one of them no longer viewed me like a gnat, at least not while she wanted to gain something from me. "Thank you. If you could come by tomorrow at noon?"

"We will be there," Kole agreed, for there was no way I could go anywhere without my trusted guard.

"Thank you." She dipped her head again and smiled fully before leaving the small room.

Iver leaned against the far wall next to the door. "You were clever today."

Both Kole and Edda looked between the prince and me.

"How do you mean?" I asked.

"The whistle, knowing a Lysian could pick up the sound without you needing to exert the energy of yelling. The way you tied off Erik's leg to keep him from losing more blood. Helping when the healer was working on him," he rattled off a shortlist.

I shrugged a shoulder. "I did what I could."

Iver pushed off the wall, brushing past Edda as he approached with such ease only a Lysian could master. Smoothly, he knelt before me, balancing on his toes. Gray eyes settled on mine. "Because of your actions today, my brother will live another day. I am in your debt and will be forever grateful for this."

I found myself stunned.

Edda scoffed. "How about you thank her by setting her free?"

Iver's lip curved up in an amused smile, though his gaze remained holding mine. "You don't need to be a Seer to know she will one day be free of us."

It took everything in me not to react to that comment. Did he know what Edda was? What we planned?

He rose to his feet, turning to Edda. "Ariana looks as though she desperately needs a bath and some rest. Time to leave her be."

Edda held his gaze, eyes narrowing.

She then turned to me, possibly surprising the entire room, for she said, "The Lysian is right. You are a Leader Superior now and need to take better care of yourself."

I expected her to demand to remain with me, but she did not. She withdrew from me. Whatever worry she felt was sealed away. When she spoke, a degree of separation remained between us. She was not my Edda, not even my friend. Just simply an adviser. That was the role she had made very clear that she wished to play. If only it did not hurt my heart every time.

Iver and Edda left together, leaving Kole and me in the sitting room.

He sighed after some time. "They are both right. You look terrible. You should go get cleaned up and get some rest."

I stood then, taking my leave, for it seemed that just looking at me was too much for anyone.

The night was restless, and the next day was no better.

I met with the healer and showed her what I knew. She scribbled down notes, thanking me wholeheartedly for sharing my knowledge with her. However, it was not till sometime in the evening that I finally saw Erik.

I spotted him from a distance as he walked with his brother Edmond down a hall. Erik stood on his feet, moving with the same predatory grace I knew him to always have. It was as if the last twenty-four hours never happened. As if Erik's life never hung in the balance. Seeing him whole shook me. Then he rounded a corner with his brother and was gone.

35

ARIANA

E islyn and I sat with our backs to a building on a small hill watching the sunset. My muscles were sore from the training we just finished. It started hand-to-hand and ended with using wooden staffs.

The setting sun warmed my face, and I tried to focus only on that feeling to clear my mind. Lately, the only time I felt at peace was when I physically or mentally exerted myself. Resting was no longer a solace. My mind raced during the quiet moments, diving deeper and deeper into the worries brewing within. Over and over, I replayed the scenarios of my approaching escape.

I also thought of Erik, wondering why he had not yet made time to see me. Those thoughts had me feeling foolish. I was a prisoner. Why would he make time for me when he had more important things to do?

Iver's comment the other day perhaps caused me the most unease when he casually stated that one did not need to be a Seer to know that I would soon be free of the Lysians. Though he had never mentioned it again, I was terrified to ask him what he meant by it. I could not shake the feeling that he somehow knew what I was planning.

Eislyn picked up one of the staffs, absentmindedly balancing it horizontally on one of her fingers while observing the view. "You have done well with training." She turned to me while keeping the staff balanced.

I scoffed. "Yeah, sure."

"You disagree?" She let the weapon roll off her finger and fall to the ground.

"Lysians have no weaknesses," I pointed out.

"That isn't true." She smirked and asked, "In a fight of a Bavadrin against a Lysian, who would win?"

"C'mon." I did not answer, for it was apparent.

"What? Not sure?" Her voice then got louder. "What do you think Iver?"

Surprised, I turned and found the prince stepping out from behind the building.

"You're getting good at that, Eislyn." He smiled, joining us, though he remained standing and leaned against the building while we sat. Eyes that now seemed even more clever than before viewed me from where he stood.

Did he know I did not intend to return from this next trip home?

It was impossible, unless he was also a Seer?

"Well?" Eislyn turned to him. "Lysian or Bavadrin?"

"Lysian," he answered.

"Clearly," I commented, rolling my eyes while trying to get the thoughts of Iver being a Seer out of my head.

"It's to your advantage that everyone thinks this." Eislyn smirked.

"How so?"

"Who has more to lose?" she pointed out.

"The loss would be the same for either side," I answered. Whoever lost would do so with their lives. The cost was the same.

Iver joined in to help lead me to the answer they both wished for me to find. "Sure, but who truly has more to lose? Think of who everyone expects to win . . ." He laughed when he saw the look of confusion on my face. "You have more to lose, and so in a fight, you will invest everything you have. A Lysian fighting you will never truly give it their all, and that gives you a chance. *You* would fight like your life depends on it while the Lysian may get distracted, arrogant even, and make a fatal error."

"A Bavadrin's only hope is to fight a Lysian that is too cocky and thus makes some sort of fatal error." I couldn't believe that this was his logic.

"It would be a benefit, would it not?" He arched a brow. "As long as neither has conjuring capabilities."

"So basically, I would only stand a chance if fighting you?" I said, trying to present a casual demeanor while within I feared the things he may know. Iver snorted, and I added, "It would be better to not rely on an opponent's error."

"Well, life is not fair." He then turned to Eislyn. "Is it?"

"I'm not in the mood, Iver." Eislyn's voice was indifferent; however, her gaze turned cold as it cut toward him.

"Tell me, is it pleasure or pain that stimulates your mood this evening?" Unfortunately, he did not seem to care enough to heed her warning. I was thankful that she took his attention away from me. Even as the air around us turned cold and heavy with tension.

"Go away before you regret coming here," Eislyn replied curtly.

Iver viewed me. "You appear confused. Do you not know the history yet?"

"Iver," Eislyn warned.

"What history?" I couldn't keep myself from asking.

"The history of my friends Kole and Eislyn." He spoke casually while Eislyn's jaw clenched. "Well, allow me to enlighten you. You see, Kole and Eislyn were once madly in love and were due to be mated. In fact, that shoulder she always keeps covered bears his mark, a claim as her mate forever imprinted on her skin."

Iver continued, "But first, there is something you need to know. When he was a boy, Kole used to be head over heels for my sister. Would follow her around like a puppy dog. And eventually, as any neglected pup would do, he finally found someone who gave him the time of day, and his attention switched to Eislyn. Now my sister is lovely, but she is not without flaws. Jealousy overcame her, for even though she did not love Kole, she did love having his eye. So, she set up a plot where she could be alone with him, and she kissed him. But this plot included not only a kiss; she also meant for everything to be seen by the one who held his attention."

Iver's gaze cut to Eislyn as he continued speaking of her. "But that person could not handle such pain and lashed out. She found some skinny Lysian tart and slept with her, thus breaking Kole's fragile heart." Iver looked at me and laughed. "I know you Bavadrins are rigid when it comes to sexuality, but here we are not. One can be with whomever they desire. Eislyn here cares more about fitting with her partner on a personal level rather than caring for their anatomy. Though I doubt the tart was picked for anything other than ease of wielding her into a blade that sliced into Kole's heart."

Eislyn moved so quickly I did not even have a chance to be startled. She used a wooden staff to sweep at Iver's legs, bringing him to the ground. Moments later, she straddled him, pressing the staff into his neck. His hands gripped the wood, keeping it from crushing his throat.

"If you see me as the evil one who destroyed poor Kole's heart, then you know *nothing*," she panted, tired with rage.

Iver growled before maneuvering out of Eislyn's hold. They went round and round. The way Iver moved with effortless grace made him appear untouchable. Eislyn was not as light on her feet nor as quick, though she got out of every one of Iver's assaults until he finally pinned her to the ground, her face in the dirt. He twisted her arm back, and she hissed in pain.

"The entire thing was staged, Eislyn. Iona wanted you to see her kissing him," Iver growled, anger rippling through him.

"Was it staged for him to kiss her back, for his hands to move over her lower back as if welcoming the embrace?" She bit the words out as if they tasted sour, the pain still raw. It was a wound that had festered, never closing. I imagined that it at times scabbed over only to be picked at and re-opened, never healing.

"It is time that the two of you let this go." Iver spoke through clenched teeth, and it was the first time I had ever seen him anything other than calm and collected. For some reason, he was furious.

"If you don't break my arm, then I am going to kill you with it," she growled.

Iver twisted her arm further in response, until Eislyn cried out. There was no hesitation in his gaze, only an icy determination. He truly was going to break it. They were going to destroy one another.

Without thinking, I reached for a staff and stood, pointing the end at Iver's throat without touching him.

Surprised, he eased the pressure from Eislyn's arm, and her body relaxed underneath him.

"A Bavadrin standing between two Lysians. That is bold of you," Iver said, his attention entirely on me. "Just because you did not die last time you faced a Lysian does not mean you are equipped for such a challenge."

"Please. Stop hurting each other." My words were a plea.

Iver released Eislyn and rose to his feet. I moved as well, keeping the end of the staff pointed at his throat without touching him. Eislyn rolled to the side and onto her feet as soon as she was able.

My hands hurt from the hold I had on the staff, knuckles

turning white. I was so rigid that I did not have the capabilities to release the weapon when Iver reached out. Taking it in his hands, he yanked me forward. By the time I released it, I was already flying towards the Lysian. He threw the staff to the ground as the distance between us shrank. His hand gripped the back of my neck, keeping me from backing away. Strong fingers curved around the tendons of my throat, controlling my head, and forcing me to meet his eyes. I was in the clutches of power, and the only hope of escape was the fact that his King did not wish for my death.

"Why did you do that, Ariana?" Iver's voice was incredibly calm.

A tremble scampered through me.

"You were hurting her," I answered.

"Iver, let her go," Eislyn cut in, though he did not seem to hear her request.

"And you are not concerned whether I may hurt you? You care for her enough to risk your life?" Gray eyes bore into mine, demanding an answer.

"I hoped I was not truly risking it."

Surprise touched his features. "By threatening me?"

"That was not my intention. The staff was meant only to provide a buffer between us, to protect me were you to react unfavorably. It was never intended to be used if unprovoked. I never touched you with it."

Iver smiled and suddenly released me.

I had been trying to pull away from him so when the pressure of his hand on the back of my neck vanished, I had to catch myself from completely falling backward.

"Let's go, Ariana." Eislyn picked up the sparring sticks and turned to me, completely ignoring Iver.

For some reason, I found myself looking to Iver as if asking for permission to leave.

He jerked his head to the side, gesturing for me to go. "Hope you two have a lovely evening. And do yourself a favor and don't involve yourself in future Lysian conflicts. Unless you happen to have a protective form of conjuring."

Somehow, I managed not to stumble at his choice of words, schooling my expression into a mask of calm. I did not respond.

He watched us as we made our way through the small field.

"What in Spirit's name were you thinking? Just because you helped Erik the other day does not mean that Iver will let you behave as you wish towards him," Eislyn hissed when we were nearly back at the building where my room was.

"He was hurting you," I pointed out, surprised at her anger.

"He would not have broken my arm. I would have been fine." Her gaze cut to me. "I have known him for a long time. He uses words to torment others. He does not enjoy inflicting physical harm." The two of them had been friends at some point. That was news I needed a moment to get used to.

"Why does he speak that way to you and Kole?" I asked. Iver enjoyed pushing getting a rise out of them most often.

"Iver speaks that way to everyone. But he is perhaps upset with the two of us." She looked back over her shoulder where we came from, but he was gone.

"Upset?" I asked.

A deep sigh escaped from her. "The three of us used to be close before what happened. Well, I guess if I were to include Erik, then it was the four of us. But, after everything, Kole and I became cruel to each other. Iver ended up being, in a way, stuck in the middle, which he hated. So, he removed himself from everything altogether."

So that was Iver's pain, the root of his anger. He lost two of his friends without physically losing them. Just as that loss tormented him, he now tormented them in return.

Eislyn stopped at my door, waiting for me to enter.

"I'm sorry," I said to her, feeling guilty.

"Just don't get between Lysians again. That's not wise," she said, still waiting for me to enter the room.

"Thanks for training me." I finally opened the door.

"Get some rest," she said by way of goodbye, turning and walking back the way we had come.

I entered the sitting room to find Kole lounging in one of the chairs, clearly waiting for my return. He looked up from the book in his hands. He slouched to the side, comfortably passing the time while I was gone.

A forced smile in his direction was all I could manage in response to his greeting nod.

Icy blue eyes tracked me as I made my way through the small space before finding myself in front of my room, unable to go in.

A pang of strange guilt pulled at me, for I now knew a personal story of Kole's, and he hadn't the slightest of clues. If not addressed, then the guilt might quietly drive me mad. I needed to air everything out. With a deep breath, I turned to face him.

"Mind if I sit with you a minute?" I asked, already crossing the room to take the open chair near him.

Crystal-blue eyes glinted, and he shut the book in his hands, placing it on the small shared table between the two chairs.

"Sure," he said, with a look of confusion passing over him.

I licked my lips, not knowing where to begin. "There is something I need to let you know."

Kole shifted in his chair, sitting upright and squaring his shoulders. It was likely clear that I was uncomfortable, and that piqued his interest. All his attention settled on me.

I swallowed my discomfort. "I was told something that I have no right to know, for it was neither you nor Eislyn who shared this information with me, and I cannot in good conscience go on pretending I know nothing of your story," I stated, waiting for his response.

Kole's breath left him, and he leaned back in his chair, away from me.

"Iver?" he asked, his voice low.

I nodded in answer, and he cursed. "*Ashes*, that idiot can't keep his nose out of things that have nothing to do with him." A wave of anger spread through the room, stemming from the Lysian. Kole's hands balled up into fists on his lap. It was as if it was all he could do to not destroy something in the room.

I glanced at the hearth, burning with a small flame licking a nearly incinerated log. The fire danced, stretching over the dead wood. For a while, it held my attention as I waited for Kole to direct the conversation. Did he wish to talk about it, or did he want me to leave things as they were? I began growing uneasy with the passing time while he sat there, getting angrier and angrier.

I turned to him. "I don't expect you to talk to me about any of this, but I felt you should know what I have been told." I spoke calmly, hoping that it would help to ease the growing tension in the room.

"What did he tell you?" Kole kept his attention fixed on me. His face was turning red with all that he was trying to keep bottled in. Though he was massive in size, I was pretty sure he had too much rage to keep trapped within that bulk. No amount of muscle or strength could contain such radiating painful fury for very long, and I was confident that my answering his question would only fuel the flame. It was going to spill out of him.

"He said that you and Eislyn were to be mated. That his sister was jealous of no longer having your attention, and so she kissed you, but Eislyn saw," I said, deciding to give him the quickest version of the story I could come up with.

Kole snorted. "Yeah, she saw alright. And did he tell you what happened next?" His words grew bitter.

My heart rate increased.

"He said you found her in a bed with another," I answered.

A cruel smile found its way to Kole's lips, and he appeared genuinely terrifying. "Yes. She could not wait to destroy me." His nostrils flared as if he couldn't pull enough air into his lungs.

There was so much pain hidden within him.

I contemplated leaving Kole to himself. Even though he remained seated, his breathing pattern changed, becoming shallow. His eyes grew cruel, and his demeanor cold. Never had I felt such potent rage coming from him. His hands, which were balled into fists, were turning white. The small room buzzed with violent energy, and it felt as though the slightest thing could set it off into an explosion. Under normal circumstances, I did not think Kole would ever have harmed me but seeing him that way was uncomfortably precarious.

I should have left. Instead, I found myself asking, "Why do you think she wanted to destroy you?"

"How should I know? To show a force of power. To hurt me for disrespecting her." His words were a growl on his lips.

"Did you disrespect her?" I asked, keeping my voice low and calm, hoping it would somehow keep him from losing control of that rage even though I was diving deeper into his pain.

"No," he said angrily. "At least that was not the intent."

I nodded, allowing for silence to fall over us.

Several heartbeats later, he elaborated, as if needing to fill the silence. "I had always been infatuated by Iona. It was a childish emotion. But when I opened my heart to Eislyn, I believed I had truly met my person. She became my world, and I loved her. Then Iona did a stupid thing. That kiss was everything I had wanted for so long, yet at that moment, it was the last thing I wished for. Should I have pushed her away sooner? Probably. But I was shocked by the entire thing. And she is a freaking royal and a friend. So, what is the proper way to respond in that situation?"

"Did you explain these thoughts and feelings to Eislyn?" I was digging deeper, and though Kole was visibly upset, he let me.

Despite the rage and hurt he felt by reliving these vulnerable moments, some part of him must have craved to share them.

"I was giving her time to calm down. She was so angry, lost her mind. And then I walked in on her . . ." He did not have to finish, for I knew how that ended. Both of them felt the same way, too blinded by bitter anger to see the love and pain that fueled their actions.

"And you believe that Eislyn did that to hurt you and take back power?" I repeated what he had told me her reason was for doing what she did.

"Don't you?" he asked defensively.

"I do not know her reasons for her actions, for she did not share them with me. But I would like to propose a possible alternative." I waited for him to either accept or refuse the choice.

"What?"

"If I had found the person who I believed was my other half in life, if there was one person who I felt truly safe within this wild cruel world above anyone else, then I would love and cherish that bond above all else. If I then caught them doing something that went against everything I believed we were—even if it wasn't intended as a betrayal—well, in a fury of pain, I may have seen it as such. Suddenly, the safest thing about my world becomes the most dangerous and painful. That would be incredibly frightening. And if that person then withdrew from me, turned their back on me when I felt most vulnerable and did not wish to try and explain, I would be left heartbroken. I may even then ensure that I would never feel such pain again by doing something that would force all ties to be cut with that person who is now far too dangerous to be in my life."

His brows furrowed, gaze falling to the ground in thought. "You think she did what she did . . . to protect herself?" Suddenly some of that anger that had no end lost its force, and a trace of sadness moved through him.

"I have no idea why she reacted the way she had. That is something only she can answer for you, just as only you can answer for her the questions she must also carry as to why you did not try and come to her sooner."

"But she hates me." Though it was said as a statement, there was clear doubt there.

"Do you hate her?" I asked.

He was silent.

"Or do you hate that she hurt you?"

Kole's head began to shake as if he could not bring himself to believe what I was saying.

I dared to continue. "What is hate? It is a form of passion, and passion is the root that grows into all deep feelings such as hate or love. The opposite of passion is indifference. And one thing that I do know for certain is that neither of you feels indifference towards each other. But both of you do still harbor a great deal of passion."

Kole shifted his weight to the side of his seat. Unfurrowing the fingers of his right hand, he brought it to his face and then passed it through his hair. Bringing his elbow to rest on the armrest, he craned his head so that his fingers remained intertwined in his golden strands. His face was largely hidden from me. I reached for his free hand, which was still balled into a fist on his thigh.

My fingers moved over his hand until I grasped it. All I knew was that he was in pain, and I wished to help him through it. However, I had no idea how to do that other than to reach out and physically touch him, to let him know he was not alone. Kole did not respond to my touch, which I saw as a positive sign, for he did not swat my hand away.

"What have I done? I thought she needed some time . . . me not caring about her is . . ." Kole struggled finding the words. Finally, his left hand opened, allowing for mine to interlock with his for a moment. "Ariana, thank you, but I need you to leave now." He sounded defeated.

I nodded though he didn't see me do it. I no longer held his attention. Giving his hand a gentle squeeze, I rose to my feet, leaving him in the small sitting room.

Moments after I finally entered my chamber, I heard the sound of pages flapping as he chucked the book he had been reading at a wall. Sounds of chaos followed, likely the noises of furniture breaking. Kole roared in anger, and I was glad that Erik was elsewhere so that no one had to witness what was happening.

My heart broke for Kole, for the pain he felt. Perhaps it would have been better if I had not interfered and kept my mouth shut. I did not know what Eislyn's true intentions were for her past actions. The things we talked about were only to show a different possibility, that things were not always clear. Assuming to know someone's reasonings for something was not the same as truly knowing and understanding. I had hoped to help; instead, it felt as though I had done more harm. I hated that I caused Kole to question himself in such a way.

With my back to the sitting-room door, I slid down to the ground and sat there while Kole released his torments by physically destroying things.

I remained there, silently with him long after the sounds of chaos had finally subsided.

36

ERIK

I t was the day before we were scheduled to leave for the Bavadrin lands. Time since the attack passed at an incredible rate. I threw myself into preparing the forces here to stand against the fire conjuror. Which meant that I attended their trainings, demonstrating and participating for as long as I physically could. No time was left for anything else. Including my dinners with Ariana.

The Bavadrin had spent her days training with Eislyn. Ariana's movements changed with time, at least that was what I noted from the distant glimpses I got of her. She became lighter on her feet, smoother in her movements. There had always been a confidence to the way she held herself, though it now morphed into something sturdier, gaining a weight to it, an edge.

When I approached near the end of her session with Eislyn and invited Ariana for a walk, she agreed with a bright smile. Though curiosity tinged her green eyes as she joined me.

"Are you hurt?" I asked after she rolled her right shoulder for the third time, as if testing the feel of it.

"Just a little sore." She glanced at me and stopped the motion.

I only took her far enough to find a quiet area for us to rest. I sat in a partially shaded spot, leaving a patch of grass beside me bathed in sunlight I knew she would favor. Ariana lowered herself next to me. The woman seemed to always seek out sunlight. She closed her eyes, tipping her head towards the warmth and drew in a deep breath.

Ariana usually remained composed around me, hardly ever letting me scent a trace of fear. But there was often a rigidness. As if she needed to stay alert to monitor a potential threat. Now, as she relaxed into the grass, eyes closed, heartbeat steady, I couldn't look away. She was the picture of peace. There was something captivating about it, about her.

"I never properly thanked you for your actions that day," I stated, voice breaking the silence.

"You've had little opportunity," she replied, peering at me through thick lashes. In the sunlight her eyes sparkled in green hues. Never had I cared to have a favorite color before. But I think the emerald of her eyes might have been it. They shone with warmth, cleverness, bravery.

I nodded, shifting to gaze to a tree branch overhead, using my arm as a makeshift pillow behind my head. My other hand rested casually on the hilt of a blade at my hip. Never again would I be caught without it on my body. "Plans needed to be made to ensure nothing like that ever repeats." I turned back to her. "I should have sought you out sooner. I am sorry."

Her eyes widened, lips lifting at the corners. "I get a thank you and an apology all in one day from the Lysian King? Perhaps the healer missed a spot somewhere in there, leaving something wonderfully broken."

Her teasing pulled an easy smile from me. "I can admit when I am wrong and when I am thankful."

"Remind me to thank the healer." She smirked.

I chuckled, some of the tension in my shoulders easing. When had I started enjoying her company like this?

"Can you tell me about who they were?" Ariana asked, shifting the conversation.

"Distant relatives that broke away from the group a long time ago." Moving a hand from the hilt of my blade, I picked a flower of an autumn weed and twirled it absentmindedly between my fingers. "Why didn't you run?" It was a question I thought about far too often.

Ariana shrugged, glancing at the flower I held. "What good would that have done me? Perhaps I could have made it home, or perhaps Lysians would have caught me, and I would be worse off than I am now." Her gaze lifted to mine. "If I ran, then you would have likely died. I couldn't let you die like that, not when you protected me."

I would have never needed to protect her if she had been home. The thought soured my mood. Since the day my eyes first landed on her, I always had been a threat to her, and she had always helped me. She gave when she should have run, forgave when she had every reason to hate. Where I was danger, she was peace.

"Thank you," I murmured, twirling the flower in my hands several more times before finally discarding it aside. Laying back, I allowed my eyes to briefly close. "Tomorrow, we begin the journey to your city again," I commented, changing the subject.

"A couple more trips, and I'm fairly certain we could do it while sleeping," Ariana said with a small laugh.

"Indeed. Our little group is becoming more and more efficient at it. How are things between you and Edda?"

She remained silent for a few breaths before saying, "Strained. To be honest, I don't know why she even came back here with me after the Ascension."

"Because she worries for you and wishes to keep close," I answered, shifting to better view her.

Ariana stared straight ahead, though not truly focused on anything. "Edda's words, the way she behaved towards me . . . they were like daggers to the heart, and now it feels like I am bleeding out. No matter how much I try to seal the wounds, I keep getting blood all over my hands and making things worse. I'm a bloody mess that is now letting nature take its course and do what it wishes. I give up trying to understand Edda's reasons for her behavior. If she only wishes to act as an adviser to me, then that will be what it will be." Her eyes misted over.

An urge to sooth her slammed into me. *Ashes*. I wanted to protect her, to ease her pain.

I remained silent for a long moment before saying, "If I could take some of your pain away, I would." *What in Spirits name was I doing?*

Ariana broke her unfocused stare and turned to me in surprise. Apparently, she was as taken aback by my declaration as I was. Her cheeks tinged with blush.

"And what would you do with a pain like that?" She asked lightly. Playfully.

I smiled. "Why, I would put it in the royal arsenal, of course."

"Of course. Where else would it belong?" Her eyes flickered as she held my stare. *Always*, so boldly holding my stare.

"There's nowhere else that could handle it."

"You think me in such pain? Certainly, you have seen worse?" She arched a brow.

"Oh, I have seen wild and unimaginable displays of pain. However, never from someone quite as strong and bold as you. If it's something that is enough to weigh on you, then I know it is more potent than most others."

"That healer *definitely* missed something healing you," she teased.

"You think?"

Her eyes narrowed, though the corner of her mouth threatened a smirk. "You are being too... sweet."

"Oh, I can be sweet if I want to."

Her gaze dropped to my lips and lingered for a heartbeat too long. I couldn't help but smile, slow and knowing. Green eyes lifted back to mine, and she tensed, realizing she had been caught appraising my mouth. Blush further colored her cheeks. Oh, how I enjoyed this. A particular type of immeasurable tension spread between us.

Ariana averted her attention to a patch of moss on a nearby tree.

Not meeting my eye, she asked, "Do you think that we can work together freely?"

In a way, she was again asking me to release her. Was that all this was to her? An attempt at subtle seduction to get what she wanted? I couldn't blame her for trying.

I remained silent a long while, contemplating how to best answer. The entire time she continued staring at the patch of moss.

"I want to, but my people have risked so much. I cannot release you only to have you join our enemy. My world would be torn apart if that were to happen. It is simply a risk I cannot take at this time, even if I wanted to. Perhaps we can one day."

"You don't trust me," she commented, sounding discouraged. Did she think batting eyelashes and a couple suggestive glances would turn my head so far that I would lose all control and release her? I could not even fully trust my own kind. Hedrek was a problem. Something she now knew of. And the risk of trusting Bavadrins did not expose my neck alone, but the necks of my citizens. I would not risk it. Not when there was no point to, not when I already had control.

A sigh rumbled against the back of my throat. "Our story

began with us being prisoners of one another. That does not make for a solid foundation of trust. It is no secret that I like you, Ariana. I have promised no harm would come to you or yours if not provoked. But your race is known for deception. The only way for me to truly know if you speak the truth is to set you free, and that is something that I cannot risk at this point."

"You were *never* my prisoner," she said, voice colder. "If I had been the leader at the time, and you stumbled onto my territory, you wouldn't ever have been a prisoner."

"You do not know that. I am a Lysian, a threat to the Bavadrins. I certainly would not have been free in your territory," I pointed out, shifting my attention to a tree branch above. My words were complete horse shit. In my gut I knew she would never have followed in her father's footsteps. My skin would have remained pristine had she been the Bavadrin leader.

Her eyes flared as she said, "But you were never truly a prisoner, were you? You found yourself exactly where you wished to be. Even the unjust punishment you received was something you desired, at least in some ways. You always had the power to leave that cell but chose to stay."

Silence fell between us.

How could I respond when it was true. I wanted to be a Bavadrin prisoner.

But she did not desire to be mine. She wanted to go home.

"You must hate me." My words came out so low, I wasn't sure whether she could make them out.

She studied me a moment before answering. "I can understand the position you are in. Hate is not a word I would use to describe my feelings towards you. Perhaps frustrating would be a more appropriate term."

I smiled, though it did not touch my eyes. "I have been called worse."

She seemed to want to ask something else but bit her tongue.

Instead, she settled on saying, "I hope you know that I do not wish your people any harm. If you believe nothing else, please believe this." There was almost a desperation to her voice. "I do not want to hurt you or the Lysians."

I nodded in acknowledgement but said nothing in return.

Ariana sat up looking at the dimming world around us. "I'm getting tired," she stated, effectively ending the entire conversation.

I rose to my feet in a fluid motion and held out a hand to help. Her touch was warm as her fingers slid over my palm. Once standing her hand remained in mine for longer than necessary, and I held it. Searching her eyes for answers she could not provide me with. A sadness passed over her features before she tugged, and I released my hold.

I wanted to say something to comfort her, but nothing came to mind. So instead, I escorted her back to her beautiful prison.

37

ARIANA

It was my third trip home with the Lysians, but they would not make it past the city walls this time. My sweaty palms held the reins of my mount as my mind raced. Everything was coming together, a silent storm building. We all stood on the precipice, and I hoped we would all come out unscathed.

I rode Rain on my own again. She was a reliable horse with both spirit and endurance. However, by the way her tail periodically whipped and her large gray ears flickered, I wondered if she sensed the growing unease within me, making it her own.

Edda was also allowed to ride on her own, making things a lot easier, for she could separate herself from the party when the time came. And it had finally nearly come.

Shay greeted us near the city, running parallel as we approached. The wolf's movements were soundless as she made her way across the grassland, keeping pace. Erik periodically turned his head and looked at her. Our escort. He did not know that her presence meant that Willis knew where we now were, tracking our movements. Willis and the other Bavadrins would have been preparing for what was to come next.

For the first time in decades, the Sparrows lined our walls, my friend Kiora standing with them. My heart both swelled and retracted. I thought a silent prayer to the Spirit that all would go well.

Edda rode up ahead, leading the way for our small group. The Lysians allowed for it because they had me amongst them, and they likely thought that the Bavadrins would never dream of attacking them when they could kill me in a matter of seconds. Unfortunately for them, I was not the utterly helpless girl they had come to know.

When the perimeter city wall came into view, my heart rattled against my ribs. If Erik could hear it over the horse's hooves, he likely attributed the increased pulse to excitement of returning home.

"Agh!" Edda scowled from the front. "You are a Leader Superior! They know you are arriving today! What kind of welcome is this?" She made a show of pretending to be appalled that the dirt road was not lined with Bavadrins dancing with ribbons and playing their horns to celebrate my arrival.

"What, are you planning on running ahead and giving them an earful?" I commented. It was my allowing her to run, to leave me. She needed to separate herself.

"You can be sure that I am. This is completely unacceptable," Edda snapped, voice filled with scorn, and with a sharp kick, her horse sprang forward, racing towards the wall. None of the Lysians reacted or thought it odd. They had grown accustomed to Edda's strange behaviors. Then, again, they felt content having me amongst them.

I stole a quiet glance at Erik. He had a relaxed look to him, completely unaware of what was coming. Nervous energy vibrated through my being. I did not fear Erik finding me out. I feared his response.

Rain slowed her pace and so did the Lysians as they followed my lead without realizing it. I led them near the single great wide tree in the field outside of the outer perimeter gates of the city. It was a deadly tree, for it marked a critical distance. It was within the area where the Sparrows' arrows could easily find their targets; much further, and some may be challenging by accuracy. We entered the strike zone, where every archer was capable of perfection. The wall seemed so far from where we were, and I couldn't help but be impressed by the Sparrow's skills, though I hoped I would not need to see those talents this day.

Rain came to an abrupt halt, barely breaking away from the group before the Lysians all stopped, turning to face me. I gave the horse a gentle stroke along her mane before dismounting and scanning the perimeter. Edda had breached the entrance. Everyone would have been prepared now, waiting for my signal.

I felt oddly sick.

Erik's brows were drawn, dark brown hair tussled by the wind as he approached me on horseback. "What's wrong?" Concern flashed across his features. Undoubtedly, he noticed my racing pulse. It was bordering a panic.

Erik was my jailer, but he was also tormented by that fact. He didn't want to be what he was to me. I was going to release him from that burden. I just hoped that taking my freedom wouldn't be my undoing. *Our* undoing.

Trust me. Please.

Drawing a deep breath, I willed my heart to slow.

"Don't come closer," I said, taking a few steps back after hitting Rain's hide. The animal moved only several paces away, remaining closer than I wished her to be. If things got ugly, then she was liable to be injured in the madness.

Erik immediately dismounted his stallion, confusion touching his features. Sapphire eyes traveled over my body, searching for a sign of trouble, not yet comprehending that it was not I in trouble, but them.

We were separated by a few meters. Erik could close that distance in the blink of an eye. Which meant I had to act fast. I needed to shield and be ready to defend myself if it came to.

With another deep breath, I forced my body to relax. Emptying my mind of hate and fear, of everything. Burned it all away to nothing. Finally, I released the strength I kept locked deep inside, and it was gloriously sweet as it spread through me. Filling me from within, the power grew until it bubbled over, encasing me in its warmth. My hand moved toward the city's edge, and I focused on what I wanted. A shield.

"What is that?" Kole asked, his attention drawn to something moving at the perimeter gate.

Both Erik and I followed his gaze.

Mist. *My* mist.

It shimmered in the light as it sifted through the dirt, waves splashing up above the grass. I flexed my hand, flicking it up. The mist followed with the motion, and a thick wall molded outside the city's wooden one. No sooner had it formed, than archers appeared at the top of the wall just behind the one of mist. Arrows were nocked and pointed at the Lysians around me.

Erik's eyes snapped to mine, and in that moment, I saw the recognition of a threat in his stare. His gaze darkened, narrowing with frigid intensity, sending a chill crawling up my spine.

A threat. That's what he saw in me.

In my mind, I could almost hear Edda's voice urging me to take action. *Drop them all, now,* she would have said. But despite the itch in my fingers to comply, I hesitated. I didn't want to force them into submission. I wanted them to *choose,* to believe that the person they had come to know was on their side. I longed for their trust as much as I wanted to trust them in return.

"You are all free to leave, but I am not coming with you," I began, but they did not give me a chance to say more. Those still on horseback dismounted. Only Erik and Kole remained stone-still, not advancing towards me.

The other Lysians lunged.

With another flick of my wrist, a thick mist enveloped their lungs, choking off their breath. They dropped to the ground, gasping for air, while I took a few cautious steps back.

Meanwhile, Erik maintained his position. He observed his Lysians being smothered around him and then he turned to me with fury in his eyes. A dark simmering anger surrounded him, scorching away the calm, leaving a composed predator.

The way he looked at me caused unease to press into my chest. The discomfort constricted my breathing.

Relaxing my wrist, the mist dissipated, allowing the Lysians to catch their breath. "Please, just go," I pleaded, taking another step back. "The Lysians in the city will be released as soon as I return home. I don't want any of you to be harmed."

A growl from Kole caused the hair on the back of my neck to stand on its ends. His icy gaze was the coldest that I had ever seen. No longer was he looking upon me as someone he knew. Gone was any trace of possible friendship.

He was a hunter, and I was the hunted.

"Don't . . ." I warned, but it was too late.

Kole charged, closing the space between us incredibly fast, but not fast enough.

An electrical sensation spread through me, connecting me with my power. It flowed swiftly through my body like liquid over my skin. In an instant, it pooled in my palms, traveling to my fingertips and past them. With the spread of my fingers, Kole's lungs filled with moisture, and a step later, he stumbled, falling to the ground. His hand went to his throat.

I turned to Erik. "Stop this." It was both a command and a plea. I did not want to fight them, to hurt them. I only wished to take my freedom. Could he not understand that?

Please, trust me.

I relaxed the mist within Kole, and he had a coughing fit on the ground. The other Lysians regained their lung functions and stood, poised to strike. Though this time, they all held an air of caution. I was not just a Bavadrin. I was a conjuror. Instead of acting again, they waited for their King's instructions.

Erik's stillness was predatory as he surveyed me.

"Go home," Erik ordered his Lysians in a low growl. They hesitated. "Now!" he snapped, and with that, they sprang into action, following his instructions. All of them, except for one.

"I will not leave you with *her*," Kole said with venom, and I felt the sting of it.

So quickly, he turned from being a companion to someone who saw me as something revolting. So quickly, those moments that I had hoped could withstand the events of this day disintegrated into nothing of meaning. All the time we had spent together lost all significance to him as soon as I tried to free myself of their control.

"Are you kidding me?" My voice was raw in my throat. He had a lot of nerve acting as if I were the villain in the situation. The way he looked at me hurt more than I would have liked to admit. Was I foolish to have hoped for a different outcome? Were they truly going to behave as the Lysians we were told stories of as children? Aggressive and without consideration of the situation?

"I will join you shortly, Kole. I will not ask you to leave again," Erik said to his friend while keeping his eyes trained on me the entire time as he would an enemy. The Lysian King finally saw me as a worthy opponent, one deserving of his full attention. Though a fight was not something I wished for.

A minute later, we were alone in the field with hundreds of Bavadrin arrows pointed our way.

Thoughts raced about my mind. There was so much I wanted

to say to help him see I was not a threat. I hoped for a chance to spare our fragile relationship from crumbling altogether.

Sadly, I did not have the chance to tell him anything.

One moment we were standing in the open field, and the next, he was before me.

Had he always been this fast? The thought flickered through my mind before adrenaline drowned it out.

Erik grabbed me and slammed me against that single massive tree. Hard. His large hand caught both of mine, and he nearly crushed my wrists above my head into the rough bark, holding me firmly in place. My back stung from being shoved so forcefully that my breath was briefly knocked out of me.

His gaze pierced mine with fierce intensity. He barred his teeth. Had his canines always been that frighteningly sharp? In that moment, Erik was far more predator than King.

He caught me so easily.

Stupid girl, you should have just dropped him to his knees when you had the chance, I heard Edda's voice chastising me.

38

ERIK

Ariana trembled, her body pressed against mine, her hands locked above her head. My senses were ablaze, focused entirely on her. The archers she had hidden away were of little concern; they wouldn't risk harming their leader with me so close. They lacked a clean shot, thanks to the wall she'd conjured and the shelter of the tree. This allowed my focus to remain solely on the Bavadrin girl who surprised me to the point of breathlessness.

With her hands locked above her head, I doubted that she could conjure. Though she had shown herself to be shockingly powerful with her gift, able to build a wall against the one already there to offer her people protection from my flames. Then, to have kept it in place when focusing on my Lysians was incredible. Never had I met another conjuror with such abilities. It was impressive. However, it also fell short.

Ariana was true to her kind. The cunning Bavadrins. She had me completely fooled from the start. I always saw her as irrationally confident and brave, but it was never really irrational, not when she harbored such a strength within her. A power that she had done well keeping secret, pretending to be no more than a girl. It took little to fool me, for I never challenged that thought. She was small and slender, a woman who was no true physical threat to me or my Lysians. I could not have been more wrong. Her mind I knew better than to underestimate, and yet I found myself doing just that.

Ariana was powerful enough for her plan to have worked.

She could have survived her little stunt.

If only she had not made two mistakes.

First, she allowed me to get too close. My senses and speed surpassed hers, a fact she knew well. She should have kept her distance.

Second, she hadn't mastered conjuring. It was clear she was not fully trained, using her hands as a crutch. Her mist moved with each twitch of her fingers, a telltale sign.

Conjuring often began with the body directing energy. It was easier to control and focus that way. She should have trained to let go of that crutch, to conjure with just her eyes or even her mind. Maybe then she wouldn't have found herself trembling in my hands, her green eyes wide as they looked up at me.

The smell of fear surrounded her. Its sweet scent filled my lungs with every breath, and just like that, we became what we always were. She was the rabbit and I the wolf. It took her only a few moments of struggle before her body stilled the way a rabbit would. It was a survival instinct to freeze. No point in fighting when there was absolutely no escape. Don't fight the predator, and he might lose interest. Unfortunately for her, I was no wolf. I was worse. My interest was not easily lost.

I shifted my hold on her hands, and she winced in pain. *Good.*

My free hand slid around her throat. Her breath hitched at the contact, my fingers running across the tender skin at her neck. Her pulse thrummed beneath my fingertips, blood rushing as it pumped adrenaline through her body, needlessly fueling her muscles, for she had nowhere to go.

Anger rippled through me for the position we found ourselves in. I hated her for the trust I built with her. Trust that crumbled as if it were made of soft dry sand blown away by one strong gust of wind. What other ways had she fooled me? Shadows of doubt were cast upon every moment I shared with her, and it infuriated me. I refused to allow her to make a mockery out of me. I never wished her any harm, yet now I nearly relished it. That fact only angered me more, for I had become the monstrous Lysian the Bavadrins told stories of.

"Erik," she spoke my name, no more words necessary. There was no apology. No plea for mercy. Only her gaze, locked on mine.

I growled, my anger spellbinding. What a fool I had been.

Rage rippled through me once more, but it did not feel powerful. Some of its strength was stolen by the knot in my stomach, which only grew by the second.

I had two options.

Killing her would regain control, the safest choice for my Lysians. Edmond and Jorn would approve. Yet the thought turned my stomach.

Or I could set her free. She claimed to want to help, but her sincerity was a mystery. I wished to believe her, pathetic as it seemed.

Another growl escaped me. Killing her felt wrong, but her deception cut deep. She had the power and cleverness to be lethal.

My skin grew hot with frustration, fire burning for a release. So, I released it.

A circle of flame surrounded us and the single tree in the extensive field. Its heat brushed up against my skin, hot enough to be uncomfortable to all except for the one wielding it. My conjuring would not harm me. Unfortunately, the same could not be said for her.

Ariana's heart fluttered like a hummingbird's wings. Death by fire wouldn't be a painless one. Still, she remained silent as her large green eyes remained locked on me.

"Go ahead." My voice was a snarl. "Put the flames out, *conjuror*." I commanded her to do something I was fairly certain she could not, not while I held her hands pinned above her head.

She tried to move her hands anyway, her crutch, but could not free them from my hold. I then felt her try anyway. I sensed tiny wisps of moisture lick the flames from their base on the ground, but it was too little to ever hope of putting a dent in the fire surrounding us.

Sweat beaded on Ariana's forehead with both effort and the heat of the blazing fire. Finally, the little bits of moisture she could conjure died out. She failed.

In the distance, yelling erupted from the perimeter of the Bavadrin city. Panic had grown, yet they remained sealed away. Ariana was not only using the barrier to keep me out, but she was also using it to keep them in, keeping them away.

Briefly, I glanced at the wall she created for her people, surprised to find it still fully erect. There was no sign of weakening. If she were to release her hold on it, then maybe she could hope to survive my flames. Certainly, she must have known most of her energy was keeping the wall up. Conjuring anything while maintaining such a thing would prove to be more difficult.

"Spare them," she said when noticing my attention was on the village beyond instead of her. "This wasn't their doing."

Ariana was unlike the others of her kind. She unquestionably was cunning, as was warned of the Bavadrins, but they were never known to be selfless. They were painted as greedy and selfish. Yet there was a nobility to Ariana, like a cloak that perpetually hung around her. *Noble.* A word I never even dreamt of equating to a Bavadrin, especially one who was so capable of fooling me.

My anger shifted its attention from her onto myself. I had been the monster who took her from her home and tried to force her to do my bidding. She may have hidden her conjuring from me, but she only used it in an attempt to come home, never against me or the Lysians except now to protect herself. Yet when the roles were reversed, I used flame to burn her city and her people. I would have destroyed everything in my path were she not brave enough to pull my attention and give me her father. I was the Lysian the Bavadrins warned their children of, but she was not the Bavadrin we had been told of.

The surrounding fire vanished, and I looked at her once more.

Her breath was shallow and quick with the panic she was trying her best to control. The scent of fear clung to her. She thought I may end her life, and suddenly both sadness and regret flooded me.

I leaned closer, her breath hitching. She should fear me. The monster who trapped her. If it were Edmond in this position, then he would have snapped her neck without hesitation.

"You need to keep a larger distance from your enemies, and you need to learn to conjure without the use of your hands." I gave her two bits of advice before releasing her.

Her large green eyes stared at me, yet she did not move a single muscle.

I would have preferred to put a healthy distance between us, but the archers going mad on top of their walled perimeter kept me confined to the shelter of the tree. I could only take two steps away from her. Like a caged animal, I searched for an escape, finding no good option. Everything was too open in the grassland. I could try to run. I was fast, but I did not know how skilled the archers were. There were stories of Bavadrins annihilating droves of Lysians with their deadly arrows. I did not know if those along the wall were still as skilled as their ancestors. I could attempt to encase myself in flames until disappearing from view. That would likely be the best choice given the situation.

Ariana brought her hands together in front of her, rubbing her wrists. Her eyes averted, a look of confusion passing through them. I wondered what she was thinking at that moment. Her hand then moved, her focus shifting to the wall that separated us from her people.

I tensed, expecting the barrier to drop, for her people to swarm out and try to imprison me for my actions. Many of them would not survive such an attempt, but they could certainly try.

To my surprise, the wall only grew, rising further into the sky, blocking the archers completely.

Just as I released her, she was releasing me.

The sounds of flustered Bavadrins rose over the barrier Ariana created. They did not like losing sight of their Superior.

"You are not my enemy, Erik," Ariana said, turning her attention back to me. Though she was very much the same girl who had been living under my roof that entire time, she appeared different. In a way, she appeared more whole. The puzzle of who she was became less of a mystery. Her courage and strength ever since I met her now fit with the person standing before me. No longer was it misplaced.

"That is still to be determined," I commented. Only time would tell whether I was making a mistake in releasing her.

She remained standing with her back to the tree while I walked from her.

Mounting my horse, I rode off without another word, leaving her with Rain as a parting gift.

Ariana's gaze followed me as I moved further and further across the lands until we were no longer able to see one another.

39

ERIK

I found myself thinking back to all that occurred since I first crossed the Bavadrin border a few months ago. Every memory, every interaction with Ariana replayed in my mind as I searched for where I had gotten sloppy and stopped viewing her as the threat that she indeed was capable of being. During her time in the Lysian lands, everything I observed led me to lower my guard. I always harbored a sense of caution when things involved her, yet it was still not enough.

Those final hours of traveling from the Bavadrin lands after the unexpected turn of events were quiet. The trip home was uneventful. No one made a sound, not even Kole. My mood did not welcome anything other than complete and silent obedience.

Unfortunately, my brothers did not harbor the same intellect and began an assault of questions as soon as we returned.

Hours passed, and I allowed them to berate me with their opinions and demands for action. We sat together in a large room that had been made stuffy by the bickering. There were maps and papers with all the information we had on the Bavadrins and the Siddhe laid out on three large tables. Much of it was outdated information from long ago. I had the documents brought up as soon as we returned and had been looking through them till the arrival of my brothers. That was when all planning went out the window, and an argument regarding their appetite for blood ensued. Eventually, we called for Kole and Eislyn to be brought to the meeting. I was most curious to hear their opinions on the situation.

They entered together, clearly noting the tension in the room.

Kole tilted his head towards Eislyn. "What is she doing here?" The disdain which usually accompanied his words towards her was missing. Or perhaps the squabbling between myself and my brothers had warped my view of disdain.

Eislyn raised an eyebrow. "I suppose your teeny tiny brain is not large enough to be of use, and so they called me for backup." It appeared she at least had not lost her bite. Usually, a comment like that from her would send Kole fuming, but he remained oddly composed.

"That's enough." My voice was not loud, yet it commanded submission.

It was not my favorite idea to have Kole and Eislyn together in one room when emotions ran high. Especially when Iver was in that same room. Such an environment was typically not conducive to progress. But in this case, it was necessary.

"You two are as feisty as the day you both broke up." Iver grinned, though I caught his eye remaining on Kole. Had he too picked up on the change and was trying to elicit a response with his words. Perhaps there indeed was something different about Kole's demeanor towards Eislyn.

"Stop being a child," Edmond growled, not wanting to deviate from the reason we were all gathered.

"Careful, brother." Iver turned casually, viewing Edmond from where he sat.

"What are you going to do? Challenge me?" There was the

barest hint of a growl in Edmond's tone. His control was slipping, made clear by the way his entire body tensed.

Iver stared at Edmond with boredom, his demeanor unruffled, though he did not continue to provoke. Finally, a wise action from him. Usually, he always threw caution to the wind.

Ignoring them, I addressed Eislyn. "Ariana is gone," I informed her what everyone else in the room already knew.

"What do you mean?" Eislyn stepped forward as if the action could clear her hearing. She likely wished to have misheard. She glanced at Kole, who kept his attention ahead, waiting for me to elaborate.

"Ariana has re-taken her city," I informed her.

Eislyn's jaw went slack, and in that moment of uncertainty, she again looked to Kole for answers.

I gave the barest tilt of my chin to Kole, allowing him to provide some clarification.

"Ariana is a conjuror. No Lysians were killed during this," he informed. It was the first time in a while that they exchanged words so cordially.

Turmoil had a strange effect on relationships. Usually, many shattered under pressure. But some grew stronger, the force turning the bond into something powerful enough to withstand the turning tides. It was unexpected to see the two of them able to interact without their usual revulsion when blame was easy to throw, for Kole had been Ariana's guard, and Eislyn had been training her to fight. They both were left with plenty of ammunition to use against one another.

"What kind of conjuror?" Eislyn asked in disbelief.

Kole turned to me, for it was not something we had ever seen before.

I answered the question with what little I understood. "I am uncertain. It seemed like mist but stronger, capable of choking the air out of someone's lungs, and capable of creating a barrier around her city."

"Did she attack you?" Eislyn asked me, her head tilting in wonder.

"No."

Her lips curved ever so slightly, eyes narrowing. "You attack her?"

"Not really."

She remained silent for a moment. "Could you have killed her?"

"Yes," I answered and felt Edmond's gaze cut to me, his eyes filled to the brim with anger he struggled to control.

Eislyn's attention dropped to the ground in thought. "I see. So, what, Kole and I are to be some sort of character witnesses for Ariana or something?" She looked back at me, and a flicker of hope passed over her before being replaced with an unreadable calm. "You want to let her go."

Iver's eyes brightened. "You are smart, but I am a little surprised. I thought I sensed relief from you. Do you really wish to spare the Bavadrin?"

Eislyn kept her attention on me, not even acknowledging Iver's comment, making no attempt at answering him.

Iver's head tilted. "Excuse me, are you ignoring me?" When she did not reply, he snorted. "That's a bit childish."

She turned to him then. "And here I thought one of the best ways of interacting with children was to do so on a level which they may understand."

"Are you calling me a child?" Iver smirked.

"Am I speaking to someone else?" she snapped.

Jorn sighed. "The sooner you all focus, the sooner we can go our separate ways." He shook his head, mumbling to himself that he could not believe he was the voice of reason.

Edmond leaned forward. "You are correct, Eislyn. You and

Kole are character witnesses of sorts. Outside of Erik, the two of you have spent the most time with Ariana. Erik leans towards trusting the Bavadrin. We would like to know if you both would have chosen the same."

"What would our answers change?" Kole asked.

"Perhaps nothing or perhaps something," Edmond responded without actually giving an answer.

"There is talk about potentially attacking the Bavadrins and reclaiming control," I informed them, conveying what Edmond's and Jorn's wish was.

"Would you kill her then? If control was taken back?" Eislyn asked.

"That is not of your concern," Edmond stated flatly, not liking that she seemed troubled by the Bavadrin's life being taken.

"Actually, it is," Eislyn replied curtly. "Because despite her being a Bavadrin, *I* trained her. She—"

Jorn grunted a laugh, interrupting Eislyn. "C'mon, she is not Lysian. You were not actually teaching her anything."

"And yet she learned," Eislyn stated dryly, before turning her attention to me once more. "You know I do not take on trainees lightly. Even though Ariana is a Bavadrin she has the drive and determination of the strongest of us. She does not give up. I would trust her at my side if we had to fight side by side against a common enemy."

"You cannot be serious. I thought Iver was just kidding when he said you favored the girl. You, a warrior, are putting your trust in a Bavadrin!" Edmond yelled, a crazed look in his eye as if he could not fathom what was being said.

"Yes, I am," she stated without an ounce of hesitation.

"I never thought you a fool, but this—" Edmond's lip curved up as if he tasted something repugnant.

"You all asked for my thoughts on her. Ariana has the heart of a warrior. Of what I have been able to learn of her, she would never stand with the Siddhe." There was a certainty to Eislyn's words that gave me more relief than she would ever know.

"You would bet your life on this?" Jorn asked, a frown on his angular face.

"I would." Eislyn lifted her chin defiantly.

"Would you bet Kole's?" Iver asked. Despite everything going on, my little brother remained as intrigued by the relationship between Eislyn and Kole as he was by the decision about Ariana.

"I would," she answered, refraining from looking at anyone but me.

I turned to Kole. "And you, what do you make of Ariana?"

"I feel betrayed, for she saw me when I never truly saw her," he answered, and I wasn't sure what to make of his comment. "But I do not wish to be the first to throw the stone. If we go to war with one another, then it should be her decision, for that outcome would be better than if we were to annihilate innocent people for no reason."

"Unbelievable," Jorn growled, looking to Edmond, who mirrored his shock.

"You would risk your own to protect her?" Edmond ground out, his fingers wrapping around the arm of his chair, turning white from his tightening grip.

"To attack may be a greater risk if they do not intend to betray us," Kole stated, eyes slicing to Edmond. "I saw them on the walls of her city, archers. They had not been there when we first took control of the Bavadrin capitol, and yet somehow, they have gathered there now. They were good enough to regain control from our soldiers, injuring them if needed, but without killing. If those archers are a fraction as talented as the old stories paint them to be, then we would lose many of our own in an attack now. And for what purpose? Just to flex our muscles. Ariana knows who we are, and that we are capable of kindness. She will not turn her back on that."

"She has burrowed into your mind, poisoning it," Edmond stated flatly.

Kole shrugged. "In a way, perhaps she has, but the poison there was my own. She helped to clear the fog created by my mind. Someone who can show that kind of patience, to care enough to help the male who is keeping her prisoner, is someone worthy of my faith."

Iver scrutinized Kole a moment before his features smoothed, and he again took on a casual and relaxed demeanor. "Well, that settles it. She will be free to decide her future without our attempt at forcing her hand." He then turned to me. "Unless you disagree?"

"We will wait and see what happens," I stated.

Edmond's eyes grew wide, as if he could not believe what was being said. He had not expected Eislyn and Kole to both agree with me. "You have spent far too long with this Bavadrin, brother. She has clearly wormed her way through your brain. Have you forgotten the entire reason she was here? That our sister is out there somewhere while we sit here entertaining protecting some enchantress!"

A growl rumbled through my throat. "Mind who you are speaking with, *brother*. For I am first your King."

"She needs to be killed, if not for our sister, then to free you all from her spell." Edmond seethed.

"If not for our sister?" Iver exclaimed with mocking surprise. "Spirit knows Iona is a troubled soul. But I doubt our sister would desire the blood spilled from an innocent girl in her name. Especially one who may yet be a powerful ally."

"You truly agree with him?" Edmond looked at Iver while pointing a thick finger at me. It took all my strength not to reach out and snap it in half.

Iver shrugged indifferently. "If you are looking for a brotherly vote on this subject, then I am afraid it's looking like it would be a draw. But we do not vote in such manners. Our *King* decides."

Somehow, Iver and I found ourselves on the same side of something. He likely enjoyed watching Edmond crumble from the situation he found himself in.

When had Iver decided to give the Bavadrin such a benefit of the doubt? I heard Ariana and him speaking that night when they slept by the fire outside the tent after her Ascension. He did not torment her, nor did he show any aggression towards her. On the contrary, they seemed to genuinely have enjoyed each other's company. Was it possible that they found an odd friendship in one another?

"*Ashes*, she has completely wormed her way into your head too!" Edmond exclaimed.

Iver laughed, which only further fueled Edmond's anger. "The only person who could handle being inside this impressive skull is me." He tapped his head with a finger. "My brilliance is too powerful. It would turn any other brain to mush."

Edmond stood abruptly, his chest rising and falling in quick succession. "I'll take care of this Bavadrin witch as we originally planned." Without waiting for a response, he flew across the room, fully prepared to track down Ariana and end her life.

"Edmond!" Jorn called out in warning, which was not heeded.

"Brother," I spoke with a deathly calm.

Edmond broke his march, wavering just enough to hear my words.

"If you take another step, then I will see it as a challenge for the throne." Though my voice was low, the weight of the warning riding on my words was heavy enough that it felt as though I had yelled them.

Edmond froze.

The King's decision was not to be defied, and I had decided. Acting against my desires at this point was a challenge for the throne itself. And if it came down to that, then it would end in his death, for never again would the option of an exile be viable. Not after the last one led to the problem we now had with Hedrek and his followers living in the mountains.

Edmond spun around on his heels, facing me. "You choose that little sorceress over your family?" he yelled, angered by the invisible shackles he thought I had just put him in. But those shackles had always been there, tied to a rope that at first was held by our father, and now me. He was never free to decide such things.

"I choose not to unnecessarily ruin innocent lives," I stated.

"What of our sister's innocent life?" He was blinded by rage, unable to see the complete picture.

"I intend to find her, but I refuse to do it through the murder of someone not deserving of it. Our forces are still growing and in training. Preparing to defend our home from two fronts. Once they are ready, we will reach out to the Bavadrins to request access to move through their lands, and then we will attack the Siddhe. The goal is still to free our Lysians and our sister. That has not changed."

Edmond did not respond, and for an entire ten seconds, we simply stared at one another while he fumed within. His hands balled into fists that he was powerless to throw.

Through clenched teeth, he finally spoke. "May I be excused?" It was about time he remembered his place in this family.

"You may, but I do not want to hear another word of attacking the Bavadrins if they have done nothing to provoke such a response. This is the last we speak of this."

"Fine." He turned on his heels and marched out, taking most of the tension in the room with him.

Iver released a low whistle, leaning back in his seat. "Now that was exciting."

"I don't have the patience for your games, Iver." I glanced at him while he smiled.

He shrugged a carefree shoulder. "It's no game. I agree with you, Erik."

Jorn chortled. "To see the two of you agreeing on a matter like this—" He shook his head.

My attention shifted to our brother. "If you dislike my decision, then the invitation to challenge is open for you too."

"No, Erik. I will not be challenging you. We both know I stand no chance against you. I just hope you know what you are doing." Jorn rose to his feet to leave. He likely wished to console Edmond.

"Killing the girl would deprive the world more than it would do anything to help bring our sister back," Iver commented as he watched Jorn walk away from us.

Jorn stopped, turning to view our little brother. "Deprive the world of what?"

Iver appeared to think it over a moment. "Someone kind, intriguing, and clever."

Eislyn looked at Iver as if he were crazy. "Kind? Since when do you place any value in kindness?" she asked, unable to keep the surprise from her voice.

A broad and cavalier smile crossed Iver's face. "Just because I do not care for it much myself does not mean that others cannot provide it for people."

"You couldn't care less for the weak. Isn't that what you always thought? That kindness only benefits the weak," Jorn pointed out.

"Oh yeah, the weak are of absolutely no use to me. The world would probably be better off getting rid of most of them. But it's also nice of Ariana to be willing to help those less fortunate. I certainly have no intentions of doing it myself." He stroked his chin. "Also, I would like to amend my previous notion, for the strong can also benefit from kindness. If it were not for Ariana's kindness, then we may have lost our King a few weeks ago."

"You are remarkable." Eislyn shook her head in disbelief.

"Thank you." Iver grinned, knowing fair well that she was not complimenting him.

Jorn grunted a laugh, shaking his head as he left the room.

"Erik," Eislyn said while glancing at the tables covered with paper. "Mind if I look through some of these things."

"Help yourselves."

Both Eislyn and Kole went to separate tables.

"What?" I turned to Iver, who was the last of my brothers left in the room. Yet, he was strangely staring at me.

"You surprise me," he stated, tilting his head. "I would have never thought you would let a threat go, no matter how small. If we are wrong, then she is much more than a simple small threat. You know this. You have already considered all possibilities, yet you still let her go."

I smiled tightly. "And look at you, cruel Iver caring about a weak Bavadrin woman."

His eyes narrowed. "We both know she is not weak. As for me being cruel, I am certainly capable of it." He looked at Eislyn and Kole. Though the two of them were not interacting, they were in the same room with the furniture still intact. "That's new." He nodded to them before turning to me once more. "I think our Bavadrin friend may have had something to do with this."

"How would she?" Kole and Eislyn had been at war for years. We all felt the effects of their broken relationship. When their bond broke, it reached my brothers and me as well, cracking ours. We all used to be one unit, and now we were always divided. After what happened between Kole and Eislyn, there did not seem a force powerful enough to quench the raging fires within both of them. How was Ariana, someone who had not known their history, able to have a meaningful impact?

"I told her what happened between them. And now, several days later, Kole seems to have lost some of that deep-seeded rage.

Do you think it is a coincidence? He even commented today that Ariana saw him for who he was, that she helped to clear a fog in his mind." Iver smiled. "Anyway, I am famished. See you later, *my King*." He dipped his head in an embellished performance before taking his leave.

When Iver left the three of us, I too took to one of the open tables, combing over the documents. Hours passed, and each of us had not even reviewed half of the papers on each of our tables.

With a grunt, Kole's hands slammed on the wood. "How can there be so much paper with such little information about the Siddhe."

With a sigh, I took a seat, still holding several sheets in my hands. His frustration was something I was deeply familiar with. I had examined all these same documents for months now, always hoping to find some new bit of information that had previously been overlooked. It constantly felt like I was on the edge of that discovery only to find myself unable to grasp at anything substantial.

"Go take a break. None of this is going anywhere," I said, answering his anger with a knowing sigh.

Kole nodded with an air of defeat.

"Here, I could use a break too." I stood, discarding the sheets onto the table, and titling my head towards the door in invitation. Kole followed a step behind me, but when he moved towards Eislyn, his pace slowed. Once in the hall, I turned to look at him, but his attention was not on me. He stopped.

Though he did not say anything, Eislyn went still, clearly sensing that he stood somewhere behind her. She kept her eyes on the table before her while he kept his on the wall by the door, even as he spoke to her. "There is something I need to say, or I am afraid I may not get another chance to say it."

There was a brief moment of hesitation before he continued. "Years ago, I found something in you that made me feel more alive than I had ever felt in my life. You didn't just see me; you *saw through me*—every flaw, every fear, every broken piece—and somehow, you chose to love me anyway. And I swore to protect you till my dying breath."

He paused for a heartbeat before continuing. "Then Iona happened. I never expected her to . . . I did not know how to react. You were so angry, and I gave you space for your anger to subside. That decision is now the greatest regret of my life." Kole raked his hands through his hair as if frustrated.

I should have left. Let them have this moment in private. Yet I could not bring myself to move. They had not spoken in years, truly spoken. The risk of this going horribly wrong kept me in place.

Kole's gaze fell to the ground as if the weight of his words were too heavy to keep his head up. "I swore to protect you, to put your heart above all else. And yet, through my silence, I made you feel as though I didn't care. My silence became a weapon, a wound I never intended to inflict. The anger I've carried for so long blinded me, made it easier to ignore the part I played in what came after. I see it now—I was the one who first broke the vows we made. The one who failed you."

He drew in a heavy breath. "This knowledge haunts me. It's a torment I cannot escape. I wish to apologize, but no words could capture the depth of my regret. You need to know this, Eislyn: you are the only one I have ever truly wanted in my life. I would have died for you then, without hesitation, and I would still lay down my life for you today. My heart has always been yours, and no anger, no pain, could ever fill the void you've left behind. Not anymore. I'm so sorry, Eislyn" He then simply walked out of the room without even waiting to hear a reply. Kole did not meet my eye when he strode past me.

Eislyn stood utterly still for several heartbeats before finally placing her hands on the table before her. She shifted her weight so that half of it was distributed to her hands as if her legs could not hold her anymore. A tremble shook through her.

I went to her.

"Hey." My hand rested gently on Eislyn's shoulder, a small gesture that shattered the fragile dam holding her together. She spun toward me, her face crumpling as the weight of it all hit her. Her legs buckled, and I caught her, pulling her close. "It's okay." Never in my years of knowing her had I seen a single tear from her, even as children, until that very moment as she sobbed in my arms. She began shaking.

"I thought he didn't care," she whispered between breaths.

"He has always cared," I said. She pushed me away. Regaining the strength in her legs, she paced towards the exit.

Once at the door, Eislyn turned back around with a look of horror in her tear-filled eyes. "What have I done?" Her hand went to her stomach. It was as if, for the first time, she realized she was not the only one pained by the events of their past. "I'm going to be sick." Distressed blue eyes looked back up at me. "How can you not hate me? He is your best friend."

"You both are," I answered.

"Erik, what have I done?" The tears spilled over, running down her face. I moved towards her, but she stepped out of reach, shaking her head in disbelief. "I should go." She pivoted, racing out of the room.

Years had passed since the icy anger first crystallized between Eislyn and Kole, growing colder and more unyielding with time. At first, I had hoped it might thaw, that the tension between them would ease. But instead, the frost only deepened, and the dust of neglect settled on that impenetrable wall of ice. Their pain, sharp and bitter, fed the divide, refusing to fade—until now. At last, that dreadful wall had melted, but it left a raw, aching heap of unre-solved pain.

40

ARIANA

I sat on the floor of an empty room with my legs crossed, hands folded in my lap, and eyes shut. Power thrummed within me. Like oceanic water, it rolled in waves before crashing against my internal control. Focusing, I pushed it beyond of myself. My eyes slid open. Waves from within move out in misty sprays. The entire room filled with a liquid fog that touched everything but me. My gaze drifted up, and my conjuring followed. It condensed and shifted, forming a wall. All of it was done while my fingers were firmly closed into fists.

Clapping came from behind, echoing through the empty space and stealing my concentration. The mist lost its formation, falling into liquid pools before vanishing.

"You're getting really good at that." Landin's voice reverberated through the room.

"Still not good enough." I rose to my feet, turning to face him after wiping the sweat on my brow with my sleeve. "Are we prepared for tomorrow?" I asked. It was the first time we would go through the Lysians' white night without the protection of the treaty. A night when they became more instinctual and less predictable.

He nodded. "Of course we are. We are always prepared for the white night." His smile faltered a touch. "Any word from your . . . *friend.*" It was a bit of a culture shock to stop referring to the Lysians as animals when I first returned home. After all, if we were to be judged by how we cared for our prisoners, the Bavadrins were far less humane. At least in the days when Fraser ruled. Those days were no more. We were going to change the way we viewed others. We were going to change a lot of things.

"No word," I replied lowly. I wondered who would reach out to whom first. Erik wanted my help, didn't he? I expected him to make contact, but he didn't. After my escape and my return home three weeks ago, I heard nothing. It was as if the treaty was never broken, and the boundary between our lands was not to be crossed again.

A part of me longed to go to the border that night. Erik told me that during the white night, he patrolled the edge of his territory. I wondered if that was still true. He probably would think me mad for going there alone on such a night. The thought nearly brought a smile to my lips.

My attention refocused on Landin. He stood stiffly, rubbing the back of his neck.

"What's wrong?" I asked, closing the distance between us. I was in an abandoned building in the woods just outside of our city's border. It was a trek to get there. Landin would not have come all that way if he did not have something he needed.

"Well, nothing that I know of," he said while retrieving something from his pocket, holding it out to me. "This arrived for you." He held out a neatly folded piece of paper, sealed with silver wax. There was no seal imprinted on the wax. It was simply melted onto the paper. My name was written on it.

My pulse spiked.

"The Lysians?" I asked him, taking the letter.

He shrugged, watching me. "I'm not sure. It was brought by bird—" He paused as if he didn't know how to say whatever was on the tip of his tongue.

"What? Tell me."

Landin scratched the back of his head again while shifting on his feet uncomfortably. "Well, it got delivered to some kid who said it arrived by a paper bird."

My brows rose in surprise. "A conjured bird?"

His hand dropped to his side. "Don't know. I was not present when it arrived. I only have what the child said to go from."

I frowned, looking at my name written on the paper in neat handwriting.

Flipping it over, I slid a finger beneath the wax, breaking the seal.

Ariana

I have heard such remarkable stories of you and am dying to know whether they are indeed true. And so, I would like to extend an invitation to dinner in the Siddhe territory. Please feel free to bring a handful of Bavadrins with you, as I do not expect a woman such as yourself to travel alone.

No harm will come to you or your companions on this night as long as there will be no aggression from them. This is something that I will swear to you.

I understand it is roughly a three-day trip from your home to mine. Therefore, I will allow for an appropriate time for you to prepare to make such a

journey and ask that you arrive ten days after receiving this letter.
I highly look forward to meeting you.
-Clause, King of the Siddhe

The letter held a blood smear to seal the promise he made.

Landin swore under his breath, having read it along with me.

"Where is Edda?" I asked while re-reading the note, as if there may have been something I missed or misread.

"I will find her." The sense of urgency in his voice was evident. He certainly had questions floating around in his thick skull but was too surprised by the turn of events to ask any.

"Tell her to meet me in my room," I ordered and ran out of the building with Landin close behind.

Moments later, I was on horseback and riding home. Rain, the horse Erik left behind and the fastest we had on our side of the border, sprinted full speed. Her hooves hit the dirt with powerful grace, sending bits of grass and rock flying. She brought me home in hardly any time.

Running through the building, I hoped that Edda would be there, somewhere. She wasn't. After a thorough search—I looked into some rooms a few times—I finally retreated to my quarters to wait.

After three minutes, I nearly ran back out to recheck all the rooms again. An uncomfortable nervousness took hold of me. It was torture having such a spike of adrenaline coursing through me without having anything to physically act upon. And all of it stemmed from a single letter.

Clause, the ruler of the Siddhe, was calling me forth to dinner.

It was not something I had ever heard of happening before.

I could not imagine what being in the Siddhe King's presence would be like. Did he know the Lysians were after him and that I believed there may have been truth to their accusations?

Edda entered my room with no warning, marching straight to me. She did not ask whether something was wrong, for she could read me like a book. Silently, I held out the letter. She took it in her hands, her eyes flowing over it. When she finished, she released a sigh and sat down on the edge of my bed.

"Well, you must go," she said simply.

"You aren't afraid of what may happen if I do?" I couldn't keep the surprise from my face, for she had decided so quickly.

Her lips pinched, as they often did when she considered how much she wanted to tell me. Were there things she knew of him? "He swore with blood. The letter is sealed with it. The Siddhe King will not break his promise as long as you do not break it either. You should probably prick your finger and mark this too, for good measure." Concern shadowed her features. Edda's gaze flowed over the letter for a second time.

"And you think that will work?" I asked. She spoke as if she knew him, though that was impossible. Did she see him in visions of the future? If she had, she never shared that with me.

Edda shrugged. "Blood oaths worked to keep the lands here separated from the Lysians and Siddhe for millennia until that one Lysian King made sure the treaty broke."

That logic was faulty, for if the Siddhe had been stealing Lysian and Bavadrin citizens, then the treaty was broken long ago. We just had not been wise enough to realize it.

"But Fraser was not killed due to its breaking," I stated. There was still a price to be paid for the breaking of the treaty. The Spirit indicated that *I* was the curse. Though I did not understand how.

"Was he not?" Edda raised an eyebrow.

"Things could have happened the way they did without such a

treaty," I stated. Without Fraser's willingness to even hear others out, his own actions alone sealed his fate, treaty or not.

She shifted the conversation away from the treaty and onto the matter at hand. "You will not always understand. There may be things that turn out not as you expect, but they will be the way they should. I am certain that the person who wrote this letter will not bring you harm, at least not while within the rules of this agreement. Clause is dangerous, but he is also a man of his word."

Edda had always been my protector. However, a strange rift grew between us ever since the Lysians entered our lives. She created distance but without actually leaving my side. Edda was family to me. It was a bond that I thought would never be broken. However, those were childish thoughts, for there were no bonds that could never be broken. Everything breaks with the right amount of pressure.

Still, I trusted her. If she believed it was safe to go, then I would.

I nodded, agreeing to the dinner. Intrigue partially overrode my fear. What would the Siddhe territory be like, what Clause would be like? Would one dinner help me learn whether he took Bavadrins or Lysians?

"But, as soon as the meal is over, leave," Edda warned, looking from the letter back to me. "This says nothing of protection or safety if you spent the night there. Do *not* linger."

"Of course, I wouldn't spend the night." That was something she did not have to worry about. "Will you accompany me?"

Edda hesitated. It was the first time I had ever in my life seen her waver about anything. In all the years I had known her, certainty always guided her. She had eternally known what she wanted to do or what she believed should be done. Her gut was steadfast and fearless in its guidance.

"Yes. For you, I will go," she finally said, placing the letter on the bed and stood.

She walked across the room and paused at the door. "Are you planning on seeing your friend tonight?"

I could never in my life get one over on her.

"Yes," I told her. There was no use in hiding it. If before I was just contemplating going to the border, then now, I was certain. Erik needed to know what was going on. We needed to stop avoiding one another.

"Good," she said, surprising me yet again. "Make contact, but do not tell the Lysian King of that letter, not on a night like tonight. It isn't safe. Set up a different time to meet with him."

"You think he will try to hurt me?"

"The Spirit releases the Lysians tonight. News that will disturb should be given when he has better control of himself. Trust me on this." Her onyx gaze observed me. "Be careful."

"Is that why you never taught me to conjure without my hands?" The question had been gnawing at the edges of my mind every day since my return.

Edda arched a brow, a faint, knowing smile curving her lips. "Clever," she said simply, offering no further explanation. But that single word—her subtle acknowledgment—nearly floored me.

I watched her in silence, my thoughts tangled. How had we ended up here? Then again, I realized, this was how it had always been. She led, and I followed, unquestioningly. "You always knew the Lysians would come."

"No," she replied, her tone turning sharp. "I knew it was a possibility, one thread in a web of futures. But I also knew this—if you ever found yourself at the mercy of the Lysian King, your survival would hinge on him believing himself superior. His kind thrive on control and power." Her mouth twisted into a cruel smile. "Don't look so horrified. If you had kept your distance and forced them to their knees, all would have been well. I gave you options—more chances of survival, depending on the choices you made."

"Why not tell me any of this?" I demanded, the hurt in my voice cutting through the space between us. "Do you not trust me?"

"It's not about trust," she snorted out a cruel laugh. "It's about the danger of tampering with fate. You would have tried to change it, and that is far more perilous than you realize."

"And what is my fate?" I pressed.

"You know enough of it already," she said, her words final, a quiet weight settling in the air between us.

"And the Siddhe King?" I asked after a beat.

"What of him?" Her expression remained unreadable.

"If you know things, then *tell me*." The rumors of his immortality rang in my ears, a constant hum of mystery surrounding the man.

Edda exhaled, her lips curling into something that wasn't quite a smile. "The Siddhe King cannot be contained, and you cannot hope to control him. He does not share the simple, brutish mind of a Lysian, nor does he rely solely on physical strength. He is far more dangerous than that. Let him too close, and he will destroy you. Do not try to understand his motives for *anything*. You may think you want to know, but you do not."

She turned as if the conversation were over.

"Did you know he was taking our citizens?" I called after her.

Her steps slowed, but she didn't face me. "Do you know for certain that he is?"

And then she was gone, leaving me alone.

41

ARIANA

I sat in a field on the edge of the border while Rain indulged on grass several yards away. The night did not seem so dark under the light of the white moon. I wondered what Erik would be like under such power. He always seemed in control. Everything intentional. Would he become more free-spirited?

That was if he actually showed.

Since the treaty guarding against border crossing was no longer in effect, there was a possibility that he may no longer protect the boundary. I sighed, searching for any sign of movement ahead.

Minutes passed, bleeding into an hour, and then another. The morning sun was likely to rise sometime soon, and I was losing faith that he would ever appear.

Was all of this just a waste of time?

Movement at the edge of the woods snagged my attention, and I jumped to my feet. Someone or something stirred amongst the trees, close enough for me to notice but not for me to make out what it was. A breeze blew from my back, carrying my scent in their direction. If they had not heard or seen me yet, they undoubtedly smelled me now if they were Lysian. Whatever it was stopped, and the night turned incredibly still. I took a tentative step back, away from the forest, wondering if I made a mistake in coming here.

I was prepared to bolt in Rain's direction when another movement drew my attention. A Lysian stepped out into the clearing, dark eyes focused on me.

Erik.

I nearly sighed in relief.

He stood there for what felt like eternity before slowly closing the distance between us, though there was nothing casual in his movements. I was used to him being quick when he was so alert. This was almost worse. It gave me time to watch as he drew nearer, a predator taking its time, closing in on its prey. My heart jackknifed in my chest.

I took a small step back in apprehension, and it was an effort not to take more to keep the distance between us from shrinking further. *I had come to see him. He will not harm me,* I told myself. *Edda would not have allowed me to go if she saw it as dangerous.* I said these things to myself to quiet my growing nerves.

Erik stalked closer. His focus remained entirely on me. When I stepped back, his gaze tracked my movement before finding my eyes once more, pinning me with his stare.

"Hi," I managed to say.

He stilled. Standing under a beam of moonlight, as if the Spirit itself had blessed him with eternal light. The sight of him was breathtaking.

"Why have you come here?" His voice was cold, distant.

Squaring my shoulders, I kept my chin lifted. "I have been working on what you said to."

Erik's head tilted to the side inquisitively. I did not need to elaborate, for he understood what I meant. Without twitching a single finger, flames came from the ground, but instead of circling around us, they formed a line between us.

Without moving a muscle in my hands, the energy of my power flowed through me. I harnessed it, condensing it, sending it out towards the flames. Fire hissed when mist intermingled with it. Sending more of my strength towards it, I focused on the flames, and soon they shrank in size before disappearing into smoke altogether.

A muscle in his jaw flexed. "Appears you have been learning. However, you still let me get too close."

"I am not a threat to you," I said. For the only reason he would have been one to me was if he thought I was one first. Erik was not a monster that killed for sport. Reason controlled his actions. At least on normal nights.

Without responding, he continued moving forward, further closing the distance until we stood just out of reach of one another. His scent enveloped me, a heady mix of earth and fire that made my head spin. It was not until that moment that I realized I missed the smell of him. What an odd thing to realize.

Eyes so blue they looked like deep dark pools in the night, lifted to the moon. "Why have you come here?" he asked, attention dropping to me. Again, his tone was uncomfortably cold. His broad shoulders remained tense.

I bristled. "I couldn't have simply wanted to see you?" The reason for my presence did not shadow the fact that I also *wanted* to see him. Over the past few weeks, my thoughts often slipped towards him. I was curious to know what he thought of how I took my freedom back, of my being a conjuror.

"You should not have come." His gaze flickered to my throat. "It's dangerous." Those eyes then drifted down my body before rising to meet mine once more. Predacious power circled him. A vortex of energy that pressed into me. The night made him feel more menacing. Or had I forgotten what being around him felt like?

"I'll be fine," I said, though I wasn't sure if I was trying to convince him or myself.

He scowled, looking back at the moon. Was he searching for answers up there? My attention lifted to the star flecked sky finding nothing out of the ordinary. Though with Lysian vision, perhaps he saw things up there that I was blinded to.

"How have you been? How is Kole?" I asked, my attempt at having him open up.

"Fine," he answered flatly.

"You're angry?"

"No." Again, he answered with a single word.

"Why are you so distant?" Erik had seemed more welcoming when Fraser had him locked up in prison than he was now. "I thought you wanted my help?"

He observed me. "You know what I desire. The way I see it, the next decision is yours to make. You tell me when you are ready to help, if ever."

"I don't understand why you are behaving like this. . ." I stopped myself from finishing the thought, for it sounded pitiful. Despite everything, I believed we had been forming a friendship. That was true, wasn't it? Yet now, it seemed like he did not want to acknowledge any of it. It was as if he had built up walls in the few weeks I had been gone, walls primarily against me.

"Despite everything, I actually liked you." I shared a bit of truth, hoping it would warm him towards me.

"You actually liked me." He parroted, as if trying to understand my angle. If it was possible for him to tense even more, he did.

I blew out a breath. "Are you trying to pretend that you did not like me too? That I was just a prisoner and nothing more?"

He moved so fast. Suddenly his hand was around my throat. Instinctively I recoiled, and when I couldn't step away, I gripped his forearm. My pulse beat against his palm as his fingers tightened, though not enough to cut off my breathing.

I was too stunned to voice any words, especially when Erik leaned closer. He drew in a deep breath, as if inhaling me. The gesture was oddly intimate. His lips were close enough to be dangerously inviting.

Danger. My senses screamed. But the warning lost itself to the heat burning beneath my skin. Something darkly thrilling shot through me, drowning out thoughts of reason or caution. It was as if I grew drunk by his proximity.

My breath hitched as his free hand slid to my hip, his fingers biting into my flesh with a possessive touch. The corners of his lips lifted. His smirk was infuriatingly confident as his gaze roamed over my face, devouring me. He drew me closer till his lips were just shy of mine. With his hand at my throat, I was completely at his mercy. Except, I could still conjure. I *allowed* him to hold me like this. His eyes barely widened, as if realizing the same thing, before they narrowed.

His breath ghosted against my cheek as he said, "I want you gone." He released and shoved me away.

As quickly as it began, it was all over. The emotional whiplash was nearly too much. Was he toying with me? Trying to scare me?

I stumbled, catching myself.

My attention fell to his feet. An uncomfortable fervor coated my skin in embarrassment. What was I supposed to say to that?

Silence spilled between us until he finally spoke again, his voice taking on a gentler tone. "As much as I would like to walk you home, especially on a night like tonight, I cannot. Your men will see me as a threat, particularly on this occasion. I will be taken as an immediate risk. They will attack, and I will defend myself. You will be forced to protect your own. So, it will come down to you and me at odds. Blood will be spilled. This is where we are, the world we live in." His dark eyes continued to cut into me. "You should not have come here and on the night of the white moon. What if another Lysian approached from the border? What if they attacked you? Would you have killed them to protect yourself? Where would such an act have left us then? You are being irresponsible to both your people as well as mine. I never thought you this foolish."

I stared at the ground like a scolded child.

"You're right." It was stupid to have ever imagined anything other than what he described. Still, disappointment settled in my stomach. I had been eager to see him, to be near him.

I felt him watching me as shameful embarrassment washed over me.

He sighed, reaching for me again. Warm fingers curled around my forearm, sending a jolt of awareness through me. His touch was gentler this time, enough to tug my gaze back toward him. Our eyes locked, his stare piercing.

"I wish things were different," he said softly yet with an edge of something that almost seemed like... desperation? His voice touched me where his hand didn't, and my skin felt as though it had been set on fire again. Surly he knew the effect he had on me.

"You push me away, and then say this, as if you..." I shook my head. "What is it that you want from me, Erik?"

His hand fell from my arm. Instead of retreating, he took a purposeful step towards me. I kept my feet firmly where I stood, refusing to retreat from him. He did not touch me again, yet I *felt* him in that space. His presence filled it, as if he set the air itself ablaze. Authority rippled off him, the force of it delightfully commanding. His eyes bore into mine as I held his gaze.

His head tilted while he viewed me, the movement wolf like. "I want you to run from me," he admitted, his voice almost daring. Without restraint, his eyes roamed over me in a way that had my face warming, especially when they paused a beat too long on my lips. "I think I would really enjoy catching you."

I felt the heat of his unhurried appraisal in my bones, in the way my pulse spiked.

I could no longer draw breath. And as if to prove a point that I did not fear him, I reached towards him. Erik stood deathly still as my fingers trailed the edge of his hand before gliding up his arm. I traced a path up to his shoulder. His collarbone. Down his chest.

Erik's hand wrapped around my wrist, stilling me with my palm pressed to his chest. Over a heart that beat unbelievably fast. "You're playing with fire, Ariana."

My skin prickled with awareness. There was *definitely* desire in those dark eyes.

So, feelings were reciprocated after all.

The double entendre wasn't lost on me, and I couldn't help but feel a surge of warmth flood my body. "I like the heat," I answered, surprising myself with the boldness of my words.

"You're making this difficult," he muttered, his voice coarse. He released my wrist and my hand fell to my side. But neither of us moved away. The air crackled with tension.

"Sometimes I rather enjoy being difficult."

He exhaled a shallow breath, face tilting towards the moon. "Ariana." The sound of my name coming from him in that tone did things to me. "I need you to leave." His attention dipped to my lips, remaining there. Something painfully desperate shone in his eyes when they lifted. "Please go."

"What if I don't want to?"

His entire body went rigid, a myriad of emotions playing across his face in the moon light.

"Are there not enough Bavadrin males to entertain you?" he replied sharply, his tone hacking through the charged air like a blunt knife. Erik stepped away, withdrawing. "This is incredibly stupid of you." It was as if he slapped me with those words. His lips curled, flashing his elongated canines.

"You're hot and cold," I said, keeping the hurt out of my voice.

"One moment you're pulling me close, and the next you're shoving me away. I don't understand."

Erik's jaw clenched. "We live in different worlds. This . . ." he gestured vaguely between us, "it can't happen."

This time I was the one adding more physical distance between us as I stepped back. He had me standing before him, feeling rejected and foolish, when he was the first to start blurring the lines. This was not a game I wished to play. "There is something I need to talk to you about, but it isn't appropriate for tonight. Though it is urgent, so the sooner, the better."

"What—" He stopped himself, evidently holding himself back from asking for more information, and probably understanding that there may have been a good reason for me not to wish to share more on the night of the white moon. He nodded. "Meet here the day after tomorrow in the afternoon?"

"Will you be able to get home and back so quickly?" I asked, surprised.

He smiled wickedly, lifting a dark brow. "You truly underestimate the stamina of the Lysians. I will be here, along with my brothers."

I did not let my mind flirt with the word *stamina*, he said so pointedly it was most certainly flirtations. The white moon version of Erik played mind games. Not that he likely wanted to. It was wholly clear he was being pulled in various directions and did not have the slightest idea of which path to choose.

"I'll see you then." I turned, swinging myself onto Rain, annoyed by this entire encounter. He ignited a fire, stirring desire within the both of us; I felt it, saw it. Then he shoved me away, leaving me confused and embarrassed about this entire thing.

"I see you have been taking good care of Rain," Erik noted, appraising the horse as if he were making sure she was still healthy. That only angered me more. Of course, the horse was cared for.

"She was abandoned. I'm fairly certain she likes me better than her previous owner, anyway," I commented, turning her towards home.

His lip twitched. "And who was her previous owner?"

"A Lysian with poor manners," I replied, no longer looking at him.

Rain sprang forward, moving into a gallop as we began our long trip back. I kept her running full speed until I no longer felt those dark eyes watching me.

42

ERIK

We did not have to wait long before catching sight of Ariana and the others on horseback. It brought me an odd sense of pleasure to see that she still rode Rain and that the horse continued to favor her. The animal did not bond quickly with riders, yet she had formed a steady one with the Bavadrin Leader Superior. It was enough that the horse remained with Ariana instead of following the rest of the Lysians home.

Seeing Ariana on the white night was startling. I could not deny that it was good to be near her. With that defiant look in her eyes, refusing to fear the things she should. Never had I imagined seeing her at the border on a night such as that. Still, she continued to act recklessly bold, even for a conjuror. What if Hedrek had come down from the mountain with a pack of Lysians and attacked her? It was as if that possibility never crossed her mind. The entire time, she just assumed that if she encountered any Lysian it would be me, and even that should not have been a comfort to her. She had grown too comfortable around us.

Ariana did not arrive at the meeting alone. Landin, Edda, and two other Bavadrin men I never noticed before accompanied her. Wolves approached from the distance, keeping a large berth between themselves and the Bavadrins, though it was apparent they followed them.

The Bavadrins all dismounted, joining us on foot. Ariana stood with an air of unintentional allure, her riding leathers hugging her body in ways that made it impossible not to notice every curve. The fitted shirt accentuated her frame, while the pants followed the lines of her legs with maddening precision.

Her cloak, clasped at her throat, billowed slightly in the wind, offering glimpses of the figure beneath as it moved. The fabric framed her like a shadow, the hood hanging loose against her shoulders, exposing the windswept strands of her hair that tumbled in defiance over her shoulder. While the other half of her hair remained intertwined with stones and gems as was custom for their Leader Superior.

"Thank you for meeting with us. There is something I wanted you to see," Ariana greeted us briefly before holding out a sheet of paper. There was none of the warmth coming from her that was present the other night. Her entire demeanor was rigid.

I took the paper from her, noticing the blood on the bottom first. By the smell, I knew it was hers mixed with someone else's. My eyes glided over the words, and I could not keep the growl from my throat. Handing the letter to the nearest of my brothers, I then looked into the unwavering green eyes staring at me.

"When did it come?" I asked.

"Morning of the white night," she answered. That left just a few days until she needed to leave if she intended to go.

"You plan on meeting with him?" Iver's eyes drifted over the letter in his hands.

"It's an opportunity to get a better understanding of Clause and much-needed information. Our knowledge of the Siddhe is dangerously limited. Most of it is ancient or collected from Seers over the years," Ariana pointed out.

"We know he can take a conjuror's powers," Edmond stated. "Seeing as he's also someone to play tricks, you don't want to spend much time around him, for obvious reasons." Edmond paused then. "We also know he's an ancient conjuror, hundreds of years old."

Jorn shrugged before voicing his thoughts. "I don't see what the problem is. I say let her go. If she dies, it's no skin off our backs, but if she returns, then she may have useful information."

A growl rippled through me.

Edda smiled wickedly. "Clause does not take the powers of a conjuror. He just mutes them. Conjurors do not affect him, but he in return has a lot of power over them," she corrected Edmond, who narrowed his gaze on her.

"How do you know such things?" Iver asked.

"She is a Seer," Ariana answered, as if that was enough of a reason. "Well, I have said everything I needed to." She reached for the letter as if preparing to take it and leave.

My voice stilled her before the paper touched her fingertips. "That's it?" I could not believe that was all. She dropped this in our laps, and then wished to leave without sharing her plans. That would not cut it.

"What more is there?" Her gaze sliced towards us, hand falling to her side, and I realized she was angry, though I was not sure exactly about what. "I wished to keep you apprised, as this may affect your future plans. That is all."

I took a deliberate step towards her, gaining her full attention, ignoring the way Landin inched forward as if prepared to shield her if I were to attack. "You are just going to march into this Siddhe Kingdom and hope he will allow you to leave?"

"Does it look like I march anywhere? I was thinking of taking more of a strolling pace," she replied flippantly, and Iver's lips twisted into a smirk.

Another rumble traveled up my throat. This was not a joke.

"Clause is a man of his word," Edda stated, "Though he is indeed dangerous, he will uphold his promise. She will be released unscathed as long as he is not threatened." The old woman's willingness to agree to such a thing only further infuriated me. Being a Seer, shouldn't she know the immense danger Ariana would be in by being within reach of the Siddhe King?

"The ancient stories told of him painted him as cruel, powerful enough that even time could not touch him, for age never wore him down. Years of life only hardened him, and he had lived long enough for several life spans." I warned of the little we knew. My attention turned to the old bat. "You said you would protect her. That you would not allow harm to come to her."

Edda's lips flattened into a straight line.

"I am capable of protecting myself," Ariana stated curtly.

"She certainly is. After all, she bested you, didn't she, Erik?" Edmond smiled bitterly. Still cross with the choice of releasing her and the Bavadrins from our control, choosing to see it as a weak decision on my part.

Iver surprised me with the caution in his voice when he asked Ariana, "You are certain you wish to do this?"

Her gaze shifted to him, as stubborn as it had been when viewing me. "Not at all. But it is the choice I made. I only hope to come back with some answers for both you and me."

"You think he'll provide you with answers? That he'll just come out and say he's abducting Lysians?" Jorn folded his arms across his chest.

"If we assume that he is a collector of conjurors, what makes you think he won't add you to his collection?" I asked. Unease held me in its grimy grip, and I did not seem able to shake it off. She was willingly placing herself in danger, just as she had when she stepped into my cell after Fraser's lashings. But not every caged beast responds identically. Just because I spared her did not mean that the next would do the same. She was gambling with her life as if it were nothing.

Ariana leveled her green gaze at me. "Careful, you almost sound worried about a Bavadrin."

Iver snorted. "He worries, alright."

Her delicate jaw clenched at Iver's comment, and she turned to him, taking back the note, folding it, and placing it in a pocket. "There is nothing to deliberate. I am going. As a sign of respect and hope that we can form some sort of cooperation with one another, I decided to share this information with you." She walked over to stand beside Rain, running a hand down the side of the horse's neck.

"I will come to your city before you are to leave, and I will stay there until you return from the Siddhe," I informed her. There would be no budging from this.

Her gaze narrowed. "Why?"

"To know as soon as possible what this invitation means." My hands curled into fists at my side.

"And to make sure you do not betray him," Edda added.

Ariana waited for me to deny the Seer's comment.

I didn't. Not because I did not trust Ariana, but because this was how I was going to ensure that I got my way.

Ariana threw her horse's reins down. Anger radiated from her. She stomped towards us until she stood nearly toe to toe with me. Though she had to look up to meet my eyes, the anger mixed with raw willfulness somehow made her seem taller. "After everything, you still do not trust me? I did not need to share any of this with you." Her voice was a soft snarl, breath becoming uneven.

Jorn stepped towards us with open palms, as if that would

placate her. "Listen, it doesn't have to be Erik to go. I will go in his place if you prefer. We realize that it is not exactly only my brother's decision. It is yours as well. But if we are to work together moving forward, this is what we need. Good faith alone is not enough. My sister's life hangs in the balance. We've never had this kind of an opportunity before." He was trying to play to her kindness.

"But if you refuse, we will assume that you have sided with Clause. You will be an enemy," Edmond stated, offering a different incentive. We were pressuring her.

I did not deny his words. Though I did not know how much I agreed with them. The one thing I did know was that I would be there when Ariana left her city and when she returned. One way or another.

"You cannot be serious." She turned to me with wide eyes.

"I very much am." My tone was final. Were she a Lysian, she would have agreed at once and perhaps even asked forgiveness for denying me my wishes. Instead, she stared right at me defiantly, fury swirling magnificently in those green eyes.

Landin joined the conversation for the first time. "You do not have the authority to tell her what to do."

Iver answered his comment with a relaxed smile. "We are only offering options. Cause and effect. Allow for our involvement, and the bond between our nations can begin to form. Keep us at bay, and some will be left to assume the worst and prepare for that outcome as well."

Ariana's face was reddening. "Fine. Erik is welcome to come stay in the city for a short time." Her gaze pinned me. "And one other Lysian of your choosing can accompany you, but that is it. Be aware that while in *my* home, you will have no say in anything. You will follow *my* lead. Are these terms agreeable?"

I restrained a smile at the victory. "Yes."

Her gaze narrowed as if doubting I could follow those terms.

"Very well." She mounted her horse, and the other Bavadrins did as well. "You know the way to the city," she stated, letting me know we would not get an escort from the border, not that we needed one. Ariana did not wait for a response before they all took off.

A minute later, we began heading in the opposite direction.

43

ARIANA

Shay sensed Erik's approach first. The wolf informed Willis, who told me in turn. Erik had chosen Kole to accompany him, and I hardly managed to refrain from going to greet them. I told the Lysian King they would not have a guide, and I certainly refused to trouble myself to act like one. So instead, I paced around the entrance to the Superior's dwelling, the home I had grown up in, thanks to Fraser.

A tendril of nervousness wrapped around me, and no amount of pacing would loosen its grip. Erik was going to visit the city, genuinely visit, as a guest. And Kole was with him. I wasn't sure which I was more anxious about.

"You are going to wear a hole in the floor," Landin mused from where he leaned against the wall, arms folded across his broad chest.

I pivoted. "I can't help it."

"Too excited to see your... *friend*?" He raised a brow.

"If you cannot play nice, then you can leave." I shot back, though the heat in my tone wasn't quite sharp.

Landin snorted in amusement. "You play nice enough with him for all of us."

I paused at that.

"What?" Landin laughed. "Don't look so shocked. I've known you since we were little, Ariana. You're my best friend—I can read you. And it's painfully obvious you like him, in more than a diplomatic way."

"I don't know what you mean," I said stiffly.

Landin pushed himself off the wall, his arms falling to his sides as he closed the distance between us. "Are we starting to keep secrets from each other now?"

"No," I said quickly, shaking my head. "It's just... I've barely gotten out from under his thumb."

"And now you want to get under a different part of him." His grin was teasing.

"Landin," I snapped, managing to keep my jaw from dropping, "is this how you talk to your Leader Superior?"

"This is how I talk to my best friend."

"You keep reminding me of that, as if you're worried about losing the title." I viewed him skeptically. "And since when are you so tolerant when discussing Erik?"

He rolled his eyes. "I enjoy reminding you because you were my friend before you became my Leader Superior. And for the record, if the Lysians harm you, all tolerance is gone. Until then, I'm trying to follow your lead. And Willis's, I suppose. Just know that if it comes to acting in your best interest opposed to the greater good of *whatever*, then I will choose you."

I narrowed my eyes at him, though his words struck deeper than I cared to admit. "That's a dangerous sentiment."

"I will *always* choose you," he said firmly.

"Don't say that," I said quickly, the weight of his words tightening my chest. "You are Bavadrin." The reminder meant as much for me as it was for him.

"You're family," he shot back. "And don't pretend you wouldn't do the same for me. You already have."

The words twisted something inside me. "Landin..."

His eyes softened, filled with understanding, as he pushed toward the memory I wished he hadn't brought up. The night I gave up Fraser. The night I chose Landin over my duty. The night I defied the Bavadrin ways to save him.

Before either of us could say more, a firm knock interrupted the moment.

Willis stepped inside. Behind him, two Lysians followed. Both were imposing, their gazes immediately pinning me in place. One's eyes were dark pools of blue, the other's cold as ice.

Regaining the movement of my legs, I strode towards them.

"The Lysian King and his travel companion have arrived," Willis stated the obvious, as if I had not known that they approached.

I smiled politely. "Thank you. You may go now, Willis." I twisted around, adding, "you too, Landin."

Landin slowly made his way to the exit, as if to make sure I was confident that I wished to be left alone with the Lysians. He left when I did not change my mind.

Erik glanced around the room before his gaze slid back to me, and he commented. "Leadership suits you."

I scoffed. "As if you would know what kind of leader I am."

"I do," he said with a certainty that begged to be challenged.

Instead, I addressed the other Lysian in the room. His thick blond hair was pushed back by the wind of travel. "Kole, it's good to see you."

He nodded, his icy blue gaze sliding over me to my toes before traveling back up to my face. "You hide some power in that little Bavadrin body of yours." There was no trace of that anger he had directed at me the last time we had been together. When he viewed me as an enemy.

"I never wanted to hurt you," I said, remembering when I took the breath from him, causing him to keel over.

Kole stiffened and frowned. "You didn't." Still, he did not like appearing weak in any way.

I smiled. "Either way, I am sorry."

"No need for that." He stood up straighter, folding his arms over his chest. It was the same Kole I had grown to know in the Lysian lands, the brooding guard. And when he looked at me, it was with the same crystal eyes I found a comfortable familiarity in. I stared at him till he asked, "What?"

"I could have sworn you would have been furious with me."

"Well, that's what you get for assuming all Lysians are just angry, menacing animals."

A new smile pulled at my lips, and I did not conceal it. "Come, I'll show you to your rooms." They followed as I led them through the building. Wooden floors creaked under our feet, while stone walls stretched before us with nooks carved out for candles to provide light.

It felt odd, the change, going from the Lysians leading me to the opposite.

"Do you stay in this building as well?" Erik asked casually as I escorted them up the stairs and down the hall.

"Yes. If you need to find me, then Kole can probably help you," I stated. Kole had been the one who gathered me when my world came to a screeching halt due to the Lysian with fire dancing over his fingertips. The same Lysian I now welcomed into my home. What a bizarre turn of events.

"If you're here somewhere, then I will find you," Erik said casually, though it sounded as if it were a promise. My face flushed.

I delivered them to their rooms, one hall off from my own. "Are either of you hungry?"

"Not really," Kole answered. Erik didn't disagree.

"I need to head to a meeting, so you both are free to explore your rooms, bathe, and rest."

"We aren't tired and would love to join you." Erik held my stare.

I refused to back down. My gaze narrowed. "I imagine it's difficult for you to do what you are told instead of doing whatever you wish. But you are a guest in *my* home. As such, you will have to learn to back down when you don't get what you want."

He chortled. "I still insist we join. Especially if this meeting is about the Siddhe."

"No." It did not matter what the meeting was about. This was my home. I did not need Lysian shadows following me everywhere. Though they were guests, they were *not* in control here.

Kole rubbed the back of his neck. "May I be excused from this little spat?"

Erik dipped his chin in agreement and Kole disappeared into his room. The challenge in Erik's gaze did not waver. Did not budge.

"Listen. You must stay for now, but I will make you a deal: after this meeting ends, there's somewhere I would like to go. It's a place important to me. Few have ever been there. If you behave now, then I will take you with me when I go."

The male stared at me, pondering this. As if he had any choice. Begrudgingly, he agreed, and I left the Lysians in their rooms while I went to prepare for my looming departure.

44

ARIANA

When I arrived to gather Erik later in the day, he opened the door without my having to knock. He was dressed in clean clothing, and his brown hair was pushed back out of his eyes, still wet from bathing.

"How did you know it was me?" I asked curiously.

"Your steps." His lips twitched up as he followed me into the hallway.

"You remember the sound of my movements?"

"I remember a lot of things." He held my gaze. Had he decided a path he finally wanted to take or was he still pulled in various directions? I tried to ignore the way my pulse spiked, peeling my eyes from him to focus on where we were going.

He kept pace beside me, cautiously observing the surroundings. Neither of us spoke as we passed beyond the city wall. By the time we arrived where I was bringing him, the sun had nearly set.

I took Erik to someplace meaningful, wanting him to see it. Wishing him to understand an intimate part of myself. A strange vulnerability came with inviting him to join me that I nearly stopped and took him back home. However, my feet continued forward, walking past the insecurities, until we finally made it to our destination, and there was no going back.

"A tree house?" Erik asked, looking up at it before turning to view the field towards the single tree in the distance with a scorched ring around it. His lips curved up ever so slightly.

"Amused by a memory?" I asked, looking from that distant tree to him.

"Very." He smiled fully, exposing those sharp teeth. I used to find them repellant, though they no longer bothered me. They were simply a part of him. If anything, they intrigued me.

"Let's go." I nodded towards the wooden ladder. Taking hold of the withered wood, smoothed by age and use, I lifted myself, climbing to the top.

It was exactly as I remembered. Parts of the floorboard were broken, making the path precarious, so I needed to watch my step to make it through the space.

Erik silently moved through the area, taking in the crystals and stones strung up on strings and draped from the ceiling at the edge, which overlooked the field beyond the forest. There was a hammock weaved together by my mother's hands still hanging on the side of the room. I used to come up to the tree house and lie in that hammock, swaying ever so softly for hours. Now and then, I got to a place where if I closed my eyes, I could imagine my mother was swaying me herself. My throat ached with the memories.

"This used to be my mother's little escape. It's pretty much everything I have left of her now," I informed Erik as I walked to a small table with a couple of her books and a small jewelry box void of any jewels.

"Did she live here?" he asked, looking around the room.

"You know, I don't actually know. We used to come here sometimes when I was little. It was our special hideout. After she was taken from me, I would come here to feel close to her. It always felt like a safe place. I never brought anyone here before."

"Not Edda or your two Bavadrin guards?" He turned to me.

"You mean Landin and Willis? No, none of them. I'm sure Edda knows of this place, but if she does, she has never mentioned it to me before. Landin and Willis know of it, but they too have never actually been here."

"Then why did you bring me?" he asked, surprise coloring his features.

"I wanted to come before my leaving, but I didn't want to come here alone tonight." I walked around the small room, touching weathered wood and ripped fabrics, indulging in the memories. I could have brought Landin or Willis with me, though that was not who I wanted with me this night.

Erik tracked my movements with a peculiar look on his face.

"What?" I glanced at him.

He shrugged, lips curving up. "People look different when they are at home."

"In what way?"

He had seen me in my land before, though always under his control.

"Their guard is down," he stated simply.

"Should it not be?" I turned my full attention to him. Once upon a time I would have seen his comment as a threat. Now it was nothing more than words that fascinated me.

"You think having your guard up would protect you from me?" His eyes glinted, the air around him growing heavy. He was still very much the predator he had always been.

"I think I have proven that I have no issue protecting myself from you." I smirked, pretending that the look in his gaze and the way the world around him responded to his presence had no influence on me.

I will be impenetrable to his effect.

"You think so?" His smile grew, exposing deadly teeth.

My heart did something strange in my chest.

I will be almost *impenetrable to his effect.*

"Is that a challenge?" I stepped to the side, slightly bending at the knees in anticipation.

He saw my physical stance as an invitation to try.

"No conjuring," he stated, and everything around him dimed even more. As if he could control not only flame, but light itself.

"Okay." I grinned before lunging. The Lysian King was not going to get more warning than that. It was a rare chance to get a sense of his physical abilities for myself up close. I had seen him in action when the outcast Lysians attacked, and Erik was extraordinary. Yet, there was a difference between witnessing something and experiencing it for yourself.

Erik evaded the attack with an embarrassing amount of ease. His movements were swift, and he made them seem effortless and natural, even with the hazardous and uneven flooring. It was as if he sensed the world around him without even having to look at it.

His hands touched me only to guide me away from him. I found myself pushed to the side, facing a direction not intended, with Erik behind me. Spinning around, I found him in a casual stance.

Straightening, Erik squared his shoulders and waited for me to charge again. It irritated me that he did not take a more offensive position, though I was pretty sure our little match would come to a quick end if that were to happen. Lysians really had an unfair advantage in a fight.

I took two small steps to the side. His full attention remained on me, following my movement. There was no way I stood a chance with all those superior senses of his focused so intently. I needed to distract him.

A thought crossed my mind, and I suppressed a smile.

My gaze settled squarely on him. For several seconds, neither of us moved. Then my attention shifted abruptly to the space out over the makeshift treehouse balcony behind him. My eyes winded in startled shock. Erik turned to see what had caught my attention so suddenly, and at that moment, I sprang forward. Lunging for him, I prepared to shove him. Perhaps if I could just startle him, get him off-balance, I would be able to...

He stepped aside. Stopping me short, his hand snatching mine in a way that I was the one who lost my balance, literally falling into him. My back hit his chest. It happened so quick, yet I felt everything in such detail it was as if the single moment endlessly stretched. Fingers gripping my hips, momentarily tightening before relaxing. A hand glided across my abdomen, pressing me into him. Arms circled me, capturing me. I breathed in the scent of earth and fire. His heartbeat thrummed strong and true at my back.

He leaned into me, sending a shudder through my body. "How devious of you," he murmured in my ear before releasing me.

Without fully regaining my balance, I charged away from him. My foot jammed in one of the uneven floorboards. Stumbling, I caught myself and turned once more to face him. He stood staring at me again, a confident smile on his lips.

He lunged first this time, his speed forcing me to leap back. The boards creaked beneath my boots as I sidestepped.

"Come on, Ariana," he taunted, his voice a rumble that sent shivers scurrying along my spine. "Is this all you can do?"

Pivoting, I slammed my shoulder into his chest, managing to knock him off balance. His eyes flashed with surprise as he faltered back a step before dropping. With a twist and a sweep of his leg, Erik took me down. I hit the floor with a grunt, the impact rattling the boards beneath us. Before I could recover, he straddled me, his weight pinning me down.

His smirk deepened as he leaned forward, bracing his hands on either side of my head. "Looks like I win, princess."

I glared up at him, my breathing uneven but my resolve unwavering. "Not quite."

From the pocket of my pants, I drew a slender blade and pressed it to his throat. The cool metal glinted in the moonlight, and his smirk faltered for just a heartbeat before returning, this time with an edge of admiration. We agreed to no conjuring, not no weapons.

"Clever," he murmured, his voice low and velvet.

"Iver and Eislyn taught me the power of being underestimated," I replied, my lips curving into a smile.

Neither of us moved. His sapphire eyes held mine, their intensity a match for the blade at his throat. For a moment I thought he might lean closer. Instead, he climbed off me, offering a hand. I accepted it, letting him pull me to my feet. His grip lingered, strong and steady.

He glanced to my other hand; at the blade he gifted me at my Ascension. "You keep it on you?" His hold loosened before he finally let go.

"Did you expect me not to?" I sheathed the dagger in the blade pocket at my thigh, brushing off the dust from my clothes.

"I wasn't sure what you would do with it. But I like that you keep it close."

I looked at him, but he was no longer focused on me.

His attention moved over the space once more. "So, this is a place you go to feel safe?"

"Sometimes." I watched him as he drifted through the room before exploring the small outdoor balcony, which dangerously had no railing. It was strange, having someone else in a place that had been singly my own for so long. I felt as if I stood on a ledge, fearing what he would find, while hoping his interest would remain held for a while.

Erik paced over to the edge of the balcony, looking towards the moon. "The best way to feel safe is for you not to go to the Siddhe," he said casually. Of course, he could not easily let it go.

Sighing, I joined him outside. "This allows me an opportunity to learn something of the Siddhe, maybe find out if what we think is even true."

"It is," he stated, refusing to allow room for any other possibility. The stern opposition he had to Clause's invitation did not align with his goals of freeing the Lysians. He probably was afraid of losing an ally in my people's leadership.

I viewed him. "Then this meeting may be fruitful. I know you are concerned for your sister, and I told you that the Bavadrins will help. If anything were to happen to me, then the Siddhe threat would be seen as very real. Whoever the next leader is to be, they will join forces with you. You will have the support of the Bavadrin lands. I can promise you this." I tried to ease his worries. Erik's goals would still be pursued, even if I was no longer around.

A look of disgust passed over his features, and he looked away from me once more. "Do you think me so vile as to not care at all what happens to you?" The coldness in his tone surprised me.

I, too, peered out at the sky. It seemed so quiet out there, yet it was a peace that would not last. I felt it—an ominous presence that did not belong. Something loomed over my people and me.

"There is no shame in worrying about those you rule over and your family," I stated after a moment. Erik had his goals, and there was no problem with that.

He released a low, cruel laugh and pivoted, pacing several steps into the tree house. "You are correct in assuming that that's something I care for. However, you are wrong in thinking that it is the only thing that has me uncertain about your trip. I do not simply care about what happens to you for the Lysians' sake." He turned those sapphire eyes back towards me. "I do not wish for harm to fall to *you*. Specifically you. The thought of it alone is enough to make me wish I had the power to destroy the Siddhe without your involvement. You have done nothing to warrant taking such a risk."

Warmth swelled in my chest, and I tore my eyes from his. "I thought we were not even capable of a friendship. That was what you said the other night." I had to force myself to turn back to meet his gaze, feeling so incredibly irrational for that single interaction to have upset me the way it had.

"The look on your face when I said some of those things... I regret my delivery. But what could I have done? You had just wandered towards the border all alone on the white moon of all nights. And then you, what, wished us to simply exchange pleasantries? I wanted nothing more. Yet I had my duty to protect the perimeter, and you now know that the border may be threatened by Lysians who are not under my control. The risk you were putting yourself in was reckless, and not to mention my self-control was..." His voice briefly trailed off. "I needed you gone. So, I said what I needed to get you as far away as quickly as possible."

My heart as it skipped a beat. I tried not to think of how he likely heard it do that. "Where exactly does this leave us, Erik?"

He was a Lysian King, and I was the Bavadrin Leader Superior. For the first time, we were both free, standing on our own two feet, our actions no one's but our own. What he said before placed invisible walls between us, though the way he spoke now, it was as if the only thing between us was air.

He looked around playfully. "It leaves us in this here tree house, I suppose."

He pulled back, turning the conversation light, but I did not want to go down that path. I wished to continue the uncomfortable one, where we could show one another our truths.

"You know." My tongue flicking out to wet my lips, which had gone dry under his piercing gaze. His sapphire eyes followed the movement, dipping to my mouth before returning to meet my stare. "I care about you, too." My voice was soft but steady, a quiet admission that felt like pushing open a door—a door I feared would be slammed shut in my face. Again.

Over the days I'd spent among the Lysians, something shifted within me, between us. The Lysian I once feared, who threatened my entire world, had become something else entirely. I did not know when it happened, or perhaps I was afraid to see the truth and thus blinded myself to it.

But like a sapling drawn irresistibly to the sun, I found myself drawn to Erik. His presence magnetic.

"I know," he said quietly, his voice stripped of its playfulness, leaving only sincerity.

I leveled my gaze, meeting his. "How do you know?" It felt as though I stood on the edge of a cliff. If I jumped, would there be anything to catch me?

He angled his head, a trace of a smile lifting at the corners of his mouth. "You mean, besides when you tended my wounds in that Bavadrin prison?"

I nodded, though that moment hadn't meant anything specific —just a helping someone unjustly injured.

Erik took a step closer, and suddenly the air between us became thinner, harder to pull into my lungs. His presence was overwhelming, as though he had summoned every ounce of his power into this moment. "When you cooked that favorite meal of yours," he said softly, "there was a light in your eyes when you watched me take that first bite. I'll never forget it. It is a fond memory." His smile deepened, though his tone remained serious. "When you escaped, you did so with care—not harming any Lysians. And you released me when you had every right to imprison me. Even to kill me." Another step. "That wasn't even the first time you spared my life."

My pulse quickened, betraying me.

"And," he continued, his voice dipping lower, "there's the way your heartbeat races every time I near you."

My heart stuttered, as if responding to his words directly. "I thought it was just fear."

His mouth twitched, holding back a smile. "It's not fear."

He stepped closer again, and the space between us nearly disappeared. The raw power coming from him was palpable. He was an imposing force—his heat, his strength, his sheer authority pressing in on me.

His presence didn't terrify me like it once had; it consumed me. His gaze was a physical thing, searing over my skin, while his scent, rich and heady, wrapped around me, drowning out the world. The sight of him was breathtaking. He held my senses firmly captive, and I wanted him to take two more. To touch him. Taste him.

I rooted myself in place, refusing to back away, refusing to create space.

Erik's hand moved with a deliberate slowness, his fingers grazing my hip. The touch was light, almost tentative, testing—offering me a chance to retreat. His hand slid upward, leaving a trail of fire in its wake, every brush of his fingers igniting something deep within me.

When I didn't pull away, he closed in.

I stared straight ahead, unable to look anywhere else. It was as though my body had forgotten how to move, how to breathe. My gaze fixed on the rise and fall of his chest, his broad, muscular frame a wall before me.

Erik's hand drifted upward, gliding over my arm, before settling at my neck. His thumb pressed softly under my chin, tilting my face upward, and I found myself locked in his dark eyes. His gaze blazed, unnerving, yet impossibly warm.

I was so hopelessly drawn to him, every part of him.

Spirit, help me.

It was as though he sensed my thoughts. The energy

surrounding him shifted again, slowing further, becoming heavier, more intimate. My breathing faltered under the weight of it.

When I still didn't move, still didn't run, he leaned in. Unhurriedly, carefully, his head dipped, and he stopped just shy of my lips. He didn't close the gap—waiting, silently asking for permission.

Drawn like a moth to a flame, I rose onto my toes, closing that final sliver of space between us.

My lips brushed against his, soft and searching. He kissed me. It started tenderly as if he was afraid he might hurt me.

But I was not made of glass.

My lips parted for him, inviting him in. His tongue swept through, exploring and deliciously thorough. The taste of him only made me hunger for more as my tongue met his stroke for stroke. His tenderness transformed in response. Feather-light touches gave way to something deeper, hungrier, rawer. With every heartbeat, the kiss grew in intensity, a wildfire spreading between us. I matched his fervor, meeting him with the same untamed need that clawed at my chest.

His lips trailed down my jaw, my throat. My breath hitched as his teeth scraped along my neck before he found my mouth once more.

It was as if he wanted to devour me, and I wanted to be devoured.

Our tongues collided and I nearly lost my mind with the divine taste of him. Erik pulled me against him.

The more I tasted, the more I craved. My senses narrowed, sharpened to a single point. I could see nothing but him, feel nothing but the heat of his body, smell nothing but the enticing scent of his skin.

His breath became mine, or perhaps mine became his—I couldn't tell. There was no Erik. No me. Only *us*, tangled in this fiery, overwhelming moment. He consumed my doubts and fears, swallowing them whole until nothing was left. Every worry, every thought, every bit of hesitation dissolved. The Lysian King holding me became my entire world.

My fingers tangled in his hair, deepening the kiss. The low, guttural growl that escaped his throat sent a pulse coursing through me.

His hands tightened, strong and unyielding. The pressure of his touch was possessive. There was no escape—not that I wanted one.

I lost myself in him, and it was the most exquisite kind of oblivion.

Until he let me go.

Erik pulled away, breaking the kiss. His touch lingered, reluctant, before finally releasing me. He retreated a step, and it felt like a chasm opened between us. Dark eyes scanned my face, searching for any sign of discomfort or regret.

He would find none.

"I don't want you to leave. I don't want you to do this with the Siddhe," he said, his voice low, carrying an edge of frustration.

I swallowed, steadying my ragged breath before replying, "Trying to seduce me into compliance?"

A wry chuckle escaped him, though it lacked any real humor. "If only it were that easy."

"My decision is final. I am going, Erik."

His jaw clenched, hands fists at his sides. It was probably difficult for him to not have complete control. He hated my decision.

He shook his head and glanced to the field outside. "It's late. We should go." His voice was barely more than a whisper, strained and distant. When he glanced back at me, the fire in his eyes shone. That hunger, that longing—it still burned, unquenched and undeniable.

For a moment, I couldn't find my voice. All I could do was nod.

Erik turned, walked to the balcony, and *jumped* from the tree house. My heart nearly stopped. But then again, he was Lysian and landed on his feet with effortless grace. I raced over and peered over the ledge as he looked up at me.

"I'll catch you," he offered with a daring smile. Gone was the moment we just shared as if completely evaporated.

It was an effort to make my jaw work to compose a response.

"No way," I answered, moving to take the ladder instead.

He chuckled softly.

When I finally joined him at the tree's base, neither of us mentioned what just occurred. We walked back to the leader superior compound, parting ways to our separate rooms as if nothing had happened between us.

But while I lay in bed, I could still feel the lingering touch of his lips on mine and how my body bent around his.

It was real. It happened.

It was beautiful and unexpected, though I did not know what it meant moving forward. I only knew that I had one more day at home before leaving for the Siddhe lands. I planned for what was to come while the Lysians stood idly by, waiting to learn what the outcome of the trip would be.

When life stilled, in those moments of waiting for a meeting to start or while lying in bed, worries entered my mind for the unknown. What would the Siddhe be like? Edda warned me that Clause would want to observe my conjuring. She advised me not to let him see it easily, that he would try and test me somehow, and when I did finally conjure to use my hands as a crutch, so he would see the false limitations of what I could do. She also advised me to cover my skin so that he could not easily touch me, though if he wished to touch me, I was to allow it. He would not harm me. That was the safety the letter he had sent offered me.

Edda shared that though Clause stated I could bring along whomever I wished, only those who could conjure would be able to stay with me. She knew so much through her sight, and I was glad to have her guidance even though our relationship strained. Even so, the fact that she would be beside me during the meeting with the Siddhe king offered a great deal of comfort. I continued to feel a sense of safety in her presence.

The notions of what was to come swirled in my mind. Concerns for the future kept me from settling. The only other thought strong enough to push those concerns aside was the memory of that moment with Erik in the tree house. The way it was to be in his arms, to regard them as a safe place. Strangely, he felt so familiar, though we had never embraced like that before.

In those still moments in the dark, I was torn between two unknowns: the mind and the heart. My mind spun webs of fears of the Siddhe while my heart dared to hope for a different future.

45

ERIK

I knocked on Ariana's door before I could talk myself out of it. Darkness still lingered outside, but the sun was not far off. With the morning light, she would leave. Too soon. By the sounds of footsteps within her room, it was a sleepless night not only for me.

Her steps stilled their pacing, briefly frozen by my disturbance. Slowly, she approached the door, cracking it open. Wide green eyes looked at me in surprise.

"Erik." Her voice softly murmured my name before she glanced down the halls, noting the guards at the ends standing at attention. None of them moved but were ready to, should she call for them. There was no one else walking the halls at this hour. Only me.

My gaze traveled the length of her. A loose silk robe cinched around her waist. The material ended at her thigh, showing off her long, lovely legs. The fabric hugged her curves in the most appealing of ways. Waves of brown hair flowed down her back, spilling over a single shoulder, half braided with little stones inter-twined in long strands, as was customary for their Bavadrin ways. I had to admit, that look was particularly attractive on her. It added an almost savagery to her otherwise elegant appearance.

Stepping aside, she let me enter her room. "What are you doing here?" she asked after closing the door.

"I couldn't sleep either. Figured it may be more enjoyable to visit with you than for both of us to pace around alone until sunrise." The sheets on her bed were pushed aside, evidence of her failed attempt at rest.

"You crave my company?" She arched a delicate brow, a small smile curving her lips.

"I crave it so much that I rather you not leave once the sun hits the horizon," I answered, focusing my attention on her.

The smile slipped from her. "It's one dinner. We have gone over this. Edda ensures I will be alright. I am not discussing this any further."

She was being so stubborn. And so was I. "How much do you trust Edda's visions? Seers rarely see the future clearly. Their visions are often difficult to interpret."

Her jaw clenched. "I trust Edda's guidance. She has not steered me wrong yet. She said I would be alright when your Lysians came, said I would return, that I would be the future Leader Superior. She was not wrong about any of those things."

"Does not mean she is right now." Despite Edda's certainty that Ariana would be safe, I felt in my gut that this would not go well. It put me on edge.

Ariana folded her arms across her chest. "Are you trying to start a fight?"

"No." I sighed, running a hand through my hair. I wished there was more I could say to stop this from happening.

Her gaze narrowed. "Why are you even bothering to waste your breath on this again?"

"It's not a waste if it keeps you safe."

Her head tilted, and more of that silky hair flowed over her shoulder. "You kissed me the other night and practically ran away from me after that. Now you want to talk about your desires to keep me safe? I do not have time for these emotional games, Erik. Neither of us do."

The boldness of her words caused me to straighten. "I did not run away. I just prefer more time with you without this trip of yours casting shadows. This is not a game."

She stepped to the side, attention never straying from mine, arms remaining folded across her chest. Her stance was a barrier, closing herself off from me, preparing to dispute my opposition. Narrowed eyes pierced me as if my answer was not quite enough for her. "Why did you come here tonight?"

"To keep you from leaving tomorrow," I answered honestly.

"Your words won't change my mind." She shook her head slowly from side to side.

"I am not opposed to chaining you to the bed," I stated, another honest thought. If words wouldn't do, then that was another option.

She released a low laugh, arms falling to her sides, exuding pure confidence. There was that same spirit which drew me to her from the moment I first laid eyes on her. But her heart skipped an actual beat at my comment. "Even if you were to succeed with something like that—"

"Oh, I would succeed." I cut her off with a smirk. How delicious it would have been to have her at my mercy like that. Vulnerable.

Tension thickened between us, filling the room. Ariana's gaze continued to hold mine. "You are but one Lysian. Conjuror or not, you alone cannot withstand all my Bavadrins, the Sparrows. And I doubt you want to burn everyone to bits if you need us to fight a war. And that is *if* I spared your breath." Though her words challenged my suggestion, her heart beat harder. Like the suggestion did something to her.

"A minor oversight on my part," I replied.

She laughed, the sound brilliant and light, drawing my smile to the surface. "Again, we are back to you being left with nothing but words to sway me. Like I said, that won't work. I have no interest in arguing with you over this."

"Then let me convince you another way." I approached her. She stilled, apart from the rise and fall of her chest with every breath. If she didn't want words, then I could find other ways to sway her. If she wanted to throw herself into chaos and play with danger, then I was more than willing to be that for her.

She caught the attention of the Lysian King. If she let me, then I would have her playing with fire.

I reached out, fingertips along her jaw, before brushing her hair back over her shoulder. The touch was featherlight, yet electric. As if just touching her could have been fatal. As if *she* was more deadly than I ever imagined. And I wanted to tangle with that threat. To make it mine.

She swallowed, her throat bobbing. I wished to run my lips and teeth over that throat.

"Convince me how?" Her voice grew breathy, but her stare held mine with so much certainty that flames burned through me. Her confidence was exquisite. She never shied away from me like so many others. Her boldness did things to me.

"I'll show you if you let me." I closed in and stole nearly all the space between us, crowding her.

She craned her neck, viewing me with zero hesitance. "How big of a hit will your ego take when you cannot convince me? Because come sunrise, I am leaving."

Lethal.

This woman was lethal.

I smirked. "I welcome your challenge." My lips landed on hers, stealing her breath. *Spirit*, the taste of her was as delicious as I remembered. Better even.

Briefly, her body tensed, as if surprised when my arms wrapped around her. A heartbeat later she relaxed into me. Her lips parted, letting my tongue swipe through her mouth. The kiss was slow, thorough. I savored the taste of her. Ariana's fingers threaded through my hair before running over my shoulders, pulling me closer.

My hands explored her, traveling over the elegant curve of her back, her thigh, moving up her side, grazing her breast. I mapped her body with my touch, memorizing the feel of her as she pressed against me. She breathed a strangled moan into my mouth. I *felt* that sound. It ran through me, flooding my veins and drugging my mind. And we were still fully clothed.

She was unlike anything I had ever experienced.

The air grew thick with desire.

Somehow, we had traveled through the room till I pinned her between me and the window, her backside propped against the sill, holding some of her weight.

The scent of her arousal enveloped me, and my thoughts became harder to control. I fought my urge to take her fully. That was a choice we would both make one day and not under the duress of a threat. This night was meant as just a taste of what she could have more of if she stayed. And I only had minutes to sway her before sunrise.

I traced the hem of her robe, hand slipping underneath, running over soft skin. My movement stilled in surprise. She was not wearing *anything* beneath the robe.

Ariana released a throaty chuckle, the sound sultry and devastatingly effective, blazing straight through me. *Lethal woman.*

My mouth reclaimed hers. As my hand roamed higher along her thigh, I was met with the intoxicating heat of her. Her breath hitched before she slightly parted her legs, a silent invitation that I accepted with an eager greed. I slid one finger inside her, and the sensation was so maddeningly intimate that jealousy flared, envying my own hand.

A low, moan rumbled through her, back arching, breath hitching in sync with my movements. The restraint I clung to frayed with every sound the woman made, every shift of her body. She was unraveling me, piece by piece.

I traced my lips along her jawline, teeth scraping down the column of her neck, until I reached a spot that drove her wild. I fisted her hair, tugging, forcing her to expose her throat to me. Her nails dug into my shoulder. She was going to leave marks. The thought only spurred me on.

I added another finger, stroking her. Her hips rocked, moving against my hand, drawing me deeper into her. The way she felt, the way she responded—it was indescribable.

A groan escaped me as my lips captured hers again, swallowing her gasps. When I freed my hand from her hair, my fingers brushed along the curve of her neck before wrapping lightly around her throat. The soft pressure elicited a moan, raw and primal, vibrating against my mouth. The sound sent a shiver of satisfaction through me, and a slow, wicked smile curved my lips.

So, she liked a touch of dominance.

I could more than work with that.

I squeezed. Not enough to hurt her, but enough to tease, to threaten. Beneath my touch, her pulse fluttered like a bird's wings, fast and unrelenting.

Between her legs, I maintained the rhythm she enjoyed, driving her towards a fast approaching the edge. Ariana trembled, her desperation spilling out in those exquisite, breathless sounds that made me ache for her.

I could feel the tension in her body coiling tighter and tighter. Her heart thundered, her breathing shallow and ragged. Her hand clamped down on my forearm, while the other gripped my shoulder.

And then, she let go.

Release washed over her, consuming her entirely. Her body arched, nails digging in just enough to sting as she shattered, trembling and writhing in my arms.

Just as the first ray of morning sunlight broke over the distant horizon, casting a golden glow across her skin, painting her in hues of fire.

46

ARIANA

For the first two days of travel my thoughts wavered between concerns regarding the trip and thoughts of Erik. His hands on my body. His mouth on my neck. His eyes consuming me.

The man touched me with the most delicious form of possession. One that somehow brought freedom with it instead of suffocation. I felt safe. Wanted. Freed.

Erik tried to hide his disappointment when I readied to leave. As if he truly believed there was a chance I would stay because of his touch. But it only made my resolve to go that much stronger.

We were blind against Clause. All we knew of the Siddhe were muddled fortunes from past seers and records from before the division and safety of the treaty. The chance at gaining insight was not something we could pass on. Not when we desperately needed information.

An escort greeted us at the edge of our border into the Siddhe territory early morning of our third day of travel. We were going to make it just in time for dinner with the Siddhe King, which would be followed by a long night of traveling back to our Bavadrin lands before ever resting. There was no way we were going to stop moving until within the shelter of our territory again.

The escort waited patiently on horseback while we drew near. He appeared to have been alone. The closer we came, the more evident were the scars on his sandy golden skin. They were everywhere, nearly covering every inch of visible skin, markings deeply etched into flesh.

"Only those with any conjuring abilities are permitted to continue beyond this point," he stated without ever giving his name. His voice was neither friendly nor menacing.

That was not the deal, though Edda had already warned me of as much. "In the letter, Clause stated I could bring whomever I wished," I countered anyway.

"And you have. Those who remain here will be offered the same protection, and no harm will come to them. However, only those with any conjuring or otherworldly abilities may continue beyond this point." His attention drifted over our small Bavadrin party before returning to me.

Edda viewed the escort without a trace of anything other than a dull look. "Well, appears as though it's just us three from this point forward." She agreed to the limitation she had always known would be.

I caught Landin's eye, for he would be joining us. Though he did not have developed conjuring abilities, he possessed the slightest sway over the wind. It was what made him one of the best archers in our city, at least before the return of the Sparrows. With some practice, he could join their ranks someday, if he wanted to.

I addressed the three Bavadrin guards who were going to be left behind. "Wait here. We should be back before sunrise."

They grunted in response, remaining on horseback while Landin, Edda, and I followed the guide.

The Siddhe moved at a reasonable pace for a terrain that took us higher and higher into the mountains. The wind nipped at the three of us as we followed in silence, our hooded cloaks pulled up to keep what little heat clung to our bodies from escaping.

The cold did not seem to bother our guide, for his hood remained down. His hair was dark and clipped close to his head, allowing visibility of the scars there. A lot of them seemed to result from true wounds and self-inflicted ones, as there was a pattern to them.

I had never seen anything like that before, but I had heard of it.

The Dunes Clan who once lived in the Bavadrin desert were said to have markings carved into the flesh, though the people disappeared years ago. The belief was that they had rejoined with the Spirit, that their gifts and life had opened a door for them that others could only hope for. Yet, if our guide was really part of the Dunes Clan, then we had been mistaken. Erik was always correct, and we were just too blind to see what was in front of us the entire time.

The Dunes Clan was said to have marked their skin because it was a part of their conjuring. Like any other, their unmarked skin was easy to cut with a blade, and easy to harm. However, if injured, the skin would heal vastly stronger. The markings provided permanent skintight armor, for a knife no longer could cut them. That was not their only ability. They could also communicate through thought with one another—at least the stories had always said so. The leader could command his clan without speaking a word. I was not sure how dynamic that ability was for them. They had disappeared before I ever got to see any of the clan.

Glancing back, I caught sight of Landin, who also seemed focused on the stranger we followed. A look of scrutiny etched on his face, with his eyes narrowed and brows pulled down.

When the trees became sparse and the ground of the steep

incline more uniform, I drove Rain forward till she kept pace with the guide and his horse.

"Do you mind sharing your name?" I asked him, noting his hands. There were scars there too. Three per finger, starting from a point just beneath the tip. They ran down over the knuckles and over the back of his hand, all the way to his wrists. The fabric of his cloak started there, obscuring the rest of his skin, though I knew in my gut that the marks continued further.

His brown eyes turned, appraising and unreadable. "My name is Soren," he simply stated after a moment.

I offered him my name in return, to which he replied, "I know who you are," without giving me another look. He certainly was not trying to come off as warm and welcoming. Unfortunately for him, that would not prevent me from asking the questions I longed to know the answers to.

"The scars covering your skin—are they self-inflicted?" I asked, my gaze dropping to his hands once more.

His attention remained on the mountain before him as he answered, "Some."

I glanced behind me. Both Edda and Landin were watching my interaction. Landin evidently grew more rigid. Edda's lips had the slightest downward curve, the only sign of displeasure she showed. She undoubtedly had the same concerns as I, that the Siddhe guide was, in fact, a member of the Dunes Clan. A Bavadrin.

"Where are you from?" I asked, turning back to the guide.

"I live here." Again, he kept his attention trained ahead. Was he hoping that if he acted indifferent I would go away? He would learn that was not to be the case.

"That is not what I asked," I pressed.

He turned then, brown eyes studying me as if seeing through me. "You know the answer, Bavadrin Superior." He said it with the slightest tinge of distaste. It felt as though the air got even colder around us. Why would someone like him feel anything negative towards me or the Bavadrins?

My mouth went dry. "You are of the Dunes Clan?"

"We no longer go by that name," was his admission.

My heart beat harder in my chest. The Lysians had been right. Our conjurors were taken. Instantly I felt shame for not realizing such a thing sooner. Why did all the Bavadrins always believe that the reason some conjurors disappeared was because of some sort of blessing from the Spirit? We could not have been more foolish or wrong.

I licked my lips, which grew dry from the frosty wind. "Why are you here? With the Siddhe?"

Again, he did not look at me as he answered. "Seems as good a place as any. We are useful here."

"You left the Dunes on your own free will?" I asked him, not knowing what answer would be easier to swallow. If they were taken against their will, then I would do everything in my power to free them. However, if they left on their own accord, then why?

"All of life is a choice," he said with a frown, and his horse picked up its pace, slowing only once it was ahead of me. The message was received: the conversation over.

I fell back in line behind the guide, and we continued to follow him in silence.

If the Dunes Clan was under the Siddhes' control, then were other Bavadrins also with the Siddhe? The Dunes Clan were never technically Bavadrins, but Bavadrins had a symbiotic relationship with them developed centuries ago. They lived in a territory where most Bavadrins did not wish to reside, so they were allowed their own freedoms and customs. When the great war occurred, they fought alongside the Bavadrins, both benefiting from the support of the other. I never knew of anything happening that would have pushed the Dunes Clan to leave their Bavadrin shelter for the Siddhe.

The pines of the forest cleared, and there was an enormous castle in view, etched into the mountain itself. There were too many peaks to count on the face of the fortress as it reached high into the sky, as if competing with the mountain itself to touch the clouds. The setting sun glistened off the many windows, none of which appeared to be plain glass. Instead, the windows shone with shards of color. It was the most remarkable thing I had ever seen.

Soren came to a stop, dismounting and expressing no interest in the breathtaking view. "I will take your horses so they may eat and rest. They will be returned when you are all ready to leave." He waited patiently for us to follow his lead.

I hopped off Rain with a frown, patting the side of her neck. Through my mind, I told her to be careful, to not eat or drink anything they gave her. By the shake of her head, it seemed as though she understood. It made me feel a sliver better to pretend that was the case.

"Welcome," a calm voice intoned, smooth as silk and unyielding.

We spun around to see a Siddhe emerging from the castle's entrance. His hair was so pale it seemed almost bone-white, framing a face that was strikingly handsome—sharp angles softened by a strong jaw and full lips. His ears tapered to elegant points, and his deep gray eyes, darker than any storm, held a weight that was almost oppressive.

As he approached, his movements were so fluid it seemed as though he were gliding rather than walking. His gaze drifted over the three of us before focusing on me. The air around him grew unnaturally still, heavy with the deep, ancient power that radiated from him.

"It is a pleasure to finally make your acquaintance, Ariana," he said, his voice measured and precise, as if every syllable carried significance. He held out his hand expectantly.

I didn't need an introduction. I knew who he was. I could feel it in my bones, a truth whispered by the air itself. Still, I had to temper my surprise. The Siddhe King standing before me looked barely older than I was. Yet if the stories held truth, then he had walked this earth for centuries.

Beside me, Edda went ridged.

"Clause," I said his name in greeting. I was not planning on reciprocating the pleasantries, for it was *not* a pleasure to be standing before him, not when I did not know why he wished to have a meeting.

I slid my hand into his, and the corners of his mouth turned down, for my hands were covered with gloves. In fact, my entire body was covered, except for my head.

The guide collected all our horses and took them to their stables.

"Come, let's get you out of this cold." Gently, Clause led me towards the entrance, gray eyes observing me the entire time. The authority coming from him was unnaturally intense. Even the air around him did not stir, and I now moved through that stagnant zone. It was as if nothing could touch him, not even a breeze if he did not wish it to. His presence was one of absolute control. And the way his gaze was leveled at me, stalking me as I moved, it felt like a heavy shackle. Everything became more complex, even breathing.

I had to suppress the shiver running down my spine.

Clause stepped aside and motioned us to enter the castle. My jaw nearly dropped when we walked past the open, thick wooden doors into a hall that led into a magnificent room. I had never been in another room like it. It was extraordinarily massive and surprisingly warm. Large stained-glass windows blended effortlessly with the colorful walls. The soft glow of hundreds of candles framed the room within their golden wall nooks. Infinitely large, vaulted ceilings enclosed the chamber, and it was not a simple ceiling. Thousands of variously colored glasses covered the top in an extraordinary mosaic of a serpent in the center, surrounded by gold and blue shards. There were two stags at the far side looking incredibly regal, and to the other side a lone white wolf. There was more detail, yearning to be admired, but I tore my eyes away from the exquisiteness of the ceiling when Edda coughed under her breath.

"See something you like?" Clause asked, watching me with clear curiosity.

"It's beautiful. I have seen nothing like this place before," I answered in truth, and his head tilted to the side as if he couldn't quite understand something.

"Please, take a seat." He gestured to the table, which I had not even noticed within the great room. His gaze followed me as I walked through the space.

I sat between Edda and Landin while Clause took his seat directly across from me. Food was immediately brought out. The servants did not meet the eye of anyone in the room as it came to life with their swift and silent movements. It was as if the only thing they were allowed to look at was the table before us or the exit. Of those whose ears I could see, I took note of the points, marking them as Siddhe. They all vanished as quickly as they had appeared. Once the table was nearly overflowing with bread, meats, cheeses, and fruits, we were left to ourselves again.

"Help yourselves to whatever you like," Clause offered, moving a hand openly over the table. We did as instructed, filling our plates with various foods; though, I found myself hesitant to try any of it.

"This room is a work of art, is it not?" Clause averted his attention, beholding the mosaic on the ceiling. "The craftsmanship is exquisite, standing the test of time."

Briefly, I followed his gaze. "As I have said, it's beautiful.

Though I doubt you have asked for me to come here to show off your decor."

His gray eyes dipped back to me. "You are not interested in culture or history?"

"I am far more interested in what you hope to get out of this meeting."

He smirked, holding my stare. "Interesting choice of words. 'What I hope to get out of this meeting.' What makes you think I wish for anything other than simply to meet the new leader of the Bavadrin people?" Resting his elbows on the table, he clasped his hands before him.

"You have never extended an invitation to any of the previous leaders," I pointed out, trying not to think that he could have likely invited *several* of the previous Leader Superiors, for he was said to have been that old. He may have a handsome youthful face, but that had nothing to do with his true age or the powers he was rumored to possess. If Edda's suspicions were correct, then I might soon get a glimpse of some of those powers.

Clause's attention dipped to our plates. "None of you have touched a thing." It was an obvious change of subject.

But before any of us even had a chance to pick up a single utensil, the door to the room swung open with force and a woman sauntered in. Her skin was incredibly fair, her blond hair pulled back with a thick braid running down the middle of her back. Pale eyes met mine coolly before finding Clause and softening, visibly favoring the Siddhe king. The way she moved, with a predatory grace I had come to know well, I did not need to see her teeth to know she was a Lysian.

But that was not what disturbed me the most.

The metallic smell of blood accompanied her, so pungent that even my Bavadrin nose could scent it.

47

ARIANA

The Lysian female sauntered closer.

"I cleaned up the mess on the outskirts as request-ed," she stated with a sickly sweet voice. That was when I noticed the sword strapped to her hip and the blood dripping from it. Her pale gaze turned once more to me, noting my atten-tion on her wet blade, and she smiled callously. "The great Bavadrin Leader Superior," she mocked, coming to stand beside Clause and folding her arms over her chest. "You look no more than just a meek little Bavadrin."

Clause clicked his tongue, leaning back in his chair with an arrogance only a King could have. "Behave yourself, Malavika. These are my dinner guests." He pretended to lightly reprimand, though by the glint in his eye, he was clearly intrigued. There was something unyielding to the Siddhe King. His presence and control had a finality to it. There was no way he did not know the Lysian would enter the room, and that she would be displeased by my presence. In fact, he likely orchestrated it all, but to what end? Allowing someone to insult his *dinner guests* did not seem like a good way to make friends. However, I did not know if friendship was even his goal.

"My apologies." She flashed a hostile smile. Not at all sorry. Her gaze drifted over me once more, full of judgment. "So, let's see your conjuring. It must be spectacular for someone like you to have single-handedly freed yourself from the control of the Lysians."

They knew so much about what had happened. With dread, I realized that someone must have shared the information with the Siddhe.

Could they truly have spies in my lands?

"I am not here to entertain you," I stated dismissively, wondering whose blood left a trail behind the Lysian. Whose blood still dripped from that blade on her hip?

She ignored my words. "Why did it take you so long to finally free yourself? Was it because you couldn't get enough of the royal Lysian brothers? Tell me, did you sleep with all of them like a true Bavadrin tramp?"

Heat flared in my stomach at her words.

Landin's gaze drifted to me as he clenched his jaw. Thankfully, he remained silent and seated as Edda and I had instructed before we ever came to the Siddhe lands.

Clause kept his focus on me the entire time, monitoring my movement and the emotions that he would not see because of my wonderfully schooled features. I had years of practice controlling my face to hide the thoughts that passed through my mind.

It was clear the Siddhe king wanted Malavika present. He wanted her to burrow under my skin, likely hoping to anger me into using my conjuring. I expected him to at least ask to see my gifts first before trying to force them from me. He did not even give me that chance. Instead, he decided to play things out by force. That only irritated me further, for I did not appreciate their games. I was not a puppet. And if they wished to fight dirty, then I could do that too.

Clause was said to collect conjurors, so what was Malavika's gift?

The Lysian smiled smugly before her gaze drifted to Clause and softened. Her liking of him was her weakness, and I was going to press into that.

Reining in my anger, I smiled pleasantly. "You flatter me, for a Lysian royal could never find such favor in a simple Bavadrin like me. Though I'm sure I could learn a lot from someone as interesting as you, Malavika. Tell me, after you open your legs to your Siddhe King, do you weep sad tears because you know you will never be more than a pastime to quench his utter boredom?"

Her jaw clenched while Clause smirked darkly. It was clear she cared for him and what he thought of her. Though by his reaction to my comment, it did not seem like he cared all that much for her feelings in return.

"Bitch," she seethed.

I did not know why she hated me so instantly. It was not my choice to visit the Siddhe territory. I probably wished to have been gone as much as she wanted the same of me.

"Mirror is that way." I nodded to an area behind them where a part of the wall was decorated in a starburst pattern with broken mirror shards. She should have taken a good look at herself before she began throwing insults.

There was a momentarily sweeping silence in the room. Then the Lysian moved as quickly as the ones I had grown to know, grabbing the dinner knife from Clause's dining set. She shoved it forward. Despite the table distance between us, a shimmering distortion flickered around me, and four blades appeared within inches of my throat. By reflex, I pushed myself from the table, the chair screeching horribly as I stood.

The knife in the Lysian's hand vanished to the hilt, while four identical blades formed around me. Was it her conjuring gift? I had never seen anything like it, to take one of something and make copies of it at a distance.

Landin unsheathed his sword, rising to his feet a fraction of a second behind me. Only Edda and Clause remained seated.

If I had not moved when I did, then the Lysian would have cut me. Anger rippled through me, and power instantly ran over my skin and down my veins. It pooled in my palms, and I thrust my hand forward, shoving mist into the Lysian's lungs. She lost hold of the blade in her hand, and it clanked on the table before her. The four knives around me disappeared. Her hands instinctually went to her throat for breath which was no longer where it should have been. She tried to gasp, but one did not come. Her hand found Clause's shoulder, panic in her icy gaze. She was reaching to him for help.

He looked at her with a dark sparkle in his eye as she crumpled to her knees beside him. Only then did his knuckles brush over her skin, and even though I had not released my conjuring, she began coughing, gulping down one greedy breath after another.

I couldn't help but glance at my palm, still feeling the power very much alive in my fingertips, yet the effect on the Lysian vanished. Clause may have seen a glimpse of my conjuring, but I also just caught a glimpse of his. He only had to touch her, and it completely nullified the effect of my influence on her.

"I must apologize. Mal can have quite a temper at times. She will not upset you again this evening, for she was just leaving." His blatant excuse of her was calm, though she flinched as if he had yelled it.

Malavika stood once she regained her bearing. Her eyes met mine once more, and she snarled, her teeth flashing before she turned and left. It was impressive, for the control he had over her was strong. Malavika did not seem like someone typically easily dismissed.

"She gets awfully spirited at times, but I would never have allowed her to truly harm you," Clause commented, taking a sip of wine before gesturing for me to take my seat once more.

Landin looked from me to the King. A deep frown etched onto his face, and he glanced at me once more. He hated everything about what was going on, that I was being tested by someone we knew so little about, someone who likely posed a threat. His jaw clenched, and I knew that he was making a great effort not to say a word. As long as the promise Clause made was upheld, then Landin's purpose was for moral support, not to get involved. He sheathed his sword when I gave him a small nod. However, his entire demeanor remained rigid. Following my lead, we both returned to the table, his hand resting on the hilt of his blade the entire time.

Landin's eyes promised of death as they stared at the Siddhe King. Quick, shallow breaths caused his chest to rise and fall with furious anger. He did not like me threatened, but we also knew that the Siddhe King would likely try to see my conjuring. It was all orchestrated. Landin knew that as much as I did. His hand was in a fist under the table, and I reached for him. My touch did nothing to relax him. When his fist did not relent to allow my fingers to slip through, I withdrew from him, hoping he could keep it together just a little longer.

Clause took a single bite of chicken while his gray eyes studied me the entire time. Being under the watchful eye of a Lysian was uncomfortable, but this was so much worse. It was as if I was there merely for the purpose of him to observe and be entertained at my expense. I had the urge to gouge out those eyes so that he could no longer view me in such a superior manner.

I did not exist for his pleasure.

"So, tell me, Ariana, are the rumors true?" he asked casually. It was another game, he was toying with me. Giving me just enough to force me to follow. He could have been alluding to anything.

I swallowed a single red grape. It seemed the safest thing on my plate to try.

"I cannot confirm nor deny, for I do not know what rumors you speak of." I reached for the glass of water before me, my throat incredibly dry.

A smirk pulled at the corner of his mouth. "Why, the ones that say you killed your father."

I nearly choked on water, and he tilted his head, a full dark smile appearing on his lips.

"I can assure you that I have not killed anyone." It was an effort to keep my jaw moving, to keep my teeth from grinding.

His gaze held mine. "But you *are* responsible, are you not?"

What was I to him? A source of amusement? He invited us to this meeting, the first of its kind as far as I knew, and now he asked of such personal things. He had no right to expect an answer to such a question. I owed him no answers. Yet he, too, owed me no answers, but I refused to leave without getting some.

"I'd like to ask *you* of a rumor," I said, not answering him, for two could play at this game.

"Please." He was still smiling, gray eyes darkening.

"Do you have a Lysian by the name of Iona hidden somewhere amongst your territory?" I asked of Erik's sister, sitting back in my seat. I would never cower to him, no matter how cold and powerful his presence was.

Edda froze mid-chew, turning her onyx eyes to me. Though she said nothing, I felt her scorn. She didn't want me to push the *hospitality* of our host.

"You intrigue me," he said as if it were a compliment. "I swear to tell you mine if you tell me yours first." There was a spark of enjoyment in his gaze.

A moment passed between us, a silent standoff.

"I could have saved him but chose not to," I spoke of Fraser.

Landin's head swiveled so fast it was likely to come off. I was a Bavadrin, sworn to protect the Leader Superior, and I hadn't. In fact, I had wished for his death more than anything else in the entire world. And now, I announced that truth to someone we could not trust.

"Why?" Clause asked, curiosity dripping from him.

"Why?" I was taken aback by the question.

"Yes, why did you do such a thing to dear old dad? And do be honest, or I won't tell you mine." He observed me as if he were consuming me with a look. There was no escape. I felt surrounded even with him just sitting before us.

"Because he butchered my mother in front of me," I answered flatly.

I expected Clause to smile in response, but for the first time, he didn't. Instead, he appeared somber, the shine in his gaze blackening.

"I'm sorry." His voice was low but clear.

I didn't know what to do with that. It was not expected. There was the barest flicker of kindness in the response and even his eyes. We stared at one another, sharing an odd and unexpected moment of understanding. He viewed me with absolutely no judgment. A strange and tortured sympathy came from him.

Clause then blinked several times in succession, as if clearing his mind, and withdrew. When his gaze found mine once more, his demeanor shifted back to a more playful one. He reached for his wine, twirling it lazily in his hands.

"Iona is around here somewhere," he confirmed before bringing the glass to his lips.

The Lysians had always been right. I bit my tongue to prevent myself from asking about her further. The last thing I needed was for Clause to discover just how desperate I was to learn everything about where she was or what had been done to her.

"You built a wall of mist to protect your people when you escaped from the Lysians?" he asked. There was no doubt that someone had fed him this information.

"Yes," I confirmed.

"Intriguing. How did someone like you go unnoticed for so long?" His gaze slid to Edda, who sat beside me, watching our interaction.

She hardly touched her food, nor did she make a single sound. I wondered if Clause knew what she was, what form her conjuring had taken. That she was a Seer. He never asked about her or Landin's abilities. His attention was mainly my burden to bear.

"You know, you and I are a lot alike." He turned back to me. "We both killed our fathers."

He seemed stuck in the dark and gruesome. I did not respond because I did not want to admit that we could have had something like that in common. My hands were not responsible for Fraser's death, but my actions placed the blame on my shoulders, anyway. Were it another Bavadrin being put to death by the Lysians, then I would have tried to save them.

Clause moved his arm, reaching out before me, palm up.

"May I have your hand?" he asked.

Goose bumps spread over my skin at the request. For a moment, I hesitated, my instincts screaming at the dangerous presence. One heartbeat, two, I relented, sliding my gloved fingers into his waiting palm.

Even through the fabric his touch was cool, almost unnervingly so, yet his grip was firm. He observed my hand in his, running a thumb over my knuckles. Then, without a word, he began to tug on the fingers of my glove. The movement was unhurried, intentional, as if savoring the act. My pulse quickened, each tug sending ripples of tension through me.

I could pull my arm away, but then he would be left holding

the glove alone, the bare skin of my hand exposed. I remained frozen.

He was going to touch me. I had no idea of how truly potent his abilities were but I desperately did not want to find out this way.

I wanted to glance at Edda, to seek guidance or reassurance, but my gaze refused to stray from my hand in his, from the glove slipping further and further away.

My heart pounded, each beat louder than the last.

This was a game for him, cat and mouse. He was seeing how far he could go. But if he thought me a simple mouse, he was mistaken. If Clause fancied himself a predator, then so was I. He was not *my* King. I would not tremble before him.

Landin shot to his feet, his sword drawn in one swift motion. The gleam of steel caught the light. It was dangerously close to breaking the agreement that we had signed. Clause had not harmed me, not yet, but Landin's actions carried the threat.

"Landin, sit down," I commanded, my voice sharp, my gaze never wavering from the Siddhe King before me.

Clause stopped what he was doing, gray eyes flickering to Landin before narrowing ever so slightly. He did not speak, but his presence seemed to swell, pressing down on the room.

Landin remained rooted in place, his knuckles whitening around the hilt of his blade. A charged moment stretched between us, brittle and trembling on the verge of snapping.

Finally, I tore my eyes off the threat before me to look upon the threat next to me. "We had an agreement coming here. It has not been broken, and you certainly will not be the one to break it. Is that understood?"

Landin glanced back at me defiantly, jaw clenched.

"Better do as she asks." It was the first time Clause had genuinely spoken to anyone other than me. "Patience is not a strong suit of mine, and I will not be threatened in my home again. This is the only warning you will have, boy." His voice was calm, though the weight of that warning was immense.

"You are threatening her," Landin snarled, a storm of anger and a need to protect fueling him.

"While it is true that my touch can be seen as a threat," Clause agreed, his thumb moving over my nearly ungloved hand, "I swear to the Spirits that I wish Ariana no harm. I only hope to understand her more."

"Landin," I said his name through clenched teeth, pulling his attention. Finally, something clicked in that stubborn skull of his. He sheathed his blade, and his butt found his seat once more.

The glove was removed a mere second later, and my hand rested in Clause's. He shifted his hold so that his fingers brushed against my wrist and his lip curved up.

"Your pulse is racing," he commented.

48

ARIANA

I was suspended in a strange state of alarm, waiting to feel something foreign, but it did not come. Instead, Clause tortured me with the unknown while he lazily examined my hand.

His touch was deliberate, flipping my palm up, as if memorizing every curve and line. His thumb traced my wrist once more. While I wore gloves, his touch seemed cold, though now, it was as if it burned, heat seeping into me.

Edda breathed out heavily beside me. She stared at Clause with dark, dangerous eyes. She looked at him as if that moment was personal to her, like she knew the Siddhe King before me. Had she wanted me to be in such a predicament? Had she foreseen everything and guided me down that path in an attempt to eliminate me for the treacherous act against the Leader Superior I had committed?

Landin shifted his weight in his seat, and it creaked with the movement. He had drawn his sword moments ago and nearly ended the agreement which kept us safe while we were in the Siddhe lands. Was he in on it with Edda? The both of them did not see me as being fit for leading the Bavadrin people for what I had done to my father.

Father. I never called Fraser by that name. Not in a long time.

I looked back at my hand and the Siddhe holding it. He wanted to kill me. I knew it in my blood to have been true.

No.

The thoughts and feelings racing around my mind were not my own, at least not exactly. Clause was drawing them out, maturing small insecurities into something significant.

A smile grew on his handsome face while a frown solidified on mine.

"Please stop. I can make my own decisions without your input." My words were spoken through clenched teeth.

Clause withdrew his hand and with it the amplified thoughts. I failed to suppress the shudder moving through me. Nausea brought the taste of acid to my mouth. It was extraordinary, the impact of his touch. Had he been able to read my thoughts? Forcing a steady breath, I tried to keep the panic from taking over.

"Very interesting," he commented while I shook with the feeling left behind. His power had slithered around me. It glided over my skin, tightening and releasing. The sensation was revolting.

"What is?" Edda asked, sounding curious. This was the first time she spoke to the Siddhe King.

Though Clause replied to her, he kept his eyes fixed on me. "Everyone always accepts my influence as their own, for it stems from your own insecurities. No one has ever recognized it as foreign the way you just did."

I had no response, for I still did not quite understand what had occurred. It was seamless, his influence. There was no odd feeling, nothing that let me know he was doing anything until he finally withdrew.

"She knows who she is," Edda stated.

"Indeed, she does," he agreed.

"What *exactly* did you do?" I asked when the repulsion within finally subsided enough that I did not fear hurling when my mouth opened.

Clause reached for the wine before him without looking at it. "What do you know of what I can do?" The wine swirled in the glass before he took a sip.

I glanced at Edda, unsure how best to answer, so she answered for me. "She knows you can affect others with conjuring abilities, lessening them or igniting them."

"That doesn't explain what just happened," I stated, slowly regaining control of my racing heart.

"Does it not?" His gray eyes sparkled. "Is conjuring just a skill you turn on and off, or is it always there?" His smile widened when I did not answer. "Conjurors have an attachment to the Spirit realm, drawing power from it. Once that door opens for someone, then it is forever opened. The gifts of conjuring enter, seeping through a being. It intertwines itself in your thoughts, breath, and even the beating of your heart. And I can influence another's conjuring."

He watched closely for my reaction to what he shared, but didn't receive one. I simply stared right back at him while the magnitude of the power I now sat before threatened to change the world I had come to know.

"Can you read people's thoughts?" I asked.

He laughed, the sound echoing through the room. "Now that would be an ability to treasure, but no. I can feel calming thoughts, negative ones, passion and so on, and I can bring them forward, amplifying them. However, I do not have a way of knowing exactly what they are."

We endured the rest of the meal with meaningless small talk. There was no substance to any of it. It was as if Clause used the first half to get all the answers he craved from me, and the rest was just to pass the time. When it was all over, I could not get away fast enough.

Unfortunately, we were forced to endure his presence longer.

Walking from his castle with us, Clause had someone fetch our horses. My muscles had grown stiff from sitting after the days of riding. I didn't mind stretching my legs before beginning the ride home, though I could have survived without the company of the Siddhe King.

He lead us only a short distance, though our path was lined with others who appeared to have been of the Dunes Clan. Scars intricately etched into their skin. At least a hundred of them lined the way, with Soren at our backs. There was no need for such a display in his own lands. The three of us did not pose any threat. The guards were completely unnecessary.

"It's beautiful up here, is it not?" Clause asked casually.

"The air is a bit thin," I stated flatly.

He chuckled dryly.

"Why are those of the Dunes Clan here?" I asked as my gaze drifted to them. They stared straight ahead, ignoring us. Their bodies were marked like Soren's.

"They wish to live here and serve me." He walked with his hands in his pockets, utterly unconcerned by my question.

"And what if they chose not to serve you?" My feet stilled, and Clause pivoted to view me. I was not stupid. I knew some choices were not a choice at all, not if one wished to keep living.

"Why do you seem to assume it is only under malicious circumstances that they would decide to serve me?" In the darkness of the night, he appeared even more dangerous. His bone-white hair glowed with the light of the moon, and the features of his handsome face were sharper, crueler.

"I doubt that it is your winning personality that has them following your rule," I stated, and he smiled, taking absolutely no offense to my words. "It was clear the Lysian tonight cared very much of your opinion of her, yet you care nothing for her feelings. You do not come off as someone who cares anything for anyone but yourself. There is no reason all of these people would want to follow someone like that."

Edda's stiff fingers wrapped around my wrist, a silent command for me to shut my mouth.

"It is not so bad to follow someone powerful, capable of offering protection." His gaze narrowed.

It was clear I was tiptoeing close to a sharp edge where he was concerned. Perhaps I should have heeded Edda's silent warning to stop, but I could not find the strength to pull in my disgust and anger any longer. He admitted to having the Lysian princess somewhere in his lands. He had the Dunes Clan under his command. There were likely many others under his control, and I doubted they had much of a choice in the matter. And the way he behaved that night, the arrogance in how he viewed the world, was repulsive, as if everything in it was his for the taking.

I forced my spine to straighten, head held high as I replied, "Fraser ruled through fear and a false sense of overwhelming power. He was a monster, and now he is dead, and the world is a better place for it."

The surrounding air went electric with my words. Edda's hand fell from my wrist, probably shocked by my bold statement.

Clause did not respond right away, though it was evident that I hit a nerve by the apparent frown on his face. "Do not pretend to know me. I am not your worthless father." His voice was even, and though he did not step towards me, the darkness in his gaze felt as though we stood toe to toe. His power slithered around me once more, even though he had not touched me. It glided over my skin, tightening its hold.

His cold eyes shifted to something in the distance. "Your horses have finally come."

Turning, I saw them approaching. A child strode towards us,

the reins in her hands. I got a closer look at her. Her skin was darker than a Siddhe's, her ears slightly pointed. It was not the typical sharp Siddhe point. She was mixed blood.

My body turned cold.

"Do you have Bavadrins as slaves?" I asked, looking from the child to Clause's unreadable face. He didn't deny it, though he did not respond. "Are they here against their will?" I tried to keep myself from lashing out.

His lips twitched. "I don't care to know such things, against their will or not. They work here. That is all."

"Is there any way you would free them?" I asked, realizing I was not yet in any position to demand anything from him, but I could not simply leave without knowing what his price would have been, if he had one.

"Ariana." Edda spoke my name in warning.

"Perhaps, I may agree to release them if you agree to something yourself." When I did not respond, he continued, "Come stay here with me for a little while. Let me show you what it's truly like in my lands. You may learn that it is not as terrible as you assume."

"Like hell she will," Landin bit out, unable to keep silent any longer.

Clause looked at him with sharp distaste. "What is this person to you, Ariana?" He turned to me then. "This Bavadrin is someone who is holding you back while I can help you grow. If you come here, I could help you cultivate your power. Those you seem to surround yourself with currently will only stifle your gifts. Take this one, for example." His head inclined towards Landin. "He thinks you are too weak to even make your own decisions."

"I will not leave the Bavadrins to be enslaved," I said, ignoring his jab at Landin. "But if you free all who wish to leave, then I may be persuaded to visit."

"How long would the terms of this visit be?" Edda began asking as soon as I finished speaking, her eyes wide.

Clause smiled knowingly and took a single step towards me, raising his hand as if to touch my cheek.

Landin drew his blade and lunged between us, forcing me back.

Time slowed to a crawl, yet there was not enough of it to stop what was happening.

Clause's expression twisted with disdain. He barely spared Landin a glance before lifting his hand and touching him—just the faintest graze of his fingertips.

A touch deadlier than any blade.

Landin crumpled to the ground like a marionette whose strings had been cut, his sword clattering from his grasp.

He lay motionless.

I took a step toward him, but Edda's hand shot out, her iron grip anchoring me in place. She took a deliberate stance in front of me, placing herself between me and the Siddhe King.

Ice crawled down my spine, sinking deeper and deeper until it shattered something within me. My mind rejected what my eyes saw. A touch shouldn't have been capable of that. It shouldn't have been possible.

Landin's body lay on the ground. Too still. The eerie silence of something that no longer clung to life. My chest tightened, breath growing shallow, each sharper than the last.

Though I hadn't touched him, hadn't checked for a pulse, I knew. Deep in the marrow of my bones, I knew. No breath filled his lungs. No heartbeat echoed within his chest.

Edda released me when I fell to my knees. Shock wrapped itself around me, thick and suffocating.

Tears blurred my vision, and the world became a watery haze. No sound escaped my lips, not even a whisper of grief. It was as though the enormity of it all stole my voice, leaving me with nothing but silence and the unbearable ache of loss.

Clause spoke without moving from his spot beside Landin's body. "I will not give up anything first. You will have twenty days to get your affairs in order and then return to my home as a guest. If you do not, then I will assume you have sided with the Lysians. Independent, neither of you poses much of a threat. Unified, you may cause some trouble. Therefore, if you do not agree, then I will have no choice but to see you as a threat and you will be eradicated. I hope it won't come to that, for there is so much I wish to share with you."

Clause paced forward, past Edda, who watched with wide eyes as he raised his hand, the same one that had just stolen Landin's life. With the back of his fingers, he grazed my cheek. At that moment, all the pain I was feeling was taken away. Breath found my lungs easier, and I finally lifted my head and met his gaze.

"I can help you with your pain if you wish it." His voice gained a soft edge. Edda placed a hand on my shoulder as if she thought I might leave with him right then and there if she did not tether herself to me. "I look forward to seeing you again, Ariana. There is so much you are capable of. You truly do not know."

His touch fell away from my face and every painful emotion slammed back into me. It was so potent, knocking the air out of me. As Clause walked away, the Dunes Clan began escorting him, leaving Edda and me alone with our horses.

My attention dropped to–

I couldn't think.

On hands and knees, I crawled to Landin's still-warm body. My trembling fingers found no pulse.

He was gone.

My best friend.

No more shared jokes. No more nights of conversation. No more promises.

Gone.

The finality of it tore me open.

It was then that a scream erupted from me. Horrid pain melded with a rage so great. The anguish in my chest twisted, morphing into something darker. My power surged to life. It shot through my icy veins, doing nothing to warm the cavernous cold in my chest.

I snapped my hand forward, and with it came a torrent of mist, thick and suffocating, a force so powerful the ground trembled. The mist hurtled toward Clause, a raging wall meant to break him, to crush him. To end him.

The impact should have sent him flying, should have shattered bone and spilled blood.

Clause didn't even flinch.

His steps remained poised and purposeful. It was as if he were a ghost. My wall of mist flew through him, slamming so hard into the tree before him that the sound of it cracking shook the mountain.

Gray eyes glanced over a shoulder at me, the faintest flicker of amusement tugging at the corner of his lips. The Siddhe King chuckled, low and soft. Without a word, he turned away, continuing his path forward as if I hadn't just tried to kill him.

TO BE CONTINUED...

Thank you for reading!

If you enjoyed the story, I'd be truly grateful if you left a review. Your feedback not only means the world to me, but it also helps the book reach other readers who might love it too.

ACKNOWLEDGMENTS

Thank you to my husband Josh, for being my partner in life. For letting me run with my passions and for all the support and love you provide. Thank you to my daughter, for making my life so much more interesting, and granting me a love unlike any other. To my parents who made immense sacrifices in their lives in order to give our family a chance at a better future.

Thank you to the friends who have supported me through this process. To Carolina, for reading the roughest of the rough drafts, and enjoying it enough to keep going. To Helen, for encouraging my bravery enough to take certain risks. To Danielle for the endless support, the walks, the book chats, and for believing in this story. To Chelsea for your encouragement, conversations, and our shared love of reading. To Morgan, for letting me pick your brain when I need to bounce a thought off someone. To Stephanie, for your attention to detail and wonderful support. To the book club girls, the gathering I look forward to each month, and the escape it provides.

To the readers, thank you for taking a chance on this book. You are the breath that gives life to the characters, and I thank you for it.

THE BREATH OF MIST TRILOGY:

Breath of Mist
Heart of Torment
Soul of Carnage